THE DA VINCI STAIRCASE

Love and Turbulence in the Loire Valley

Bruce Fink, in collaboration with Héloïse Fink

SPHINX

Any resemblance found here to people living or dead just might be intentional.

He who thinks about finishing before starting, finishes nothing.

Sine labore nihil.

CONTENTS

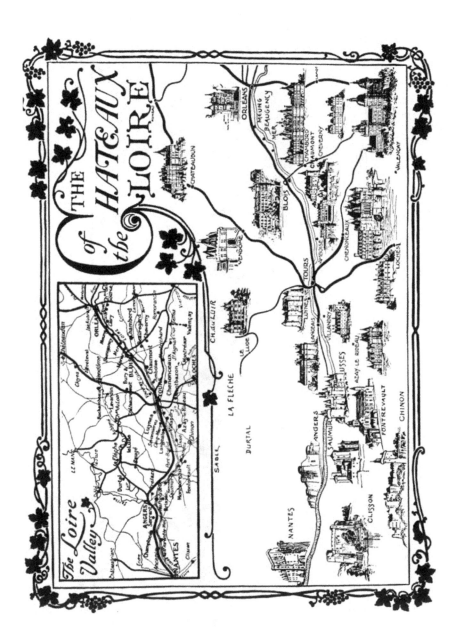

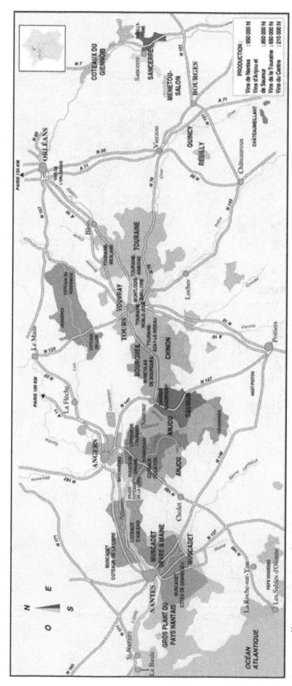

Loire Valley Wine Producing Regions

Veüe du Château Royale de Chambor du côté de l'Entrée

CHAPTER ONE

Chambord Castle

Music and architecture are the supreme arts.*
—A certain French psychoanalyst

The dreamlike village was floating in the clouds. Its sculpted stone dwellings were glowing in the mist, their color a cross between snow and buttercream. Steeply sloped slate ridgelines rose out of sight overhead, and domed turrets, pinnacles, spires, and the most fanciful chimneys imaginable could only barely be made out. Dense fog surrounded me as I drank in the surreal beauty, and I was transported to another time as I wandered the cobblestone lanes—yes, lanes—that lined the roof of the most astonishing palace ever built. It was as though I had been carried off to heaven and was surrounded by whimsical minarets designed by an angel, or a genie from *The Thousand and One Nights*, not by any architect of woman born.

When I finally returned to earth, I was horrified to discover that the doors were locked. I had lost all track of time. My shoes were wet, my blazer drenched, and I shivered at the thought that I might have to spend the night out there on the rooftop. It was July, but unseasonably cold and damp in the valley, as it sometimes is in the summer. I tried the hatches leading into the many different houses and towers lining the streets, but none of the centuries-old oak portals budged. There seemed

1

to be no logic to how they were laid out, and I just kept wandering around in circles trying whatever ancient iron handle came my way. The fairy-tale village in the sky had turned hostile.

I suddenly heard what sounded like a door opening and closing in the distance. I tried to trace the sound, but it had ricocheted off too many roof-lines, flying buttresses, and turrets to follow. Still, it rekindled my hope that some exit had remained unlocked. I would be able to make it back into a warm space inside! Somewhere along the way I began trying all the intricately carved mullion windows too, and finally found one that gave a bit. I coaxed it open little by little and climbed into a small room that led into a spacious apartment, the likes of which I had never before seen. It could have been a castle in its own right. And I thought I had seen all four hundred and forty rooms at Chambord Castle!*

Coming upon a tiny spiral staircase that turned in an odd direction, I gropingly felt my way down to the next landing, threaded my way through several chambers lit solely by the meager daylight the mist allowed in, and abruptly stumbled out into the main hallway. Heaving a huge sigh of relief at regaining an area I knew well, I directed my steps to the heart and soul of Chambord, not fifty paces off: the most famous staircase in the world. I paused, as if seeing it for the first time. For once, I could contemplate the enormous double spiral it formed without anyone else around … Even after my unseemly fright at having gotten myself locked out on the roof, I couldn't help it. I started to gaze and, almost in spite of myself, study its ingenious construction and intricately sculpted friezes displaying winged Cupids brandishing bows and arrows, Pegasuses unwinged, male and female fauns, mermaids, satyrs, cherubim, and dolphins galore. They had been there for five hundred years, yet had I ever noticed them all so clearly and distinctly? "Who could have come up with such an incredibly beautiful and innovative design?" I wondered for the umpteenth time as I descended the treads. "Was it the artist of artists, Leonardo himself?"

All at once, I was in severe pain. My ankle twisting, I grabbed desperately at the stone banister. "What was that?"

A body. A woman's body.

My surroundings seemed to whirl around me, and I had to crouch down on the stairs for a few moments until I felt less lightheaded. I tried to wake the woman by shaking her, but she failed to stir.

* * *

2

"This is where he found her," the night watchman told the county's prefect of police and the precinct's highest-ranking *commissaire* or lead investigator, as he led us to a second-floor landing of the iconic stairway.

"Actually, it was on the opposite side, over here," I said gently, showing them to the landing of the matching flight of curved stairs located exactly one hundred and eighty degrees from the first. "It was close to the northeast tower, but further east." The prefect, Daniel Durtal, a tall, squarely built man, seemed to take note of my attention to detail, perhaps thinking it might corroborate the implausible-sounding story that I was a former agent in the French Secret Service who now lived mostly in New York, had inadvertently stayed out on the castle roof after closing, and had literally stumbled upon the girl. His reaction to my admittedly vague reason for lingering outside so long—he perhaps believing me to be some sort of bizarre modern-day Socrates, standing catatonically in one place lost in thought for hours at a time, whereas I was more of a peripatetic thinker, as all my good friends knew—warned me that, in his eyes, I was not above suspicion. "It's an easy mistake to make," I added even more soothingly, hoping to set Lebrun, the night watchman, at ease.

Looking rather anxious, nevertheless, he resumed, "Once I called the ambulance, I tried to figure out what happened." His blue eyes, deep-set beneath bushy eyebrows, darted about. "I thought maybe she tripped—you know, got a heel caught in a crack or something. I checked her shoes, but the red soles were as new as could be, the heels were unscratched, and the nearby stone steps are pretty even. See?" he pointed and then paused—was it for effect or because the simple fellow was intimidated by his high-powered audience?—until Durtal impatiently gestured for him to go on.

"I couldn't smell any alcohol on her. Just perfume."

"Expensive perfume too," I opined. "*Chance.* By Chanel." Scarron, the lead investigator, shot me an odd look, as if no man in his right mind would know that. While observing that his leg was vibrating nervously, I mused that the scent should have been called *Malchance*, given the girl's bad luck—assuming luck had anything to do with it, that is. (You'll find that I adore idioms, whether highbrow or low, feeling they are the very soul of a language, and play mercilessly with words.)

"Seeing as how she looked so graceful-like lying there," he continued, "I reckoned she blacked out—you know, had some kinda stroke or heart attack, and then fell." At this, the heavyset man took out his cell phone and showed Durtal and Scarron a few pictures he had taken of the singular position she had been lying in, her torso spilling down the stairs.

"Anything else?" Durtal asked him condescendingly. "Did you hear anything?"

"No, but then I says to myself, what if there was some sort of struggle? A girl looking like that could, I reckon, get herself into a heap of trouble. So, I check to see if there are any scuff marks or blood in the area, but find nothing," he commented, shaking his head. "Then—what, no purse, no phone? How weird is that? No violin case neither, like all them musicians who have been coming in and out of the castle all week? Zilch."

I raised my eyebrows at this. "Is it possible," I asked, "you are talking about the acclaimed Chambord baroque festival?"

"Started two days ago already," Lebrun replied as if any moron would know that. This was, after all, the center of the universe to him. "Don't you hear them playing right now?"

I didn't. Was my hearing that poor or had he just heard them earlier and believed they were still performing out in the courtyard?

The gendarmes looked at me askance, as if wondering how anyone could be interested in such prehistoric music. I didn't let that stop me from thinking about the festival while Lebrun insisted on showing them the remainder of the snapshots he had taken. How could I have overlooked it, having always wanted to attend?

"Text those to us right away," Scarron almost barked, "and I'll have them run through the computer along with the ones we took at the hospital." The wiry, tousled-haired lead investigator struck me as a no-nonsense sort of guy, so why was he snarling at a simple security guard? There was an edge in his voice, as though he were trying to contain something and succeeding only partially.

"Through the computer?" I echoed. "What do you hope to find out?"

"Who the girl is," Durtal replied. I stupidly assumed they had already established her identity when they met the ambulance at the hospital. "We can't find any record of the unpronounceable name she gave us—no passport, no residence permit, no employment or medical history, nada."

"Probably was high as a kite on coke," Scarron remarked. "Seems to have hit her head pretty badly and has both retrograde and anterograde amnesia," he added, seeming to want to impress us with medical jargon

4

I was sure he didn't understand. "Why can't they just plant silicon chips in everyone at birth?" he sneered, a bit too loudly I felt, half his face contorting, as if he had Bell's palsy. "Would make our lives a hell of a lot easier!" His phone buzzed, he looked at the screen for a moment, and then gave the Loir-et-Cher county prefect the thumbs up while tilting his head in my direction. He had, I was sure, been told to run my profile, something they probably would have done even if I had had my old badge on me that evening, which I didn't. His braggadocio didn't stop his leg from vibrating nervously.

Ignoring Scarron's totalitarian dream, I turned to Durtal. "I fail to grasp why the chief of police is personally involved in a case that may be nothing more than an accident—if we can accept, even provisionally, that there is such a thing as an 'accident.'" The coppers eyed each other quizzically, obviously having no idea what I was talking about. I had expected as much. At least I had gotten their attention.

"You mean you, too, have heard about the mystery of the staircase?" the night watchman's voice suddenly resonated in the vast hallways. "The secret code built into it that puts a hex on people who examine it too closely? It's no accident!" Listening to him, I reflected that the unheralded grandeur of the place could make one imagine almost anything.

Scarron rolled his eyes and opined, "Probably just tripping her brains out on acid." His other leg began spasming now.

Lebrun, who was looking at me, not the lead investigator, blustered on, demonstrating that he, like the others, had failed to grasp my point, "All the Loire Valley castles have mysteries built into 'em, and Chambord contains the biggest one of all."

A polite silence ensued. I smiled inwardly, having heard the many legends the mythical palace had inspired.

"Chambord is not a hunting lodge," the security guard continued. "That lie has finally been ..." He seemed unable to find the word "debunked" or "exposed" or the expression "laid to rest." "The whole castle is one big church, shaped like a Greek cross. And there's a code that was built into its staircase by Leonardo da Vinci himself." His sunken eyes rose in their orbits, as if to the celestial vault.

"What a ... !" Scarron began emphatically.

"Go on," I encouraged the security guard who had clammed up at Scarron's aborted insult. The castle is, after all, shaped like a Greek cross (think of a plus sign, +) inscribed in a huge square, with large

5

round towers added at each corner, and the double-spiral stairway located right smack in the middle of the square. Durtal, Scarron's superior in both age and sagacity, firmly gestured to his lead investigator to humor me.

"I've been working here for over twenty years," Lebrun resumed proudly, feeling encouraged by my words, "usually the day shift, but often the night shift, and believe you me, I've seen it all!" His eyes swept the enormous corridors around us. They were almost glowing in the dark, so white were the limestone walls. "People from every different continent slipping, stumbling, and banging into things, completely oblivious to where they're going as they stare at the ceiling." At this, he pointed to the high coffered ceilings sculpted with the sometimes solitary, sometimes interlaced initials of the king and queen, fantastical creatures, dolphins, and intricately etched knots, alternating with crowned salamanders, symbolizing François I—it was, after all, and still is his palace. "But—" he trailed off, glancing now at the huge stairway as if it were a beautiful yet menacing beast.

"But?" I prompted him.

"The only people who really get hurt are the ones who stare at the staircase for too long. The ones who get completely absorbed in it."

It wasn't easy to keep a straight face, but I tried.

"My family has lived near the castle forever. You know, Chambord's got the biggest forested park in Europe," he went on, suddenly waxing professorial. "The whole city of Paris could fit in it, and it's surrounded by a twenty-mile-long wall." He made a grand sweeping circular gesture with his arm as he repeated facts he must have overheard castle tour guides tell their flocks. "Even the queen of England's estate isn't as big."

He was a true-blue Frenchman, I thought silently. Has to get one up on the Brits!

"But ever since Thibault the Trickster killed the church's priest here a thousand years ago for starting Mass before Thibault arrived, strange things have been happening, and nothing happens without us hearing about it."

Now I knew that Thibault, at least, was not a myth, but rather one of the historically attested counts of Blois. "I'm sure there are plenty of rumors about what goes on here," I remarked, having heard of his memorable punishment from one of my aunts: Thibault was forced to chase the same stag for all eternity without ever catching it. Locals often reported hearing sounds of his fruitless hunt in the park at night. "But what about the stairway?"

"It's only the people who stare at the symbols, the Bo ... , Bor ... ,'" he flailed about in search of the word, looked heavenward for divine inspiration, then found it, "Borromean knots carved into the staircase, who get more than a scratch or sprain." He pointed at a number of symbols decorating the friezes running along the outer edges of the spiral, several of which were knot-like in appearance, but not Borromean knots—knots that were considered to be cabalistic symbols by astrologers like the Italian Ruggieri who worked for Catherine de' Medici. I'd noticed real ones in a part of Chambord rarely seen by tourists as well as at other Loire Valley castles like Chaumont and Oiron, but was interested in them for reasons of my own having nothing to do with cabalism. (And not because they used to be employed in representations of the Trinity,* or because molecular Borromean rings are now used in spintronics** and medical imaging.) "They're jinxed somehow," the security guard's voice boomed again. "My guide friends here have proved they come from the crusades, Ancient Egypt, and even King Solomon's Temple."

"A load of legends and freemason mumbo jumbo," I thought to myself. I'd heard so many ridiculous things said about Chambord that I half expected he'd tell me that the *tour-lanterne* (lantern tower or cupola) that crowns the staircase, with its circular octad of flying buttresses, is actually a giant lock to which an alien civilization has the key and with which they can open the castle up and reach down into the bowels of the earth, where they undoubtedly keep a secret stash of intergalactic cash, kryptonite, or who knows what else—maybe the fabled treasure of the kings of France!

"Most people don't realize it, but the staircase is the altar of this humungous church," Lebrun went on. I sighed noiselessly. Every generation tries to make sense of Chambord, I reflected, and this must be one of the new attempts to explain the enigma. "Anybody who tries to decipher the code ends up failing, I mean falling," he faltered.

"So, you're saying there is some sort of *da Vinci code* built into the staircase?" I asked, flashing a smile at the prefect and the lead investigator, all the while tucking away in my memory his slip of the tongue. I never let a slip slide, even with my best friends. They're just too darn interesting. "A few specialists claim Leonardo designed the stairway, maybe even the whole castle, but why would he have included some

7

kind of secret code in it, much less a maleficent one?" I inquired, looking at him intently.

Lebrun shrugged his shoulders.

"What kind of message do you think is contained in it?" I continued, admittedly relishing roasting the night watchman a little. He was right to think Chambord was like no other castle on earth, but still …

Neither Durtal nor Scarron, both of whom appeared thus far to be by-the-book, police-academy-trained detectives, knew anything of my methods and I think they began seriously doubting my sanity at this point. Durtal looked exasperated, and Scarron, who, in addition to his restless leg syndrome, had "a lean and hungry look" about him, seemed to be thinking the prefect was making a career-limiting blunder by involving a loose cannon like me in the case—maybe another in a long series of blunders? Or hoping he was?

"All's I know is that it contains one of those age-old secrets, like the kind that novelist Dan Brown revealed to the world in his bestseller. I read somewhere—"

"Don't believe everything you read," I cut in, wondering how many more years I was going to have to endure such claptrap. "If you listen to Dan Brown, you might end up believing that in Paris you can see the Eiffel Tower off to the right while driving south on the rue de Castiglione from the Place Vendôme."

Lebrun flashed me a defiant look. He was not about to have his hero discredited by me, a totally unknown quantity. "I'll have you know he sold more books than … than … than anyone ever!" he protested.

"If only there were some direct relationship between sales figures and truth," I instantly riposted, not bothering to correct his blatantly erroneous assertion. "The fact is that you can't get even the slightest glimpse of the Eiffel Tower until you reach the rue de Rivoli, and you certainly can't see the Georges Pompidou Center from the Tuileries Gardens, as Brown also claimed, unless you have X-ray vision, which most of us do not have. He obviously never bothered to go to Paris." I don't know why, but that still irked me.

Lebrun was momentarily speechless. I bet he wanted to retort that Brown's novel had been made into a major motion picture.

"And he certainly never studied the history of the Louvre," I continued, unruffled by the glares I was getting and the fact that the evening was wearing on. "If he had, he wouldn't have called it a 'monolithic palace,' when it was built and rebuilt over the course of eight hundred years. Better to believe nothing you read without checking it first."

Lebrun was probably one of those Frenchmen from the provinces who had never set foot in the nation's capital, and hadn't considered for a moment that the novelist hadn't either. I was half expecting him to claim, as I've heard so many say about translators of difficult texts, that Brown may have gotten a few unimportant details wrong, but he'd surely gotten the important stuff about the "lost scriptures" right—but he just looked away, trying, perhaps, to contain his anger. I decided not to rile him up any further by telling him that it sufficed to read a well-researched biography of da Vinci, like Carlo Vecce's available in the bookshop right downstairs, to realize that virtually every statement made about Leonardo in the bestseller was flagrantly false.

"If there is a message to be found here, I suspect it lies in the empty topological space defined by the double spiral, not in the staircase itself," I added enigmatically, and was pleased to see they were all baffled by my comment. I often enjoy putting my interlocutors' imaginations to the test, even if it occasionally leaves them mystified. "I find that much more likely than the claim made by some that da Vinci had already discovered the double-helix structure of DNA."

"Be that as it may," I continued, turning toward the policemen now, "I still don't get it. Why are you two investigating something that might be no more than someone tripping on the stairs?" I hadn't yet told them that while I was stuck out on the roof, I had heard a door open and close.

Everyone was silent, and Lebrun looked ready to bite my head off. Durtal finally fielded my question. "First of all, the staff here takes great pains to ensure that no one remains in the castle after closing—well, perhaps they could do more in the future in that regard ... And secondly," he lowered his voice and I felt a brawny hand on my arm, steelily steering me away from the others, "there may be more to the story. You are quite right—normally I myself would not come out late in the evening for a trivial matter like this. I'd send an underling, not even Scarron. But ... ," he paused as if to gather his thoughts, "it occurred to me to ask my counterparts in nearby counties if they'd had any reports of similar accidents elsewhere. I had a hunch something might be amiss. They all automatically said no, yet ten minutes later the prefect of the next county over, Indre-et-Loire, had his assistant call me back. I was astonished he would admit to anything, but in fact someone had taken a tumble a couple of weeks ago at Amboise Castle—died, as it turned out. We should've been informed of it, but I'm sure their main concern was to keep it out of the papers. As you probably know, tourism in the Valley of the Kings is crucial to the economy. After Versailles, we're number one," he said proudly.

"Putting business before truth," I shook my head disapprovingly, yet convinced he was right. "So, what about the victim? A woman again?"

"No, a man in this case. But he didn't have any ID on him when he was found either. Curious, huh?"

I cocked a solitary eyebrow.

"Someone finally recognized him, and he happened to be a big-name winemaker and a professor of oenology in Bordeaux."

"An oenology professor?" I echoed. The lovely, stylishly dressed blonde on the stairs at Chambord hadn't looked like the academic type to me.

"Yes, with a funny name too, Charles Bouture," the prefect replied. "The guy was still on the young side, but he appeared to be rather out of shape and perhaps even had some sort of medical condition. The autopsy showed a fairly high level of alcohol in his blood—not that surprising for a winemaker!" he laughed derisively. Then, becoming serious again, he added, "The boys in Indre-et-Loire suspected he'd had a few drinks at a nearby restaurant, but no such evidence turned up. He visited the castle shortly before closing, and somehow escaped detection until the next morning—which is bizarre, as they don't fool around over at Amboise." He paused and then recommenced, "I know the director there—we hunt together—and they're incredibly thorough. It's privately owned, you know."

"So, you're thinking ..."

"Maybe some kid did a 'bump and roll,' deliberately banging into him in order to surreptitiously pick his pocket, without realizing the guy would career to his death, or ..."

"Or?"

"Or maybe he slipped and fell and some enterprising young soul took the opportunity to liberate him of his wallet. That seems to be what the police in Indre-et-Loir wanted to conclude."

"But you are not so sure?"

"Well," he made a face, "Scarron tells me he was no ordinary professor. He gave interviews to prominent media channels in which he repeatedly provoked everyone in the country."

"Did he, now?"

"Yes, he shocked the entire spirits establishment by asserting that wine tasting is all in one's head. A firestorm of criticism broke out recently when he proclaimed to the world that some crazy percentage, like ninety percent of our experience of wine comes from reading the label. Can you imagine a professor saying that?"

I laughed heartily, admiring Bouture's rather unmitigated Gaulish gall. "Probably not so far from the truth when it comes to Burgundy and Bordeaux wine snobs, but hopefully not for real connoisseurs," I opined, obviously thinking of myself. I had just completed a Grand Tour, as I liked to call it, of the top vineyards of the Champagne region and had tasted as many as a dozen new champagnes a day. It's beyond me why anyone would drink sickeningly sweet big-name classics like Moët & Chandon or Dom Perignon anymore, and I felt that more acutely every day I was there. To me such wines are mere relics of James Bond movies from the sixties and seventies, and will forever adorn Frasier Crane's dinosaurish wet bar (I do occasionally watch TV). For today, little known but fabulous boutique champagne houses are turning out exquisitely refined and flavorful extra bruts. But I digress ...

I was about to mention some of my favorite champagnes, like Egly-Ouriet and Bedel, when, scrutinizing Durtal's face, I realized my interlocutor was probably not a fellow champagne enthusiast and it wasn't the time or place for it. This major debate evidently amused him, but seemed not to concern him in the least. Who knew, maybe he only drank beer, maybe even just Belgium's answer to Budweiser, Stella Artois. So I confined myself to adding, rather conventionally, I confess, "Still, one can see how he would have raised the ire of many in the French wine world with an incendiary claim like that!"

* * *

I returned to my hotel, the Relais de Chambord, the only lodgings in the castle's pristine park, a park overflowing with wild boar and deer. Like a child, I always hope to see one of those majestic beasts grazing in the meadows or dashing across the road—except when I'm driving, of course, but I wasn't tonight, just strolling. None, unfortunately, appeared out of the mist.

The hotel occupies a recently renovated posthouse a mere stone's throw from the palace. It's a true oasis of style and serenity set off from the hordes of not-always-so-stylish visitors. I had promised myself I would dine there that evening—another best-laid plan destroyed, this one by "the girl on the stairs." I wouldn't have minded if a girl had spoiled my plan in some other way, if you catch my drift.

A plate of leftover charcuterie and cheese, which the late-night waiter at the bar was kind enough to scrape together for me, was fated to be my rudimentary repast. Tray in hand, I strolled back toward my wing, passing the same American father and son billiards adversaries I had seen playing pool that afternoon in the spacious, well-appointed game room near the bar. The father kept reminding his son he was stripes not solids, and to keep his eye on the ball, but their hours of practice had not changed much in the son's performance: the poor cue ball hopped around on the table this evening just as it had this afternoon, and even flew off the table altogether as I walked by. It was headed east, straight for the castle!

Why, I wondered, had the boy failed to improve despite all those hours playing with his father? Were his elder's instructions senseless or overly complicated? Or was the son unwilling? I recalled Leonardo da Vinci's preternatural powers of observation, whether it was of how different kinds of birds took flight and made use of the wind, how horses reared up on their hind legs, how the human frame twisted and turned during certain activities, or what the human face truly looked like (one never found babies with adult faces or musculature in his work, which was almost the rule in painting done just half a century earlier, something I've always found laughable). Why could one person focus so thoroughly and not another? Was it something innate, as so many wished to convince us today? Brain chemicals allowing some to concentrate and others not, as drug companies plangently proclaimed, bribing psychiatrists to prescribe their wares? Or was it simply a problem between father and son, whether refusal to please, a stubborn wish to figure everything out for himself, fear of surpassing his dad, or something else altogether—something I would never have envisioned, something elusive and almost indecipherable?

Having wended my way through narrow but plushly carpeted hallways and up improbably located staircases, I entered my room where a loud ring interrupted my speculations.

"Why don't you give us a hand?" Durtal asked without any preamble. It sounded like an order. "In a sensitive investigation like this, we could use a plainclothesman like yourself, someone who won't scare people away."

I wondered whether he wanted to keep me close because he thought I could help or because I was still a suspect.

"I'll be in the area for a few days," I replied rather noncommittally, "and don't have any very specific plans." Well, I did, but more on those later.

"Scarron can head things up at headquarters, but ..."

"But he tends to strut and flash his badge a bit?" I attempted to finish his interrupted thought for him. After all, I knew the type back in the U.S.—Olivetti, Ponlevek, and plenty of other of New York's finest.*

He seemed to concur monosyllabically.

"If I'm going to help out," I told him, "I'll need a number of things from you right away: the date, location, crash position, and autopsy report for the Amboise incident, and your best guesses as to the exact times at which both incidents occurred. Is there any surveillance video footage at either castle?" As you can see, I take my cases, like my champagne, quite seriously, and Durtal wasn't the only one who could issue orders.

Durtal said nothing, but seemed to be fumbling with paper and pen, as he cradled his cell phone and strode across a stone floor, his footsteps echoing loudly.

"I'll also want specifics about all exits to both castles, including rarely used doors and underground escape routes."

"Chambord was built on a swamp, you know," he said peremptorily.

Indeed, I had always wondered how anyone could have dreamt of erecting such a massive structure—running over a hundred thousand square feet—in the middle of a mosquito-infested marsh on oak pilings. You might just as well build the Empire State Building on a bog! The Tour de Constance on the Mediterranean coast—the defensive tower with the thickest stone walls I had ever seen—was also constructed on top of trunks of oak trees sharpened at one end and driven into the ground, but King Saint Louis didn't have much choice: that was the only practical port he had from which to launch his crusade and it needed to be fortified. King François I, on the other hand, had a choice. It was as if he had deliberately selected the most difficult site possible for the largest castle in history. Chambord was truly a dream, yet a dream come true.

"I realize it is unlike any other palace," I replied coolly, "but there is a little-known door that opens out onto the moat from the king's apartments."

"Really?" Durtal replied dryly. "Are you sure?"

"Yes. Keep in mind, too," I explained, "that an assailant may have used a window to escape, even at what most people might consider to be an unsafe height. So, we want to know if any windows are found unlocked—apart from the one I myself used to get back into the castle from the roof."

The prefect made scratching sounds, as if he were jotting something down. "You're very thorough," he remarked with a hint of ill humor and strain in his voice.

"Hold on," I exclaimed suddenly. "If the girl was in fact pushed, her assailant may still be hiding in the castle. He might be waiting for the crowds to arrive in the morning to make his escape!"

My interlocutor seemed to shudder inwardly at the thought that the possibility hadn't even crossed his mind, or that he had just brought on board someone who could foresee things he couldn't.

"Or *her* escape," I added pensively. "Can you get a team to comb through the place tonight?"

"I'll get the boys started right away," he replied, but then added, "It's going to take hours."

He began barking indistinct orders in the background and I had to yell to get his attention, "Don't let them forget the latrines in the basement of each tower."

"Latrines?" he coughed, catching his breath.

"Yes, latrines. The castle was built with the latest in Renaissance creature comforts and has an integrated sewage system. Our mystery assailant may know about it." The prefect seemed to be taking notes again when a more urgent thought flashed through my mind, "Is the staff equipped to check everyone's ticket on the way out to verify that it was purchased the same day?"

Durtal whistled. "I doubt it. And it'd be impossible anyway, since they are expecting somewhere around seven thousand visitors tomorrow."

"Yet it would make it awfully easy for us to find our assailant that way," I remarked. "Assuming he bought a ticket, that is, and didn't come in through a window or one of the lesser-known doors."

"I'll do what I can," the prefect said, sounding like he'd had enough and was about to hang up. Was he already regretting his decision to bring me in on the case? It usually takes people longer to begin to hate me, or at least have serious second thoughts.

"Wait!" I interjected. "I'll want all the information you can come up with about Charles Bouture. And a list of all the activities going on at Amboise and Chambord when the falls occurred, whether private visits, wine tastings, theater productions, concerts, lectures, fireworks, or any other special events."

"There are dozens of those every day," Durtal said. "Listen, Canal, I don't want any hysteria over a couple of falls! The Minister of the Interior will demote me to traffic cop if any of this gets out."

"Who said anything about it getting out?" I retorted calmly. "We need to see if there is any correlation between the dates of the falls and specific events being held at the castles. Speaking of which," I continued, "it would be good if I could have such lists for other nearby castles as well, not just for comparison's sake but ..."

"But?" Durtal enquired.

"To predict where we may have to expect the next incident to occur."

"The next incident?" the police chief echoed indignantly.

"Yes," I replied calmly, "*jamais deux sans trois*" (if it happens twice, it's bound to happen again). "We should be prepared for almost anything at this point."

CHAPTER TWO

Clos Lucé Castle in the town of Amboise

Details make for perfection and perfection isn't just a detail.
—Leonardo da Vinci

The warm red brick and creamy white stone of Clos Lucé Castle shone brightly in the July sun, standing on foundations dating back fifteen hundred years, to the time when the Romans still ruled Gaul. A lowly upstart built* and fortified the initial manor house in the Middle Ages (he began his career as an asscook stirring pots for Louis XI, a cruel but pragmatic king famous for promoting loyal simple folk to positions of power). King Charles VIII expanded and transformed the manor into a discreet yet elegant *château de plaisance* or pleasure palace in 1490.

Then along came François I, the Renaissance king and unsurpassed patron of the arts and gardens. He gave the exquisite Château Gaillard next door to a humble gardener who invented a way to grow orange trees in the Loire Valley. As thanks for his innovations in the art of gardening, Pacello da Mercogliano received the royal dwelling (where Mary Stuart later spent one of her many honeymoons) in exchange for a bouquet of orange blossoms every year! And in 1516 François offered the Clos Lucé to a certain Italian artist, Leonardo da Vinci, to entice

17

him to leave the mean streets of Milan for the small but royal town of Amboise to be "the king's principal painter, engineer, and architect." All *he* had to do in exchange was discuss philosophy with the king whenever the latter had a free moment! That was perhaps the first time a head of state gave precedence to beauty, art, and philosophy over war and taxes. Will it turn out to have been the last?

Leonardo ended up crossing the Alps into France on a donkey—taking the *Mona Lisa* and *Saint John the Baptist* with him in his saddlebags—and set up shop in what was to become his final home, the Clos Lucé. Would he finally have the career there that he felt he deserved?

Chatting with the ebullient concierge at my hotel that morning, I had learned that da Vinci's last residence was hosting "the most amazing and extraordinary exhibit"—dozens of Leonardo's works that had been lent by museums the world over.

"Haven't you heard, sir? It's the five-hundredth centennial of da Vinci's death in 1519."

France had turned the Florentine into the center of the universe for the occasion and I didn't know it! I had come to the Loire Valley to see the magnificent sights—I'd seen them before, of course, but not for some time—and had even been asked by a friend who published a travel magazine to chronicle my visit in the form of a multi-installment travelogue, which I fully intended to write during my spare time, or at least on the plane back to New York. So I wasn't going to let a couple of ninnies tripping on stairs at Chambord and Amboise stand in the way of my vacation plans. It's my policy to make time for fun, even in the midst of an investigation. Otherwise, what's life for?!

The concierge also promised to procure me a ticket to the concert being held at Chambord that very night at which the famously gifted Henri Wack was conducting. Every last seat had been sold out for weeks, but he would obtain one anyway.

Wandering around da Vinci's house as though it were my own, despite it being a tad overrun by visitors that day—who were all those extraterrestrials? I tried to tune them out—I drank in the serenity of the age-old rooms and furnishings, savoring the homey feel of the place. The Clos Lucé was, after all, built for a family, not for a king's entire court and retinue like Chambord was. I was very impressed by the bold, recent recreations of Leonardo's studio and study. As I contemplated them, I was transported back in time, transfixed by the soft glow of the crackling fire in the hearth. I could easily imagine him painting next to it, or perusing a worn leather-bound monograph by the light of the three-tiered mullion window.

I was less impressed by his artworks (the art establishment be damned!). They were conspicuously or not so conspicuously unfinished, as usual. It was not that I did not like some of them—and I realize that the double negative smacks of denial, but there it is all the same—yet I never thought them God's gift to humanity. I have a greater fondness for da Vinci's elaborate sketches in his myriad notebooks. So instead of dwelling on the prominently placed canvases, I spent the lion's share of my time contemplating the drawings exhibited on and around his desk in the workshop, relishing every minute there.

It was a spot where few lingered, I noted, preferring as they did to admire the pretty paint powders and brushes surrounding the master's easel. I had never before seen his sketches of the movement of water, around the piers of the bridge over the Loire River in Amboise, for example—showing in great detail the turbulent eddies and vortices that formed at the base of the piers supporting the bridge's arches—and around a wooded island in the middle of the mighty waterway. The flight of birds, the involutions of clouds, arabesques, the curls in people's hair, the turning of gears, or the swirling of fluids, whether perfectly smooth or disturbed by hydraulic friction and backflow—all kinds of circular and spinning movements obviously fascinated him. He made Descartes's cosmological vortices seem like small potatoes and would, perhaps, have preferred Blake's vortex—that obscure, all-consuming, destructive, and solipsistic center of desire from which a lover begins and to which he eventually returns.

I gazed only briefly at the scale and full-size models of da Vinci's designs for tanks, moveable bridges, bicycles, cars, flying machines, and paddle boats that an engineering-trained team of da Vinci enthusiasts at IBM had painstakingly built. I'd seen them a dozen times, they being permanently exhibited in the castle's basement, yet always discovered something new when I studied them closely. But today my stomach was growling. Out in the flower-filled courtyard, waiters and waitresses were scurrying about, serving packs of hungry tourists who were quaffing glasses of chilled rosé in the sun or in the shade of the white umbrellas. I sauntered over to the low wall overlooking the grounds below the castle and admired the view. The lawns were baking in the summer heat, just as they had for Leonardo all those centuries ago. I suddenly recalled that there was a second restaurant tucked into the woods where fewer tourists ventured.

The prospect of Leonardo's residence from the grass below was very impressive, with its high pinioned roof, and the white fairy-tale mullion windows (the ones that look like they have a big stone cross in the middle of them) contrasting felicitously with the pink brick. The place had always had a special place in my heart—I could easily imagine living there, reading by the fire, and petting the cat who could sometimes be seen dozing on the dining room table, oblivious to the tourists passing through. The greensward around it was inviting, but the woods behind it in the fanciful park were disconcertingly alive with bodies and voices today, and I was dismayed to find the second restaurant almost as crowded as the first.

Resolving to do something I never do, I walked over to a woman lunching alone at a miniscule table—a size unknown in America—at the outdoor café and asked if she would mind terribly if I joined her. (Why, you might be wondering, did I pick her table? Weren't there other singletons I could have accosted? I don't recall noticing any …) She was unusually courteous, instantly invited me to sit down, and gracefully handed me a heart-shaped menu. I introduced myself, without extending a hand toward her—in France one shakes hands with a woman only if she offers to and I always strive to follow the local codes of *politesse*—and took a seat. I then proceeded to peruse the unusually pretty menu cover to cover, hoping against hope that it might harbor a rare gem of a wine, and that she would be able to survive for two minutes without checking her phone.

Reading a book as I ate, a voice interrupted my study.

"Are you a mathematician?" my table companion inquired.

"No," I said, looking up from my book, "but I do dabble a smidgeon in topology and a number of other branches of mathematics."

"So, you're a dabbler?" she asked, with what struck me as a touch of sarcasm in her voice.

"I suppose one could say so," I replied cautiously, wondering if I was less touchy with women than with men.

"A bit like da Vinci himself?" the woman went on, grinning. She had finished her salad, having left behind a few edible flowers making her plate resemble a charming little garden, and was pouring herself water from a huge glass bottle of Evian.

"Oh, I don't think I'd go that far," I smiled broadly at this. "In our times, it is not quite so easy to be a *touche à tout*, a jack"—in my mind I imagined it spelled Jacques, for some reason—"of all trades, a polymath, or Renaissance man, as it was in his times. Milton could boast that he had read everything worth reading, but most fields have now become so incredibly specialized! In Leonardo's day, artists like Perréal, Verrocchio, and Brunelleschi were architects, engineers, painters, sculptors, military strategists, and all-purpose inventors." Those bygone days had always appealed to me. Were they now altogether out of reach? I wasn't so sure …

"I see you know your art history," the woman said, passably impressed it seemed, while I worried that my slight tendency—as I like to think of it, although it is undoubtedly an ingrained propensity—to be long-winded might turn her off. Yet she offered me some frog water (in the words of Harrison Ford, and yes, I enjoy making fun of my own country and fellow countrymen at times after so many years abroad), which I gladly accepted.

"Whenever we come here, my nephew always stands near the castle gates," I remarked with some emotion, "reading and rereading the résumé posted there that da Vinci sent to the future Duke of Milan, enumerating all the services Leonardo could propose during both wartime and peacetime. It cracks him up every time." She smiled and I sipped the cool liquid she'd poured me. "Leonardo was ready and willing to serve kings and princes as a military engineer, but also as a party planner, designing fireworks, automated puppets, and sumptuous banquets."

"Quite versatile, indeed! He was even an accomplished musician, singer, composer, and storyteller who won lute competitions and designed newfangled musical instruments, some of which were oddly macabre," she opined, an indefinable expression on her face.

"Still, his inability or unwillingness to finish things he started often held him back, despite his obvious talents. Don't you think it's sad that at the end of his life he said, 'I have never finished a single work'?"

Her eyes widened.

I warmed to my topic since she evinced interest. "Another artist had to take over many of the projects da Vinci contracted to do and sometimes even started, but did not complete. It just goes to show how crippling stubbornness" (I was going to say "neurosis," but settled on a word that was less charged) "can be even for a genius like—"

"You think it was plain old modern neurosis" (she obviously wasn't afraid of the clinical sounding term) "that stopped him from finishing things, and not his constant search for the perfect …," she looked for the right words with which to finish her thought, "… face or the perfect structure?"

21

She had rather fine structure herself, I found myself thinking, and a beautiful face to boot. Had this nymph subliminally planted that thought in my mind?

"I know he once claimed he couldn't finish *The Last Supper* because he hadn't found an ugly enough visage on which to base his rendition of Judas," I laughed, even as I wondered whether she would think me too much of a graybeard.

"I heard that too," she laughed with me.

"As if there were a correlation between outer ugliness and inner evil, or between skin-deep beauty and moral goodness!"

"If only it were true," she eyed me searchingly. "It would make life much easier," she added with a touch of yearning in her mellifluous voice.

"Yet we might just as well believe Santa and Satan are related because they're anagrams. But is anything perfect, truly perfect?" I looked skyward for a moment. "Well, maybe a few of Mozart's concertos could be thought absolutely perfect, but isn't 'perfectionism' just a polite name for pathology?"

Lord knows I shouldn't be casting stones, given the trouble I myself have occasionally had knowing when to put down the pen, stop reworking my manuscripts "twenty times on the loom,"* and send them to press. It had gotten so bad in recent years that I had seriously tried to find someone to be my amanuensis—someone to turn my notebooks full of disparate ideas into publishable texts, like Francesco Melzi was supposed to do for da Vinci. It was right here, at the Clos Lucé, that late in life Leonardo gave his brightest student instructions for putting together the "Treatise on Painting" he'd been planning for thirty years. Da Vinci secretly hoped, I suspect, that Melzi would take it upon himself to publish everything, all his planned treatises—cobbling together his thousands of one-page or even just one-paragraph reflections into something that could somehow hang together—but that didn't happen.

"Pathology!" she interrupted my thoughts and scrutinized my face. "Who are you? A mathematician, a wine connoisseur, a dabbler, a doctor ...?"

"I actually scribble a good deal—"

"Here are your desserts," came a voice, and the waiter set down identical dishes of blackcurrant sorbet in front of the two of us. *Quelle coincidence!*

We sampled the intensely flavored fare, and I lapsed back into thought. Melzi never got around to sending a single one of Leonardo's manuscripts to a publisher, despite having outlived Leonardo by some fifty years. He bequeathed the entirety of da Vinci's notes to his son who simply crammed them in his attic. ("Can you imagine stumbling upon a find like that?" I almost asked her. A sleuth with a solid background in art history could make quite a career out of attics across the continent!) An enterprising thief later stole a baker's dozen of the notebooks, had no luck selling them to anyone, and then offered to return them to the son who refused to take them back, having no conception of their value. It took well over a century* for the first fragmentary edition of a *Treatise on Painting* to fall from the presses, and there was no hope we would ever see the other planned treatises. Some claimed Leonardo wrote them and they were simply lost, but, given what was known of his life story, I considered that highly unlikely.

I glanced at my table companion. She had a strange, worried look on her face and didn't meet my gaze.

In my own case, I felt it would require such an exceptionally sharp person to serve as my amanuensis that I had rejected all applicants—so far, that is. Was I afraid of ending up with an *editio in usum Delphini*, a bowdlerized version of my earth-shattering work? Was I looking for the *perfect* interpreter of my opus? There was that damned word again! I myself had been known to criticize the notion that there could be a perfect fit between two people—as in the belief there was such a thing as Mr. Right—or, to hit closer to home, a perfect fit between analyst and analysand, and yet here I was looking for a perfect fit between thinker and scribe. How dumb was that? As if all interpretation weren't misinterpretation! (Had I been the first to proclaim it? Hardly, since it was implicit in the age-old Italian dictum *traduttore, traditore*.)

I decided to drop the subject of perfectionism. "Is it Leonardo who brings you here, or just the beauty of the Manoir du Cloux?" I queried.

"Both, I guess you could say," she replied, all smiles suddenly, her Hermès scarf quivering in the slight breeze, inadvertently revealing a hint of cleavage. She looked surprised that I knew the name the Clos Lucé went by when it was first built. "I run the place."

My jaw must have dropped of its own accord. I would have expected the director to be someone with white hair and maybe even a venerable beard.

"Well, bravo!" I enthused. "It is a delight to visit the rooms you have just redone on the ground floor. They provide so much more atmosphere—one feels like one is truly entering da Vinci's world! It's like he still lives here, and just ducked out for a quick chat with the king."

"Thank you," she replied, visibly pleased. "I did it all myself, naturally," she added, her tone and manner clearly indicating the exact opposite, as only human speech allows us to do—something I never cease to marvel at.

"Your modesty is very becoming," I remarked, and the lady without a venerable beard blushed. "I will be sure to sing your praises in the travelogue I am writing." Although she gazed at me inquiringly, I went on, looking her straight in the eyes and waxing cheeky, "Now if only you would open up the circular staircase over the chapel and the secret tunnel between the Clos Lucé and Amboise Castle, I could die happy." I guess I was being pretty obvious, but I make no excuses: I hoped to see more of her. (And you can take that however you like.)

"Few are so lucky, alas!" she laughed.

I assumed she meant so lucky as to die happy, but feared she meant to see the staircase and tunnel.

"I'm afraid that the secret passageway doesn't extend all the way to the castle, but only to an old well located in the center of town. The safety risks of opening it up to the general public have proven insurmountable, but we do allow a select few to see such wonders."

"A select few?" I echoed. "How, pray tell, does one become one of them?"

"It depends partly on who you know," she said, her expression momentarily hidden by her lemon yellow scarf which a zephyr had set aflutter.

* * *

I naturally offered to treat the high priestess of this magical locale to coffee after the private tour, and we sat on an ancient wall overlooking the grounds. I could see her face perfectly now. Throngs of people continued to spill out into the courtyard (far too many for my taste, but Durtal would be happy), and at the risk of spoiling her good mood, I asked Claudine Thoury whether the crowds were ever such that accidents occurred in the castle—people banging into each other, falling on the narrow spiral staircase up to the ramparts, and the like.

"The Clos Lucé is the fourth most visited site in the Loire Valley, you know," she replied.

"That's extraordinary," I exclaimed.

"So, yes, people do occasionally get scraped up or bruised when jostled by other tourists. It isn't easy to stop the Chinese from blocking traffic as they take selfies every five steps," she smiled mockingly, "or to stop the Russians from elbowing people out of their way."

I chuckled. "Nothing more serious than a few scrapes and bruises?"

Thoury looked a bit surprised at my insistence. "Not in the years I've been here," she replied. "Maybe one sprained ankle. I can invent more injuries, if you'd like … for your travelogue?"

I don't know why I glanced at *her* ankles at this point, but her legs looked lovely in her well-tailored dress. "I'm not at liberty to disclose any details of the investigation I'm conducting," I began, "but—"

"Investigation?" the director looked at me strangely. "Are you some sort of cultural attaché? Is that why you mentioned Perréal and Brunelleschi?"

I raised my eyebrows skyward and eventually replied, glancing at her, "I guess I'm curious, in more ways than one."

She frowned and then cried, "Is that why you've been talking to me? Trying to get information out of me?" The damsel's eyes flashed angrily.

"I had no idea who you were until you told me yourself," I replied, unruffled.

This seemed to reassure her, even if there was no guarantee it was true, so I went on, "I am investigating certain incidents in the general area for the prefect of the Loir-et-Cher, but was simply wondering if anything unusual has happened at the Clos Lucé in recent weeks or months."

She examined my face for a few moments, and then, as if overcoming some kind of fear, said, "There is something. But … "

Seeing her hesitate, I fished Durtal's card out of my inside jacket pocket and handed it to her. She glanced at it cursorily and then, looking at the people milling about, said, "Not here. Follow me."

We climbed the steep flight of stairs alongside the restaurant located in one of the outbuildings—she had me precede her for obvious skirt-related reasons, something I would have proposed anyway—and entered a high-ceilinged office with wood beams and exposed brick. "The oddest thing happened the night before the exhibit of da Vinci's artwork opened this summer," she said hurriedly, taking a seat and

25

inviting me to do the same. Her office had a true woman's touch to it, being discreetly decorated with verdant plants and lit with dimmed lamps. Stately Renaissance music was playing softly in the background. "I came to work the morning of the opening, took my usual walk through the premises, and noticed something out of the corner of my eye." She paused.

"What?" I inquired expectantly.

"It was one of the paintings on loan from the Uffizi in Florence. It seemed different to me, but I couldn't figure out what it was at first." She was obviously still disconcerted about it, whatever *it* was, her usually mirthful, teasing tone having disappeared. Could she turn it on and off at will? Yet there seemed to be no reason for her to toy with me … "Looking at it again and again, I finally realized—it was the strangest thing!—the many portions of *The Adoration of the Magi* that had never been completed by da Vinci were suddenly … "

"Suddenly?"

"There."

"'There'? What do you mean?"

"I mean *there*." Her face showed signs of stress, but she maintained her composure. "It was as though Leonardo had suddenly completed the painting." It seemed Thoury still didn't entirely believe it herself. Breaking her own silence, she added, "As though the old master had returned and finally decided how everything should look. The additions blended in beautifully with the rest of the canvas, the colors matched perfectly, and the brushstrokes were exactly like da Vinci's."

I was at a loss for words, which is rare for me.

"I was in shock," she confessed, looking at me. "I have some pictures of it here if you'd be interested in seeing them." I wondered if she was offering to show them to me primarily to prove she wasn't crazy.

I nodded and examined them for a time. "Can you please send me copies of them?"

She assented silently, accepting the card of the Relais de Chambord I extended.

"So what did you do?"

"Nothing," she replied. "We obviously couldn't exhibit the painting in that state. And we certainly couldn't return it to the Uffizi like that. They just spent years restoring it themselves. I didn't know what to do." I didn't envy her life as a curator hosting a priceless collection like

26

that. She must have had some sleepless nights worrying about it even before the incident. "Eventually, in desperation, I called the best-known restorer of Renaissance paintings in France."

"And?" A dark cloud passed overhead, eclipsing the pictures of the *Magi*.

"She finally showed up yesterday," she said, her face brightening for a moment in the penumbra. "We won't know for a while yet whether the painting has been permanently damaged or not."

I tried to lift her mood. "At least it was a painting that he endeavored to finish and not one of the sculptures on loan here. As da Vinci once quipped, painting proceeds *per via di porre*, by successive additions of particles of color, while sculpture proceeds *per via di levare*, by removing bits of stone." (Freud had once likened the latter to psychoanalysis, I recalled, employing a sculptural metaphor for once instead of an archeological one, but with much the same purport.) "Your expert restorer might be able to wipe away added particles, but it would be hard to restore ones that had been chipped away!" She seemed grateful, although it probably hadn't occurred to her before that she'd been fortunate in her misfortune. I was happy to see some of the tension in her comely countenance dissipate. "So who did the nocturnal paint job?"

"We have no clue," the Venetian blonde curator responded. "It's as if someone flew in and out, or snuck in and out like a fox. Nothing was taken, no prints were left behind. We doubled security and hired extra night guards just for the paintings on exhibit. But we have no idea who did it."

"So that leaves only da Vinci himself," I said.

"As if he returned on the five-hundredth anniversary of his death to finish what he started," Thoury proffered.

"Finish what he started …," I echoed, slowly rising from my chair, and handing her my personal calling card. "Be sure to let me know what your restoration expert finds. Maybe a close examination of the paints and brushes used can provide us a lead."

"Canal," she read my card, and paused. Her lips turned up anew at the corners. "With your knowledge of Italian art, you must be a descendant of the great Canaletto, Giovanni Antonio Canal."

"Not that I know of, but I'll be sure to look into it."

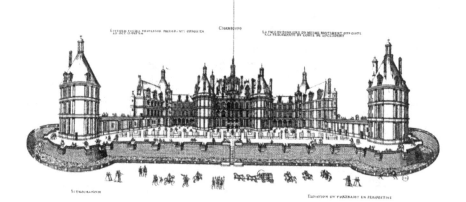

CHAPTER THREE

Chambord Castle courtyard

If you worry about finishing, you'll never start.

—François I

"Good evening ladies and gentlemen, and good evening even to those of you who are neither ladylike nor gentlemanly." A few giggles emerged around me as I ensconced myself in a folding chair in Chambord's regal courtyard. The hotel concierge had worked his magic and I was seated as close to the stage as I could possibly have hoped. Over dinner I had perused the program notes with unadulterated delectation, and was thrilled when the buzz of the crowd died out and I saw the conductor step up to the microphone.

"Despite my balding pate and brand-new tuxedo, I am not the great Avid Sapristi, but rather Henri Wack, the conductor of our little symphony."

"He doth protest too much," I reflected. "I bet he thinks he's greater than Sapristi."

"Orlando Civadin, our concertmaster, or as some of my fellow musicians occasionally say, our 'master of disaster,' could not be with us tonight, but I predict that you will witness stranger things still here, for, unless she shows up in the next two minutes, I am going to have to play the part of our talented bassoonist. Personally, I suspect she was seduced by someone in the king's apartments up on the second floor"— he pointed behind him and to the left toward the northeast wing—"and was then dragged off to the dungeon where she will be tortured by being forced to listen to my rendition of her part." Guffaws could be heard on several sides.

"Now, my elective instrument is the recorder, so I find myself in a doubly unusual position tonight, as I have never played this piece before." He turned around and looked at the orchestra. "In fact I'm not sure anyone here has." Laughter now broke out all around. "But we'll do our best to bring the program we have promised you, Lully's 1678 opera, *Psyché*, to life." He glanced off into the wings, hopefully, and then back toward the audience. "We decided to play some of Lully's music, for he himself played at Chambord on at least two occasions, perhaps in this very courtyard. So here we are, ladies and gentlemen, reliving a piece of history! Now the opera, like so many love stories I myself have been involved in, includes a great deal of tragedy instigated by Venus, demonstrating how dangerous Beauty can be."

There was a story there, I was sure.

"Which proves," he went on, "how little power to charm and harm we balding men usually have." Having a full head of hair, it was easy for me to smile at that one. "Venus, the goddess of Beauty, feels upstaged by Psyche, a mortal whose beauty she calls 'criminal,' and takes revenge on her. Tonight let us hope that it will only be Lully's tale that includes moments of tragedy, not the woodwinds." He gazed again into the wings, anxiously I thought.

"So let us set the stage: The Sun King is at the height of his reign," Wack began, donning a gleaming gold crown and picking up a scepter, "and dazzling all of Europe with his splendor. Lully, one of Louis XIV's favorite composers, had to write this opera in record time, having only three weeks before it was to be performed at the Royal Academy of Music in Paris. Not even he could compose a whole new opera in three weeks, so he recycled much of the music he had written seven years earlier for Molière's play *Psyché*. The storyline of the opera was thoroughly reworked by the librettist—yes, I do intend to bore you with the names and there will be a quiz after the concert—Corneille. Not the renowned Pierre Corneille, but his younger brother, Thomas, and this never doubting Thomas wrote the opera in collaboration with his nephew Fontenelle. But you know how it goes when you try to do anything

30

constructive with a family member: The nephew panned every line he wrote and the uncle objected to all of his nephew's ideas—at least that's what would have happened between me and my nephew! In any event, they managed to devise a fine story for the performance, one that ends well, so bravo for them!" he added, clapping, and gesturing to his musicians to clap along with him.

"You are all, I'm sure, familiar with the story of Psyche and Cupid." A number of heads in the audience nodded assent to this. "If you aren't, go to Azay-le-Rideau Castle to see the tapestries devoted to the tale in one of the bedchambers. My favorite line in the opera, and one that I would like to repeat to a very special someone," Wack looked all around the stage and audience, letting his gaze dwell on every woman on which it alighted, "is 'It is a crime for a lovable girl not to love'*—it being understood that she should love the man who truly loves her, not some random stranger."

He put his hand on his heart. "If only she would get the message!" Laughter spilled out from a few of the musicians onstage, and a man sitting in the aisle seat near me abruptly stood up and left the tent in what appeared to be a huff. "Was that the conductor Avid Sapristi?" I wondered, having gotten only a fleeting glimpse of his furious face.

"Okay, it's true," the conductor went on, "that in the opera the lovable girl is adored by Cupid, who just so happens to be a god. But we can't all be gods, now can we?" He picked up a handheld mirror at this point and frowned at his reflection in it. "The great thing about the story is that Psyche learns to love Cupid without ever seeing his real visage, which gives hope to those of us who are aesthetically challenged." Throwing the mirror across the stage in disgust, he added, "Personally, I find that a lot more compelling than the woes instigated by Psyche's curiosity in the opera, of which much is often made. But what rings universally true is how Cupid's mother, Venus, tortures her future daughter-in-law!" His face took on an indefinable expression, seeming to combine pain and malicious delight.

Then, waxing serious again, he resumed, "Lully's performance was undoubtedly attended by the very sovereign who was responsible for having disrupted the perfect symmetry of the castle around us. Go to the second floor and you'll see the humungous apartments he built for himself. I visited them earlier today and you'll never believe what I saw when I peeked under the king-size bed—genuine seventeenth-century briefs and brassieres! I have them right here, somewhere, ladies and gentlemen," he added, feeling around in his instrument case. "*Ça faisait désordre* (It looked messy) as you can imagine, and I hate messes, so I called the cleaning staff right away and gave them a good what-for." The conductor stopped looking in his case and tried his pockets, but to no avail, although to considerable laughter from the audience. Even the orchestra was cracking up now. "Well, I guess I must have mislaid them …"

"Anyway, we deliberately chose this opera by Lully because it is rarely performed. We are hoping that only one or two of you will have ever heard it before and that most of you will therefore be unable to compare our rendition to better versions of it available at nearby venues. Just a little joke to see if you are still awake!"

He gazed searchingly all around the stage and then at the audience, placing his hand above his eyes as if to help him see further. "No bassoonists on the horizon?" he asked. "No? Then I guess you'll have to make do with this buffoonist."

The audience applauded wildly, and I settled in for what promised to be a rather unusual musical event. Nor was I disappointed: from the diminutive woodwind instrument a virtuoso performance emerged!

* * *

Who could say no to an after-concert drink in the courtyard at Chambord? Certainly not me! I adore the little receptions they throw in the French countryside for the spectators and musicians.

Having approached the table where a number of professionally attired servers were pouring out glasses of top-quality sparkling wine, known throughout the region as Crémant de Loire, I was offered a libation, stepped aside to allow others to be served, and studiously sipped my drink. It wasn't champagne, but this bubbly was pretty damn good, quite subtle, with notes of apple and citrus. I was sorry not to be sharing it, on a beautiful night like this, with a friend, a female friend … A lemon yellow scarf flashed through my mind. But I was sure I would see her again. All I had to do was bust a ghost, the brush-toting chimera of Amboise, and restore a priceless painting that had been manhandled while in her care.

The conductor, mingling with several people from the audience, appeared to be holding court. Scouring the crowd, I espied the symphony's flautist, Françoise Foix according to the program, and approached her. I introduced myself with my trademark courtesy, beginning with urbane small talk about their inspired performance and the incomparable setting—the full moon making the exceptionally white stone walls of the castle glow, holding us all in awe. The brunette was wearing a snugly fitting black designer dress ("Givenchy?" I wondered) that accentuated her hourglass waist, along with a classy pearl necklace and matching earrings. Such style was rarely found among musicians, in my experience, although a few sopranos still made an effort. Looking like a paragon of good taste stranded in a sea of mediocrity, she unhesitatingly accepted my offer to have her glass refilled for her by a passing waiter. And what luck for me that she turned out to be from Saint-Rémy-de-Provence, a town I could talk about for hours, from the hiking in the nearby Alpilles to the Mas de la Dame and Romanin, fine wineries nearby.

Women are generally less inhibited and funnier after a few glasses (don't hate me for saying so), so I offered the young woman yet another refill of Crémant de Loire. I would have done so anyway out of my usual attentiveness to such things, but I also hoped the old adage *in vino veritas* would be borne out when I steered the conversation toward the missing musician. Foix didn't refuse the top-off, and I told her the story behind the libation, "This delightful wine was made by one of my favorite winemakers in the region, Vincent Girault."

She raised an eyebrow and I went on, "A man who groomed his daughter to take over his vineyard when he retired. But she went missing at the last minute. And why do you think she did so?"

"I can't guess," she replied, shaking her head, her hair moving little, however, held in place as it was by a black velvet hairband.

"The girl ran off to the big city to become a shrink, of all things!" I mean it's hard to think of two more different occupations, even if they do both involve seeking the truth.

She laughed gaily, sipped the heady elixir with renewed interest, and I added, "Speaking of women who run off, this missing bassoonist of yours, what's she like?"

"Anna Pislova?" she queried, her voice suddenly turning icy cold.

"What am I doing asking one woman about another woman?" I reprimanded myself silently.

"Close-minded and tight-lipped. From Eastern Europe somewhere."

I dared to ask about her looks, and Foix made a face. "Blonde—artificially, no doubt. Her absence tonight is out of character. She really wants to keep this job. But she'll almost certainly be excused for not showing up," the flautist opined, with a smile and a wink. "He thinks she's good-looking."

What did she mean? Who thought that? Oh, of course …

* * *

Wending my way through the warren of atypical staircases at my hotel to finally get some shuteye, my thoughts revolved around the fact that everyone seems obsessed with pictures of themselves these days. Is it just so much easier now to take and publish graven images? Musicians, in any case, have to be among the most photo-crazed, putting pictures of themselves everywhere—on posters, CDs, programs, you name it! In this case, it came in handy.

Seeing the concert program in my pocket, some force—was it rivalry?—had guided Françoise Foix's finger directly to a photo, a vanity shot of the evening's featured, albeit MIA, soloist. Imagine my surprise upon seeing the same blond hair, blue eyes, and white skin as those of the mystery girl on the stairs!

I gleaned quite a number of things from our chat, without apparently raising any suspicions, although Foix was perhaps perplexed or even miffed that I did not ask for her number after our lively conversation. Had she thought I was interested in Pislova? She might have been disinclined to give me her number—after all, stranger things have happened!—but her name was an obstacle to me: I had once dated a Françoise and things hadn't gone terribly well between us. Funny how important names can be.

The flautist told me that Anna Pislova had only begun playing with the mid-sized Symphonie de Provence recently. She was serious—many women are far more serious than men these days, after all—disinclined to mingle, and gave others little eye contact. Thought "hot" on the outside by some, she played it cool.

Quelle chassé-croisé! (What a mess!) Foix clearly envied the bassoonist, though perhaps not for her musical ability. When I jokingly asked her whether she thought the bassoonist had any enemies, she laughed and replied, "You mean apart from me?" I noticed her watching Henri Wack as he scanned the crowd for someone, even as he bantered with his admirers. So the flautist was in love with the conductor, and he was smitten with the bassoonist …

Does love always have to be so complicated?" I wondered, as I entered my room. "Or is it something other than love? Lust? Prestige?" My speculations were interrupted by a loud ring of the telephone.

"*Âllo oui?*" I answered. "*Déjà?*" I exclaimed (Already?).

"No rest for the weary," I muttered to myself as I pulled my blazer back on and gathered my keys.

* * *

An hour west along the Loire lies a little town, complete with cow pastures and an ancient church, which is dwarfed by the hulking castle that gave the burgh its name (or, rather, changed its name): Villandry. No one comes for the cows or for the august, well-proportioned Romanesque church built around a fifth-century chapel—it's the castle's myriad extravagant and meticulous gardens that are a magnet for tourists from the four corners of the globe.

As I drove there in the dead of night, I tried to recapitulate the facts and then let hypotheses come to mind as they might. A winemaker had died at Amboise Castle a couple of weeks ago, a "ghost" had finished one of da Vinci's paintings at the Clos Lucé Castle a week ago, a musician had taken a dangerous fall at Chambord Castle yesterday, and someone had suffered a lethal plummet at Villandry this evening. An old castle was involved in each case.

The events at Amboise, Chambord, and Villandry had occurred in alphabetical order, but the quick jump to Villandry didn't leave much room for a continuation of the possible series, assuming there would be one. Actually, there was another castle by the name of Villesavin in the area, I suddenly recalled. I'd have to look that one up. But the incident at the Clos Lucé didn't fit in alphabetically. In any case, it seemed so qualitatively different from the others that it couldn't possibly be related.

Were these events somehow tied to something fantastical like the history of the castles? Did the series run, for example, from the oldest to the newest? But which is the oldest? Even the most professional of historians would have a hard time answering that one. Each of the structures has elements from different centuries, having been built and rebuilt over the years as architectural and artistic tastes changed, as did their owners' fortunes. Indeed, almost nothing in Touraine escaped that fate, the area having been prosperously inhabited forever, which was not the case in most other regions. That made dating the castles difficult if not downright impossible. Should I pick the year construction began in the Renaissance? The year each edifice was finished? The age of the oldest known structure on the site? Or—why not—the date of the first blood shed within its walls?

"There's no beginning, there'll be no end," I thought unexpectedly, a song from the sixties echoing in my head.

Chambord Castle was the simplest, having been begun in 1519, after total leveling of the prior hunting residence of the Counts of Blois. And I had read that the majority of the work had miraculously been completed by the late 1540s. Still, end dates for such massive palaces were especially difficult to determine, and several subsequent kings had continued the project.

Amboise Castle—a mere crossbow's shot from da Vinci's last home—was begun in 1492. That was earlier than Chambord, but Amboise's origins are prehistoric, people having occupied the promontory on which it sits for thousands of years. If I were to base the order on precedence, Amboise would beat Chambord hands down. For while a simple lodge existed on the site in Chambord already in the tenth century, Amboise's fort had already been burnt to the ground *and* rebuilt by the ninth.

Work on Villandry, according to the *Guide Bleu* I kept in my car, began in 1532. Yet five centuries earlier there had been a castle mound on the site* and later a defensive castle. At least the Renaissance construction start dates of the three castles were in the same order as the incidents … Not surprisingly, the Clos Lucé did not fit into this chronological series, and I decided to put this obscure line of inquiry on the back burner for the time being. I began thinking I should have had a cup of coffee before leaving the hotel, especially since the driving conditions were worsening, the moon now being eclipsed by dark menacing clouds.

Might there be something connected to who built the palaces? But why would anyone base a series of crimes on something as bizarre as alphabetical order, construction dates, age of sites, builders, or architects—and why not throw in the king's mistresses, while we're at it? Lord knows he'd had scores of them! "Well, odder things have been known to happen," I thought, reassuring myself that I wasn't merely spinning my wheels as I recalled cases of serial killers I'd heard about. Maybe, I reflected, returning to a line of thought that had occurred to me before, we were going from the castle where the least dramas had occurred to the one boasting the most. Behind their perfect facades, horrific scenes of every kind had occurred …

I realized full well, naturally, that all such cogitation was premature, but I always speculate first. Generating as many suppositions as possible allows certain so-called facts to become visible that I might otherwise overlook.

"What about the dates on which the incidents occurred or the intervals between them?" I couldn't help but wonder next. The one at Chambord had occurred on July 3rd, and tonight's had occurred on either the fourth or the fifth—I'd have to ask Durtal about the probable time of death. Three and five were both prime numbers—indeed, "twin primes," those separated by just one other integer—as was 29, the date of the incident at the Clos Lucé. But I did not know the exact date of the fall at Amboise—had it been on the 17th? If so, we might have to expect further incidents of some kind in just a couple of days: on the 7th and possibly on the 11th and 13th of July. I would not be able to calculate the intervals between each pair of successive events until I knew the exact dates, but one thing was clear: they were getting closer and closer together.

"Was it some sort of kangaroo Fibonacci series?" I wondered, as a rectangular sign announced that I was entering the world-renowned town of Villandry.

CHAPTER FOUR

Villandry Castle

Watch out for that first step, it's a doozy!

—*Groundhog Day*

It was pitch black out when I reached the castle and a light rain was falling. Actually, it was more like a mist or what people in Normandy call "spittle," better known here as *bruine*. I stumbled through the thick shadows to the castle entrance where I found Durtal, who had just arrived, leaning against a towering stone wall and complaining about the weather—I wondered where he was from, as no one from the Loire could be outraged by meteorological conditions so typical of northern France—to a tall man and a slightly younger woman with a very serious mien. The man turned out to be the castle owner, Hervé Castillo, whose name was synonymous with the most famous gardens in France. He designed them to be environmentally cutting edge and to shimmer with ever-changing colors throughout the year, and still found time to head up a prestigious national association of castle owners, *La Demeure historique*. He looked young, and his youth contrasted sharply with the venerable dwellings over which he presided.

The woman proved to be Scarron's counterpart in the next county over from the one in which Chambord was located, Indre-et-Loire—or should I call it the rival county? When Durtal introduced her to me, he seemed pleased that Jeanne Le Coq was filling in for her boss (his counterpart) who was on vacation. "Were they an item?" I wondered, glancing from one to the other. (I'm nosey, I admit it.)

Le Coq shook my hand professionally, yet warmly somehow, and looked me in the eye as she did so. I noted this perhaps all the more markedly since it has become so rare among young folk today whose social IQ has, in my not-so-humble opinion, declined by at least two standard deviations and who can't address anyone, no matter how distinguished, with any other greeting than one that sounds like what people feed horses. (I'm persnickety, too, I know.)

The castle owner peeked at me out of the corner of his eye as he shook my hand a bit limply. He looked somewhat haggard and disheveled, like someone who had been yanked out of bed in the middle of the night, which is precisely what had happened. One could immediately sense the difference between him, a civilian used to undisturbed sleep, and the police officers who had seen years if not decades of late night emergencies. (I later learned he was jetlagged from a recent trip to America.)

The head commissioner—a woman with a perfectly round face and auburn hair peeking out from under the hood of her raincoat—looked wide awake and had been the first to arrive. She was based far closer to Villandry than Durtal or myself, and she had already been to the scene of the incident, something of which she seemed quite proud. She, Castillo, and the night watchman—who had seen nothing until he almost tripped over the body during his rounds—had set up some spotlights to help us survey the damage, as it had occurred out of doors. A tarp had been thrown over the body—to protect it from the rain, I wondered, or to protect us from the sight of it?

Le Coq pointed to an ornate white stone balustrade high above us in the brume. "It's been raining for a while here and he probably slipped. But he might have jumped or been pushed."

"What the hell was he doing in the park so late after closing?" Durtal asked Castillo, looking the man who was just as tall as him straight in the eye. "Doesn't your staff sweep through the grounds to ensure that everyone has left before dark?"

"Actually," the soft-spoken castle owner replied factually, and we all turned toward him in the soggy stillness, "at Villandry, we allow people to leave whenever they like. There is a gate over on the far side of the park," he pointed westward, "through which people can exit after closing time." He seemed to enjoy saying the unexpected. "No one else does it, but that's our policy here. Some visitors stay to watch the sunset from the terraces, stroll in the perfumed evening air, and even admire the stars from the *jardin d'eau*, the Louis XV-style pond."

"Doesn't that lead to complications, Sir?" I asked.

"It hasn't until tonight." Castillo turned toward me and his dark eyes took on an indefinable expression. "The only people who have ever overstayed their welcome were a man and a woman who hid inside the castle itself because they had always wanted to spend a night here."

I laughed. He looked sober and cerebral, but had a sense of humor, I thought.

"I hope you charged them the going rate for a five-star hotel," Le Coq chipped in mercenarily, evincing little in the way of poetry.

"No," the mild-mannered owner replied, looking toward the exit and reverting to his polite yet distant demeanor, "we just sent them on their way. A few ghosts may overnight inside as well, as late-shift janitors occasionally report odd noises and the smell of cigar smoke, but I haven't yet seen any of them myself even though I grew up here," he added modestly in front of the stately, regal palace that looked even grander by night.*

Durtal seemed appalled by such a stance. "So after hours there could be no one in the park or five hundred people, and you'd never know it?" he asked, staring incredulously at Castillo. "My ex-in-laws were here last week and said the gardens were packed!" He shot a glance at Le Coq and then hastily added, "You must get thousands of visitors a day here."

"We don't count them on the way out, if that's what you're wondering."

"You at least count them on the way in?" the prefect asked, somewhat aggressively and haughtily.

"Those who are kind enough to buy a ticket, yes," Castillo replied quietly, seeming to be more awake now and enjoying shocking Durtal. "A few undoubtedly scale the garden wall in the less frequented parts of the park." Looking the prefect in the eye now, he added, "We don't have barbed wire fences and guard towers around the perimeter of the property, if that is what you were expecting. We leave the German shepherds to others."

41

Durtal would have liked, it seemed to me, to upbraid the man for his lackadaisical attitude, if not for his sarcasm. But whether it was because Villandry was not his Loir-et-Cher turf or because Le Coq and I were present, he refrained from doing so.

"You'll be happy to hear that they do have a video surveillance camera at the ticket office," Le Coq proffered, as if to appease her ruffled colleague.

"Great," Durtal remarked petulantly, "that will allow us to narrow down the list of suspects to three or four hundred an hour—assuming we can identify them with facial recognition software—plus every guest who came in over the garden wall courtesy of Monsieur Castillo."

"Do we know who he is?" I asked the young commissioner, pointing at the supine body.

"He had no papers or wallet on him," Le Coq informed us. "He isn't a pretty sight ... "

"Well, let's have a look anyway," I suggested. I knew the Loire well, but had never conducted an investigation here and wondered if it was typical for people not to carry ID. "I would at least like to check out his crash position to see if it can tell us anything about whether he slipped, threw himself off the terrace deliberately, or was pushed into the void."

Le Coq removed the tarp, revealing a middle-aged man lying on his back, his head soaked in blood.

"Rather unusual crash position," I commented. We all looked up at the railing of the equivalent of a seven-story building and tried to picture it. "Any idea of the approximate time of death?" I asked.

"My guess would be shortly after midnight. The body was still warm when I got here," she said, seemingly pleased to be better informed than her male interlocuters. "I'll ask the boys in forensics to look into the crash position."

Castillo had been gazing intently but had remained silent since the tarp was removed, and all at once I grew afraid he had been more than a little troubled by the sight of the dead body. "I know who he is," he suddenly said. I was wrong, thinking him too moved to speak. We all looked at his serene face.

"You *know* him?" Le Coq inquired.

"No, he is not even a casual acquaintance," he assured her, glancing again at the body in what seemed to be calm horror. "But I know his work. He's a well-known figure in the world of mathematics. Won the Fields Medal, the Fermat Prize, the Henri Poincaré Prize, and a slew of others." My eyes widened. "I've often seen him on television, and I even have a couple of books on my shelf from a series he edits." He pointed a wet finger to a distant window—his study, perhaps.

"You mean Sidney Lavillaine?" Le Coq blurted out.

"Exactly."

"You've heard of him?" Durtal asked, unabashedly giving the attractive officer the once over, although there wasn't much to see, dressed as she was head to toe in loose-fitting bright yellow raingear (yes, I'd already looked).

"Of course. But I never fell for his studied eccentricity," she replied coldly. "I had heard he sported shoulder-length hair and always wore a brightly colored *lavallière*," she pointed to the rather elaborate looking, old-fashioned cravat around the dead man's neck. "Also pinned a large brooch to his jacket representing some sort of invertebrate, like this octopus here," she said, pointing again. "I should have realized who he was right away." A smile then appeared on her stern face. "Even fancied himself a politician in recent years. Just ran for office in a part of France he never lived in."

"Like every other French politician today," Durtal grumbled, standing up straight as if to show off his already considerable height. To whom? And wasn't his own job rather political?

"He's not your run-of-the-mill politico, however," remarked Le Coq.

"No, he certainly isn't," the castle owner interjected. "Few of them imitate John Napier, the Scottish mathematician who never went out without a black rooster perched on his shoulder."

"Claims not to be on the right or the left, but not in the center either," the commissioner added.

"Original," I proffered. "Sounds more like a poet than a mathematician," I said with a laugh despite the solemnity of the scene. I believe Edgar Allan Poe had something to say about such people. I, naturally, had never heard of Lavillaine, spending as I do most of the year in New York, and avoiding television like the plague—hadn't it once been called a weapon the Russians invented to destroy American education? The French have managed to convince themselves that TV in their country is educational and even highbrow, which it may have been once upon a time. Today it's either politically tendentious or just as vapid as anywhere else, even when they make a show of interviewing novelists and scientists.

43

"Comes from a long line of painters and writers, according to what I heard," Le Coq conceded. "But prides himself on the speed with which his mind works, and drives racing cars to keep his reflexes quick."

Eyeing them both closely, and tucking away for later contemplation the fact that his family included artists, perhaps even nocturnal ones, I asked, "Would either of you happen to know anything about his area in mathematics?"

Le Coq, who seemed to know everything, said, "Mr. Castillo is a highly accomplished engineer and a nationally ranked chess player." She bent over the corpse and covered it anew with the tarp. Finally. "I bet *he* knows."

"Lavillaine works in many areas," Castillo answered my question, silently and self-effacingly correcting my naïve presumption. "I mean he *worked* ... I still can't believe it ...," he said, glancing back toward the tarp, and trying to regain his self-composure. "Started out in cryptography, if I recall correctly, but then moved on to entropy, chaos theory, and models of turbulence. I saw him on TV just the other day talking about airflow and jet engines." He paused for breath. "Also promoted a whole line of popularizing books on mathematics, a number of which center around the Riemann zeta function and prime numbers."

"Prime numbers ...," I mused distractedly. Speaking up, I asked, "Do you know of any enemies he may have had?"

"Enemies?" he echoed, shrugging his shoulders. "Some researchers feel he had sold out."

"You didn't answer my question."

"One thing is for sure: he was such an attention whore—if you'll excuse the phrase, for it really fits here—that one journalist dubbed him the Lady Gaga of mathematics." He said this in the same tone of voice in which he said everything else, never letting on that he was about to deliver the punch line. "Personally, I have mixed feelings about him, if one may say so in such circumstances," he added, looking away, toward the river.

I encouraged him to go on for the good of the investigation.

"I have sometimes said he is to mathematics as Michel Onfray is to philosophy—it's not as glitzy a simile, but just as damning." He looked around to see if any of us had caught the reference, and seemed pleased when he saw that Le Coq and I had. "To his credit, Lavillaine actually proved some theorems, and he prided himself on explaining things clearly and simply, something which may well have vexed his fellow professors. French intellectuals tend to prefer to make students feel stupid instead of smart. To their way of thinking, the point of writing and lecturing is not to teach but to cow and impress."

"Really? I never heard any such thing about the French," I remarked disingenuously, having been accused of it myself in what seemed like a former lifetime, when I traveled in rather different circles. The fact remained that I did not share Castillo's typical post-French Revolution belief that it is possible to democratize knowledge, and have always relished Mencken's quip that "Democracy is a pathetic belief in the collective wisdom of individual ignorance."

"It's a well-known fact—ask any foreigner studying in France. Lavillaine, for his part, strove to write in such a way that the reader feels like a genius." The castle owner paused, gazing up toward the terrace above us. "In any case, he was surely envied by many in the mathematics establishment for his media attention. But could we call them enemies? Rivals maybe ..."

* * *

I wondered how many steps it took to go from "rival" to "enemy," letting my mind wander as I drove back to my hotel in the dense darkness. It would have required great strength to lift someone over the crenelated parapet around the castle keep near the famous love garden, but the momentum of a few short steps would suffice to push someone, who was resting or admiring the view from the north terrace, over the fairly low stone balustrade there.

If it had been suicide, it was rather flamboyant given the location, but then that fit the man's persona. And a mathematician like him would undoubtedly have calculated the height of the terrace in advance. Only his crash position still puzzled me.

Castillo's grandfather was a famous war hero shot by the Nazis, I suddenly remembered, in honor of whom the family had erected a memorial in the castle's park right near that terrace. Is that why his grandson had mentioned a hatred for barbed wire?

The few cars on the road were moving fast as the lights of the city of Tours—the capital of the region known as Touraine, where a Celtic tribe known as the Turones settled some twenty-five centuries ago*—began to appear on the horizon. All at once I realized I had forgotten to tell Durtal something. Accidentally? On purpose? Accidentally on purpose?

45

It was about the identity of the amnesic girl. The old saw, "a little knowledge can be a dangerous thing," floated through my mind.

I had always felt knowledge was best reserved for the worthy. Misguided scientists ended up splicing fish genes into tomatoes, cloning sheep, and designing superviruses for biological warfare, like they did in Lyon's P4 laboratory, Maryland's NIH labs, and at dozens of universities around the world and certain Chinese research centers. Employing so-called gain-of-function to weaponize existing scourges, such madmen made them so infectious, airborne, and lethal that no safety measures could contain them.* It was only a matter of time before they would infect and kill most of their creators, and hundreds of thousands along with them. The insane engineers who built atom and neutron bombs would likely be responsible some day for the deaths of millions, if not billions. They were, as I'd heard one scientist with a good head on her shoulders say, like children playing with matches and gasoline, foolishly hoping they won't burn down the planet.

Science sans conscience n'est que ruine de l'âme (Science without conscience is but the demise of the soul), the world-famous Dr. Rabelais had said. The man occasionally flew off on drunken rants and tangents, but he still knew what he was talking about. Five hundred years of so-called progress had repeatedly proven the Renaissance physician's point. The YouTubeification of knowledge was decidedly not my cup of tea, even if it was Lavillaine's and Castillo's. I preferred Mariage Frères! Keep knowledge out of the hands of unscrupulous scoundrels, I always say. But then it wasn't always easy to know at the outset who would prove to be one and who wouldn't …

On the main highway, I recalled something else I had failed to tell Durtal and should know why I didn't know why I hadn't failed to—. What? Too many negatives!

Was I really convinced that the sound I had heard on Chambord's roof had been nothing more than the wind blowing open and closed a window I myself didn't try? After all, there were thousands of panes that I couldn't even see in the thick fog, much less reach.

I told myself things were moving so fast I didn't have time to think of everything. I had forgotten to ask Durtal whether they had found any unlocked windows or doors at Chambord during their search. But deep down I knew I had avoided broaching the topic so as not to feel obliged to mention what I myself had heard. Was I determined to solve the Loire Valley castle case all by myself?

XVI Siècle. CHÂTEAU D'AZAY LE RIDEAU,

(Touraine.)

construit par Gilles Berthelot,   Trésorier de France.   restauré à M. de Biencourt.

CHAPTER FIVE

Azay-le-Rideau Castle

Une femme, ça ne s'invente pas.*

—Anonymous

The town was long known as Azay-the-Charred. A bloody battle for the throne pitted young Prince Charles (later to become King Charles VII, of Joan of Arc fame) against his powerful vassal, the Duke of Burgundy, a man who committed the cardinal sin of trying to crown a Brit king of the Gauls, England being France's hereditary enemy! Their soldiers duked it out, so to speak—far from Burgundy's renowned vineyards, whose reputation is second only to Bordeaux's—in Azay-le-Rideau. It was referred to as *Azay-le-Brûlé*, Azay-the-Charred, for many years thereafter because the teenage prince achieved what most adolescent boys can only dream of (and practice tirelessly in their video games): total destruction. His men burned the ancient fortress there and everything around it to the ground.

A century after that somber episode, the castle was completely rebuilt (much of it, too, on oak pilings), and today it stood glittering like a flawless Renaissance diamond in the bright summer sun, yesterday's Norman spittle having finally ceased. The extremely elegant outbuildings added later sparkled with their black slate roofs and gold-leaf

49

covered finials rising high into the sky. I was so right to come see the castle today! It was finally freed from the scaffolding that had obscured it for the past couple of years, and the scintillating façade had been restored to its rightful splendor, exactly like Gilles Berthelot, its owner and builder, had imagined it in his dreams.

He was one of those rich, daring fellows who—like Jacques Coeur, Semblançay, and Fouquet—took it upon themselves to finance a French king's extravagances and wars. And like them, he made no distinction between the royal finances and his own. The fiscal whiz should have realized it would be impossible to explain how he could afford a more sumptuous and avant-garde palace than the king himself, even though his fortune had been made legally. Yet he, like the other central bankers, as we would now call them—there was no such thing as the Banque de France, Federal Reserve Bank, or Bank of England back then—just couldn't help but show off his wealth. All of them ended up fleeing the country, suffering imprisonment in austere Alpine bastions, being forcibly exiled, or even being hanged like mere riffraff. They seemed, at the time, to be a necessary evil. "Were they still today?" I wondered.

Berthelot's five years of insane extravagance, from 1518 to 1523, had proven saner than sane in a way, however, because he bequeathed us one of the crown jewels of the Loire Valley. I had every intention of visiting his unfinished architectural fantasy before the concert that was to be held in the castle's park that evening, one in a series being given by the Symphonie de Provence before its inexorable trek southward.

I was also hoping to pick up the trail of something there, having spent the night dreaming of really big prime numbers, black roosters, and Fibonacci series bouncing around like the cavalry attacking Roland in Roncevaux. The dead mathematician had no surviving family and the deceased winemaker's home lay far away, near Bordeaux. Bordeaux is fine, don't get me wrong—even if its bottles are often overpriced and its vintners are totally intoxicated by their status as the wine captains of the known world—but a trip there would require me to leave the Loire for at least a day or two, whereas the crucible of the action appeared to be here. Maybe I could convince Durtal to send Scarron there ... with a little expense account for vino as an inducement. It might even help the lead investigator burn up (or remedy) some of his nervous energy— well, maybe if he traveled the two hundred and fifty miles by bicycle.

Some might object to my method of working, especially if they are familiar with how mathematicians tend to approach problems.

They slave away night and day for weeks, months, and even years at the same theorem, single-mindedly enlisting prodigious powers of concentration on a problem—Doxiadis's *Uncle Petros and Goldbach's Conjecture* may be fiction, but it's no joke. Maybe you've heard that Grigori Perelman, who sketched out the solution to one of the past century's biggest brain teasers—the Poincaré Conjecture—and then refused all the prizes that were showered down on him for it, secluded himself for seven whole years, telling no one what he was up to. (It took four long years for various teams of researchers simply to check the internal coherence of his proof!) Mathematicians like André Weil vaunt the lucid state of exaltation they occasionally fall into as one astounding thought after another miraculously presents itself to them, some even saying it's better than sex because it can last for hours, even days. One has to wonder about that claim—at least wonder about what it means for those who would endorse it ...

My working methods are altogether different. Emptying my mind plays a crucial role in them, and I prefer to rely on waking up in the morning after receiving what I once heard a Fields medalist refer to as a person-to-person "call from the god of mathematics," the answer bubbling up from the unconscious. And as is typical of what emerges from the deep, the answer is often the exact opposite of what I am expecting and trying to demonstrate. So don't think for a minute that I was slacking off by going to concerts, drinking sparkling wine, and chatting with pretty women. All in a day's work!

* * *

I had, in fact, put some time into the investigation that morning, and had even breakfasted with the polizei, or at least its local incarnation. Not that I had planned to ...

Upon awakening, I tried to check the Symphonie de Provence's concert schedule to see if it coincided with the "accident" a couple of weeks earlier at Amboise, but my brochure only covered this week's performances. Why couldn't the ever-so-sophisticated French produce brochures with real coverage of events? Did they schedule absolutely everything at the last minute?

I dialed my favorite extension and asked the canny concierge to secure me a seat—and perfectly rainless, windless weather, naturally!—at the outdoor performance of garden-themed music that evening in

51

Azay's enchanting park. The celebration of flowers in the Loire Valley reminded me of a quote I had heard attributed to Freud, which I suspected was apocryphal: "I have wasted my time; the only thing that is important in life is gardening." Such a remark would have sooner passed my lips than his.

A table on the hotel's magnificent patio with the most unobstructed view of Chambord awaited me for my Sunday morning repast. I had, of course, picked it out in advance in my hyperlucid mind, this form of exaltation being more my speed. To my left was the comely canal supplying water to the moat around the castle. It had picture-perfect stone bridges over it. And right in front of me was the edifice, glowing the creamiest of whites in the morning light.

While tarrying in this oasis, I flipped through a book on Chambord's architecture and construction history that I had espied and eagerly picked up in the lobby. It turned out to be one I already knew: *Chambord: L'œuvre ultime de Léonard de Vinci?* (*Chambord: Leonardo da Vinci's Last Work?*) "Interesting coincidence!" I thought.

Turning the pages, I stopped short, the words "Hold your horses" flashing through my mind, and leafed back a bit to my favorite part. A French researcher* had been virtually laughed out of academia for proposing what was eventually proven true about the original design. He'd had the gall to base his discovery on the latrines and septic tanks— funny how we so often make discoveries through the lowliest parts of a building! Every guidebook and video now loudly proclaims the truth he dredged up, demonstrating that sometimes you have to be dead and buried for your ideas to be accepted. Or is it just that no one is ever accepted as a prophet in his own land? Maybe if he'd been American or German ...

As it turned out, the initial palace design called for a spinning structure, like a gigantic helicopter with four independently rotating blades, ready for liftoff! People then immediately assumed it must have been da Vinci, finally conceiving the ultimate spiraling machine, who proposed it. Domenico da Cortona, who purportedly built a wooden model of the place, could not, they claimed, have been its sole designer.

A bird flew overhead and attracted my gaze to the castle anew. Every other castle is just a castle, but there is only one Chambord! I was willing to credit Leonardo for the advanced sewer system and the water-tight roof design, perfectly suited to a land of endless fog and drizzle like this valley. And I was even willing to admit that the arcades that encroach on their superimposed architraves (long horizontal stones, for the architecturally challenged—you'll be quizzed at the end by Henri Wack) on Chambord's third floor façade—designed to make all three stories appear to be the same height even though they aren't—were prefigured in his sketches for the Medici Palace in Florence (a distant world for the barbarous Frenchmen of the time); as was, possibly, the unusual idea of including massive corner towers on a square or rectangular structure (he had seen small ones at the Palazzo Ducale in Urbino while working for the manic-depressive Cesare Borgia).* Still, nothing doing—I couldn't be convinced that da Vinci was the main architect, having my own ideas about why each tower had been intended to rotate ninety degrees with respect to its neighbors, and I toyed with the idea of discussing them in my travelogue—even if it would make me the next victim of academe's derision ...

The sky blue book lying next to me was more captivating than anything by John Le Carré, revealing as it did many secrets of the unique layout. One of the beautiful blueprints in it suddenly reminded me of Villandry. Its love gardens were set out in the exact same rotational pattern. Was that a regular feature of gardens back in the day? I'd have to examine the myriad drawings in Du Cerceau's renowned tome on architecture.** Glancing up, I felt I could sit there for hours cogitating, sipping the best coffee I'd tasted in weeks from a porcelain cup decorated with gold *fleurs-de-lys*.

All at once, the image of a dark staircase appeared before my mind's eye, the one I had felt my way down from Chambord's roof. In medieval times, spiral staircases turned in such a way that a righthanded soldier could run down from the highest point in a castle brandishing his sword in his right hand and gripping the handrail or steadying himself against the wall with his left. The assailants, forced to fight lefty, were at a disadvantage. At Chambord, built during the Renaissance when defense no longer dictated design, all the spiral staircases I had hitherto taken—admittedly, not all seventy-seven of them—turned the opposite way. But the one I went down that fateful night followed the usual medieval model. That could mean one thing and one thing alone: I had found my way back down into the castle through the northeast tower. For the prescient scholar had been right: the entire floor plan, including the direction of all the staircases, had been reversed in that tower in order to allow the northeast wing containing the king's apartments to be added on, a decision made after construction had already begun.

53

The northeast tower was therefore the mirror image of the originally intended one, something no casual visitor notices. And Leonardo da Vinci wrote backwards—right to left—such that most ordinary mortals could only read his handwriting in a mirror. Thus while it was at least plausible that this supremely enigmatic building, designed like a flying machine and intended to be symmetrical in such an unusual way, had sprung from da Vinci's hyperactive imagination, it seemed more than just plausible that, if he had been asked how to extend the castle to satisfy a royal whim, he would have simply held up a mirror to the blueprints of the northeast tower. Presto chango! "When exactly had that decision been made?" I wondered.

Mirrors ... Da Vinci was fascinated, as I myself had once been, by concave ones—although he probably had no need to use one as he wrote or read his own writing. He obviously used a mirror to draw his self-portrait. If, indeed, it was a self-portrait! Funny that everyone pictured him like that, whereas he had always been clean-shaven, dyed his long graying locks blond, and only decided late in life that he wanted to look like a druid or a Greek sage—Pythagoras or Plato. My mind began to wander, from the sign over the door of Plato's Academy—"Let no one ignorant of geometry enter here"—to what it would be like to view a Fibonacci series in a mirror. I now recalled that Leonardo, too, had read Fibonacci's work.

"Canal, are you in a trance or what?" boomed Durtal's deepthroated voice.

"No ..." I started, looking up at the neatly dressed prefect.

"I figured I'd find you dawdling. You have it pretty good here," he added, with a sweeping gesture encompassing the whole of my little paradise.

"Well, I may have just solved an architectural conundrum of some not inconsiderable moment," I proffered. Being a stickler for ceremony, I stood as I shook his hand warmly. I frowned inwardly, suddenly realizing that da Vinci couldn't possibly have weighed in on how to extend the palace, a decision apparently made after work had already begun, since he had died a few months *before* construction began at Chambord. So much for solving an architectural riddle! Unless the experts were wrong, I reflected, grasping at straws to try to preserve my lovely hypothesis.* Or, if they were right about the actual construction start date, maybe his fascination with mirrors had rubbed off on his fellow castle designers? On François I himself?

54

"What about *our* conundrum?"

"Won't you join me?" I asked, pulling out a chair for him.

He seated himself and surveyed the scene. "What are you waiting for?" he asked as though I had no right to eat.

"My low-cal breakfast," I explained emphatically. "The service here can be on the slow side when there are this many people," I said, gesturing toward the patio around us that was now packed with chic foreigners and Frenchmen. "Would you like to order something yourself? My treat."

"Maybe just some coffee, thanks," he replied. "You and Le Coq both seem to know the same celebrities," he added with no lead-in.

"Aren't you confusing me with the handsome, cultured Castillo? He was the one who knew Lavillaine. And, personally, I wouldn't recognize Lady Gaga if I ran her over with my car," I said without thinking, only realizing afterward that it was a rather odd trope, "even if I do know she has a reputation for flamboyance."

"Okay, fine, but you mentioned some guy by the name of Humphrey and she ate it up." Durtal adjusted the plump cushion behind his back to make himself more comfortable.

"Castillo was the one who mentioned the attention-hound pop philosopher." I prefer never to mention such people by name—it makes them exist when they don't deserve to.

The prefect blatantly shrugged off my comment and, a waiter appearing out of thin air, ordered *"deux doubles express, sans lait ni sucre,"* totaling four shots of strong espresso, taken black. Whom could he need a jolt like that for this morning, I wondered, or was it every morning?

"You thought she was interested in *me*?" I asked.

"I'm sure she was," he replied.

"We can be mistaken sometimes, you know. Even Socrates, who bragged he always knew who was in love with whom, may have been wrong now and then." I did not think it was the time or place to mention that the Greek philosopher may have misrecognized his own feelings for someone, leading him to misrecognize that guy's feelings for him and for a third party. Did you follow that? I confess, I do go on at times …

"Not me," he asserted baldly, ignoring my free association. "It's possible she was taken with Castillo, the man who has everything," he acknowledged. "Women have eyes only for brains and prestige, in any case."

55

"So women never look at you? You're the last man on earth women notice, Mr. Chief of Police of the entire county?"

"Exactly. Especially since my wife left." He paused to take a breath. "When I meet girls now, I compliment them constantly and try to ingratiate myself with them, laughing at all their jokes, funny or not, and agreeing with everything they say, no matter how dumb."

"So maybe they sense you are not really interested in them, just wanting somebody to plug a hole in your life."

He looked aghast for an instant. "You think women can pick up on that?" he asked anxiously.

"You think they can't?" My eyes widened.

"I guess I hoped they couldn't ..."

I nodded. People really kid themselves, I reflected. It never ceases to amaze me.

"I keep looking, hoping," the winsome prefect uttered.

I glanced to my left toward the edge of the immense forest. "Like Thibault the Trickster, you're doomed to hunt the same deer for all eternity?" The prefect laughed suddenly at this. At Villandry last night, he had told me I could just follow his car home, since he lived a few short miles from my hotel, just outside the Chambord Castle park walls, inside of which he had hunted ever since he was old enough to lift a rifle. "The one that can fill the gap in your life?" (I didn't mention to the forlorn fellow that we pretty much all feel we are missing something, and wistfully imagine a time when we weren't, when something or someone made us whole—psychoanalysts claiming it was when we were being fed at our mother's breast, the gnawing feeling in our stomachs being filled by the milk and other suffering being offset by the warmth of mom's body and the comfort of her arms. Some envision "true love" as what can make us whole again. Others hope that the emptiness inside and longing can be filled by prayer, repentance, Brahma, the Holy Spirit, or some other incarnation of the godhead.)

He scrutinized my face. "They never do. You think you've finally bagged the broad you'd always been looking for, but either you never really catch her or she turns out not to be who you thought she was."

"Or you turn out not to be who she thought you were," I opined.

He sipped the steaming royal coffee that had just arrived, cautiously at first, then more greedily. "You mean I lead them on or dupe them into thinking I'm someone I'm not?"

"Don't you? Don't you try to convince each of them that you're crazy about her and her alone?"

"Isn't that what they all want to hear?" he queried cantankerously.

"Maybe not, if it isn't true. Perhaps you are *dur avec elles* (hard on them), Durtal?"

"Me?" he exclaimed. "Nah. Anyway, I don't think I'll ever understand women ..." The prefect looked off into the distance for a moment and then brightened. "Did you hear the one about the righteous man who'd been divorced three times?"

"I don't believe I have," I replied, glad to see the morose mists lift.

"God offers to grant him a wish, so he tells God he's afraid of flying." Durtal was now smiling broadly. "Could God build him a bridge from France to Martinique so he could drive there? God objects to the environmental impact of such a long bridge and inquires whether the man might have a different wish. The serial divorcee then asks God to explain women to him."

I guessed that joking made him feel better about his own failure (or resistance) to grasp even the most elementary facets of female psychology. Women, I reflected, must feel crushed when he tries to get them to shoulder the burden of his desperation and to heal it for him.

"To which God replies, 'How many lanes would you like on that bridge?'" he continued, laughing loudly even before he finished delivering the punch line.*

"So not even the Almighty understands women, but you're sure they don't want to hear the truth from you?"

"If they knew the truth, they'd never ... ," he trailed off.

"It's that bad?" I inquired gingerly.

"Well, let's just say they all complain sooner or later, and they all leave me at some point," he added, gazing at the delicate, feminine cup in his large ungainly hand. "I keep looking for someone who will fit me like a glove, and instead," he went on, blithely changing metaphors, "it's like trying to ram a square peg into a round hole."

"Maybe the hole is not as round as you think," I proffered, looking at him out of the corner of my eye, thinking it was, indeed, a rather tawdry and even parlous state of affairs, and recalling for some reason Renyi's quip that a mathematician is a device for turning coffee into theorems.

"Huh?" His brow furrowed.

"Maybe the hole is so convoluted that only a hugely complicated object could fit into it, as complicated as the one it would take to fill the space inside Chambord's double-spiral staircase."

My giant truffle and herb omelet finally arrived and Durtal stared in amazement as a smartly aproned waitress grated a generous quantity of thin black truffle slices onto it. The spectacle, the aroma, and the magnificent dish itself drew glances from people at nearby tables.

"That's some 'low-cal breakfast'!" he laughed sarcastically as I dug in.

The waitress gave the prefect the once over, he obliviously polished off his caffeine fix right in front of her, and pushed his chair back from the table as if to leave. The man was blind! I had the sense, moreover, that he had forgotten the point of his visit. Unless he had merely wanted to talk about women.

"Aren't you forgetting something?" I asked, as he began rising to his feet.

He looked puzzled. "No, nothing has come out since last night," he replied, still gazing at my plate. He stood up, took a last glance at the castle glowing in the morning sun without blinking, and suddenly struck himself on the forehead. "Oh right. There's this so-called expert who studied each of the major castles in the Loire Valley this past spring in order to locate their vulnerabilities to terrorist attacks. Part of the 'Sureté Vigipirate Program' (akin to Homeland Security), the boys in Paris told us. He has a weird sort of name ..."

I waited expectantly.

"As if they could stop terrorists!" he boomed. A few frightened faces turned toward us. "It's a scam to make it look like the government is doing something when, frankly, there is nothing to be done in such wide-open spaces," he added, barely lowering his voice.

I began to rise to my feet as he resumed his seat, as I always do, even for cops, although not for three-year-olds.

"Hervé Castillo's comments reminded me of the program last night, and that got me thinking."

"So this so-called expert?" I asked, as I tasted the fresh, fragrant herbs straight from Chambord's own garden that complemented the eggs and fine, lacy slices of *tuber melanosporum*, the "black diamond of the Périgord." The dish was scrumptious! I knew it would make Durtal's account of terrorism a lot less dull.

"Vellimachia's his name. His goal was to help us safely welcome as many visitors as possible, but," the prefect gave an uncomprehending snort, "he spoke about crowds at the castles as if they shouldn't exist."

"He would want the deaths at the castles publicized as widely as possible ... Are there any known anti-tourism, ecoterrorist groups in the area, like in Barcelona and Venice?" I asked, finishing off the cool pomegranate juice I'd been served in a spectacular tulip glass. "With ninety million tourists a year in France, you'd expect there to be some."

"Ecoterrorism? What the hell is that?" he asked peevishly.

"We need to check, too," I went on, following my own line of thought, "where this Machiavellia fellow was the day the incidents occurred. He may have deliberately omitted to mention one or two potential weak spots in each castle."

"I see you're thinking in an awfully devious vein, Canal!"

"Can I assume the cashiers have records of credit cards used for payment?"

"The guy would have been smarter than that. He would either have paid cash or simply come in through an unguarded entrance he had deliberately failed to tell us about."

"Or given, if not sold, his information to others, maybe even to Castillo."

"Why Castillo?" Durtal queried.

"He seemed to know all the leaky spots in his own system."

"I wouldn't mind taking that know-it-all down a notch!"

"Have you run any sort of background check on Vellimachia?"

"Not yet, but I will tomorrow morning. I'll call his office and try to sweet-talk his secretary into telling me where he's been the past few weeks. I want all the dirt on that damned Castillo!" He pushed his chair back decisively and stood up.

I wondered, as I rose to my feet, how a man with so little self-confidence when it came to women imagined he was going to sweet-talk a perfect stranger. Was it his appearance that he was foolishly unsure of? Or some sort of desperate look on his face? A woman on the phone wouldn't be able to see that, after all ...

"You're a crackpot, Canal," he opined. "Ecoterrorist groups—really!" And with that parting remark, the prefect seemed sufficiently pleased with himself to take his leave of me.

* * *

59

The oddest thing happens to me whenever I go to Azay-le-Rideau Castle: just as people like Durtal often get me sidetracked, I have been getting waylaid at Azay ever since they moved the ticket office into the boutique. I wander aimlessly around the shop—which tops them all, being truly gorgeous—even before buying an entry ticket, and glance at all the new and old titles on display in the natural light streaming in through the enormous windows. It's terribly inconvenient, because then I have to lug whatever I buy around the castle for the next couple of hours. But there it is—I just can't help myself! (A friend of mine once admitted to liking the boutiques more than the castles themselves, but that's a sign of something else, in my view: an advanced case of shopaholism.)

Most castles in the Valley now trick you in the same way, and it's pretty easy to guess why. After visiting, people are generally thinking only about lunch or a chilled glass of chenin blanc somewhere, so they try to lure you into the gift shop before hunger or thirst has a chance to strike. On this occasion, after wending my way through tables laden with mysterious and unexpected objects, my eyes alighted on a colorful volume on the mistresses of François I and I just had to have it. The man was well known to have been not only good friends with Leonardo da Vinci, but also a *coureur de jupons*, an incorrigible skirt chaser—almost right from birth! It was even said that once he became king, François attacked Milan, not so much to take possession of the city, as because of rumors he had heard regarding the beauty of its female inhabitants!

The coin of the realm having changed hands, I abandoned the boutique for the castle park.

Words could never do Azay justice. I generally despise everything that was done in France in the nineteenth century, but I have to admit that the idea of building a reflecting pool right next to the Renaissance castle was a stroke of genius. Seeing that giant frosted birthday cake right side up on land and upside down in the water is a sight to behold! I never know whether to begin my visit by circling the pond to see the many-faceted jewel from every angle or whether to head directly for the first ever indoor/outdoor stone staircase in France, with its elaborately sculpted ceilings, which divides the main wing of the castle in two. I usually let the weather determine my choice, starting inside if it's raining, outside if it's not.

The sun was shining today, the white stone walls blinding me so totally I had to don my Ray-Bans, and a busload of tourists was scurrying toward the main entrance, so I hightailed it in the opposite direction. I directed my steps toward the far end of the gardens where construction workers were assembling something. It was the wide-open stage for the evening's open-air concert, set in a park spanning several acres in which even a rhinoceros could escape detection. It reminded me of Durtal's words, striking me as a perfect target for certain groups (which didn't exist, according to the prefect) used to operating in the great outdoors …

I prefer not to indulge in unpleasant thoughts, so I retraced my steps to the castle, ascended the staircase—the second most famous in all of France—and admired the view of the reflecting pond from the first landing, which is glassed in (unlike those that give out onto the courtyard, which are exposed to the elements). Surrounded by such beauty, I began to wonder why I had allowed myself to get roped into this investigation, helping pampered people who are lucky enough to live here year-round. It was starting to encroach upon my vacation time! At least I was making room for fine concerts, but I had been neglecting my wine tastings. Did I neglect to mention earlier that that was one of the main reasons for my visit to the area? Maybe I could make it to the nearby Château de la Roche de Loire this afternoon, I thought, glancing at my watch. I couldn't skip that one. After all, they'd been making wine there for centuries, and supplied it to the Sun King at Versailles. Not to mention that it was right next door to the stately Château de la Cour au Berruyer and just uphill from the Azay Castle lookalike, L'Islette—not a winery, but well worth taking a look and an hour to lazily drift past its dreamy watermill in a rowboat on the Indre.

Anyway, one castle at a time. Following my own bent—instead of the signs indicating the designated order in which people are supposed to visit Azay (the French aren't terribly obedient, and I guess I'm rather French in that regard, doing as I damn well please)—I climbed the oddly shaped and incredibly worn smaller staircase to the five-hundred-year-old tangle of oak timbers in the recently opened attic. It resembles the inverted hull of some great sailing vessel from the Spanish Armada and was built to last a millennium, putting our modern building techniques to shame. Decorative touches—coats of arms and sculpted beams—popped up where no one could expect them. Gratuitous beauty—now that's something you don't see every day! The wood had come from the forest right nearby and the exact year of the castle's construction had recently been determined using dendrochronology. I extracted a pen from my pocket and jotted down the date on my entry ticket.

Coming back down to earth, or at least to the floor below, I passed precious minutes in the king's stately yet charming bedchamber and antechamber (with beams that used to be painted like the ones you can see in the celebrated Portrait Gallery at Beauregard Castle near Blois and at Plessis-Bourré Castle, a fortress of former double-drawbridge fame, further down the Loire near Angers). So what if the king only spent one night there?* It can still bear his name. Then, in a flash, I was on the open-air loggia of the main staircase, buffeted by the four winds, which men in tights and women with generously exposed breasts had crossed for centuries in the dead of winter, pretending they lived in southern Italy. Then again, the indoor temperature was probably not that much higher in the winter than the outdoor temperature! In any case, it was a beguiling time when beauty reigned supreme over comfort.

I entered the Great Hall and ogled its impressively high windows on three sides, its seventeenth-century parquet, and its glorious *plafond à la française* (French ceiling with beams the size of five-hundred-year-old oak trees). After peeking out a *jalousie*—a tiny opening in a carved wooden shutter, allowing me to observe people in the park without being seen by them—I passed, as though I were some kind of ethereal time traveler, from its brightly lit vastness into a dark and intimate space: the bedroom where the dimly lit Psyche and Cupid tapestries hang. After a long look at love and hell, or the hell of love, some might say, I ended up in the bedchamber of the lady of the house, Philippe Lesbahy, a.k.a. Madame Berthelot (no, she wasn't in bed, if that's what you're thinking). I felt they shouldn't have covered the walls there with floor-to-ceiling braided reeds, even if they did have evidence that this was the way the room looked at some point in the castle's history. Yes, okay, it contrasted with the appearance of the other rooms and perhaps provided a rather cozy space when the unobstructed winter chill crept into the old stone structure, but the sixteenth-century insulation left me cold.

I was examining this unusual sort of "wallpaper," and considering whether I would do better not to mention it in my piece for the travel magazine, when someone banged into me, almost knocking me over. So there were modern-day sentient beings here! Regaining my balance, I looked at the distracted visitor who apologized profusely, so profusely indeed that I recognized the voice.

"Monsieur Wack," I said, accepting his apology with a formal nod, "how fitting to run into you in the lady of the house's bedchamber.

62

I suspect you have already looked under the bed to see if you could find any more of those old-fashioned briefs and brassieres." I myself had admired the *lit à quenouilles*, a four-poster Renaissance bed there—intricately sculpted with the faces of bearded men with long flowing hair, and sporting purple velvet curtains for privacy and plump pillows of hews unusual in our times—although it hadn't occurred to me until just then to glance underneath it.

"Do we know each other?" he asked, grinning a bit disconcertedly, as if his thoughts had been light-years from our present surroundings, perhaps in some distant musical universe.

"Not yet," I replied, "but I have been a fan of your work for many years, even though I reside primarily in New York. I have all your recordings there! And I was lucky enough to hear you conduct last night—"

"Oh, you heard that train wreck of a concert?" he interrupted, his expression belying his words.

"You must be extremely hard on yourself if you call that extraordinary performance a train wreck," I proffered, secretly wondering at his false modesty.

"Hard? No, just realistic. I'm going to *kill* that girl when I find her!"

"*Cherchez la femme, pardieu! Cherchez la femme!*"

He looked flummoxed, perhaps not having caught my reference to Alexandre Dumas père. I have to admit that I said it a bit automatically, if not altogether wantonly, but he seemed to be troubled by the fact that the literal meaning of the phrase, "find the woman," was somehow eclipsed by its metaphorical meaning, "the woman is the key to the mystery."

"*Kill* that girl," I repeated softly, musing that the more emphatic the phrasing of the anger, the greater the love hidden behind it.

"Yes, I'd like to subject her to Chinese water torture, and then wring her neck with that bassoon of hers," he added in an indescribable tone of voice where it wasn't clear if he was more interested in throwing her on the Renaissance bed and kissing her lovely neck or mangling it in a dark hallway.

"Have you tried looking for her?"

"I wouldn't even know where to begin," he replied as we exited the bedchamber and proceeded down the stairs and out into the courtyard. He paused to stare at the rear end of a scantily clad girl heading up the stairs.

63

"Have you called anyone she knew? Her family?"

"Family?" he asked, turning back toward me.

I had the sense he had never before thought of her as someone who might have one.

"Friends?" I queried.

"Orlando Civadin?" he said contemptuously, almost spitting out the name of the concertmaster. "I'd rather wring *his* neck! I certainly wouldn't ask him."

"Why wouldn't you?"

He looked at me curiously for a few moments and finally replied, "We had a falling out some time ago. There's no love lost between us."

The man didn't seem to feel much need to hide his dislikes and displeasures, I reflected.

Noticing a small group of tourists gathering near a door in the courtyard, he abruptly left my side, waltzed over to the group, and in a stentorian voice announced that he was to be their guide for the day. "We're going to begin our tour by taking a short swim in the canal right over here, in which flow the sometimes troubled waters of the Indre River. But don't worry," he reassured them, "I am a certified Water Safety Instructor, and can fish out anyone, especially ladies, who can't make it over to the stairs located a bit upstream from here," he said pointing toward the gardens.

You can imagine my surprise.

"You can leave your clothes over here by the wall," he indicated to his ever more perplexed audience, a few of whom were laughing at this point.

"Just kidding, just kidding," Wack finally admitted. "Your real guide is this fine gentleman here," at which point he had the chutzpah to point at me.

I shook my head in denial—I'm sure I looked serious and staid compared to him—their actual guide showed up, and the conductor shouted to them all to "Carry on!" He was obviously used to commanding, even when the troops weren't his.

He returned to my side and resumed walking as though nothing had happened. "You were saying?" he asked.

"I wasn't," I answered. "You were saying *I* was their guide. And that there was no love lost between you and your concertmaster."

"How true."

Noticing a candy wrapper on the ground off to the left, he ran over, picked it up, and stuffed it into a nearby garbage can. "People are such oinks," he remarked. "I'm trying to keep Touraine clean—it's *le Jardin de la France*, the Garden of France, you know."

"So I've heard," I replied, finding it hard to hide my mirth. "I've never met Civadin. What's he like?"

"A pretentious prick, if you'll excuse my French. He won a prestigious competition back in the day, and now he thinks he knows everything!"

"I myself prefer those who embody Nicholas of Cusa's dictum that nothing becomes a man more perfectly than to be found very learned in ignorance itself, he being the more learned the more he knows his own ignorance."*

The conductor eyed me narrowly for a few moments and then quipped, "Civadin acts more like he's learned in everything *but* ignorance. And His Majesty always makes it sound like he's taking the moral high road by refusing every form of support the French government gives artists. He turns away the richest of violin students." He interrupted himself to fiddle with an outdoor light fixture that appeared to be loose as if he knew how to repair it, and instead knocked it over. I half expected him to electrocute himself. "Instead, His Fabulousness flies, does free climbing, jumps off things, swims—"

"An athlete, then?"

"No, a geek: always up on the latest developments in windmills and solar energy, and buying extravagant cooking gadgets for meals to which I have never been invited."

I looked at the maestro and reckoned that, given his attitude, he wasn't about to be invited to spend Christmas at Civadin's house. I couldn't help but think of Don Quixote when he mentioned windmills, but tried to keep him talking. "Sounds like he spreads himself a bit thin," I opined.

"And yet each activity feeds the others, making him still more conceited, ambitious, and ..."

"As if that weren't true of virtually every professional musician, and undoubtedly of Wack himself," I laughed to myself. "And?" I echoed aloud, trying to keep a straight face.

Wack eyed me a bit warily.

Noticing tables set up outside a café—recently opened in the perfectly symmetrical outbuildings—that I had never had the opportunity to try, I invited him to have a drink with me. At first he begged off, saying he never drank before a concert, but when I mentioned it was teatime, he acquiesced. We selected a table with an umbrella, the mid-afternoon sun having heated things up considerably, and Wack plopped down onto a chair like a great big walrus.

I don't know what it is about me, maybe it's my oversized ears (I mean that figuratively, of course), but people often end up telling me things they wouldn't tell anyone else. Maybe it's my relaxed demeanor, maybe it's the fact that I always order a nice bottle of wine and tempt the recalcitrant into having a sip, "just one little sip." Who knows? I might have mentioned to the conductor that the concert didn't begin for another five hours, and I did admittedly ask the waiter to bring over two glasses ...

After we had been served (and may God forgive him for order-ing a pastis—he was from Provence, after all), I reminded him that he had been saying that the concertmaster was "conceited, ambitious, and ..."—at which point he had broken off. It's always significant when people break off like that. I looked at him expectantly.

"Wants my job. He can't bear that I'm in charge, not him."

"Hmm."

He shifted in his chair, stretched out his legs (kicking me in the pro-cess), and his virtuoso hands began nervously tapping what seemed to be a soulless gigue on the table. "He wouldn't even want it if he had it," he opined, willingly allowing me to pour him a taste of the effervescent Vouvray I had ordered—a 2007 Philippe Foreau brut that I especially like, which they miraculously had on the menu. "No matter how much recognition he'd get, it would never be enough for him. What he really wants—and I'm absolutely sure of this—is a career as a soloist. He just loves the spotlight."

This from the very man—no, rather, stand-up comedian—who hogged the limelight at last night's concert for at least ten minutes and then played the bassoonist's part himself ... He had been self-deprecatory in his words, it is true, but actions speak more loudly, don't they?

His muscular fingers encircled his champagne flute as if it were an antique recorder played by Handel or, more likely, an elusive female. Taking a long sip, he gave me a significant look and nod, judiciously set aside his pastis, and gave his undivided attention to the Loire Valley's best-known form of bubbly. "Aaaaah," he exclaimed, toasting me with his glass in the air, but then immediately turning his attention to a short-skirted woman walking by.

"I couldn't help but notice that there were two musicians missing last night," I reopened the discussion.

"If only *he* could've gone missing! Went to see his mother in Paris, supposedly, but the royal pain in the ass will be back tonight for another three-year stint with us." He held up his glass, "Here's to his disappearance!" He took a long draft and I refreshed his drink. "Then, maybe …," he trailed off.

"Maybe?"

"Oh, nothing," he shrugged his shoulders.

I took a stab in the dark, willing, like Hamlet, to risk slaying Polonius when it was Claudius I was after, "Then maybe, just maybe, you could have her to yourself?"

He almost fell off his chair. Once he had settled back down, looking red in the face, he eyed me suspiciously and asserted, "I said no such thing."

"No, I did," I admitted conciliatorily, not mentioning that his constant scanning of the crowd even after the concert ended had spoken volumes.

"I could say good riddance to them both!" The maestro raised his glass again, but then suddenly looked all forlorn.

"But if there wasn't a girl in the picture, why would you care whether Civadin wants your job or not? Doesn't every concertmaster secretly or not so secretly want to conduct?"

He listened, a smidgeon admiringly, I thought.

"Isn't that something virtually every conductor takes for granted? Doesn't the number two man always want the number one man's job?"

He tilted his head sideways noncommittally, gazed at the blithely effervescent Vouvray, and took another long draft. "*Le boire est bien le propre de l'homme*," I thought to myself (Drinking is truly what makes man who he is, constructed like Rabelais's *Le rire est le propre de l'homme*, laughter is what makes man who he is, or what distinguishes man from all other beings).

"Nothing to have a falling out about, is there?" I went on, hoping to prod him to open up.

His mouth opened, a smile was emerging, and I could sense a silly joke coming when all went dark. I never saw the face he was about to make.

67

I hoped it was a woman, and the softness of the hands covering my eyes suggested it was. Simultaneously, I heard music. The unpredictable maestro had begun loudly whistling an air from *Psyché*, so loudly, indeed, that everyone at the café stopped talking, apparently turning our way and embarrassing me, which was probably the swine's aim.

"Probably fantasizing you'll have as many mistresses as he did," came a voice. The book I had purchased at the castle boutique was lying next to me on the table and whoever it was—the timbre sounded familiar—had obviously read over my shoulder. "Go ahead, guess who it is," she ordered.

"Françoise de Châteaubriant, *la mye du roi*?" I said (the king's sweetheart). "Anne de Pisseleu d'Heilly?" Getting no response, I tried yet another well-known mistress, "The Countess of Thoury?"

"I see you know them all! But you were right the first time," she giggled, removing her hands so I could see it was the flautist, Françoise Foix—not Françoise de Foix, which was the Countess of Châteaubriant's maiden name, but pretty darn close. In contrast to the regulation-black number she had worn last night, which still baffled me, she was wearing a no-less-chic sheer white muslin summer dress and elegant dangling earrings that jangled with every shake of her head. "Fancy meeting you here, Monsieur Canal," she added, smiling broadly at me, and tilting her head to make her shoulder-length hair—which was lightly curled today and not held in place by a headband as it had been the night before—move fancifully, as only women know how. "It's a lovely spot you have found, but I'm afraid that the company you keep …"

"What about the company I keep?" I asked as I stood up, prepared to shake her hand with great formality—too much for the occasion, clearly, but I like it that way. Instead she leaned in to kiss me on both cheeks, putting her hand on my arm.

"Well …" she cackled like anything but a professional musician.

Françoise was perhaps not unlike her namesake. I had never entirely understood François I's taste in women, but his first long-standing mistress, the Countess Françoise de Châteaubriant, must have been quite a looker. Having heard tell of her beauty and culture, he lured her and her husband to his court, sent her husband off on a "delicate mission" to the furthest reaches of Brittany, and set about wooing her sedulously. Quite a stratagem! It was the king's first serious love affair …

No royal gentleman, he, the witty lout Wack did not even stand up when she approached to exchange kisses on alternating cheeks—she didn't seem to mind in the least—three times, as they do in the south. Or was it four smacks? It was four somewhere in France, anyway. Or was that Italy or Belgium? Maybe she had just given me two: I had been too surprised to keep count when she unexpectedly started.

"You must join us, Françoise de Foix," I insisted, swiping an empty chair from an adjoining table and holding it out for her in my most chivalrous manner. "A little Vouvray?" I asked, gesturing to the waiter for an extra glass.

"I never drink," she replied as she wiggled into the treacherous wood-slat chair.

"Yes, you do." I was momentarily startled, I confess, by the minx. "You drank with me at Chambord."

"Oh, that was different," she explained. "I never drink white wine."

"Yet it was white bubbly that we drank together."

"But at night I can't see the color."

"You dislike the color?"

"I like red," she looked me in the eye. "And I hate bubbles!"

The waiter set a glass down in front of her.

"So I shouldn't pour you any?" I concluded.

"Of course you should, Monsieur. Do you mind if I call you by your first name?" I had seated her midway between Wack and myself, but she immediately moved her chair much closer to mine.

"Not at all."

"But you didn't tell me what it was at our last tryst," she complained. "It isn't fair—you've seen mine but I haven't seen yours."

Attentive as he was, Wack didn't even crack a smile at this. I had no intention of dating a musician, and it was clear, in any case, that she was playing me. Putting on a rather fine show, too. There truly is nothing new under the sun.

"It's Quesjac," I told her. "I know, it's a bit unusual, but it's not unheard of in Dordogne where part of my family comes from." Okay, so I was being a bit disingenuous, but that's what I always say to appease the uninitiated. If your name was as prosaic as Jacques, wouldn't you shake it up a little? "Now if I were king and you, lovely Françoise, were from Dordogne, I'd send your husband off on a mission to the furthest reaches of the Périgord Noir, so I could keep you for myself."

"But I'm not married," she effervesced, taking my hand and rubbing it while tilting her head a bit toward my shoulder so that a whimsical wisp of her hair brushed against my cheek. She even re-crossed her legs so as to ostentatiously brush her bare foot up against my pants leg, the coquette having slipped off one of her white Ferragamo pumps sporting refined tiered bows.

All at once, the conductor came to. Françoise and I could do nothing but listen while he talked about anything and everything—Psyche, love, music, poetry—interspersing compliments with sexual innuendo, and quoting François I's dictum that "a court without women is a garden without flowers, a spring without roses."

"*Bon Dieu!* Does he realize I am still here?" I wondered after a few minutes. Having almost been asleep, in a matter of seconds the man seemed to have gotten high on himself!

Wack seemed to have found something utterly intolerable. His self-effacing onstage persona had given way, revealing the inner attention freak. "The human comedy goes on," I told myself.

* * *

As I settled into my chair that balmy evening and perused the concert program, I recalled the fat contracts that winners of classical music competitions often receive and wondered what could have held this extraordinary Civadin back. Wack had said little of value about his second-in-command, a man he had just signed up for another few years with the symphony—an odd fact. The printed bio indicated that the concertmaster had won the prestigious International Tchaikovsky Competition in Moscow in 2006, which would typically have catapulted him into the stratosphere of soloists—something Wack believed he wanted more than anything else—but for some reason had not.

Turning the page to Wack's bio, complete with a glossy photo that glowed strangely, the words "pretty ballsy" came to mind. The erudite and virtuoso conductor had struck out on his own after a couple of years working under the famous Avid Sapristi, and had founded his own symphony. Had Wack felt that Sapristi was holding him back?

The recorderist was a consummate clown, inveterate jester, and all around dissimulator. He engaged in brief acts of seduction that he apparently could not control, like this afternoon's command performance for a woman whom he had barely even noticed before—not that different from the king who reigned here five hundred years earlier, according to my newly purchased account.

70

An usher walked by—at least he might have been one of the contemporary sort, accoutered as he was with rather tight-fitting black clothes head-to-toe and spiky hair—and I asked if I might please have a program for all of the Symphonie de Provence's performances that year, not just this one.

"If you must. As if my sorry excuse for a life didn't suck bad enough already," he said with an almost imperceptible foreign accent and went to fetch one. "I'm the sound engineer," he made sure to tell me upon his return, "not an usher at this dumb castle."

A hydra with nine vicious heads peeked out of his shirtsleeve as he dropped a rather glossy brochure in my lap. It confirmed that the Symphonie was giving several concerts in the Loire Valley that summer. But they had not given any concerts at or near Amboise in June—indeed, at that time the orchestra was about as far from the Loire Valley as one could get and still be in France: in the Basque country near Spain.

* * *

A rapt hush fell over the gardens as the period instrument orchestra struck the first note, a deeply pitched A above middle C tuned to 415 hertz as Wack had ordered, a frequency rarely used in the New World. The wind instruments rose and fell in imitation of birdsong, tastefully rendering the pastorale in the sensuous night air. The conductor, wearing a dark red shirt, cast a fleeting glance at the flautist, who seemed out of sorts and pretended not to notice. But a few moments later, she stole a look at him as she played the melody by Delalande.

"Why was it that as soon as Wack thought Françoise and I had something going on, the die was cast?" I asked myself. I couldn't help but wonder how the two had spent the remainder of the afternoon. I guess the only quality Foix had been missing to show up on Wack's radar prior to today was that of already being taken, of being another man's woman. Wasn't that just so typical?

It certainly didn't bode well for the future of their ... could one call it a "relationship"? Well, I'd played my part as the ever self-abnegating Cupidos, god of love—the rest was up to her. Would someone like her know how to keep a man like him interested? Would Helen of Troy? Look, another glance! There were women with such a knack—Anne d'Heilly had done so for almost twenty years. But was that love? What is love?

71

I was suddenly jolted by a jarring hiccup in the soulful, passionate music with multiple voices responding to each other. Had I fallen asleep and a bomb had gone off? No, it was just a horribly wrong note. Wack looked like he had to rein himself in in order not to march over to the concertmaster and break his bow in half! I hadn't really observed the "geeky" Civadin before, but did so now. He was tall, of athletic build under his black blazer, and had shoulder-length wavy hair. He deftly got the violins back on track and gave Wack a quick but dirty look.

The last strains of the heady period instruments ended all too soon and the entire audience, young and old, was standing, hands red hot from clapping and throats hoarse from yelling "*Bravo!*" and "*Bis!*" (*Encore!*). The maestro then announced quite composedly that they had prepared a mere thirty-seven encores, and the crowd went wild.

Mr. Life's-a-Bitch, looking like Dostoevsky's man from underground, ran over to the stage. Even before the fans had stopped applauding at the end of the third and final encore, he helped the flautist down the few steps to the grass. "Where did he learn such good manners?" I wondered. The sound engineer offered her a glass brimming with bubbly, but she immediately began to speak with someone else. Was he yet another hunter of elusive prey?

As at Chambord, Wack was king, surrounded by his courtiers with Azay in the background, but he was a very contemporary sort of king, with an agent, secretary, and public relations staff schmoozing with different music festival directors, cell phones glued to their ears. The concertmaster, however, was standing alone near the stage. Wack might see me, but I sidled up to the blond, broad-shouldered man anyway, introduced myself, and complimented him on his euphonious performance that evening.

"Yes, I thought I played rather well tonight," he concurred. "As for the others ... ," he trailed off. He wasn't exactly deep in his cups, but an empty glass stood on the stage next to him, and a half-empty glass was precariously perched in his left hand.

"They didn't hold up their end of the stick?" I proposed.

"Oh, most of them did, but the conductor messed up repeatedly, as usual."

"And tried to blame it on others?"

"And tried to blame it on me!" He squeezed his wineglass so tightly I thought it would break, then took a choleric slug of the fine chenin blanc from Saint-Just-sur-Dive they were pouring that evening. I was enjoying a coupe myself, but doubted Civadin was doing justice to the exceptional Crémant de Loire by the inimitable Arnaud Lambert. "But there's nothing unusual about that—he's been doing it for months."

"Months?" I echoed.

"Ever since ..."

"Ever since?" The man seemed a bit hard to read, both self-assured and bitter, wanting to talk yet taciturn. I tasted the wine again—light, tangy, very refreshing.

He seemed to choose his verbs carefully. "Ever since I started receiving attention that he felt he deserved," he said with a grand swish of his blond mane, leading drops of bubbly to fly out of his glass like furious thirty-second notes.

"Hmm."

He appeared to be wondering what I was thinking and weighing his next words.

"Monsieur Canal," a woman called out in a plangent voice.

I considered her for a few moments and concluded that I'd never seen her before. No one knew of my presence in this small town tucked between two ancient forests.

I excused myself with a gesture to the concertmaster—I find it terribly impolite when people do nothing to apologize, leaving you abruptly or answering a phone call while you're midsentence—and walked over to the woman.

"You must be a man of consequence," he commented, when I returned to take my leave. I appreciated his nineteenth-century turn of phrase, but never know what to say when people make such inane observations (unless to make a joke about "Truth or Consequences," which my interlocutor would surely have never heard of, whether the TV show *or* the town in New Mexico).

I extended my hand to shake his. "I hope we shall meet again soon."

"I, too," he said, perhaps having mistaken my politeness for sympathy with his plight.

CHAPTER SIX

Langeais Castle

Ah, qu'en amour le plaisir est charmant,
Quand la tendresse est égale
Entre l'Amante & l'Amant.
(How wonderfully pleasing it is when lovers adore each other
equally.)

—Lully, *Psyché*

"We have got to stop meeting like this," I said to Le Coq when I saw her standing on the drawbridge, her slightly curly auburn hair falling gently down her back as far as her waist, which is all too rare a sight these days, I feel. The bridge was surrounded on both sides by Langeais Castle's massive, forbidding towers, overtopped by a menacing sentry walk, where arrow slits, loopholes, and machicolations awaited intruders. Designed to forever protect France (the little there was of it at the time, that is) from Brittany's expansionistic military aspirations, the medieval fortress was illuminated from the base of its hundred-foot windowless walls. Bright light rose high into the crenellated battlements.

As I approached, the commissioner's lips sketched out a tenuous, tense smile. She was not enveloped in bulky rain gear on this warm, pleasant evening as she had been the night before. Indeed, her khaki pants and sleeveless white top were form-fittingly pleasing to the eye. She looked like she was dressed, not for a crime scene, but for a casual night out on the town—"with whom?" I wondered, sounding to myself a bit too much like Miss Marple. She extended her hand to shake mine and guided me—like Umberto Eco's medieval sleuth, William of Baskerville—over the drawbridge. We had to mind our step in the dark, as there was a considerable drop-off on both sides and only a flimsy, dangling chain guardrail, and then passed through the long tunnel-like gateway leading into the courtyard.

Our gaze was suddenly met with a most striking contrast. For Langeais is actually two castles in one—the outside saying "Go away!" and the inside, with its elegant Renaissance façade, saying "Come right on in." The ever-conniving Louis XI had the imposing fortress at Langeais built by his faithful captain, Jean Bourré. But by the time the first towers were finished in 1466, the political winds had changed and he gave the burgeoning fortress to a cousin* of his with decidedly less militaristic views.

Overlooked by the majority of tourists, this mammoth structure, located right in the middle of town, was one of my personal favorites. A secret marriage took place here one frigid winter morning in 1491, forever linking Brittany's fate with that of the kingdom of France. (Need I mention that Duchess Anne of Brittany had already married someone else—the future emperor of the Holy Roman Empire—by proxy a year earlier, a stand-in having symbolically placed his leg over her exposed thigh? They weren't going to let a little detail like that get in their way.)

But Le Coq was once again all business, and I'd have to return another day to tour the place in peace. "The medics arrived at the same time as me and are still up there," she said, pointing toward a strange, craggy, austere form on a promontory a couple of hundred yards behind the "new" castle. I looked around to get my bearings and focused on the exceptional edifice, arguably the oldest keep in the world, built by the most implacable, bloodthirsty Count of Anjou ever, Foulques Nerra— Fulk III, the Black. He erected it on land pilfered from his archrivals, the Counts of Blois, Eudes I and II, and it was the first of dozens of strongholds he built. He designed the rectangular keep in Langeais to be impregnable, and history proved him right. It never succumbed—at least not until the Hundred Years' War centuries later, when it began to flip back and forth between the English and the French. Tonight it appeared to have taken yet another victim.

We directed our steps through the garden and up the path to the proud tower that had been dominating the Loire since 990. "The night watchman noticed something dangling over the edge of the observation deck at the top of the old keep and went up to investigate."

I was annoyed there had been yet another victim. Who would it be—a doctor, a lawyer, an Indian chief? And yet another night watchman? Not again!

We climbed the several flights of unlit stairs up to the observation deck, which boasted a stunning view of the surrounding cedars and sequoias, and of the Renaissance façade, courtyard, and French gardens below. Had it been daytime, we could have seen the mighty river rolling by, but at this late hour it was just a dark gash between two dimly lit banks.

One of the medics was helping the victim sit up, and we were able to talk with a British tourist aged seventy-three, who told us he was staying at a hotel in nearby Tours. Tall, lean, and with a long Don Quixote-like face, he was dressed in bright green overalls a Frenchman wouldn't be caught dead in. He claimed to have arrived at the castle late in the day and climbed alone to the top of the keep despite the afternoon heat. He did not recall seeing anyone either on the steps or up on the observation deck before he got there. Indeed, he said he remembered nothing, leaving us to conclude that he had passed out as soon as he reached the landing.

"Most likely a vasovagal syncope," one of the medics proffered.

"To the layman?" the commissioner asked.

"Something like heat exhaustion," he replied, "or possibly ..."

"What?" I asked.

"A mild heart attack."

"Hmm," I uttered in the explosive humidity of the night.

Conscientious as usual, Le Coq examined his foreign ID and jotted down a few details, after which we left the medics to their difficult job of conveying him down to the ambulance. "Looks like we caught a break here—nothing to investigate."

In the dim light, I stole a fleeting glance at an entry ticket I had picked up that had fallen from the Brit's pocket. I made out the words July 4th, *Nuit des Mille Feux*.

"No new crime to add to our Fibonacci series," I mused to myself. Then audibly, "Durtal will be relieved. Where is he, by the way?"

"He didn't answer his phone," she replied. "When the people at your hotel told me you were just fifteen minutes away, I didn't bother trying him again or his lead investigator."

I didn't know if I should feel flattered or not.

"You are easier to deal with."

I was right not to feel flattered. I wondered what the prefect could be doing this time of night. Hunting like Thibault, only hinds instead of stags, does instead of bucks? "Durtal is probably out raising hell somewhere," I said, testing the waters.

"Yes, just the type," she said, giving a somber smile (if there be such a thing), as we descended the treacherous path near what seemed like a small pile of rubble. It was the remains of a long-lost chapel erected a thousand years ago, in fulfillment of a promise made in Jerusalem by Foulques Nerra. To atone for having killed his wife? I forget … something like that.

"What sort of type do you think he is?" I asked.

"Offhand I'd say he's the strong, serious, but not too brainy type." She rushed on, "That's okay, though. A prefect needs to be someone who looks good in front of a camera and is reassuring to the public—that sort of thing."

"You don't like them brainy?" I asked as we approached the long arched stone carriageway through the highly decorated Renaissance façade back out to the austere medieval façade.

She ignored my question. "Few of them have much upstairs."

"You're the brainiest?"

"Well, almost. But the dumbest, too …" I looked at her curiously and was about to ask why, but she suddenly scooped up my tie with her hand and, examining it in the light of the carriageway, declared, "This tie was given to you by a lady friend, wasn't it?"

I hadn't expected the question, and had to think for a moment before replying, "Yes, as a matter of fact it was."

"It doesn't suit you at all," Le Coq proclaimed, looking at me reproachfully, and speaking in serious tones again. "I bet she never got you."

"You're quite right," I admitted, even as I thought her a bit cockily self-assured in sartorial and amorous matters for one her age. The tie was made of pure silk, but the hues were all wrong for my coloring and

I didn't even know why I had brought it with me on this trip. I had, no doubt, been reminiscing about the giver who never got me. Pretty foolish ... "Taste and brains," I remarked, smiling at Le Coq.

We crossed the drawbridge anew, descended the stairs over the erstwhile moat, her heels getting caught in the cracks between the stones, and headed toward an old half-timbered house near the main square. Its ground floor hosted the only café that was still open in the sleepy little town, dwarfed into virtual nothingness by the towering fortress. We found an outdoor table and sat gazing at the fearsome fortress. She ordered a glass of rosé. I didn't request my usual late-night libation, but just coffee, for I had a fairly long drive ahead of me. I began wondering what it was like for a woman to be so much smarter than her man—I'd known a few women who acted as though they were whereas it wasn't crystal clear to me, and I seemed to recall such couples fought a lot.

A loud boom of thunder interrupted my irreverent thoughts and the heavens opened.

Le Coq scooped up her handbag, I grabbed our drinks, and we dashed for the door. But we were already soaking wet by the time we crossed the threshold.

It was a very quaint place, dark but welcoming, with old oak beams and polished wood tables. "The gods have sent us a sign," I bantered.

"That we're not smart enough to have seen it coming," she bantered back. "At least I've figured out the first incident," she added defiantly as she sat down, as if challenging me to a duel. Our table was near the door and she sipped her beverage gravely, staring out the window at the pouring rain. "Just before visiting Amboise, Charles Bouture, the oenologist, had been at an important wine expo in Paris. Nobody even bothered to look into it." She spoke to me like I was Durtal. What gall!

Was she boasting? Or did she want me to praise her?

"He got into a furious fist fight there with Herbert Couard," she went on, "owner of the prestigious Lansquenet Vineyards." I couldn't help letting out a long whistle. "He's one of the biggest of the bigshots in Bordeaux's Saint-Emilion appellation, the eminence grise of something called the Jurade—"

"*Oui, ma chère, je sais.* The ancient fraternity of Saint-Emilion winemakers meets in the castle keep built by Richard the Lionhearted."

I could tell I had scored a point in our duel. "Well, it was positively insane. They had to call security on the two grown men, one a Ph.D., the other a world-famous château owner!" She finally looked me straight in the eye. "I talked to someone who saw the whole thing. Bouture had clearly had a few too many, and dared Couard to a blind tasting. Claimed Couard couldn't tell a white from a red without looking at his glass." She seemed simultaneously shocked and reluctantly entertained by her tale, which I myself was enjoying immensely. "Bouture then bragged that he'd given a posse of award-winning sommeliers a blind tasting of a half dozen Bordeaux and they'd all rated Couard's dead last. He even accused Couard—in front of dozens of international movie stars and prominent retailers—of bullying and buying his way into the coveted Class A Premier Grand Cru category of Saint-Emilion wines."

"How could he buy his way in?" I asked, as the waiter set down our respective second rounds before us, mixing them up at first. I couldn't help but look at the bottle from which he poured her pale rosé, even as I listened to one of the juiciest *vitis vinifera* stories I'd heard in a long time. The back label claimed the wine was "jovial" and "adored pizza, salad, sunny cocktail parties, with broad smiles and peals of laughter."* Only the French could come up with descriptions like that. And get away with it. Such musings made me forget where I was for an instant.

Le Coq's voice boomed, breaking into my reverie. "By changing all the rules about who qualifies for the lucrative designation." She'd done her homework. "Bouture embarrassed the hell out of Couard by telling the glitterati that, owing to his new rules, he'd been able to skyrocket into the Bordeaux stratosphere with a taste score from the judges of only six out of twenty!"

"Wow, you'd think it should sink Saint-Emilion," I exclaimed, all ears again. "So what *does* it take to become one of the world's richest winemakers?" Personally, I wasn't a big fan of Saint-Emilion wines, but I knew they were widely considered a flagship appellation of the Bordelais and had been served to many a U.S. president on official business in Paris. I myself vastly preferred Haut-Médocs.

"Nothing involving grapes." The coffee I was imbibing almost went down the wrong wine-loving pipe. "Discreet lighting in the tasting rooms, attractive pourers, and a well-appointed seminar room. Next, you need brand-new storage cellars, convenient vehicle access and bus parking to accommodate free-spending tourists, and paid product placement in television shows and movies. Those now count for fifty percent of the total score. So many points are now given to a vineyard's appearance and notoriety that Lansquenet's F minus in taste still managed to earn it Class A status."*

"Something nobody knows, naturally," I concluded. It may not mean much to you, but to the French, Class A Premier Grand Cru is like the Nobel Prize for winemaking and commands top dollar!

I thought I detected an odd blend of bitterness and sadness regarding the human condition in her voice, mixed with joy at telling me something I hadn't heard. "Nice to know that all the best restaurants will now be stocking Lansquenet because of its commodious parking lot!" I scoffed.

"To top it all off," she paused to sip her jovial rosé, "Bouture informed Couard he was about to publish a tell-all book about it, and had already had it translated into English and Chinese. That's when the punches starting flying." She smiled. Wine has a tendency to take the edge off.

I frowned for a few moments. "Still, when you think about it, it is obvious that Saint-Emilion wines enjoy such an iron grip on people's minds that all the bad press in the world won't overpower simple psychology," I proffered. "When people see his label, they swoon—it is a well-established Pavlovian response. Even a hothead like Couard would realize there was no need to silence the voice of one calling out in the desert."

She put her glass down, opened her mouth, then closed it. "So perhaps I have not solved anything ...," she murmured modestly.

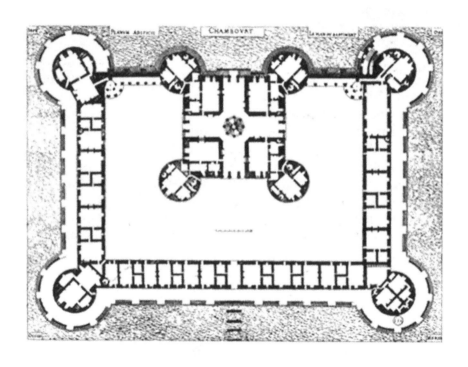

CHAPTER SEVEN

A rainy day in the Loire Valley

L'Amour fait perdre le repos. (Love makes us lose sleep.)
—Lully, *Psyché*

Once again, I made it back to my hotel in Chambord after one in the morning. Having provisionally pilfered a compilation of da Vinci's notebooks from the hotel lobby, I opened it at random to a drawing of four sets of staircases around what was either a solid central core or an open stairwell—it wasn't clear which. On the following pages were studies of water in motion and the flight of birds. They preoccupied my thoughts for I don't know how long.

When I finally awoke in my quiet room, it was so late that I had to ask the kitchen staff to extend the breakfast window. They didn't make me beg, and on my breakfast tray I found a neatly folded copy of today's *Le Figaro* newspaper and an unexpected stack of brochures from the many castles in the area detailing their plethoric summer activities, courtesy of Durtal. As I greedily drank the Relais' exceptional coffee— not so very different from that produced by my own magical Italian espresso maker back in the Empire State—I opened the pad sitting next to the phone. Naturally, it had a picture of Leonardo da Vinci, complete with flowing hair and beard, on it. I began to make separate lists of events that had taken place at Amboise in mid-June, at Chambord on July 3rd, and at Villandry on July 4th and 5th. Amboise: regular guided tours in half a dozen languages, specialized tours focused on art and architecture, others on history, a mid-afternoon open-air concert, genuine outdoor commedia dell'arte in the evening, like every summer, and a sound and light show. A lot of comings and goings all day long and well into the evening. I sighed.

Chambord's schedule of events was even crazier and thoroughly jam-packed, the castle welcoming close to a million visitors a year—many thousands a day in the summer. The place was enormous—far larger than the peerless Castello di Amorosa in Napa Valley, built by a crazy friend of mine, which is already huge—and the various guided tours, wine tastings (several centered solely around sauvignon blanc, others around older varietals like côt and sauvignon's lesser-known cousin fié gris), seminars, lectures, architectural games for children, and musical events (some including pieces first performed at Chambord, no less) were spaced out fairly evenly on the grounds and in the many different wings and courtyards of the palace itself. So many things to do, one would have a good excuse to stay on and on! (If not for the reds … Personally, I prefer Dario Sattui's *Il Barone* to any red Loire Valley wine.)

The name Avid Sapristi on the page devoted to July 3rd caught my eye. Him again. The inscrutable guy Wack had worked under and then broken away from.

A snapshot of a beautiful, carefully made-up blonde appeared as I turned the page. It was the girl on the stairs who had been slated to play an open-air concert in the same courtyard as Sapristi, but on July 4th. "Where was she staying?" I suddenly asked myself.

Then I came to the brochure of a castle I didn't immediately recognize because of the unusual angle from which it had been photographed. Needing more of a kick start, I picked up the phone, dialed room service, and ordered another *grand crème*, France's answer to the double cappuccino. The *Nuit des Mille Feux*, the thousand-candle festival, was advertised. The festival had been held the evening of July 4th, complete with actors dressed in period attire, strolling minstrels, and candlelight-only illumination of the gardens, crowned with a spectacular fireworks display. Lavillaine had hardly been alone on the grounds of Villandry Castle that Saturday, even if he had been alone by the time midnight rolled around. Luckily for the crowds, the rain had not started until quite late.

The owner, Hervé Castillo, had not mentioned that major event when we spoke with him, even though he and his entire staff had been working overtime to manage the throngs of visitors. Hmm …

What was it that Le Coq had said about him? Wasn't Castillo himself a mathematician? Or, rather, a chess player? Or was it both?

* * *

Setting my pad aside, I scrutinized my tray. Croissants had been ferried to my room along with the first cup of java, and I thought fondly of a friend of mine who is ready to drop everything and drive a hundred miles to a far-flung bakery if you tell her they have authentic croissants there. The puffed pastry they are made with is, it's true, so hard to get just right; and the butter—assuming it's used—is incredibly variable in quality. It might be hard to believe that what appears to be a simple flakey dough can be so complicated, but then we similarly struggle to fathom that it takes about seven years of daily practice to correctly prepare something apparently even more basic: the rice served with sushi! The problem in recent years—at least it's a problem to me—is that the age-old profession of *pâtissier tourier*, puffed pastry expert, is disappearing. The dirty little secret of most bakeries in France is that they buy their dough ready-made from giant factories where it is kept frozen for Lord knows how long.

Today's croissants were pretty good, and the butter they had used was quite rich, resulting in the little striations and indentations that crown a perfectly made pastry. But one hotel I frequent in the Pyrenees has the *flakiest* pure-butter croissants, as well as *pains au chocolat* to die for, and I chuckled as I recalled how many of them I'd eaten one morning there! They were so irresistible, I kept returning again and again to the breakfast buffet—shame on me—even putting a few in a napkin to eat later. Is that hotel supplied by the last real pastry shop in all of France? No, there is at least one more in Saumur, I remembered, thinking of Gouzy. An image of the bakery I'd discovered in Paris during my student days flashed through my mind, to which my chocolate-croissant-crazy girlfriend had become positively addicted. You might say that ours was a match made in pastry heaven.

"What had happened to us?" I wondered. "Where had we gone wrong?"

Thinking of my *pain au chocolat*-addicted lover, I suddenly remembered that I'd had a dream that morning. What was it now? A fine woman in some kind of bind. I let my thoughts drift. Bind, jam, pickle … Not much there. How about something related to bind in sound, like band—Möbius band, wedding band, Pink Floyd? Or bond—James Bond. I wouldn't mind rescuing women like he often did! Then another related sound forced its way into consciousness: blind. That instantaneously made me think of a girl I knew in college whose mother was blind—what was her name? Was it Dina? I hadn't thought about her in ages …

At that very moment, there was a knock at the door, and I was handed a large, flat package that had just been messengered over. It looked quite official. Well I'd be danged if it wasn't blow-ups of the photos the Clos Lucé's director had taken of the "finished" version of *The Adoration of the Magi*. I washed the butter and unusual *cornouille* (dogwood) and chamomile jams that had accompanied the croissants off my fingers, and all at once realized who the dream was about: Dina pointed to Thoury's first name, Claudine. Claudine was in a considerable bind at Clos Lucé Castle.

No personal note accompanied the delivery—whether on da Vinci stationary or not—so I simply examined the cache of photos, casting my mind back to Leonardo's last home. There was no secret code or message in the freshly painted parts, as far as I could tell. Although you never know, because symbolic meaning is often in the eye of the beholder, just like at Chambord, each commentator proposing different meanings for the same artistic or architectural elements, and new theories bursting onto the scene every twenty years.

The added portions fit so seamlessly into the original that it struck me as like a *tessera*, the other half of a tablet broken in two by the Romans in order to ensure the identity of their messengers—if they didn't have the half that perfectly matched your own, you knew you were dealing with imposters. Had Leonardo kept both halves? Had he miraculously risen from the dead, followed a secret passageway into the castle, and painted at unprecedented speed the other half he had always envisioned? There were brushstrokes, an apparent layering of colors, sfumato-like blurring of edges, and a handling of light and shadow that were uncannily reminiscent of da Vinci's own chiaroscuro. I reckon I was becoming delusional after spending so much time in the Valley of the Kings.

Glancing at my watch, I dialed the precious number.

"*Âllo-oui?*" came a voice.

"Am I speaking with the commander and chief of the inestimable Clos Lucé Castle, the loveliest lady of the Loire?" I asked and then immediately added, "Inspector Canal here. How are you?"

"And yourself?" she asked politely, her voice on the tense side. Had she forgotten the magic of our serendipitous encounter? I was nettled.

"Never a dull moment!" I replied honestly, and set aside my disappointment. "I was wondering if you had had any news about the canvas. I examined the enlargements you so kindly sent over, but couldn't detect any special codes or symbols in the unbelievably da Vinci-like brushwork."

"Codes or symbols?" she echoed uncomprehendingly.

"As I'm sure you know," I started to pontificate a little, but couldn't help myself, "artworks—whether tapestries, rugs, paintings, or even musical compositions—have been used to transmit messages for millennia." She fell silent. "Did your restorer find a chip or microdot embedded in the paint or frame?"

"What?" Worry permeated her voice. "Not that she mentioned … I didn't think to ask."

"Nothing to be ashamed of," I reassured her. "It's more my area than yours."

"The good news is that the paint came off very quickly and easily," Thoury said, sounding very pleased.

"Really?" I asked, skeptical that such a thing was possible.

"Yes. Whoever did it used a type of paint she had never seen before, perhaps of his own confection. Although it blended in very well with the original paints and dried very quickly, because he managed to lay down multiple layers of colors like da Vinci himself used to do, it could be removed extremely simply with acetone. So we're completely in the clear. Case closed."

Was she shutting the door to further contact with me? Her tone didn't seem to leave much room for an opening of any kind. That wouldn't do! "Interesting," I murmured (not so sure the curators at the Uffizi would agree with her if they ever came to see the pictures I held in my hands, and finding her a bit too sure there'd be no lawsuit in the offing). "What were the paints made of?"

"I don't know … Anyway, that's not my problem anymore, thank God," she responded. "It brings to mind da Vinci's debacle with *The Battle of Anghiari*, the fresco he painted in the Palazzo Vecchio in Florence."

"How so?" I queried, reclining in my chair, happy she was prolonging the conversation. I was, naturally, familiar with the cock-up in question.

"Da Vinci was always seeking the perfect concoction for his painstakingly slow painting method, which was said to be as slow as Protogenes's."

"It wasn't just his search for the ugliest face in all creation that took forever," I chimed in.

She made an affirmative sound.

"So, she remembers," I said to myself, glad she recalled our conversation about Judas two days earlier.

"Leonardo tried to rediscover a formula dating back to antiquity in which paints were diluted with melted wax," she resumed, "yet the ones he used in that fresco did not bind well to the wall. He was very proud of the part he had painted and showed it to Michelangelo and Raphael, but left it unfinished due to the smearing of the colors—well, *you'd* probably say that it was only in part due to that." She paused just as I reflected that I could listen to her with pleasure all day. "In any case, within a few years disaster struck. The paint began detaching from the plaster, and the whole thing was eventually painted over by somebody else."

"In seeking the best, he allowed it to become the enemy of the good," I quipped. "Thinking outside the box is fine if there's a genuine problem with what's in the box. But to do so for its own sake is generally vain and futile." In striving at all costs to be original, the artist fell into the trap denounced centuries later by Lichtenberg: doing the opposite of others just to be different doesn't prove your independence from them, but rather your absolute dependence on them. I know quite a few such "rebels"!

"Do you know anything about tempera?" she queried. "If you do I'll give you the keys to all the rooms visitors never get to see at the Clos Lucé!"

"Then prepare to hand them over," I joked back. "Assuming, that is, you are not talking about Japanese tempura—vegetables or seafood deep-fried in an egg, water, and flour batter—but instead about pigments mixed with egg white."

"So you know, then," she went on, "that Leonardo had a similar fiasco with *The Last Supper*. In spite of the high humidity in the refectory at the convent where he painted it, he opted for tempera instead of sticking with the tried and true fresco technique. It wasn't long before the lovely colors faded and the painting began separating from the wall."

"So our midnight artist could not have been the ghost of da Vinci. The paint he used seems to have bound to the canvas, yet it turned out it could easily be dissolved," I remarked, relishing how well-spoken she was. "Reminds me of the remake of that movie set in New York, with a scene I've watched over and over at the Metropolitan Museum of Art, *The Thomas Crown Affair.*" I wouldn't have minded showing her around that museum, just a hop, skip, and a jump from my own digs in the Big Apple (even if I didn't have keys to all the locked doors, and even if the interiors shown in the film are not actually those found at the Met), and maybe giving her a kiss in the apple orchard out back ...

"A bored multimillionaire steals an old master from a museum, paints a different old master over it, donates it to the same museum, and then sets off a fire alarm, the emergency sprinkler system washing away the acrylic paints, showing the old master to have been there all along—something like that?"

"Yes, something like that."

"One wonders whether our intruder knew the paints would come right off." After a short silence, she resumed, "You mentioned the possibility of transmitting messages via artworks ... Do you think the touch-up could have been designed to pass a message on to someone?" So, she *was* still a little rattled!

"Someone might have been scheduled to visit the castle the next day, making it impossible to establish any link between the sender and the receiver." Shifting in my chair, I added, "Maybe our mystery artist intends to complete a few other of da Vinci's unfinished paintings, like ... the *Mona Lisa.*"

I did not think it the time or place to point out that a painting Leonardo had for once finished—assuming it was, in fact, Leonardo who painted it and not one of his assistants—had been partially painted over by someone else. *Salvator Mundi,* which sold at Sotheby's for about sixty dollars in the nineteen-fifties, was auctioned off—after extensive removal of the second artist's vision, or should I say, revisions?—at Christie's sixty years later for almost half a billion.

"At least he won't have to hire musicians, singers, and clowns to get his somber model to smile, like da Vinci did," I added.

* * *

After about five rings, a voice finally picked up. "Was she alone?" I wondered.

"Quesjac here," I said aloud. "I wanted to be the first to tell you that you played beautifully, enchantingly, magnificently last night! Well, at least the first person today perhaps."

"Thank you," a sleepy and languorous voice replied.

I wanted her to know I'd done my best to listen just to her, even if it wasn't throughout the entire concert. Some musicians find it hard to meld into an orchestra and have to steal the limelight, others shy away from it and hide behind their fellow instrumentalists—I wasn't sure which kind she was yet. I'd once been to a concert near Chambord with three female sopranos, and whenever one was given a solo, the other two glared at her! Men did the same, of course, but the signs could be harder to read: clenching of the jaw, a vein throbbing in a temple … But not always.

"And you gave quite a performance yesterday afternoon, too," I added.

"I was more inspired than usual," Françoise yawned. Was her yawn part of a new game?

"I was mortally offended," I erupted. "You got my hopes up and then dashed them on the rocks of your true love!"

"*Une de perdue, dix de retrouvées*" (you may lose one, but you'll find a dozen replacements), she said in a serious tone of voice. "Who's playing games now, Quesjac? You'll find another in no time, and if you don't, I'll find one for you."

"That will be my condition for forgiving you. Can I take you out for a drink today? By the way, where are you staying?"

"We're at the Saturn in Blois," she answered, ignoring my first question, as people almost always do when I am so dumb as to ask two in a row.

"Is the whole orchestra staying there?"

A brief hesitation was followed by a joyous, "Yes, we're all here, except for that bleached blonde you're obsessed with. She's still M.I.A."

"So how about that drink?" I persisted.

"I don't drink."

"You told me that yesterday, but then you did."

"That wasn't me."

"That wasn't you? Who was it?"

"The other woman in me, the one who drinks. *I'm* really very serious."

I liked her style. So totally unlike a man! And she was onto something: there were undoubtedly two women in every female. "Well, then, we could share a Virgin Mary."

90

"That wouldn't be *bien catholique*" (literally, something good Catholics would do; figuratively, kosher), she objected.

"How about sparkling water then—Châteldon? If it was good enough for the Sun King, it should be good enough for us, don't you think?"

"Listen darling, I'm afraid it isn't going to be possible today. I'm rather ... ," she tittered.

"Tied up, right," I laughed along with her. It didn't matter anyway—I'd already found out what I wanted to know. "Well at least I'll see you tonight after the concert."

"Oh, you'll be coming to Chenonceau? How loyal of you! My *preux chevalier* deserves a *faveur*!"

"I'll wear it proudly on my arm as your knight in shining armor at tonight's joust."

* * *

The Saturn was a generic, modern hotel (not high on my list when there are so many fine old châteaux, posh posthouses, and ancient abbeys to stay at). It was located at the bottom of the hill that is the town of Blois, dominated by "the most royal castle" of the Loire river valley, each castle now having its own handle. What made Blois Castle more royal than Chambord or Chinon, I couldn't say, but I'd be sure to record its sobriquet in my travelogue.

Long before my visit, Joan of Arc was given a blessing in Blois before leading the French attack on the city of Orleans, winning it back from the English. Residing as I do near New England, I find it âmusing that, just as virtually every aged inn on the East Coast of the United States proudly announces, "George Washington slept here," every castle does its best to document the ubiquitous *Pucelle*'s (Virgin's) visit. We know she got around, rallying the troops far and wide, but I thought my compatriots were exaggerating a mite.

I left my trusty steed near the royal residence and was careful to lock all its doors. I needed to gain access to Pislova's room at the Saturn—not to look under her bed for Renaissance or other underclothing, as Wack might have—but I prefer not to show my badge whenever it's avoidable. I thought of breaking down the door, but it struck me as a bit too, I don't know ... in your face? obvious? noisy? Bruce Willis-like?

Circumnavigating the castle, I observed a jarring cacophony of styles—the different wings of the must-see palace having been built at so

91

many different eras—and was reminded of terrible murders (recounted in umpteen novels). The tall, handsome, arch-Catholic Duke of Guise, a.k.a. *le Balafré* (Scarface), a man more powerful than the King of France himself in 1588, passed its venerable threshold only to be assassinated there one fateful winter morning (I'm not saying he didn't deserve it). And Catherine de' Medici, who set off the Saint Barthelemy massacre that led many French Huguenots to their death, is said to have kept vials of poison in a room you can still visit today, one of which—after serving her nefarious purposes on others—may, by a twist of fate or poetic justice, have been tipped into her own fare, leading to her demise. Today it is fashionable to refer to Blois Castle as "feminine," but I think they would have done better to downplay the role played by women there ...

Long before such *femmes fatales*, the Vikings sailed up the Loire—under the command of Hägar the Horrible or one of his cousins—and repeatedly attacked the *Blisum castrum*, a fort made of wood, until they were stopped by Durtal's buddy, Thibault the Trickster, Count of Blois, whose huge fiefdom went as far north as Chartres, with its world-renowned cathedral, and as far east as Reims, including all of Champagne. Nothing seems to remain of the stone tower Thibault replaced the fort with, which perhaps serves him right. Still, everyone remembers him, his misdeeds being the stuff of bedtime stories and tall tales told around the campfire. Lebrun, the night watchman at Chambord, surely spooks his kids with gory renditions of the count's exploits. I myself can get goose bumps just thinking about how many people seem doomed to endlessly hunt for something they can never have. Brrrrr!

What *I* didn't have was Pislova's room number. When I flashed my credentials and requested the key at the front desk, the desk clerk called his manager. She scowled at me as though I had been involved in the group assassination of the Duke of Guise! Did she think I was going to paint a white cross on the musician's door, like the Catholics did to identify which dwellings contained Protestants during the Saint Barthelemy massacre?

Blois is, after all, a town that has seen more than its fair share of bloodshed, not to mention conniving Italians. Machiavelli himself visited the place twice. Da Vinci seems to have been happy to befriend him—to each his own—but he was far from my favorite author. I vastly preferred the love poetry of François I, who made Blois his main headquarters until he was imprisoned in Spain, and who planned and built the wing that dominates the Loire even as he was designing and beginning construction at Chambord. His obsession with castles became contagious in France, many even today being infected by the bug. Two pairs of brothers I know brag that they know every castle in France! Which isn't true, because there are far too many of them, but, still, you get the picture.

The décor of the room I was finally shown was contemporary and a bit spare, in sharp contrast to the opulent old town nearby. An aged bassoon over four feet long, made of beautiful wood unmarred by the unsightly metal accoutrements of contemporary bassoons, was lying in the middle of the modern space on a small sofa near the window. Flawlessly pressed clothes hung orderly in the closet, and exclusively Dior makeup lay on the bathroom counter. I found no papers or wallet anywhere, and the only purse I found, a Louis Vuitton, was empty. "What kind of a woman was she?" I wondered. I gathered together a few of her things, for which I signed, and quickly exited the hotel through a side door.

If I had had time, I would have visited my absolute favorite edifice in town, the impressively grand and magical St. Nicolas Church. Part of the incredible calm and serenity of the place may come from the abbey founded in the tenth century to which it was originally joined. The cathedral in town pales in comparison. Of course it isn't fair to measure atmospheric Romanesque (in other words, pre-Gothic) against late Gothic (especially with a nave rebuilt in the late seventeenth century after a hurricane destroyed it), but who said I had to be?

The slippery cobblestones of old town were hell to navigate in my city-slicker shoes purchased in gai Paris, but I finally made it back to my unburgled car and booted up her late-model laptop. It was password protected. A few of my usual tricks to bypass the initial level of security failed, indicating that her data was undoubtedly encrypted. I would have to ask Durtal's team to have a look at it. The region should, after all, have a few of the country's eggheads on staff from the prestigious *École Polytechnique*, France's answer to MIT and Cal Tech.

* * *

"You want to see the talk of the ward?" the stout elderly nurse at the hospital in Blois asked when I requested to see the girl injured at Chambord. "She drives us bananas. We don't even know what to call her."

93

So this was the Anna Pislova women claimed to be artificially flaxen and men subjected to Chinese water torture in their fantasies! I was reminded of black and white photos I'd seen of Charcot's hysterics at the Salpêtrière Hospital in Paris, suffering from *grand mal* or *petit mal*, their bodies limp and languishing, as if lifeless. She was un-coiffed and wearing a formless hospital gown.

"My bassoon," she cried, and lifted the heavy protective case I handed her as if it were a feather, opened it, and took out the wood-wind. She examined it carefully, then played a few dozen notes. Despite having only five fingering holes, it produced a deep, rich sound. "Why the key of E?" I wondered? "And why that melody?" The old romantic in me suddenly felt protective of this damsel in distress.

"It was in your room at the Saturn where you were staying with the Symphonie de Provence," I explained, placing it back in its case, as she got back in bed.

The nurse tiptoed out at this point, happy to leave.

"I'm supposed to be playing tonight." She spoke with just a hint of an accent.

"Do you recall where?"

"I had better get dressed and ready to go," she said, all business like.

"I'm afraid you've missed two concerts already," I told her. "There *is* one tonight, but I'm not sure you'll be feeling up to it."

"Why?" she retorted dryly, slipping out of bed. She stood up. "I'm fine," she said. "Maybe you could convince my doctor to dis-charrrge me?" She flashed me a dazzling smile and ran her fingers through her long hair.

"You had a fairly serious concussion, from what they told me." I observed her closely. Who was she? "Do you remember visiting Chambord Castle?"

The blonde didn't react.

"What *do* you remember?"

"I remember things, many things!"

"What's the last thing you remember before waking up here?"

No response.

"Do you remember arriving in Blois?"

"I know I was in Paris."

Fishing a distinctive gold tube out of her hospital gown pocket, she quickly put on some red lipstick. God only knows where she got Dior from on the ward!

The nurse who had shown me in came back to take the patient's blood pressure, and the girl greeted her as if she had not seen her since the day before. She finished pumping, released the air, noted the reading on the chart, and said, "*Au revoir*." Stealing a glance behind the nurse's back at the chart, I saw her name listed as Miss X.

"Aren't you going to take my blood pressure today?" Pislova called out loudly as the nurse headed for the door. The nurse groaned almost inaudibly and left.

"Perhaps this will jog your memory," I said, handing her the datebook I had found on her bedside table. She recognized it, flipped to July, and looked at the notations on several of the pages.

"My work schedule, I guess, Mr. ...." She looked up, as if searching in the air for my name, seeming to have grown distant again.

"Canal," I said. "What about these?" I gave her a receipt I found in the pocket of one of her jackets from a restaurant in Chambord dated July 3rd, and an early morning Paris to Blois first class train ticket with the same date on it.

She remained silent.

"Have you had any dreams since you've been here?" I asked.

"Dreams?" she queried, seeming nonplussed by the question.

I nodded.

"Dreams are meaningless," she protested. "Where I come from—"

"Have you had any, just the same?" I insisted.

Her big blue eyes fixed on me. Forehead furrowing, she admitted she woke up once during the night. "But I can't remember what I dreamt." Then, true to her probable Soviet roots, she added, "Anyway, dreams are of no importance—just random garbage left over from waking life. Dross."

Ignoring the ever-so-common reduction of everything mental to neurology, I opened her datebook and placed it next to her bed along with a pen. I realized she might be playing games, but gave her my usual prescription anyway, "Write down anything you recall if you have another one. It may give us a clue as to what happened, why you fell and hit your head." I gave her my generic calling card—the one that says nothing about what I do or have done in the past, including only my name and addresses and phone numbers in New York and Paris— and added, "If you remember something, please be sure to call me. And if you need anything, just give me a ring. The number of my hotel is on the back of the card."

"Do you know …," she trailed off.

"Know?"

"Oh, nothing," she blushed faintly.

* * *

The weather remained poor, not surprisingly. The horrible mist reminded me of Villandry, and an hour and half a million raindrops later, I arrived in Tours. It was early in the afternoon and I went straight to the University of Tours' department of viticulture and oenology, located in an ugly building constructed in the 1950s. No secretary greeted me in the office when I arrived, but a laminate door was open, so I peeked in. A man was reading at a desk in a back office—"About the ins and outs of malolactic fermentation?" I wondered, "About whether 2018 would turn out to be the greatest vintage since 2009? About Lansquenet Vineyards' profiteering since it became a Class A Premier Grand Cru? Or about the latest scandal from the Languedoc region where lesser-known varietals were being exported to the U.S. as 'genuine pinot noir' and sold for a mint?"

He looked up when he heard my footsteps. "Can I help you?" he asked.

"Professor Sarment?" I queried, having read his name on the door-plate, and reflecting once again, as I suppressed a smile, how often in France one came across people whose names seemed to have somehow destined them to follow certain careers—like Monsieur Dubois (literally, Of the Wood) whose carpentry business I had seen advertised on a workshop on my way to Tours, and Monsieur Pinard (an informal term for wine) who makes a dynamite Sancerre. A *sarment* is a small branch of a grapevine, and the complicated pruning of such branches goes back to the fifth century, thanks to Saint Martin's donkey. (The monks who tended the vines noticed that the plants the ass gnawed at, while his master was taking a nap, gave better fruit than the others, hence better wine. Saint Martin is, not surprisingly, the patron saint of Touraine.) Can your name truly determine who you become?

The man nodded perfunctorily.

I introduced myself and said, "I was wondering if you could tell me anything about Professor Bouture."

His eyes narrowed. "Charles Bouture? Last I heard he was in Italy, teaching oenology at the Slow Food University in Pollenzo."

96

He spoke elegantly (people from Touraine are reputed to speak the purest French), and I wondered whether he also taught at the *Université du Goût* down the street. It is a whole university devoted to taste, specifically that of food and wine. In true Rabelaisian spirit, they teach gastronomy and defend age-old agricultural practices designed to improve the flavor of food. The school's founder, Jacques Puisais, was a rebel like Bouture, and shocked people when he famously declared that our asepticized society is bringing about uniformity of taste, and that pasteurizing milk is tantamount to pasteurizing minds! Its faculty courageously rallied around Prince Charles of England when he came to France to publicly sing the praises of stinky raw milk cheeses made all around the country, denouncing the bureaucrats in Brussels who wanted to outlaw them all with the stroke of a pen, doubtlessly in order to please some capitalist magnate somewhere.

"Pretty nice gig," I exclaimed.

He laughed, rose to his feet (better late than never, I thought), and shook his head. "It seems that the Italians have such wildly different views about winemaking in the different regions there that they couldn't agree on a homegrown lecturer. They had to look to a Frenchman so as not to side with the Tuscans over the Venetians."

I laughed heartily, too.

"Not to mention the fact that Bouture is smart as a whip, when he isn't deliberately riling people up." He seemed to be thawing. "What would you like to know about him?"

"Well," I said, choosing my words carefully, "I am aware that he is well-known for his rather outspoken views on the psychology of wine tasting, but I was wondering if he might be known for other work."

He eyed me narrowly. "It is not common knowledge. In fact," he frowned, lowering his voice and glancing out into the secretary's office, "my journal will soon be publishing a new article by him. Why do you ask?"

"You are aware, I assume, that he is no longer of this world, and I am—"

"Right, he's become such a superstar, he's gone straight to the stratosphere," he ironized. Then he realized I was not smiling.

"He died a few weeks ago."

The professor placed a hand on his desk as if to steady himself.

"An accident, it seems, but I am not so sure. I'm wondering if his scientific work could have made him any enemies."

He paused, as if registering what I'd said, his face ashening. "Enemies? He had some rather unconventional ideas about vinification methods that could, I guess, tip over some sacred cows—but ...," he stopped short.

I showed him my badge. "I'll need to see that paper of his. It's under review, I presume?"

I didn't believe for a second that the editor-in-chief of a scientific journal wouldn't know that studies in all kinds of fields get defunded and sometimes even blackballed by all the major journals when they might jeopardize certain industrialists' vested interests, whether in pharmaceuticals, vaccines, food additives, pesticides, herbicides, radiation exposure, or—why not?—winemaking.

* * *

The duration of the rain can be tiresome at times in the Loire Valley—it is nothing like the exciting violent downpours I have grown to love in New York—but then the Garden of France does occasionally need to be watered. The unrelenting drizzle had accomplished another thing, too: it had shrunk the number of nonresident aliens at Chambord that afternoon. Attired in my London Fog trench coat, I stood alone in the majestic courtyard as far back from the castle as I could to try to take in the whole of the façade and the daringly novel design—never replicated anywhere, to the best of my knowledge—and ponder the mystery that still enveloped its architect or architects. It was referred to early on as a hunting lodge because the miles of woods around it were so full of game. But you realize that moniker is a joke when you see the place, for there's nothing rustic about it—it's straight out of a fairy tale! You have to wonder exactly what it was built for. To impress the pants off some woman? The dashing young François I certainly didn't need yet another royal castle to do that. To build the most beautiful palace on earth, dazzling visitors from the four corners of the globe? It certainly wasn't designed to be the seat of the king's power, given how rarely he actually did anything there other than hunt or survey the progress of the work.

François I spent only forty-two nights at Chambord—more, say some, than he did in bed with his royal spouse, Claude de France. He treated his chef-d'oeuvre like the most beautiful mistress a man has ever neglected.

It was widely thought that François—who wasn't called the "architect prince" for nothing, sketching as he did pictures of castles he imagined in his spare time—himself took an active part in the design at the tender age of twenty-four, along with several master masons/architects. Was Leonardo at his side, simultaneously contemplating how to throw the king's upcoming masquerade ball under a replica of the Milky Way? All the archives on Chambord's construction had been lost or destroyed during the French Revolution, so we may never know.

Architects from that time are often unknown in France—forgotten, though in name alone. Which is a lucky thing for the hapless architects who designed Beauvais Cathedral to be the tallest cathedral in France. It collapsed in 1284, not long after its completion, and again three hundred years later after they added a bell tower to it, topped by a spire, making it the tallest edifice in all Christendom, rising some fifty stories in the air—the Burj Khalifa skyscraper of its time. Such delusions of grandeur! Were they punished for attempting to build a new tower of Babel?

In Italy it was totally different. Architects of major monuments had been known and celebrated there since at least Brunelleschi's time, a hundred years before Chambord was even a gleam in François's eye. But Leonardo's contribution to Chambord's design remained a mystery, I kept having to remind myself, he having died shortly before construction purportedly began. Like researchers the world over, I couldn't help looking for clues. There were physical and virtual models throughout the castle this summer exhibiting their myriad hypotheses. The central plan, which was unique in the civil architecture of the time, and four colossal corner towers baffled everyone. Historical events may have dispersed or destroyed the royal archives, but the search was still on.

All at once, I recalled the unexpected interchange I'd had the other morning with the chatty guardian of the little church a stone's throw from the castle. He himself had just arrived, was unlocking the beautifully sculpted wooden doors, and invited me in. I still remember the look on his face when, seeing me pick up a brochure on da Vinci that was lying on a table, he remarked, "Did you know that the *Mona Lisa* was hidden from the Nazis for several months at Chambord?"

"I knew that Chambord served as a vault for artworks from the Louvre and other museums during World War II, protecting them from potential bombardments and from becoming war booty. But I didn't realize the *Mona Lisa* was among them."

The affable guardian had nodded and continued, "Thousands were sorted onsite, and many were secretly farmed out to spots thought to be safe further south, others being carefully hidden and guarded at Chambord itself in places no soldier would dream of looking."

"So, four hundred years after it was painted, the *Mona Lisa* was once again close to her creator."

"I couldn't have put it better myself," he'd exclaimed.

The *Mona Lisa* is thus the only sure trace we have of Leonardo at Chambord. And the castle itself is inextricably linked to the mysterious double spiral staircase where I had found a half-dead woman on a cold, foggy night.

Staircases have long been a sign of the times. In France, when you see one located *hors oeuvre*, outside of the main structure, in a separate tower, you can tell your friends, "This is a perfect example of medieval architecture." And when you take them to see one inside, you'll sound really smart when you say, "This is a perfect example of Renaissance architecture." That's the simple version, anyway (there are exceptions, like the staircases in highly decorated external structures at Chambord and Blois, but they are open to the elements, not enclosed towers—call them "first Renaissance").

Azay-le-Rideau's is unclassifiable. Berthelot built his indoors, yet it's an open-air number, exposed to snow, rain, heat, and gloom of night. Whoever said that beauty had to be practical? Don't we all have to suffer for it? Well, women more than men, no doubt …

When it comes to Chambord, nobody is sure of anything, which is in part, no doubt, why it intrigues me so! The double-spiral there is right smack dab in the middle of the castle, something no one else has ever dared, not even in Italy, regardless of the century. The few old drawings that remain show straight flights of stairs planned in one of the arms of the giant Greek cross. That would already have been quite odd, but hardly revolutionary. The ceilings were obviously not high enough to accommodate four interlaced staircases in the same stairwell (as seen in the sketch by da Vinci I studied that morning, which in any case had no obvious connection to Chambord)—at least if one wanted easy-to-climb, majestic staircases with adequate headroom for tall men and women sporting lofty headdresses. I reckoned that only two could be comfortably intertwined. Otherwise they would have ended up with impossibly steep interwoven staircases, like at Saumur Castle or the Tour Saint Nicolas in La Rochelle—fine for soldiers or the occasional secret visitor, but not for kingly processions. Almost no one knows about the interlocking staircases at Saumur and La Rochelle—I do, because I have friends who just so happen to be curators—but people on them can never cross paths and they can't even see each other, even if they might hear each other's footsteps. At Chambord you never cross paths either. But you can glimpse those opposite you through slit-like windows that provide certain voyeuristic pleasures. What other inspiration could there have been for such an unusual design? Didn't it always come down to finding ways to admire the object of one's affections? (There are, of course, those who strive to hide their admiration and affection from their beloved. Do we generally hide more than we show when it comes to love?)

Exploring the sumptuous royal apartments, I concluded that François must have built the place more as a symbol than as a primary residence, or even a secondary residence, since he spent most of his time traipsing from one castle to the next, his court of thousands in tow.

"Wonderful!" I exclaimed, rubbing my hands gratefully in front of the blaze in the fireplace in the hallway.

"We thought it would be appreciated by our visitors today—it's barely fifty degrees outside," remarked a guide wearing thick glasses standing nearby.

"Yes, rather nippy for July!" I concurred. "Just how heavy are those logs?"

"Heavy as the dickens!" he replied. "It takes at least two of us to carry them."

Having warmed up sufficiently in front of the flames, I told him I was headed up to the roof.

"I try to get up there every day," he said. "One of the finest parts of the castle."

It was my first trip to the roof since I had been locked out on it, and it truly is like no other roof—it's a whole town, really. Despite the rain, I was reminded of the extraordinary fairy-tale-like images of the Louvre and other medieval castles, topped with similarly fanciful roofs, found in *Les très riches heures du Duc de Berry*. It's the most fabulous late medieval illuminated book of hours—you really must see it! It will convince you that the Louvre was once a forbidding fortress, not the patrician palace we see today.

I invoke afflatus, divine inspiration, for the forest of chimneys encrusted with blue diamond-shaped jewels and turrets topped with angels and cupids that only clouds can see atop Chambord, not oriental influence. Most French castles have lost many if not all of their marvelously decorated dormer windows and vents, they being among the first things to disappear, degrading through exposure to the wind and rain, and being expensive to restore. The country is peppered with castles and manor houses that are missing one or even all of their attic windows and roof decorations. When owners are brave enough to recreate them, they transform otherwise humdrum homes into stately manors, and second-rate castles into genuine gems. The fabulous chimneys—over two hundred and sixty of them!—and turrets at Chambord are undoubtedly the finest of the fine, but their French pedigree is undeniable.* Okay, I am a bit of a chauvinist …

I could live up here on cloud nine. Which of the marvelous houses would I choose? I buttoned my coat to keep out the cold and was reminded of the sound I had heard the night I overstayed my welcome, a sound like that of a door opening and closing. It haunted me … Peering over the edge of the roof to the distant ground, I wondered whether someone might have stolen away by descending a rope or a gutter. A dexterous climber could easily get down the three stories from the roof even without a cord, clambering from one gallery to the next. In fog as dense as there had been that evening, someone could easily have scrambled down unnoticed.

Back on the third floor, I suddenly froze to the spot. I had been gazing at the many interlacing patterns carved into the coffered ceilings in the four hallways radiating out in the four intercardinal directions from the double-spiral staircase. *Entrelacs* and *lacs d'amour* (interlacing patterns) were common in French castles for centuries, and in the West since at least Roman times, but hadn't I read somewhere that certain knots Leonardo invented were known as *vinci*, or *nodi viciani*? The man certainly dabbled, long before me! And he was fascinated by repeating geometrical patterns, unusual forms of symmetry in knots, and curls in people's hair—like those in his portrait of Ginevra Benci that I'd seen one fine day in Washington, D.C.

Someone stepped violently on my Parisian penny loafer as I stood there immobilized, and I heard an oblivious voice say, "Didn't Dan Brown say that is a Patagonian symbol for the Queen of the Nile? You know, Cleopatra." I turned and saw a man pointing toward a crowned salamander, an obvious symbol for the castle's royal builder.

"No, he called it a *salbantica*—it's, you know, Etruscan," his interlocutor riposted.

102

I hadn't heard either of those select morsels of hogwash before, but wasn't that surprised and didn't bother to correct them. What had arrested me was a symbol I'd espied that I had made much of myself at one time, a *fermesse* (or *fermesse isolé*), also known as an *S barré* or *S fermé*. It's a barred or closed letter S, which is essentially a capital S with a slanted line through it: $. A *chiffre énigmatique*—that's what it started out life as. It served in the sixteenth and seventeenth centuries as an enigmatic cypher or code designed to authenticate the signature that accompanied it, signatures being the first thing one's enemies learned to forge. It drove me crazy when people wrote it as a dollar sign because it meant they had completely overlooked its recondite origins—which, effete snob that I was at the time, I never deigned to tell them.

The only French king who rivaled François I in sheer number of mistresses used it to signal the end of his letters to his lovers, aligning two, three, four, or even more such cyphers at the bottom of the text. It informed Henri IV's correspondents that if anything was found below those symbols on the page, it had not been written by him. After all, signatures were not the only thing one's enemies learned to forge.*

Another time, another king. Louis XIII often used it as a mark of affection when signing off, like certain people do today by drawing hearts, scribbling a row of Xs and Os, or—altogether disgracefully—pasting puerile emoticons in their emailed missives instead of taking the trouble to articulate their feelings in words, however unpoetic and unpolished they may be.

Some say that the cypher's meaning slid quite naturally ("metonymically") from authenticating the author to authenticating the author's feelings toward the addressee. Others that the slanted line through the S (for *semper* in Latin, meaning always or forever … yours) represented Cupid's bow, or even one of his arrows, and that the symbol as a whole was a sort of "true lover's knot," the kind found since antiquity. (Lord knows I'll have given a few generations of topologists food for thought—or perhaps, rather, headaches aplenty—with the plethora of knots I've left lying around in my cupboards—if anyone is interested enough to look, that is.)

As is my wont—call it as you like, a gift or a major character flaw—I'd given the *fermesse*, implying firmness and loyalty in love, my own meaning, one that was admittedly rather tangential. Only the very few, only the truly cultured, knew its origins. I had done the same with other symbols that drove my students to distraction, like *phi* (φ) and *delta* (δ). But put them together and they quite simply make *fidelta*, fidelity. In my defense—although why I should be defensive about it, I don't know, so I'll have to think about that—it's no sillier than the rebuses we used as kids, writing "I ♥ U" or "J&J4ever" inside a heart pierced by an arrow.

My neck was aching (like it does whenever I visit Sequoia National Park) from studying the shapes sculpted in the shimmering white ceilings, and I gave it a rest near a window as I watched a French "typhoon" (translation into American English: a light downpour) scatter the lost souls ambling about the regal gardens below. Out of the corner of my eye I noticed something carved into the stone window jamb next to me. It was hard to make out at first, but seemed to read:

> *Souvent femme varie*
> *Bien fol qui s'y fie!*

It was François I's famous line about the fickle nature of women and the folly of men who trust them! I had heard that he himself had carved it somewhere at Chambord—"defacing" his own castle—but had never been able to locate it. "Why today?" I wondered. Had I given myself more license to wander about aimlessly than usual? Hard to imagine, knowing myself as I do. In any case, every child learns the king's ditty in school. Is that what makes the French so inconstant and unfaithful, or were they already that way?

I had the sense, I have to admit, that it was the men in the present investigation who seemed fickle, not the women: Wack and his uncontrollable need for veneration from any and every source, Durtal and his torturous plugging of one woman after another into the same knothole in his being …

* * *

I finally asked to speak with the head of security. Maybe I have plain old bad luck, or maybe he was just like that—cranky and disgruntled because, unlike magistrates and wineglass blowers in France who take the whole summer off, he wasn't on vacation.

After what seemed like a laborious search through his files, he haltingly read, "No one found hiding in the castle the night of July 3–4. Window found unlocked in room 387 of northeast tower." Looking up at me, he added, "That's on the roof, probably the window through which you entered."

At least he remembered that. "Nothing else?" I asked.

"Huh?"

"No door or other window found unlocked?"

He studied his screen again for what seemed like an eternity. "A door in room 389."

"Where is that?"

After another study of the screen, he evinced the incredible generosity of uttering a few more words: "Also in the northeast tower."

"Can someone take me up there?"

"Now?" he grumbled.

"Yes, now!"

* * *

A hundred keys dangling from his belt, a fine young bearded fellow led me through dozens of rooms, following a route that seemed less designed to take us to the northeast tower as directly as possible than to show me spots he loved. Other guides I've accosted there share his fascination with the place, but not his knowledge (he even knew about the *fermesse*!). At his side, I discovered a second Chambord, one with almost perfect rotational symmetry, there being three stories of spacious apartments under all four of the steep rectangular ridgelines, each making a quarter turn from its neighbors in the rooftop village, and as many stories of living quarters under the round pepper-pot roofs coiffing the broad-based towers. And they all had their own spiral staircases that kept spinning and spinning and spinning.

My guide was so talkative—about markings on the walls, the symbolism of the palace, Masonic allegories, you name it—I almost forgot at times what I was there for. Like many others, he had constructed his own history of Chambord and even his own theory of why it was built. But since no one ever gets to see these areas, I let him parley on while discovering untold treasures.

He finally brought me to where a window had been found unlocked, room 387. We tried to locate the path I believed I had taken in the dark down one story and out into one of the main hallways, leaving the grand aristocratic apartments by a back stairway. Just as I recalled, the tight circular staircase I had taken—he said it was number 63—turned in the opposite direction from the ones in the other towers at Chambord, and we were miraculously able to retrace my steps.

After that, he led me back upstairs to room 389 in the roof-level apartment where an old weathered door had been found unlocked. It was as grandiose as the vast apartments adorning the unparalleled *Place des Vosges* in Paris! After getting a feel for the place, we examined where the door opened out onto the roof, and then reconnoitered the various possible routes between one of the lower floors and that portal—as though we were playing one of those new "escape games" that are all the rage, designed to get philistines to visit old forts and castles. I explored all the tiny staircases someone might have taken, first the ones connecting one story and the next.

"Next we have to check the *vis de fond en comble*, the ones running from the bottom of the edifice all the way to the top," my guide told me. "We have quite a number of them here at Chambord. They are the equivalent of our contemporary service stairs or elevators, which is why they aren't highly decorated. They were also," he added smiling, "climbed by more eminent castle residents for secret, late-night rendezvous."

No, they were not full of spiderwebs, as you may be thinking, but they were so dark and narrow I could hardly see how servants could have ferried silver platters laden with food and drink up and down them, while holding candelabras at the same time. They must have been highly coordinated and as surefooted as mountain goats!

We went all the way to the bottom of the *vis de fond en comble* in the northeast tower, where the almost invisible steps were dangerously worn, proving the passage of millions of feet over the centuries. Reversing course, we had almost reached the rooftop village again—I was glad to soon be seeing the sky anew!—when something glinting in the darkness caught my eye. There was a shiny object in the corner of one of the upper steps. I bent over and, placing one hand on the hard stone for balance, fished out my handkerchief. I picked it up carefully, ensuring no part of my skin touched it. The guide and I both squinted at it in the dim light.

"How often do people come through here?" I asked.

"Not terribly often, I think," he replied. "These stairs, sir, are never open to the general public—very few even know they exist!"

"Does the staff here ever use carabiners?" I inquired, for that was what it was.

He pointed to the one hanging from his belt, loaded with keys. "Almost all the guides have them. But this one looks quite technical."

"Do you buy them yourselves or are they issued by the castle?"

"By the castle."

* * *

It was late afternoon—hence cocktail hour, obviously—and I had just sat down at the Relais' curved, polished wood bar, ordered a glass of bubbly, and was minding my own business (well, everyone else's, really), when a voice bellowed, "Canal, old man! What exciting news do you have for me?" and Durtal slid onto the stool next to mine. ("Why couldn't I ever be left alone at this hotel?" I wondered to myself.) The prefect received respectful looks from the staff—I guess he was a regular, living so close to the hotel—and the barmaids appeared to be all eyes and ears. Something in his demeanor told me he wasn't genuinely interested in talking shop.

"Oh, hello Monsieur le Préfet," I stood up, shook his hand, and gestured to my server to bring him a glass of the same. I figured he would accept it, even if he was still on duty—after all, Air France pilots still drank wine in the cockpit up until a few years ago and nobody gave them a hard time about it, so why not a prefect? "News? Well, the bright, lovely Le Coq and I had a memorable evening together last night in Langeais: just the two of us, getting drenched …"

"Yes, I know. She told me everything on the phone this morning."

He loosened his tie knot slightly and shot me an inquisitive look. What he said and how he said it seemed out of joint, something that always intrigues me.

"You old Casanova!"

My eyebrows must have shot up a mile. Was he that unsure of himself with women? (And how dare he call me an "old" Casanova! I don't often bridle at such inconsiderate, insensitive comments, but I can be as vain as the next guy, and it got my dander up.) Was he envious, thinking I'd found the complicated, one-in-eight-billion key that fit my lock, the very thing he was looking for? Or had she used me—me, the Love Doctor—as a pawn to snare the prefect's interest by making it seem like she and I had something going on? Perhaps another instance of feminine wiles … Was Le Coq, trying to make it in a man's world, hunting a 16-point stag?

Our barmaid placed a coupe of bubbly in front of Durtal and he gave her the once over. "Priceless stuff about that winemaker!" he suddenly roared. "True Parisian vaudeville." Was he terrified of our modern-day Diana or just in fine fettle this afternoon?

"True," I said, "but it isn't the whole story." It seemed Le Coq had led him to believe it was, despite my reservations. "Couard, the glitzy Bordeaux winery owner in question, is a devious, scheming power monger, a bully, and probably plenty of other unsavory things. Yet I doubt he harbors hitmen in his Rolodex."

"You'd be surprised sometimes." Durtal greedily sipped the champagne the barmaid had just served and I felt reassured that Stella Artois wasn't his only poison. "It's hard to tell. When the conditions are right—or should I say, wrong?"

I held up my glass to the light, admired the amber hue and the "chimneys" (as the Belgians call the columns) of bubbles rising from deep within to the surface. "You might not know it," I remarked, "but in this glass there is both science and art. There is, of course, a science of fermentation chemistry, but there is currently no science of vinification, strictly speaking. All vintners who are worth their salt, whether they make Premier Grand Cru Classés," Durtal licked his lips at this, "or ordinary *vins de pays*, practice the dark arts of winemaking in their own way—including this one," I added. "What do you think of the result?"

"I hope it's not Cristal."

"It's even better," I reassured him, "it's made by Henri Giraud."

At this he blanched. "Even more expensive?"

"Giraud does things no one else would even dream of doing, and they work out beautifully, for a fraction of the cost." I finished my coupe—abominably small, in my opinion—and asked the barmaid to refill our glasses. Durtal drank her in with his eyes for the second time.

"In the absence of a science," I went on, "there are a few highly influential people who call themselves 'winemakers.' Bizarrely enough, they have adopted the English term—that's what we French always do, after all, when we want to give something more cachet," I nodded to my interlocutor, but he looked perplexed.

"Just like English speakers give things French names to make them sound chic," I went on, and it seemed he now grasped my point. "I guess the old tried and true *vigneron* sounded too humble or rustic to these self-anointed experts, like 'grape grower' or 'farmer.' And *maître de chais*, 'cellar-master' or 'head cellarman,' didn't translate easily enough for their taste in other countries where people don't speak French but think they speak English." I raised my glass and mused aloud, "Funny

108

how they have ended up with a term totally detached from the climate and soil, the much vaunted *terroir*, preferring something that makes what they do sound like magic! 'Winemaker' gives you the impression that they pull marvelous wine out of a hat, not out of living plants."

Durtal nodded indulgently but emphatically while nursing his drink. "You seem to know quite a lot about French wine for a New Yorker. I guess you can get whatever you want over there?"

"Hardly. I discover wondrous wines here and ship them back home," I replied, savoring the ambrosia, and asking myself if he was jealous of *everyone*. "Now, the thing is," I stressed, ensuring I had his attention, "these modern-day magicians have been selling their bag of vinification tricks for astronomical sums. They have become the new kingmakers: they can make or break the reputation of pretty much any winery in the world."

"So?"

"So, what if someone threatened to put these multimillionaire kingpins—the Michel Rollands and Jean-Luc Thunevins of the fruit of the vine—out of business?"

"Is that what Bouture did?"

"He may have. His latest research—soon to be published in the world's most influential journal of oenology—could make their methods completely obsolete, and the principal manufacturers of thermoregulated vats might be forced to close or retool fast. The vested interests at stake here make Couard's Class A preoccupations pale in comparison!"

Durtal whistled and, gazing at his now empty glass, signaled the waitress.

"There is something else …"

"There is?" He gave the barmaid a big smile this time as she refilled our glasses. "*Merci, belle dame,*" he said. She smiled demurely and returned the bottle to cold storage. He could barely keep his eyes off any pretty woman who entered his field of vision. Although he could probably charm plenty of girls, he truly seemed desperate! He wasn't the only one like that with whom I'd dealt …

"I'm not sure it really qualifies as news, but something has occurred to me."

"What?" he asked crossly.

The barmaid turned her head his way, not for the first time.

"It may be hard to do, but you'll have to try," I whispered. "Someone seems to be selecting castles at which to strike in alphabetical order.

In the Loire Valley, the next after Villandry is a small, out-of-the-way castle called Villesavin. You need to ensure their security right now. Going a bit further away from the Loire, we might even have to consider the much smaller Villeprévost Castle."

Durtal looked at me like I was out of my tree.

"Villesavin was, moreover, built by Jean Le Breton."

"So what?" he tried to whisper too.

"Le Breton was minister of finance for François I. He built Villandry and oversaw the construction of Chambord."

"Really?" Durtal interjected.

"Some say he siphoned off funds slated to pay for materials and labor at Chambord to build his own castles."

Durtal's brow furrowed. "You're saying that this Le Breton fellow could be the thread that links the incidents, even though he died like a million years ago?"

"I don't know," I replied. "But something might well happen at Villesavin on July 7th or 8th—in other words, your job might be on the line tomorrow or the next day."

"Why in heaven's name?"

"The girl at Chambord fell on July 3rd. If the coroner's report proves that Le Coq's assumption was correct, and the man fell at Villandry sometime after midnight, that would be July 5th. Three and five are both prime numbers."

Once again, he looked at me like I was out of my ginkgo.

"Lavillaine, our dead mathematician, seems to have been obsessed with such numbers, like so many before him. And seven just so happens to be the next prime."

"Aren't you making it more complicated than it needs to be? Three, five, and seven are ordinary odd numbers."

"All primes are odd by definition," I said, giving him a mischievous glance. "Well, except for the number two. But not all odd numbers are primes. Fifteen and twenty-one are odd, but both are divisible by three. Did you look up the exact date and time of the incident at Amboise for me?"

He immediately took out his phone and scrolled through a few screens. "June 17th," he said. "Is that a prime number too?"

I shook my head in the affirmative.

"The autopsy report suggested a time of death around 7 p.m., 19 heures as we put it here."

"Both prime numbers," I observed. "So the date of each incident is a prime number." I paused for effect.

It wasn't clear my words had any on the prefect. I closed my eyes for a moment, not knowing how to convey to him the mysteries and ubiquity of the primes. "Primes just so happen to be the building blocks of all other numbers and are of capital importance in mathematics. Every time you make a call with your cell phone, use your credit card, send an email, or use your web browser to buy something over the internet, randomly chosen prime numbers are involved in the encryption of your data."

"Then why did you say something might happen at Villesavin on July 7th *or* 8th?" he asked, setting down his phone a bit anxiously. "Eight can't be a prime number—it's even."

"No, but three plus five is eight."

"So?" Exasperation crept into his voice.

"They are among the first numbers in the most elementary Fibonacci series."

The champagne he was sipping went down the wrong pipe and he began coughing up a storm. "The most elementary what?" he eventually managed to enunciate.

"It's a series of numbers named for an Italian mathematician usually called Fibonacci, but who was also known as Leonardo Bonacci, Leonardo Bigollo, and even Leonardo da Pisa." He apparently came up with the sequence by estimating the number of rabbit pairs there are at any specific time if you start with a male and a female baby rabbit at time zero (1 pair) and make a number of absurd assumptions: that they reach sexual maturity within a month (still 1 pair), have their first litter consisting of exactly one male and one female after another month (2 pairs), and so on. I didn't want to confuse the issue by telling Durtal that the further the series goes, the more closely the ratio between successive numbers in the series approximates the value of the golden ratio—a ratio (sometimes called the divine proportion) thought to have been crucial to architects, artists, and mathematicians throughout the ages, and that some say influenced the design of Chambord.

"Da Pisa?"

"Yes, from the town of Pisa. Like da Vinci, from the town of Vinci."

"Meaning?" he asked, jadedly I thought—I guess I'd worn him down.

"I'm not sure, but we may well have a serial killer on our hands," I said gravely. "A math murderer."

CHAPTER EIGHT

Chenonceau Castle

He who studies many different things loses focus and momentum.

—Leonardo da Vinci

Chenonceau surprised me. I had not been back in quite a few years, and my previous visit had been magical. It was a New Year's Day morning, and it was the only castle open in the entire *Domaine Royal* (the monarch's main axis of power in the center of France). Roaring blazes burned in the enormous stone fireplaces, and visitors bundled up against the cold were few and far between. I always do my best to avoid the crowds, so I am willing to put up with a couple of frozen fingers and feet, wear gloves and a hat indoors, and tie a scarf tightly around my neck against the frosty drafts. It's worth it to be able to imagine what it would be like to live there myself, something I do in almost every castle—this would be my office, this my library, this grand space my living room, the Steinway over in that corner with the sun from the mullion window backlighting the scores, this other stately spot my dining room, with a table for at least twenty guests ... You see, I like to have the run of the place!

Why, then, you might ask, was I visiting the Loire Valley that summer, when there could be up to ten thousand people a day at a castle like

Chenonceau? I exaggerated earlier when I said I had primarily come to see the sights. Wine tasting was my main reason for being here—or for being, *tout court*, some might say. Seeing the sights and reporting on them were fun, but they came in second and third. After my Grand Tour of champagne domains from Reims to Epernay and on to Aÿ, I had been working my way up the Loire Valley from Pouilly-sur-Loire and Sancerre, via Reuilly, Quincy, and Menetou-Salon, sampling the floral sauvignon blancs of the Cher region. I hoped to make it all the way to Savennières to visit my old pal at the Coulée de Serrant, the pope of biodynamic viticulture and maker of exceptional chenin blancs, before he took off to give a talk at yet another international conference (where he'd undoubtedly lose all track of time again and almost miss his plane back—leaving all of his bottles behind for the audience to sample!).

Small vineyard owners are overwhelmed with work in the spring—pruning and replanting—and the fall—harvesting and pressing—so, since I prefer to talk with them at leisure, and in most of France you still can, summer and winter are the best. But the tasting hours in winter can be too short for me to make a full day of it and the views of the dormant countryside inspire me less than when they've donned their full verdant regalia.

I had figured I would cram in a castle or two between tastings—maybe just to walk off the effects, for I never spit out the wine when tasting it like some do—which was why I had ended up at Chambord late that first afternoon after a long, hard day of sauvignon blanc-ing. (Now don't go thinking that was why I lost track of time out on the roof and got myself locked out ...) But I never would have suspected I would be treated to so many private tours of castles after hours courtesy of the local polizei. I guess the exclusive late-night visits had spoiled me—I could get used to experiencing these fabulous palaces when wholly deserted!—and I was a bit repulsed at first by the sight of the fleets of coaches in the enormous parking lots. An avalanche of human bodies came toward me as I tried to make my way to the second most popular castle in France, and I had the sense I was entering a high-security prison or Fort Knox, except that the signs read "Do not disturb the crew, filming in progress."

"A very harmoniously constructed concert," I had remarked to my concierge that morning when he offered me a ticket to this evening's performance at Chenonceau. "How rare!"

"And the venue is indoors," he beamed, "in the Grand Gallery. I told you I'd find you nothing but the best."

Luckily, it was closing time, and only those attending the concert could now be admitted. Approaching the stately entrance tower—the sole rem(a)inder of the medieval fortress that formerly stood on the site—I veered off to the right. I was a few minutes early and, as the weather had improved slightly, I took my usual stroll along the path following the Cher to the west, and stopped to watch a spectacular sight: the pairs of resident swans were billing and cooing, dancing, as it were, around each other, intertwining their necks gracefully, exquisitely attuned to each other's movements, imitating them almost flawlessly. Nothing ungainly there!

On the opposite bank of the river, a camera crew was filming the waterfowl, accompanied by a woman wearing a camouflage jacket talking into a microphone.

I kept looking back over my shoulder to see the graceful arches spanning the major river and the one-of-a-kind gallery built above it. Has anyone ever dared build anything like it since?

The old fortress on the site was razed to the ground, its lethal loopholes and arrow slits gone with the wars, by yet another reckless man. The soon-to-be disgraced financier, Thomas Bohier (luckily for him, he died before they audited his accounts), erected a brand-spanking-new castle and then lost it all … to the most beautiful woman of the time, Diane de Poitiers, the mistress of François I's son, Henri II. It was the most sumptuous of all the gifts, honors, or titles the kings of France ever gave their incorrigibly scheming lovers. Diane was twice his age but twice as attractive as any other woman in the kingdom.

On his deathbed, François had told his son to beware of women—as they often wanted to direct the country's affairs in such a way as to make their own prosper—and to never submit to their will like he had. Yet how could he expect Henri to take to heart such "Do as I say, not as I do" advice, after setting a bad example for his son for decades? Will men ever learn?

Rain or shine, the Cher River flowing under the castle is peaceful and yet troubled, smooth in some spots and turbulent in others, as it merges with the Loire and makes its way to the Atlantic near Brittany, its waters hightailing it from there to Long Island (well, I like to think they do, at any rate). As I admired the palace I recalled some of its former owners, first a certain Dupin, who always made me think of Poe's "The Purloined Letter" (about which I had once put pen to paper, setting out a few ideas that struck many as quite odd at the time). And then

115

there was the flamboyant Duke of Beaufort, whose only qualification to become admiral of His Majesty's navy was that he had once rowed a boat under his castle on the Cher (according to the nasty Cardinal Mazarin, at any rate; I wouldn't know).

I occasionally go to Chenonceau even when I'm not especially fond of the music on offer, simply to enjoy the scenery in peace. There was no banquet or ball tonight, so there were no young women dressed as mermaids in the moats, greeting me with their singing, or nymphs flitting about here and there in the shrubbery, scattering upon the arrival of satyrs, as there had been in the castle's heyday. Indeed, all was quite quiet, perhaps like when Diane de Poitiers was forced to leave her cherished abode—the very day her lover died—by Catherine de' Medici, Henri's widow. But Venus refused to live in the fabulous castle she received in exchange, Chaumont, which she considered to be the most wretched of hovels compared to Chenonceau. She chose instead to spend the remainder of her days eating her heart out—misery is so often brought on by oneself—at her family's ancestral slum, a magnificent castle decorated by Benvenuto Cellini, who François I once called "the greatest and most universal artist who ever lived." (So much for da Vinci. Luckily for him, he was dead and buried when the king said it.)

That was the zenith of the French Renaissance, when enchanting women were worshipped like divinities and their castles and gardens were a foretaste of the Elysian Fields (not the avenue in Paris).*

The concert would soon be starting and I had to dash past beautifully carved oak doors and vaulted stone ceilings with staggered ribs and finely chiseled disk-shaped keystones on my way to the Grand Gallery above the river.

* * *

"Would you agree that a conductor's introductory words are like the label on a bottle of wine, a beautiful and prestigious label enhancing the taste and directing us to detect hints of this flavor and that, whereas a bland label or none at all leaves us in the dark and perhaps even ruins the whole experience for us?" The woman sitting on the small folding chair next to mine in the makeshift concert hall pretended not to hear me, I'm sure.

Labels—touting age-old, mythical terroirs and famous chateaux, or even just pretty pictures of castles with names you don't know—have a mysterious hold over the French mind. They can make people change their minds about a blend they initially dislike, and end up saying it's quite good, or even excellent, as happened at a professional blind tasting I attended after the bottle was unveiled (it just so happened that the at first bottom-rated wine, later declared fabulous after the label had been reverentially revealed, was Couard's Lansquenet!).

The woman I had addressed, quite out of the blue I admit, finally looked at me as though I had a polka-dotted parrot dancing the cucaracha on my head, seeming far less tolerant of my sort of eccentricity than Claudine Thoury had been.

"Might one say," I said, striving to formulate another simple question, "that the conductor's preamble has a much bigger effect on the experience of classical music enjoyed by those who assemble to hear Apollo's gift than on the experience of contemporary music?"

"Uh ... I'm not entirely sure what you mean, but we are all influenceable," she finally replied, shifting in her seat. Then, out of the corner of my eye, I saw her wild-colored pants hurry off.

"Am I as influenceable as everyone else? Even me?" I wondered as I saw her settle into a free chair closer to the stage.

The concert was disconcerting, if you catch my drift. (She probably wouldn't have.) Was it even the same orchestra? Everyone can have an off night—or so they say when it comes to famous chefs. Cooks sometimes disappoint big time after you've trekked halfway across the country to taste their much ballyhooed creations, seeming more star-crossed than Michelin-starred.

Henri Wack was not directing that night, and not a single word passed the lips of the stiff, formal concertmaster the entire evening. Universities in the States have begun grading musicians on their ability to present their music, to get the audience into the proper frame of mind, into the groove, as it were. My mind began to wander, to topics like if and where I would dine, unfortunately alone, that evening. Even when I did pay attention, I simultaneously engaged in a thought experiment: would the exact same performance be considered better if the ground had been suitably prepared, as with wine?

I tried to concentrate, but the man seated on the other side of me began snoring loudly.

Maybe the instrumentalists should have been utterly and completely exhausted ... It is a well-known fact that certain conductors can get a great deal more out of artists than other conductors can. Jordi Savall himself told me over lunch one day that he often found his musicians played with greater verve and emotion after he had relentlessly made them record take after take until two or three in the morning.

If the exact same concert were recorded twice, once by Civadin and once by our stand-up comedian Wack, would, I asked myself, people find the first recording better than the second, even though they had enjoyed the second concert more? I know a few people who would kill me if I had them listen to both versions with no prologue, orchestrating a sort of blind musical tasting with which to trap them. You too?

But maybe an engaging conductor gets more out of his musicians than a serious, yet boring one, I retorted to myself. Or does his horsing around lead the musicians to take their work less seriously? Is seriousness key to playing good music? What would the incorrigible jokester Mozart have said about that?! I found myself wondering if there were in fact anything objective about the enjoyment of music.

Strange, I thought: the names of the composers were clearly printed in large black letters on the colorful program, and their styles were thoroughly recognizable, yet I was left with an uneasy feeling ... It was as if in listening to a Beatles' song I couldn't immediately tell whether it was from the 1960s or the 1970s! I had been to myriad concerts where the conductor had been as silent as a carp, as they say in French, providing no frame of reference whatsoever, and yet the music had been exhilarating. So packaging was certainly not the whole story.

Incongruous Romantic whirling crescendos permeated one of the pieces, swelling progressively upward and then downward in range. An image floated through my mind upon hearing them—was I hallucinating, or dreaming in public? I pictured the kind of eddies that form further and further downstream of an object in a river when the current is quite strong, the eddies getting larger and larger the further they are from the object, and alternating from one side of the obstacle to the other—it's called a Kármán vortex street (or vortex shedding) in fluid dynamics. You can see them when the snow in the *Massif Central*, the mountain range in the heart of France, melts in the spring and comes careening down into the valleys, pushing against Chenonceau's arches and the piers supporting the bridge in Amboise.

Stranger still, the image reminded me of certain hysterical fits I'd witnessed, when I hadn't managed to react adroitly so as to nip them in the bud. But more on that another time, perhaps.

* * *

A stunning woman in a long red evening gown stood gazing out a window. She looked like the belle of the ball on a Hollywood set, among the hundreds of candles casting a warm glow on the Grand Gallery's white stone walls and striking black and white floor. At the far end of the football-field-long gallery, bottles were being popped open and bubbly was flowing, as the Cher's troubled waters coursed below. I helped myself to a glass, tasted the Crémant de Loire, and slowly savored the citrusy notes.

"So we meet again, Mr. Canal," a voice interrupted my appreciation of both beauty and wine.

"Indeed we do," I said, after turning and recognizing the concertmaster. I noted that he was one of those rare men who had a head for faces and names. Women always seem to remember people's names, but I myself have to make a supreme, deliberate effort to recall them even with people I like. "Thank you for a most interesting concert."

He smiled, looking pleased and relaxed tonight.

"I don't believe I've ever heard the compositions you played this evening, not a single one of them in fact. Can you point me to any recordings of them?"

"Not until my own come out this fall," he replied. Anyone else might have thought his response smacked of grandiosity, but I found it evasive. "They are exquisitely obscure pieces, and one of them—the concerto by Mozart—has never been performed in public before tonight."

"A world premiere, then! I didn't see any such mention in the program."

"You wouldn't have, of course, because it isn't there. It was a test to see if anyone in the audience would notice."

"Indeed?" I found myself wondering whether I was the only one in the audience who had noticed and if that wacky Wack might have been right when he said that Civadin was a pretentious prick.

"It's a priceless story, actually," he said quietly. "A moth-eaten suitcase containing the autograph was found just this winter in an attic in Austria," he now whispered conspiratorially. "I'm told that it made its way there from a Cistercian monastery in Krzeszów, Poland, during World War II."

I was sure I'd heard a story like that before.* "Really?"

"I'm not at liberty to say any more about it at this time. It will all be divulged soon enough, though, and you shall be able to read about it in the fullest of detail in the best papers around the globe," he assured me peremptorily. "I was fortunate enough to get a copy of the sheet music before anyone else, that's all I can say. What were your impressions?" he asked all of a sudden. The man was not just relaxed, he was ecstatic!

"I'm not quite sure yet—I'll need to hear it again a few times and try to place it in the context of his work. I wasn't sure where it was situated in—"

"I do not profess to be an expert in the dating of Mozart's compositions," he interrupted. "I leave such boring details to the bookworms with their magnifying glasses, minute studies of ink and paper production techniques, and specious speculations about evolution in style."

"In any case, the experts always disagree with each other and even revise their own opinions regularly," I remarked, noting his disdain for those who tried to establish such timelines.

"Better to let them argue it out amongst themselves," he added, shaking his abundant blond locks in horror at the thought.

I concurred with a nod, but didn't tell him I felt Mozart must have been having a really bad day when he wrote that concerto. The last piece of the evening had ended, moreover, after a dramatic pause, with a phrase of four unlikely notes.

Looking off into the crowd, the concertmaster gestured to a curvaceous woman, the one I'd christened "the belle of the ball" earlier, and she came over to join us. "Cremona, my jewel, this is Mr. Canal. Mr. Canal, my wife Cremona Civadin." I appreciated the fact that, pompous as he might be, he respected the dying art of making introductions. The stunning woman—was that dress she was wearing a Giorgio Armani?—extended her hand to me and I bent over it, sketching out a kiss.

She looked me straight in the eye. "A pleasure to meet you, Mr. Cannelloni," she said with a slight Italian accent in otherwise Provençal-inflected French.

"Canal," I said.

"Mr. Cannella," she conceded in a singsong voice. "I always feel so out of place at these sorts of functions," the revealingly clad redhead added, taking my arm in hers—so Mediterranean of her!—and leading me away from her husband, who had immediately turned his attention elsewhere. "You'd think I'd know all of the musicians in the orchestra by now, Mr. Cannelluci, but the truth is that the men all avoid me, thinking my husband is a jealous hothead, and the women all ignore me because they see me looking the way I look, wearing what they would love to wear, but can't, and consider me to be a mere housewife—as if a man like Orlando didn't require two full-time wives," she chuckled for some moments at her own joke and then went right on talking.

"You wouldn't believe how messy he is, Mr. Cantaloupi, with all those different projects of his spread out in four different offices. I am amazed he can ever find anything in them—well, in fact, I'm sure he couldn't if I didn't keep cleaning up after him." She accepted the glass of bubbly that I offered her from the drinks table, and, holding a matching red clutch in the other hand, oozed on, "They don't say a woman's work is never done for nothing, do they, Mr. Canali!" She swallowed half of its contents in a single gulp. "I mean, I know my place—I'm never to touch his precious papers or erase his whiteboards. And God forbid I should so much as look at his computers!"

I nodded, wondering how long I should listen before saying something myself, when she suddenly boomed, "No!" with the power of an Italian opera singer in full possession of her powers, a regular Cecilia Bartoli.

"Are you alright?" I asked.

She acted as though nothing had happened, and smiled at me broadly, her perfect red lipstick parting to show rows of pearly white teeth.

"Oh, I'm fine—it's just something my therapist told me to do."

My eyes widened.

"Don't look so startled, *caro mio*," she giggled, "it's standard operating procedure. Whenever I have the urge, I'm supposed to yell 'NO!'"—and she did so again, even more full-throatedly this time, turning untold heads our way—"to stop myself from smoking."

"How is it working so far?" I inquired, not knowing whether to laugh or to pity her for having been obliged to pay for such absurd advice. She gestured to me to hold her champagne glass for her.

Fumbling in her tiny handbag for a moment, she extracted a cigarette, which she immediately lit and took a long drag on. "Could be better ..." She took another drag and blew the smoke skyward. "I get so stressed out in certain social situations, Mr. Candeloro. These babies help calm me down."

"What can I do to make you more comfortable?" I asked, putting my hand on her forearm reassuringly.

"Nothing—it's the whole scene. It's not my scene. It's Orlando's and he takes to it like a fish to water."

"How did two such different fish ever cross paths—or should I say 'currents'?"

"I noticed him at a friend's party in Milan and just knew he had to be mine!"

"How did you know?" I asked, manifesting my trademark curiosity in all matters amorous.

"Oh, it's just one of those things we girls instantly know."

Funny, I reflected, how women can be unsure about so many things—their looks, whether they said or did the right thing—and still know that.

"Anyway, I had him from the moment I told him my name. You know, Cremona is where some of the best violins in the world have always been made," she exclaimed proudly. "How lucky for me that he was nuts about Cremonas!"

Her first name had rung a faint bell when her husband had initially said it, but for some reason I had associated it with Shakespeare, not violins. I must have been confusing it with Verona ...

"So violin is his true passion in life?"

"Of course not, *carissimo* Canalletti," she said lightly slapping me on the wrist. "I am! His millions of other projects are but passing fancies compared to me."

She said it so emphatically that I had to wonder who she was trying to convince—me or herself?

"So what's it like living with someone who has so many different projects?"

"I don't know, probably not that different from living with other people," she replied rather automatically.

"Does he collaborate with anyone?" I asked, she having aroused my curiosity about her one and only's host of hobbies.

"No, he works alone—unless you count me!" She laughed heartily at this, so heartily I worried the slender straps on her brightly colored yet delicate dress might snap, like they had on a friend of mine whose piano recital came to an abrupt end owing to a wardrobe malfunction. Was I wishing her haute couture evening gown would break open?

She glanced down toward the Cher. "I could fly out this window without changing clothes and he wouldn't even notice," she unexpectedly exclaimed. "He's always busy, always thinking about something, always preoccupied—well, except when he's on the phone with his *mamma*." She gave me a significant look and winked. "Gives her his undivided attention an hour a day—can you believe that?" she asked, rolling her eyes. "A grown man talking to his mother an hour a day every day, three hundred and sixty-five days a year!" Her long fingers dexterously adjusted those fragile shoulder straps, as her tennis bracelet caught the dancing light of the myriad candles in the gallery. The diamonds in it were exquisite. Tiffany? More likely Cartier since she lived in France. (Yes, I know something about diamonds and not just because I've made presents to my nieces. I've dated some wonderful women, and offered a few of them baubles, before messing things up with them in my own singular way. In search of what, you might ask? Good question ...)

"What do they go on about for so long? Do they share a great many interests?"

"I've tried to embrace his interests and learn to cook like he does, signor Cannoli, with all those gadgets of his, but I doubt his mother has. Still they seem to discuss a lot of details and strategies—isn't that weird?" She looked me in the eye, and it struck me that she was like Wack in her propensity to say just about anything that crossed her mind. "As if his mother knew jack about such matters!"

"What's she like?" I asked, ignoring the pejorative slang use of my given name, and focusing instead on the mother in question, people's mothers always being of capital importance.

"She's off her rocker, if you ask me—*pazza come una capra, folle dingue*!" she said, tapping her temple a couple of times, to indicate the woman was *toquée*, touched in the head, cracked. That's what the Italians do (some of the French too), whereas the Americans make a twirling motion with their index finger near the noggin to suggest the same basic idea. I'm not sure where either of those hand gestures comes from, but I'm sure they have a long, dignified history. (Psychologists who believe body language is the same in every culture would do well to invite Italians, French people, and Americans to the same dinner sometime!)

"That bad?" I said. "How do you deal with her?"

"She's in Paris and we live about as far away as you can get from Paris and still be in France." She opened her arms wide to illustrate how far apart they lived and spilled the remaining half of her bubbly on a passing female musician who, luckily, was dressed all in black.

I offered my handkerchief to the musician. Realizing who it was, I seized the occasion. "Françoise, my dear." I latched onto her arm. "You know Cremona Civadin, I'm sure." Françoise nodded civilly now.

123

Even when moving on at a cocktail party, I try to do so gracefully. Turning to Cremona, I said, "Will you forgive me Mrs. Civadin? There's a matter of some urgency that I need to ask Mademoiselle Foix about."

She eyed us a bit warily, and then nodded. "*Ciao, caro Canaletto,*" she said, turning away, but I grabbed her wrist.

"Have you ever heard your husband talk about the unusual concerto he played tonight?" I asked.

"Which one?"

"The one that ends with the notes C-A-G-E."

"Like *La Cage aux Folles*? No, *stupido!*" she replied, with a smile as wide as Julia Robert's.

I said I hoped to see her again sometime soon, and I meant it—she was kind of fun!

* * *

"So what did you want to discuss with me? What? What?" Françoise asked once we were out of earshot, still nervously drying her understated designer dress (Balmain this time?) with my pocket square.

"Nothing. Relax! You look great, by the way," I replied. "But you owed me a favor and now we are even."

The sudden tension drained from her face. She glanced back at Cremona and then smiled at me, as if her inner huntress had resumed its rightful place. "Good, now—"

Our brief moment was interrupted by the brusque arrival of a young man bringing Françoise a glass of bubbly and a plate of black and white petit fours. "I'm sure they're awful," he said of the original creations, "but what do you expect—they're always so cheap with us," he said, stuffing several hors d'oeuvres in his mouth at once. "Treat us like riffraff." It was the sound engineer and his jovial voice could have frozen a lava-filled piñata. Life, it seemed, gave him nothing but lemons and he preferred to let them rot rather than make limoncello.

"I don't know about you," I quipped, turning to Françoise, "but I'm having the time of my life here at Chenonceau. The food even matches the décor!"

"Oh, it's you, the one who needs everything this minute," Enrique—for that was his name—whined nasally, only now noticing me. He ignored my outstretched hand, like a cat that knows perfectly well you are standing two feet away from it but won't give you the time of day. "As if the job wasn't bad enough already, we have to put up with intruders!" He quickly darted his eyes and tilted his head to the right, apparently gesturing for me to go.

Taken aback, I still obliged him. "Please accept my sincerest apologies," I said to Françoise, "but I really must dash off." I bowed and exited stage left.

She grabbed my arm from behind and whispered in my ear, "Don't be angry. He's like that with everyone."

* * *

Thirty seconds after I entered my chamber at the Relais de Chambord, looking forward to a hot shower and even more to a nice cold glass of Monbazillac, in lieu of more solid sustenance, the phone rang. While driving back to Chambord I'd been lost in thought about the many whimsical and not so whimsical women (I preferred the former but still liked the latter) I'd recently met, and I imagined, for no good reason, that it would be one of them. Instead I was greeted by a raspy male voice telling me to come to Chenonceau as soon as possible.

"But I just left Chenonceau. I was there not an hour ago," I protested, while precariously pouring the amber elixir into a small glass with my right hand.

"We'll be waiting for you. The gate code is IBVHD."

"What kind of—" I tried to interject.

"Stands for 'I beat Versailles hands down.' Remember it or you'll never get in. Security here is extremely tight."

"What happened?" I asked, reluctantly returning the glass to cold storage in my room's minibar.

A click informed me that Scarron had already hung up, without even waiting for me to confirm. I bridled at his total lack of manners—it certainly did not make me feel any fonder of that biped. Durtal might be a by-the-book, unimaginative gendarme, but he was a human being. Scarron had yet to prove his humanity in my eyes. Then again, next to Mr. Life's-a-Bitch!

At any rate, it was of no importance in the larger scheme of things, I reminded myself. Where would we be, after all, without Neanderthals to make the rest of us look good? Or at least strive to be better …

My drive back to Chenonceau took me past the still daunting thousand-year-old keep standing alone day and night in Montrichard, the oft overlooked rustic medieval Fougères Castle, and elegant Cheverny Castle—the Tintin castle—all still lit up at this late hour. The region was truly second to none! But that could soon spell its demise, irremediably tarnishing its squeaky-clean reputation.

I was too preoccupied with other matters to dwell on those doughty dwellings. The Chenonceau gate code probably referred to some other statement than the zany mnemonic Scarron had mentioned. That couldn't be it, I thought, smiling a bit. I myself would have selected something terribly germane like the construction date of the original *moulin fortifié*, fortified watermill, built on the site. I don't know why, but 1230 appealed to me. Was it the time of Lavillaine's death, the witching hour at Villandry and Chenonceau? I found myself feeling uneasy, weary, and annoyed.

Durtal's so-called counterterrorism expert could well have been in attendance at the concert that evening, but I would not have known it since the prefect still hadn't shown me his picture. No honor—or was it honesty—among thieves? I don't know why that phrase occurred to me.

And then there was Henri Wack. I had thought he would be directing at Chenonceau that evening (the program had failed to mention he wouldn't be there, something the regulars apparently knew because "It wasn't his period," as one of them told me)—but he had actually vanished to the Alps to open another festival he directed. He was very far away and surrounded by hundreds of miles of snowy peaks, so he and his big bamboo shoot-like recorders couldn't have been involved. Why was I thinking about him anyway?

Anna Pislova, the bassoonist, was in the hospital, and Françoise Foix had been flirting with everyone under the sun, well, actually under the candlelight, all evening—at least until I left just before midnight. I wondered what time the incident had occurred?

Had I been so distracted by bewitching women that I had failed to see it coming?

* * *

"Back already? The slave drivers at this stupid castle putting you to work here now too?" Enrique, who was near the ticket booth, gibed cynically. I hoped he had not heard about the incident or my role there. "Life's a joke," he added for good measure, seemingly bewailing the human condition but with nonchalant contempt, and I wondered if he alone could pack sound equipment into a van with an attitude.

Failing to acknowledge someone is not my style. Rather than just shrug and walk on, I responded, "Then let us hope it will prove to be a sidesplittingly funny one." He looked more confused than amused, which was just fine with me.

A man materialized out of the darkness and accosted me. He claimed to be expecting me—I guess something really *had* happened there after the concert—and guided me not to the castle, but downstream from it along the same path from which I had admired the swans earlier that evening.

I espied some people a couple of hundred yards up ahead, despite the nearly total darkness. Thanking him, I continued on alone.

Approaching step by step, my eyes adjusting to the obscurity, I began to make out an odd sight: a completely drenched woman with a police-issue blanket wrapped all around her. It was a warm night and she appeared to be in fine shape, not shivering or blue like the drowning victims I had seen caught in rip tides or fished out of the water after their boats had capsized.

"Ah, Canal, finally!" Durtal, who was standing at the woman's side, said, shaking my hand. I detected some lassitude in his voice. Scarron didn't budge. Was there something about me that annoyed him? I mean, it was at least conceivable ...

"Hi, I'm Marie."

"Nice to meet you," I said in my best English, shaking the tall woman's outstretched hand, "although I'm sorry about the circumstances." The forty-something-year-old carrot-top nodded and I went on, "Would you be so good as to repeat what you have no doubt already told these two gentlemen?" I asked softly. I wasn't so sure about the word "gentlemen," but figured it was the proper term to use, given where she seemed to be from.

"I was standing in the gallery after the concert," she began coldly, but politely, shaking her hands up and down, "and as no one was around, I slipped the bolt and opened one of the windows. I know I probably wasn't supposed to," she added, "but I wanted some fresh air."

I was struck by her calm tone of voice. If she had lost her composure at some point, she had obviously regained it by now. Her apparently no-nonsense American attitude contrasted sharply with that of French women, who tend to be hopelessly hysterical.

I nodded sympathetically—having opened windows in many a monument that I'm sure I would have been reprimanded for if anyone had caught me—and she went on.

"I leaned pretty far out the window, I must admit, and was watching the water flow under the gallery, when suddenly, out of nowhere, someone grabbed my ankles, lifted my legs up, and pushed me out the window."

I could hardly believe it!

"Well," she went on more animatedly, perhaps still feeling a mite bit guilty, "you can imagine how shocked I was, finding myself in the air! Luckily the gallery is not high at all, and I'm pretty used to it."

I looked at the windows and then down to the river. Perhaps the only castle in the world to span a major waterway subject to floods that smashed everything in their path, its architects hadn't fooled around when designing the massive pointy piers on which the arches rested. Like those of the Roman-built *Pont du Gard* in the south of France, they had been built to last—they had withstood five hundred years of winter melt that had carried away every other bridge built across the mighty Cher.

The windows looked dangerously high to me and the water must not have been terribly deep this time of year.

"Used to it?" I reiterated.

"I competed as a diver for a while," she explained.

I looked at her again, speculating that there might be bulging muscles under that giant blanket.

"The water was actually quite refreshing, and the current not very strong, so it was okay. I was able to haul myself out at this little sandbar thingy over here," she said, pointing to a little protuberance of land into the Cher River just below where we were standing.

"Otherwise you might have had to swim all the way to America," Scarron teased. His legs were still tonight.

Le Coq arrived just then, slightly out of breath.

"You're the last to show up this time," Durtal observed, rather desperately, it seemed to me, looking at the radiant girl in a striking dress.

"Go on, please," Durtal said to the erstwhile diver.

"I was still scraping this slimy, rotting stuff off of me when this man appeared out of nowhere—I'm sorry," Canaples went on, addressing Scarron directly now, "I'm sure I'll get your name wrong, Inspector

Scarface?" I was impressed by her patience and fortitude. Here she was, repeating the whole story for my benefit despite being soaking wet and covered with slime.

"Sca-Ron," he tried to sound it out for her.

"Like he said."

"A stroke of luck, really! I happened to be dining tonight on duck at a small window table with my elderly father at *L'Orangerie* here at the castle," the lead investigator explained.

"Do you have any idea who pushed you?" I inquired.

"Not the slightest," she replied, shaking her head.

I was struck again by her placidity. Had her pulse returned to the athlete's usual forty heartbeats per minute? How could anyone be so calm after what had happened?

"I don't know anyone in the whole country."

"We aren't going to see the whole thing on YouTube tomorrow, are we?" Durtal asked gruffly. "Are you some sort of celebrity, or a wannabe? This better not be a publicity stunt, because if it is …," he barked.

"A publicity stunt? Now what would I do that for?"

"Well, then, what are you doing here?" I thought his tone out of place in addressing someone from France's cash cow, the U.S. of A.

"Can't someone attend a concert in this country without getting the third degree?" she now snapped.

"Of course, of course," he tried to rein himself in and smooth things over. "But what brings you to the Loire Valley, Mrs. Canaples?"

"The swimming conditions," she jokingly retaliated. "I'm doing a tell-all piece on the unsanitary water in all the principal rivers here." I smiled along with her, but I was the only one to do so. "And for your information, it's Miss, not Missus."

Things weren't going especially well and so, rather than wait until she demanded a lawyer before uttering another word, I gestured to the others and led her by the arm a few yards further from the castle, inviting her to sit with me on the low stone wall bordering the path.

I gave her some space and, as she tightened the heavy blanket around her frame, gazed out over the somber burbling waters of the Cher.

"I'm afraid I didn't catch your name," she eventually proffered with a Midwestern twang, her hands jiggling again, as if trying to shake away the tension of an upcoming two-and-a-half gainer in the pike position.

"Canal," I replied softly.

"You sound a bit like a New Yorker."

"You have a good ear, Miss Canaples. I spend most of the year in 'the city that never sleeps.'"

She digested this for a few moments and then averred, "I don't know anyone here."

"Really?"

"Why did you say that?"

"Why did *you* say that?"

"It's just that the people at the B&B where I'm staying might start worrying about me," she explained. "They recommended I come here tonight and they're the only ones who know where I am. I don't know anyone else in France."

Someone obviously knew her, given what had just happened.

"I'm just a swim coach," she added. "The head women's coach at the University of Michigan."

I studied her more carefully. "The top university swim team in the world!" I remarked.

She glanced at me again.

"Always looking for ways to improve the strokes of swimmers and cut a few hundredths of a second off their times so you can remain number one forever."

She seemed surprised to encounter someone familiar with her team in this remote French village.

"What would bring a major coach like you to the Loire Valley?" I inquired. "Recruiting some local athletes?"

"Look, it was a trip to France or nothing. I didn't have a choice," she said in an exasperated tone of voice, rubbing the bulky blanket against her dripping clothes. By this time, a swarm of mosquitoes was devouring us, but my queries seemed to bother her more than that.

"You're here on business, then?"

"No, I just came to have lunch at the *Ohbeargee due Bone whatever*."

"*L'Auberge du Bon Laboureur* is very well known in the area," I stated. "Rather expensive."

"The lunch is important. Water resistance can, you know, Mr. Canal, win or lose you a gold medal."

She might be a serious swim coach, but I couldn't connect the dots.

"In the Loire Valley?"

"No, in swimming pools."

"Oh, right," I said. "Some pools are much faster than others," I began, reciting from memory what my friend David, the swim coach, had told me, "because they are deeper at the shallow end, are fitted with overflow gutters designed to eliminate backwash, and have specially designed porous walls. People even use wave-eating lane dividers to attenuate surface turbulence. The infrastructure used to deal with it is getting more complex and expensive all the time." The image of an ultramodern pool appeared before my eyes, while sitting near Chenonceau's Renaissance gardens.

Da Vinci was certainly not the only one obsessed with fluid mechanics, even if he was among the first. Research in that field was helping catamaran builders craft faster boats and professional bicyclists refine their riding positions in state-of-the-art wind tunnels. Lance Armstrong had been fond of such research centers, even if he turned out to be at least as fond of cheating.

"Exactly," she exclaimed, and it was as if one could see gold medals, instead of the proverbial dollar signs, in her dilated pupils. "Our team sends more swimmers to the Olympics than any other university and brings home more medals than all the other teams combined—"

"Michael Phelps and company, yes I know."

"Our reputation goes much further back than Phelps. The total medal count of our team is higher than that of almost all of the countries that participate in the Olympics! A hundred ninety-six countries to be precise." She then stood up and stretched for a moment. Having shed the blanket, she looked very fit. "Can I go now?"

"Maybe you could tell me what you are going to talk about over lunch tomorrow?"

"New techniques."

"New techniques?"

"Innovative techniques, if you must know."

"Fascinating," I remarked, despite the vagueness of her responses.

"They're supposed to be based on breakthrough research going beyond Kolmogorov's theories of the turbulence of fluids. And on in-depth mathematization of the proportions of the human body," she added, glancing at my face in order to gauge, perhaps, whether or not I was following.

"Turbulence, you said?"

"In Ann Arbor we have physicists who specialize in the modeling and mathematization of fluid mechanics working with us all the

131

time," she went on. "This guy said he would give us radically new techniques—new hand positions, arm patterns, and full-body motions."

"So you came all the way to France for something he could have shown you on a computer screen?"

"He also said," she added, "he could sell us information about a new stroke. We would be the first to know about it."

"So it was business!" I concluded silently. I nodded, impressed. "Rather brazen of you to come all by yourself, don't you think?" I commented aloud.

"The contact seemed to want me and me alone," she said, tilting her head and sitting back down on the wall. "Maybe because I know a bit more about math and physics than the men's swim coach or the athletic director."

"Enough to know if what he is selling is worth the investment?"

"He wants millions."

So it was not only a business meeting, I recapped silently, but a big one. "Millions of honorary degrees? Gold medals?" I bantered.

"Dollars," she rejoined.

"I guess he realizes the U of M has deep pockets."

She shrugged her shoulders condescendingly. "We spend millions just heating the pools every winter. And plenty more on meditation classes, mindfulness training, and the latest in high-tech swimwear."

"I thought those special low-drag bathing suits had been outlawed by the IOC," I remarked, cocking an eyebrow.

"They were," she responded, "but then they were allowed again, then disallowed, and now we are allowed only the small ones, not full-body suits." She massaged her thigh for a few seconds. "The fabric mimics shark skin. Sharks predate the dinosaurs, you know. Among the oldest creatures on earth," she added. "And they've learned to reduce their turbulence in the water over millions of years. Their skin, I mean the new fabric, even firms and strengthens a swimmer's muscles."

She sure knew her stuff. "So the women get more help from it than the men, since their bathing suits cover more acreage?" I joked.

She looked at the castle suddenly. "I never thought of it that way."

* * *

"The American was probably high on PCP or NBOMe, like they all are," Scarron said. "Thought she could fly!"

"She seemed to me to be in full possession of her faculties," I riposted as we walked back toward the castle, a bit behind the others.

"Probably pushed by some practical joker," he suggested, changing tack completely, "or one of those kids who can't resist doing what they see all the time in cartoons."

Pointing to the castle's unique series of arches spanning the river, I said, "Just one window to the right or left, and she would most likely have hit the edge of one of those mammoth piers protruding beyond the width of the gallery."

CHAPTER NINE

The town of Chenonceau

All communication is miscommunication.*

—A certain psychoanalyst

The sun was shining the next morning and I decided to take advantage of the Relais' magnificent patio. I hoped to be alone with Chambord as my sole breakfast companion, and my wish came true. My gaze was drawn anew to its formal French gardens, which a rich American—as fanatical about the castle as I was, no doubt—had just recently donated millions of dollars to recreate exactly as they had been during the reign of the Sun King, complete with manicured lawns, boxwood bushes, lemon trees by the hundreds, flowerbeds, and four of the most enormous *fleurs-de-lys* you've ever seen. (They are, of course, the main symbol of French royalty. To see them properly, you really have to be in a hot-air balloon—hovering over Santa Fe!) Louis XIV was never one to scrimp when it came to adorning his royal residences—just consider what he did at Versailles, which actually did start out life as a rather rustic hunting lodge built by his royal dad.

Once again, I hadn't been back in my room five seconds when the magic was spoiled by the ringing of the phone.

The prefect hadn't been able to reach the bewildering counterterrorism expert in Paris, and the only person who had his schedule and cell number was away on vacation for three weeks. Why call to tell me that?

Annoyed, and thinking that there must surely be other ways to reach him or at least run a background check on him, I asked a question of my own, "What time did you receive the call last night?"

"Very late."

"Before or after midnight?

"After midnight."

So July 7th—another odd number, but also another prime, I reflected.

Durtal promised again to get me a picture of the expert, Vellimachia, but there was an anxious edge in his powerful voice. "Your idea about lunch at the *Auberge du Bon Laboureur* is a great one, Canal. The defenestrator may have seen Scarron, but he'll never suspect me or Le Coq. Everyone will think we're on a date, not a couple of cops," he remarked. "But what if the stuck-up doll can't stand me?"

Maybe *that* was why he had called.

* * *

I slowly replaced the receiver and asked myself how the straight-up prefect (was he?) could know my every move. No one could be tracking my comings and goings—except for the ungainly longhaired handyman who always seemed to be tinkering in my historic hallway—or listening to my conversations by hacking my cell phone since I didn't have one. I checked my hotel phone and room for bugs (not bedbugs, perish the thought, but those little GSM or RF listening devices) and, much to my chagrin, found one behind the mini-fridge. That led me to change into some old jeans and a T-shirt—bet you didn't think I had any— borrow a flashlight from hotel maintenance, and examine the bottom of the Alfa Romeo I had been renting since I left Paris. It took a while, but I eventually located a tiny rectangular box magnetically attached to the chassis. It wasn't the kind of tracking device some rental car companies use so they can retrieve vehicles that get stolen—it was far smaller and almost undetectable, so well did it blend in with the color of the automobile's underbody.

I have to admit I was somewhat miffed by the techniques being employed. Who did they take me for? They were a little too obvious.

I had to wonder if, as sometimes happens, transparent things were being done to hide the fact that less transparent surveillance was also occurring. Some spies leave blatant traces of surveillance—bugs, cameras, tracking devices, etc.—to discourage people from looking further, deliberately make it look like they tapped into the wrong wires or placed obvious listening devices in the wrong person's office to suggest incompetence, or leave some messiness at a crime scene or break-in to make it look like it was someone else, whether some other secret service or a specific individual. But when you investigate more deeply, you find that things have actually been done properly, botched facsimiles having been left behind as a smoke screen. Sometimes facsimiles are even deviously covered over in a clumsy manner, leaving a trace of another trace, both of which are designed as lures or decoys.

So, too, people—and not always just conmen—at times pretend to be naïve in order to all the more thoroughly dupe us with a complex strategy. Maybe I was going too far, imagining an adversary worthy of my own convoluted metathinking. But such things are common enough in the relational realm. I recalled someone I had formerly worked with whose strategy with women was so complicated that—once we had finally peeled back the layers of his conscious bullshit about what he was up to, and taken a long peek under the hood—it turned out to involve four people in all: himself, an older man, and two women, one under the legal age of consent and the other substantially older. The orchestration of his scenario invariably took months to play out. Another guy I knew would hit on one woman in order to get her best friend interested in him, and the best friend had to already be seeing someone else. Buyer (of the BS) beware: you never know what sort of murky scenario you might be drawn into!

I changed rentals and, *la mort dans l'âme* (with a heavy heart), left my beloved Relais. As I checked into an off-the-beaten-track B&B, a funny remark by Paul Erdös, a mathematician I had read about, popped into my mind: "Another roof, another proof."

Durtal wasn't going to be happy, but I'd just fend him off with the ol' saw, "Don't call us, we'll call you."

* * *

If you thought I was going to hand the job at the *Auberge* over to two coppers, you haven't yet cottoned on to my modus operandi.

As Edgar Allan Poe knew ages ago, the police are often unable to see what is in plain sight (like da Vinci's stash of dough, which he placed in little blue and white packages and left out in the open). Not that it did any good to tell them that!

I, too, lunched—secretly and not badly, I might add—at the same restaurant. But first, I stopped off at the *Orangerie*, which is located right on Chenonceau Castle's premises. A faint murmur could be heard down the hall, but there was no one around to man the welcome desk, so I peeked at the neatly tucked away reservation book. I saw only a profusion of foreign-sounding names and some quintessentially French ones like Durand, Dupont, and Dufour.

"Oh, your friend Monsieur Scarron—we know him and his lady friends well," replied the woman I finally found who worked there. "He was here with a girl I had never seen before. Came in for lunch, after two, if memory serves, and begged us to seat them despite the late hour."

In Paris such information would cost you at least a C-note, but out in the country things are simpler and people not so guarded. (On the flip side, everyone knows everyone else's business and talks about it openly, the anonymity of the big city being completely unheard of here. Which I personally appreciate, feeling there is far too much anomie—as Durkheim famously called it—in our contemporary world, but it can occasionally make my own secrets harder to keep!)

I thanked her (would she later wonder why I'd asked?), wandered out through the well-tended gardens behind the restaurant, and leisurely made my way toward the *Auberge* through the lovely little village of Chenonceau, the site of the fateful shoot-out between Diane de Poitiers and Catherine de' Medici that forced Diane to pack her bags. Wasn't dealing with women already difficult enough, without them fighting amongst themselves? Well, maybe that was part and parcel of life with women. With men, too, for that matter …

Had Scarron, I reflected, been on a hot date? With a secret lover? Or an inflammably jealous one? Preoccupied by my peripatetic meditations on illicit love, I was barely aware of the hotels and restaurants around me overflowing with flowers. Suddenly I had to jump onto someone's stoop. I had only a second to glance and utter a few choice imprecations in English at the driver as he skid in his sports car around the corner I was near, expertly breaking and gunning the engine almost simultaneously. Not your average French driver, or even your typically impatient and impetuous Parisian or Marsaillais.

* * *

Now I have to admit that I am no Fantômas, a true French master of disguise of the silver screen, but I can fool most of the people most of the time and enjoy doing so. The woman at the *Orangerie* hadn't batted an eye at my unkempt hair—a wig, obviously, as it's not a good look for me, in my humble opinion—and scraggly beard.

Squinting at the menu through ridiculous black-rimmed sunglasses, I ordered what struck me as the finest bottle on their extensive list. The expression on the sommelier's face was priceless—a nice little amuse-bouche—when I chose it over an exorbitantly priced Premier Grand Cru Classé Bordeaux. I affected a thick-as-pea-soup American accent and made it appear as though I had alighted on that particular domain and vintage somewhat randomly, for the French are generally convinced Americans know nothing more about wine than the names of a few world-famous varietals like chardonnay and cabernet sauvignon, whereas I've met many who are far more knowledgeable than your average Frenchman. Frogs tend to be quite indiscriminate in their drinking habits, as long as a showy castle and the word *Bordeaux* are prominently splashed across the label—they unfortunately consider that to be a sure sign of quality.

I had reserved a table under the simple name Humbert H. Headshrinkski (unlike Scarron, I had at least had the courtesy to reserve—so what if I use a different alias every time?) at the far end of the courtyard. Having been to the *Auberge* before, as you can imagine, I knew the layout, but had no idea where the punter would be sitting. I opened anew the book on François I's devastatingly beautiful mistresses that I had picked up at the boutique at Azay-le-Rideau Castle, hiding the cover from view whenever the wait staff came near, the volume being in French, after all. Such reading was usually catnip to me, but for once I couldn't focus on women, famous or otherwise. I kept thinking about the comment once made by the inimitable Richard Feynman: that turbulence was the most important unsolved problem in classical physics. It still brought down trees, bridges, and dams, not to mention jumbo jets.

139

Just like women often did to men. I guess I *was* thinking about women after all. I knew scores of men whose lives had been turned upside-down by them! Not that women had a monopoly on making mayhem ...

A few red drops materialized just then on the page before me. Last night's bubbly might have turned out to be my last, God forbid, but instead I'd escaped the reckless road hog with just a couple of scratches.

"As a small child, François I," I read, "shared a bed with Mademoiselle de Polignac, his father's former mistress. When the Marechal of Gié, his governor, tried to pry him from the influence of women at age seven and make a man of him—seven being thought to be the age of reason—he promptly climbed in bed with his mother, Louise of Savoy. In the end, Gié had to have someone break down the door to the latter's bedchamber and forcibly remove François from her bed, telling him he was too old for that sort of thing."

"In his early twenties," I read on, "François could barely control himself in the presence of Mary of York,* the beautiful young wife of his aged father-in-law, King Louis XII, and almost ruined his chances of acceding to the throne of France. He would have spoiled them had he gotten her pregnant, for it would have given his soon-to-be-dead royal relative a legal heir to the kingdom—and Louis XII wouldn't have wanted to know or believe the heir wasn't really his. François's mother had to harangue him to keep his hands off Mary and, realizing that was insufficient for one as 'hot to trot' as he, organized an around-the-clock guard to keep him away."

Flipping to another section, I learned that "Anne de Pisseleu outshone all the beauties of her time, but was never really in love with François I." Interesting ..., I reflected. "She was even in bed with another man once when he knocked at her chamber door. The man promptly hid in the unlit fireplace and the king, affecting a need to relieve himself, urinated on the man's legs and feet. The importunate interloper never returned."**

Glancing up from my book, I saw the coach being seated by the maître d' at a table that had undoubtedly been reserved sight unseen, weeks in advance, by the athletic director's secretary in an office in Michigan. The American was dressed in full jock regalia: brand-name sweats that befitted her role. She certainly wasn't trying to hide her supposed mission in life.

Durtal and Le Coq were soon directed to a table almost opposite me, a deplorable location for surveillance. The female gendarme was well put together, but Lord knows the male portion of the brains and brawn equation could have made more of a sartorial effort, what with his conspicuously untucked shirt and overly tight pants. Despite my Einstein-like wig and ungainly beard, I was sporting my regimental jacket and tie. After all, if we don't maintain standards, who will? It's ridiculous when the wait staff is better dressed than the customers. Pretty soon even Michelin-starred restaurants will be serving guests in shorts, flip-flops, and baseball caps, I reflected, as I glanced at the portrait of the sumptuously attired François I on the cover of my book. Why his horse had more panache than the prefect!

The other tables began to fill up with people of all nationalities, businessmen, families, and—who knows?—maybe even undercover lovers. I had already been served two glasses of Château de Villeneuve's fine chenin blanc and enjoyed a complimentary savory *crème brulée* with *foie gras* served in a miniature soufflé dish—life was tough—when the supposed super genius arrived. I only saw him from behind as he stood and then seated himself. He seemed stiff, yet unable to sit up straight— "from poring over his calculations too much?" I wondered.

Right from the beginning, it was not the talkative Midwesterner who had the floor. But I could hear nothing amidst the French, Russian, and English conversations around me. The man imperiously waved the waiter away with a dismissive gesture. He was there to talk turkey, not eat it.

In vain, I listened for the words "fluid mechanics" and "human kinetics"—how to get beings like us to move like dolphins, sharks, endangered bluefin tuna, or swordfish, as if we, too, were meant to live in the water. Was he speaking only of cold cash?

His unusual ponytail barely pivoted, so with no regret, I left untouched the "deconstructed lemon tart" dessert (the word "deconstructed" to describe something edible is always a red flag, in my view) and directed my steps into the restaurant, as if I needed to wash my hands. Near the fireplace, I did an about-face and peered through the glass door. The man was looking down at his plate, not at Canaples, but his lips were moving. Waiters and busboys kept flowing in and out, forcing me away from the door, but the fair-haired man finally looked up for a moment and I saw his face.

* * *

Da Vinci would, I thought, have found sufficient inspiration in the man's mug to paint the fallen disciple in *The Last Supper*. One look at that face and the artist would not have had to model Judas on the prior who had been asked to remind him that he needed to finish the mural painting. Did Leonardo find him hideous solely because he asked the Florentine to hop to it?

I don't know who or what I had been expecting.

The commissioner's loose curls were dancing back and forth as she listened to and laughed at Durtal's undoubtedly scintillating repartee. (At least he wasn't trying to ingratiate himself to Le Coq by laughing at hers.) "Those two were useless, just as I suspected," I reflected, a mite smugly, I confess, as I witnessed the contact's discreet exit. I wouldn't have put much stock in the report they'd have given me anyway, all communication being miscommunication, a pitiful game of telephone, all information misinformation, if not disinformation, all recognition misrecognition. I'm sure I wrote something like that many moons ago … And it's as true today as ever.

I placed some bills on my table and parted, determined to tail the ponytail. I naturally had no idea where any of this would lead, but, as Einstein once put it, "If we knew where we were going it wouldn't be called 'research'"—or in my case, it wouldn't be called an "investigation."

Exiting the *Auberge*, I was preoccupied. Something was ringing a faint bell.

* * *

"That's when I told the mayor to take a hike and let *me* talk to the Press." Le Coq was hanging onto Durtal's every word as women are wont to do, at least when they first meet a man. Their untouched desserts—which appeared to be the "deconstructed" *clafoutis* with Reine Claude plums and the "revisited" *tarte Tatin* I'd seen on the menu, a magnificent hot apple upside-down cake when made in the traditional Loir-et-Cher manner—were undoubtedly cold by the time I'd done all the tailing I could, and had returned to the restaurant accoutered as the nosey parker they knew.

"No Brad Pitt, that date of yours," the prefect addressed the American, after we joined the badges. Le Coq covered her mouth with her white linen napkin to hide what appeared to be a cruel grimace.

Canaples didn't seem to appreciate his typically French sardonic sense of humor. "Pretty intense guy," she said in a dignified manner.

I signaled the waiter and ordered a sweet wine. Marie looked at me like I was insane.

"In what way?" I asked kindly.

"Difficult to follow," she said. "Had a very thick accent, for one."

"French?"

"More Slavic than that, I'd say. There are a few foreign swimmers on my team, but I'm no expert on accents. I don't speak anything other than English, and some say even my English is ...," she gestured vaguely, taking a sip of the Sauterne, something she'd never do in Ann Arbor but would undoubtedly tell all her friends about.

"Athletic?" I ventured politely.

She seemed happy to accept the characterization and tasted the wine appreciatively again, appearing to conclude it was legit to do so. France has that sort of effect on people! It might soon be the perfect time to ask her more delicate questions.

"You said he was intense, Ms. Canaples?" the commissioner asked.

The Midwesterner flushed and took another gulp. "He threw around a lot of terms and equations I'd never heard of—singular value decomposition and navy strokes, I think—and spoke very excitedly, as though he had squared the circle or something!"

I didn't bother to tell her that it had been proven in the nineteenth century that the old dream of squaring the circle with just a compass and a ruler was a pipe dream, even if many, da Vinci included, believed they had done it at one time or another.*

"The Clay Mathematics Institute in Oxford," I began, "recently designated the Navier-Stokes—not navy strokes, but your interlocuter was apparently not a native English speaker—existence and smoothness problems as among the seven most important unsolved problems in mathematics today. They are included in their Millennium Prize Problems, and a hefty award goes to whoever can prove that solutions to the equations always exist in three dimensions and, if so, whether or not they are smooth."

No one said a word.

"Your mystery man may have obtained the proof somehow and, not content with the forthcoming million dollars, immediately put it to marketable use," I went on.

143

Not a word passed their lips, so I moved on: "What about the new stroke he supposedly invented?"

I looked at the coach and thought I saw top podiums lining up in her eyes like lemons in a one-armed bandit. "Called it the 'inverted fly.'"

"So have you decided to accept his offer?" I asked.

"Hard to know exactly what it looks like or whether it could truly become an Olympic event, but a lot of surprising things do—think of curling!"

"So does he want the millions wired to some offshore account somewhere?" Durtal asked.

"No, he wants payment in the form of a *Cray supercomputer*."

* * *

As everyone rose to leave, I urgently placed my hand on Le Coq's arm and asked her to stay behind for a few minutes.

"So what did you think?" I asked as the two of us regained our seats.

"Um, if you mean the food, I hardly noticed," she replied. "And I didn't even see when Canaples' contact left … ," she added sheepishly.

"That's okay, it was part of my plan."

"Ah … What?"

"There's hope for us all," I said (no matter how serious or lovelorn, I added to myself). "I knew Durtal would have your full attention."

The usually serious girl said nothing, so I drew an object from my leather satchel, one I hope never to be seen with again in public—obviously not the book on François I's mistresses. "I found this laptop in the hotel room of the girl I discovered on the stairs at Chambord. I need your tech team at headquarters to hack into it. And I want answers, not monosyllables."

She came crashing back down to earth. "You mean you know … ?"

"Yes, I know who she is. Her picture is in half the concert brochures in the Loire Valley. Goes by the stage name of Anna Pislova. Which is not the name she gave Durtal and Scarron at the hospital."

"Why didn't you give the laptop to Durtal and have his team examine it?"

"I haven't yet told him who the girl is."

"You haven't? Are you playing games with us?"

"Are you playing games with *me*?" I showed her the tracking device. "I found it on the chassis of my previous rental car." She looked at it blankly. "My hotel room was bugged, too."

144

I ignored her furrowed brow, finished my Sauterne, and then began, "Try to stay open-minded, even if this all sounds a bit improbable or completely crazy: A professor of oenology is attacked at Amboise Castle, which is right smack in the middle of a wine producing region, the vineyards starting just a few hundred yards from the town center."

"You really are obsessed with wine, aren't you?"

I shushed her and went on, "Chambord is the most whimsical, the most poetic, one might even say the most musical castle ever built, and who should get pushed down the stairs there but a musician? Villandry's gardens are among the most mathematically laid out gardens in France—most of the flower beds there follow the same pattern of rotational symmetry as the keep at Chambord Castle was originally supposed to, and our victim at Villandry is a math whiz. Chenonceau is located right on the water—it literally has its toes in the Cher River—and the person attacked there is a swim coach."

"So you're saying that the victim," she articulated slowly, "always has some connection with the location."

"Let me remind you that our victims are no slouches. All of them are prominent figures in their fields. Well, I'm not so sure about Pislova—I haven't had a chance yet to look into her background or musical accomplishments."

"We certainly aren't dealing with a representative cross-section of Loire Valley tourists," she conceded.

"Now, there are undoubtedly other crimes being committed in these parts every day, and maybe we shouldn't be focusing solely on renowned castles." I scratched my head for a moment. "You and your colleagues can help us out with that, checking if strange incidents have been occurring elsewhere as well. But the choice of venues thus far seems to be anything but random. Just as the dates of the incidents all seem to be prime numbers."

"Prime numbers!"

"I asked you to try to stay open-minded. Do we now know Lavillaine's probable time of death?"

"The best guess is 12:15 a.m.," she replied.

"So July 5th, as we suspected."

"We? As *you* suspected. Are you interested in places or numbers?"

"Now, in thinking about who could be next, we must try to discern what is specific to each of the castles in the area—"

"There are scores of them," she scoffed.

145

"We may have to expect further incidents on either the eleventh or the thirteenth, if not both."

"You think you know the exact dates of upcoming crimes? How could you?"

"Villandry's victim may have been a clue of some kind, selected by the assailant to tip us off."

"Tip us off?"

"Yes."

"Or lead us astray," she objected.

A busboy noiselessly refilled our water glasses and strode off.

I smiled, being all prime numbered out and ready to forget about them myself. "You're beginning to think like Dupin."

"Huh? Arsène?"

"No," I reassured her, "not Lupin, the gentleman burglar. *Dupin*, the master crime solver in Poe's mysteries."

"Ah!" She reddened slightly.

"Flattery is not in my nature. I call them as I see them."

She smiled and flushed more deeply.

Embarrassment is generally far more enjoyable than most people— Le Coq undoubtedly included—are willing to admit. "I assume it's too soon to have a forensic medical report on the mathematician's unusual crash position?" I asked, moving on. I had thought it an impossible position in which to land from the outset, and now I had a further reason for thinking so.

"Maybe today, maybe not 'til tomorrow."

"What if I told you Lavillaine is alive?"

"What, are you crazy?"

"A man in a convertible almost ran me over a few blocks from here."

"It can't be him!" she blared.

The few people still lingering on the patio turned our way. "Can't it?" I asked quietly, facing Le Coq anew. "How close a look did you take at the body you found at Villandry?"

"Close enough! The pool of blood around him spoke for itself."

"Did you see the coroner's report?" The gory image failed to move me this time.

"No," she admitted, and then whispered, "I didn't think to ask for it."

"You know as well as I do that plenty of drugs can slow your pulse and breathing to the point that they're virtually imperceptible. The man may have poured animal blood on his head for good measure." I myself

146

had at first wondered if I was dreaming when I saw him at the wheel of the car. But it seemed incontrovertible: the shoulder-length, light-colored hair, the brightly colored thing around his neck, the odd pin on his jacket …

"Lots of people have staged their own deaths before," I went on, "usually for highly specific reasons." I glanced up at the foliage above our heads and then looked her right in the eye. "Some for greater notoriety. Others to expose people who have been trying to kill them, like that Russian agent Babchenko who faked his own assassination and gave a press conference the next day. Still others do it to discover who their real friends are by secretly attending their own funerals and observing people's reactions."

The commissioner listened, her face pale.

"Or to dodge taxes or alimony. A staged death would explain the unusual crash position," I added, stroking my chin. "It probably sounds farfetched, but I keep trying to find a *mathesis universalis*, something that ties all of these incidents together and explains them, instead of having to come up with a *mathesis singularis*, a different explanation for each incident."

Le Coq's spoon, which she was mechanically dipping into the left-over limoncello sorbet the swim coach had ordered, slipped out of her hand and clattered on the ground. "Do you always talk like that?" she finally asked, looking up.

"Like what?" I replied with a question, preoccupied with the thought that nobody I'd encountered thus far seemed to fit the profile of a killer—may Agatha Christie be forgiven, but not just anyone can be a killer, except perhaps under extreme conditions like war (you and I are not killers, I hope) or bizarre experiments à la Milgram. Yet someone had nevertheless pushed Canaples out the window. "What kind of automobile did Lavillaine drive?" I added.

"I'm afraid I don't know."

"Well, it's our job to know such things!"

"I do know *something* you don't know," she said nervously. "Rumors are rife that Lavillaine had just been fired by his university. Seems his research was funded by a foreign military power. A plane ticket to Shanghai was even found in his glove compartment."

"Maybe Lavillaine's still planning on catching that plane to Shanghai," I remarked incisively, "with part of a Cray supercomputer in tow, to work from China with love. What was the date on his ticket?"

"I, um, I'll have to check that for you," she said abashedly.

"Yes, that too."

After a moment, I put my hand on her forearm. "Sorry about that," I apologized. "I guess I'm mad at myself for not having figured things out yet." I was undoubtedly being captious—how could we have anticipated such crazy events?

She blushed slightly—on my behalf?

I gave her the make, model, and license plate of the odd crossover vehicle Canaples' contact had just sped off in and asked her to look up the owner. "Speaking of planes," I resumed, "have you noticed anything unusual about our swim coach?"

Le Coq seemed to rack her brain. "No," she finally drawled.

"She shows no signs whatsoever of fatigue," I said flatly. "There is a six-hour time difference between Chenonceau and Ann Arbor, and yet she doesn't show the slightest trace of jet lag."

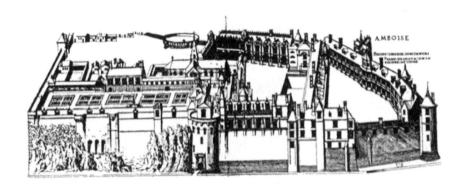

CHAPTER TEN

Amboise Castle

He who thinks little, errs much.

—Leonardo da Vinci

He who thinks much, may err still more.

—Anonymous

Were these crimes, or just practical jokes in bad taste? Given how a dead man seemed to have if not nine lives like the fabled cat, at least two, I wondered if I shouldn't just return to my wine tastings. We nevertheless decided that I would go back to square one, because while Anna Pislova may have simply tripped on the stairs at Chambord (even if the unlocked door in room 389 of the northeast tower was redolent of foul play), Marie Canaples may have deliberately jumped out the window at Chenonceau, and Lavillaine may have faked his own death, someone *had* actually died at Amboise Castle. That was our terra firma, our bedrock.

The head commissioner placed a call for me to the director of that oh-so-chic château where they were hosting an elaborate Leonardo da Vinci exhibit, jointly with the Louvre in Paris. He made no promises, but graciously offered to have the staff buzz him when I arrived—if no one was available, he'd cancel a meeting and accompany me himself. I appreciated the fact that the august owners of Amboise had not allowed their castle to be run by an ill-bred lackey.

I felt like indulging myself and forgetting about these extravagant incidents for a few minutes, so I took a slightly roundabout route in order to glimpse a number of more humble abodes for a change, jewels like Civray-de-Touraine, or Pray where a nice bottle is always to be had. The contrast is quite striking, these family castles having been built on a rather more human scale, and when I imagine myself living in them, the choice of rooms in which to locate my study, bedroom, and piano is more limited, but at least within pecuniary reach.

I drove, too, past altogether different sites where sprawling castles had been dismantled stone by stone and sold off by the *Bande Noire* (unscrupulous French-revolution-era speculators and liquidators of confiscated and indebted estates)—like the Château de Chanteloup, where the only thing left was the funny towering eighteenth-century Pagode—and reflected that the Loire Valley was truly the Valley of the Kings. France's sovereigns had built myriad castles there themselves, and their courtiers and ministers had built untold more nearby in order to be close to their lieges. Not just out of friendship or fealty, naturally— often their motives were more mercenary than munificent.

Even after the kings had gravitated north toward Paris, the Garden of France continued to attract everyone with its charms. Hadn't Mick Jagger himself bought a small castle a mere stone's throw from Amboise? ("Does he actually speak any French?" I found myself wondering, having heard he even had a recording studio in his digs. "Has he ever written songs in French? Should I mention him in my magazine piece?") Castlemania had reached such a climax near the equally royal town of Chinon that one cannot drive half a minute without spotting another glittering castle or manor house.

I was counting in two-minute intervals the time it took me to drive between stately homes today, whereas Cray supercomputers calculated in nanoseconds. Someone with exceptionally developed math and science skills wanted one, someone with ambitious projects, giving rise to a need for speed. Who would want a computer that could perform so many trillions of operations per second?

The owner of Villandry might have the brain power to put such a behemoth to use and he certainly had all the room in the world to house it in his palace. A brand-spanking-new Cray with performance in the petaflops would be worth upward of ten million smackers, but Castillo would probably know that various groups around the world also owned older models—ones that could run at forty teraflops, performing "only" forty trillion operations per second—and might be willing to spare one of their antiquated adding machines.

If it was Castillo, was he hoping to discover, just for fun, new prime numbers beyond the last one discovered in 2018 (which is 23,249,425 digits long)? Maybe he was drawn to them, believing them, like some, to be "the most arbitrary and ornery objects studied by mathematicians, growing like weeds among the natural numbers,"* or thinking them, like others, transcendental.

I slammed on the brakes and dove into the only café in the tiny village I was traversing. I asked to use the phone and dialed Le Coq's cell number.

"I need you to contact border control to find out when Hervé Castillo last went to America."

"The owner of Villandry?"

"Yes, none other than him. And check the date of the last meeting of the board of directors at Longwood Gardens in Pennsylvania," I went on.

"Pennsylvania?"

"I want to know where he went during his last trip to the U.S.—New York or Massachusetts may have been the real reasons for his trip."

"Don't you mean Michigan?" I guess she'd been contemplating a possible connection between Castillo and Canaples.

I instinctively glanced around the café to see if anyone could hear me as I talked a bit excitedly, "There are dozens of secret math and science societies in Boston and the Big Apple, including geniuses of all ilks: top professors, Nobel prize winners, crackpots, hackers ..."

"You mean, like think tanks?"

"A bit, but more like private old boys' clubs. The members often have common interests, which may or may not be humanitarian." I took a deep breath. "They're highly selective, politically connected, and defend their associates' activities, no matter how—how shall I say?—tawdry or nefarious."

"So?"

"So, while Cray and IBM have been waging a battle of the Titans for decades to see who could build the fastest supercomputer, neither of them seems to care what the teraflop terrors will be used for—good

153

or evil, a better mousetrap or gain of function for biological warfare. They're perfect illustrations, my dear, of Rabelais's famous quip about 'science without conscience' leading to 'the demise of the soul.'"

Radio silence.

"Castillo may be a member of one of those exclusive clubs and could have been asked to trade some of their innovations to get ahold of such a weapon. Lavillaine may be a member of the same club—they're both confirmed jetsetters. Maybe there was bad blood between them …"

"Weird," Le Coq exclaimed. "But why would Castillo put his prize possession in jeopardy? Villandry's reputation could be tarnished for years, for no one would believe that a murder committed in his gardens—assuming there had been one—wasn't somehow connected to him," the unimaginative commissioner continued. "If implicated, he would lose face in France and the States."

* * *

Passing a huge roadside ad for the Clos Lucé along the country lane I was following, my thoughts veered to the nocturnal paint job that presumably owed nothing to supercomputers.

Someone could have silently scaled the wall or dropped in by hot air balloon, used some kind of skeleton key, and locked the door on the way out. Or done it by remote control from Nevada or India with some sort of brush-carrying drone or robot apparition. Even the latter would have had to enter and exit the castle somehow. Unless it was disguised as one of da Vinci's inventions in the basement. Or hidden inside one of the larger ones. Maybe it had been installed months earlier, had been radio activated once the painting had arrived from the Uffizi, and was still there. I should ask Thoury to let me go through the place with a fine-tooth comb.

I reflected that there was something curiously positive in all this: not understanding what was happening allowed for hope, for it proved it was having an effect on me. In any case, like everyone else, I never understand anything other than what I already have in my head. It's only confusion that can force me to come up with something new.* Hard to accept sometimes, but true …

Over the years I had worked with myriad detectives who vaunted their so-called intuition, thinking it crucial to solving mysteries. I have never lent much credence to the idea of intuition, preferring to trust in the awe-inspiring human ability to generate multiple hypotheses

154

and the cooperation of my unconscious that assembles incongruous things and silently works on them while I sleep—yes, sleep. There is an impressive number of mathematicians and scientists—people who tend to laugh disdainfully at any mention of the unconscious—who nevertheless admit that they struggle for days, weeks, or even months with a problem, only to wake up one morning with the solution. Some find it in a dream: a snake biting its own tail (or was it six snakes biting each other's tails? I've heard both versions!) in a dream allowed August Kekulé to discover the hexagonal structure of carbohydrates. Others find the solution in an odd word or phrase they find floating in their minds upon waking, having no clue where it came from. I might have to hope for something similar ...

* * *

Before me now stood the very first Renaissance castle to be built in France, located atop a hill dominating the Loire for miles. I stopped my car, after taking yet another detour in order to arrive in Amboise from the north, to admire the view of the town from the right bank. The royal river itself is often as wide as the Mississippi, silver as the sky in winter, and deep as a bathtub (bet you weren't expecting that, but it's true in the summer when rain is in short supply).

The very first King of France (Clovis) and the King of the Visigoths (Alaric II) feasted together and promised each other eternal friendship and perpetual peace in the year of our Lord 502 on the island in the middle of the river in Amboise, L'Île d'Or. It lasted less than five revolutions of the Earth around the Sun. (I guess it was more like a pinky swear.) For millennia, the Loire served as a virtually impassible barrier between north and south, which was no doubt why the two hirsute, bloodthirsty monarchs—one Frankish, the other Gothic—met in the middle of it. Even now, those who have the good fortune to live south of the Loire rarely consort with those who live north of it. (Poor Mick Jagger.)

I crossed the impassible barrier of yore and arrived at the exact spot to which the Vikings twice rowed their ninth-century ships all the way from the Atlantic Ocean. Why? To pillage, sack, and burn towns like Amboise and Blois to the ground, naturally!

The Vikings' ability to navigate virtually any waterway under the sun made me wonder whether King Charles VIII's fantastical plan would have actually made the soaring citadel at Amboise invincible.

He wanted to dig a moat so deep around the castle's promontory that a portion of the Loire's waters could be drawn into it, totally isolating it from the town. François I and da Vinci were not the first to have entertained mindboggling dreams at Romorantin and Chambord of diverting powerful rivers from their wide and native beds, Canal-izing them, as it were.

Next I made a sharp right on the left bank, along which Joan of Arc had led the ragtag French army on their way to liberate Orléans in 1429. "How many different peoples had fought battles here?" I wondered. The Germans attacked and captured the hilltop castle during World War II, which was then bombed by the Allies. I hoped the burg today would be more the way the austere King Louis XI—who was the opposite of François I in just about every respect—saw it when he chose it as the perfect permanent residence for his wife and children, wishing to keep them above the fray.

Instead of oozing tranquility, however, the Amboise I encountered today was jumping. It was, after all, high season. Foulques Nerra had certainly never seen crowds like this when he controlled the town a thousand years ago—he'd probably have run them all through.

Parking spaces were few and far between, so I left my new trusty steed (actually an orange Toyota) near the *mail*—the raised promenade along the Loire, a bit west of the center of town—and plunged into the maze of tiny streets. They were bedecked with flags and banners boasting bounteous *fleurs-de-lys*, so many that I had to wonder if the French Revolution had somehow overlooked Amboise. I passed in front of an upscale grocery store and was suddenly transfixed by a striking sight in the window. It was a green vegetable shaped like a large conch, which had the most astonishing patterns of bumps arranged in spirals around and around the outside. The elaborate patterns appeared to be fractal in nature, repeating over and over again on a small scale within larger ones. I don't know what impelled me to count the number of rings around the several larger and smaller specimens on offer, but lo and behold, they were all Fibonacci numbers! I knew that such series appeared in nature, like in sea shells and thistle flowers, but I had never seen one in the vegetable kingdom. I should cook more, I told myself.

The greengrocer I accosted inside called it a Romanesco broccoli, saying he thought it originated in Italy ("How fitting," I thought), and I asked him to put one aside for me, not wanting to lug the lovely legume around all afternoon. I resumed my peregrinations through time along the cobblestoned streets, reflecting that if we really were dealing with a series of crimes of some kind, then we were no longer talking about a Fibonacci sequence. For the latest incident had occurred on the seventh of July, not the eighth. If these incidents were connected to each other and formed a deathly mathematical series of some kind, it appeared to be one involving prime numbers. Would they—like the primes themselves, according to the ubiquitous and prolific Euler—turn out to be "a mystery that the human mind will never penetrate"? Wasn't it another mathematician, Erdös, who said "something strange is going on with the prime numbers"?

So lost in thought was I, reveling in the divinely incomprehensible nature of numbers, that I was quite surprised to find myself in the main *place*—one shrinks from calling it a square, given its long irregular shape—where the ever-popular Bigot chocolate shop/tea house has been handed down from mother to daughter for generations, and promised myself a refreshment or divine fruit sorbet (almost a hundred percent fruit) there after visiting the castle. I knew I shouldn't, but I knew I would stock up on my favorite treat: homemade milk chocolate pralines they call "Léonards." And why shouldn't they? It's da Vinci's town, after all. A thousand calories of pure gastronomical (which is, after all, astronomical plus a g, as in g-spot) delight!

Walking toward the long stone incline up to the castle, I regarded from afar the ominous narrow tunnel that led up to the butte—the Vigipirate-crazed would have nothing to complain about there. No wonder Amboise Castle had served as a slammer for so many years after its heyday, hosting bigshot rebels like cardinals, dukes, and princes. Some of them had been incarcerated here even after Louis XIII's prime minister, Richelieu, ordered the castle's fortifications razed to the ground in the 1630s,* but not before Louis XIV ordered the town's defenses to be rebuilt, probably thinking that you never knew when an impregnable fortress might come in handy. It always did!

Like in 1661, when his trusty musketeer d'Artagnan, the most famous of the *Three Musketeers*, escorted an ill-fated mega-financier by the name of Fouquet here. The banker had built a flamboyant palace that eclipsed anything his poor turnip-eating sovereign, Louis XIV, yet owned,** and invited the king to the party of the century there—can you get any dumber than that? It naturally incited the Sun King to accuse him of misappropriation of funds, throw him in jail, repossess his riches, and build his own even more sumptuous residence: the palace of palaces—Versailles.

At the base of the incline, I noticed a new wine store and—well, you know me, I just had to stop. It was tucked into a cheery old half-timbered house, which today undoubtedly looks almost exactly as it did when Thomas Jefferson saw it in 1787. He was completing his *Tour de France* (long before there were bicycles on this fair planet) in quest of the country's best wines, coming in peace up the Loire Valley from Nantes, to Angers, Tours, Amboise, Blois, and on to Orléans, a town where prestigious wines adorning the King of France's table used to originate, and where a few intrepid winemakers were rebuilding vineyards from scratch. Jefferson's Grand Wine Tour lasted four whole months, handily beating any I'd ever taken. It makes me jealous! Could he have been even more of a wine aficionado than me? He did spend a never rivaled percentage of the White House's budget on French wine.

My *vitis vinifera* expenditures were quite high, too, naturally, and as if to remonstrate with me for spending too much on such tipples, the shop was closed. I gazed longingly in the window for a while, and then ascended the incline, working up quite a sweat in the late afternoon sun. With each step through the *Galerie des Blasons* (Coat of Arms Tunnel), I went back further and further in time, feeling like the man from Monticello myself, or even d'Artagnan.

The naturally cool boutique was located near the ticket office in a series of spacious, stately, brick-vaulted rooms one would never suspect to be hidden within the massive walls. I looked about—for you never know what you might find, from seeds with which to grow ancient herbs to a genuine goose quill pen to give my nephew. Yet, my attention was, as usual, drawn most to their huge array of books. They had some of the same ancient and modern works I had noticed at Azay and at the Clos Lucé, but some novel ones too. *A Treatise on Sculpture* by Leonardo da Vinci himself was for sale. Boy, was I ever right to come to Amboise!

I'd never known the Florentine to write anything longer than what fit on a single page, text and drawings combined. Was I dreaming? A barrage of thoughts rushed through my mind all at once, vying for attention. It was rumored the artist had published a book of sketches of Rome's antiquities, and that a few visitors had seen a book of anatomical drawings on his desk when they dropped in on Leonardo at the Clos Lucé, but that was it.

I opened the precious volume at random and my eyes alighted on words to the effect that the sculptor frees the figure trapped in a stone, but gets terribly dirty and smelly in the process, sculpture being so much harder physical work than painting—I had certainly read those before in da Vinci's notebooks!

The cashier, seeing what I was holding in my hands, came over to me and indicated that it was hot off the presses. The preface, she told me, indicated that it was a compilation (prepared by none other than da Vinci's faithful student and amanuensis, Francesco Melzi). And that it had recently been exhumed somewhere in Italy—she flipped through the first pages looking for the name of the place—and had been painstakingly transcribed and simultaneously published in French and Italian.

"What about the publisher listed on the book's spine, TTT?" I asked. TTT was spelled out on the inside in Beneventan script as Trulli Turbolenza Taviano, an odd name if ever there was one.

"The copies were delivered in person because TTT wanted to immediately get the book into the souvenir shops of all the Loire Valley castles commemorating the five-hundredth anniversary of da Vinci's death," was her courteous response.

As I was to discover in the tourist office later, there were a lot of castles doing so. "I'll take one," I said. Handing her my business card, I added, "If you receive any more of them or see the distributor again, please give me a ring." I wasn't sure she would, but I noticed that her eyes lingered on my name—or was it my address in Manhattan?

The director must have told the entire staff that he was expecting me, for the tall employee immediately offered to call the guide the director had managed to free up to show me around. I acquiesced—having held out a faint hope he would show me around himself—paid for my mysterious find, and waited.

Marie Gaudin, for such was my guide's unexpected name, was a young brunette. She was dressed in horrible contemporary French fashion—half-red, half-orange pants weirdly stopping some four or five inches above the ankle, and a top that descended half-way down her thigh, being an odd cross between a laboratory coat and an apron. I resolved to try to focus on something else about her—her beautiful mind, if she had one, for example—as she instantly bubbled over with

159

stories. Guides usually believe no one knows anything about art, history, or architecture, and grandstand about all kinds of things in which they themselves have little to no expertise. The girl probably thought historical tidbits would suffice to entertain a moron like me. Luckily, she had merely been instructed to answer whatever questions I might have. I could go wherever I liked and peek behind every door. It was like being a kid in a deluxe candy shop!

We crossed the majestic esplanade situated high above the village. From every angle I could see the steep-roofed white houses strewn at our feet like black-slate-hatted dwarfs needing protection, and the Loire beyond, shielding the town from all enemies coming from the right bank. It is said that its riverbed used to be far smaller, much of the water flowing north into the Seine and then into the English Channel, but that was eons ago. Today it was dotted with old-fashioned flat-bottomed sailboats made of weathered wood, some anchored and gaily whirling in the wind, others carefully navigating the treacherous sandbars that define its ever-shifting countenance, living proof of Heraclitus's claim that you can't step into the same river twice.

"No, sir," she replied condescendingly (unlike her counterpart in the boutique) to my query, "we have never found any evidence of what you are talking about."

The rumor had remained alive for five hundred years that there was a tunnel from Amboise Castle to the Clos Lucé, a secret passageway that François I took when he paid visits to Leonardo da Vinci.

"It's just a silly rumor," she went on, "you shouldn't believe it for a minute."

Despite her denials (and Claudine Thoury's too), I reserved the right to believe the tunnel might still be discovered someday.

"Well, many things get unearthed at these ancient sites."

"There is," she admitted, "a half-mile-long underground passage traversing the entire prominence on which the castle sits that was built by Louis-Philippe, but it only dates back to the mid-nineteenth century. And there are plenty of underground chambers beneath the esplanade, but none that connect with the world beyond the mesa."

She then had the audacity to roll her eyes when I mentioned the far longer tunnel supposedly built by the Duke of Choiseul in the eighteenth century leading three whole leagues from Amboise to his former Chanteloup Castle, after he had convinced King Louis XV to turn the prodigious property he had purchased in the area into a duchy for him.

"Your name," I changed the subject, "is curiously connected to the life of François I. Is that a coincidence?"

She had no idea—or at least pretended to have none—that Marie Gaudin was the name of François I's first mistress, who later became the mistress of both the Holy Roman Emperor Charles V and of Pope Leo X.

The girl led me to the tiny chapel where Leonardo's remains are buried, his final resting place being right here in France, not Italy. I'm not sure what da Vinci would have thought of the green antlers protruding from the chapel's rooftop spire. My guide explained that the chapel was dedicated to Saint Hubert, the patron saint of hunting, so they made some sort of sense. I suspect the artist would, after having been treated so well by France, be happy to be resting for eternity in such an exquisite chapel, loftily perched and visible from afar, even if the antlers might have offended his aesthetic sensibilities.

"It's the finest lace I've ever seen," I exclaimed once inside the chapel. We were surrounded on all sides by the loveliest of lace—I mean, it was stone, but it was sculpted in such a light, delicate, and intricate way that one could have sworn it was designed for the cuff or collar of a King's fancy dress shirt or a princess' ball gown. How anyone could have worked stone into such airy, fragile frills was a mystery I hoped to look into.

A horde of tourists flooded into the precious stone jewelry box, so I hurried back out into the blazing sunlight, leaving Leonardo to the cackling crowds. A mere hundred paces from da Vinci's tomb, I stopped in front of a locked gate and pointed at some ancient stone stairs behind it. "This looks like it goes to the base of the ramparts closest to the Loire."

"Nobody has a key to this gate," she immediately retorted and tried to steer me away from it.

Still squinting, I stood rooted to the spot and considered it carefully.

I surmised that the steps led to an open air rain gutter that ran from the gardens right in front of the castle to the base of the fortress walls two hundred feet below us. I vaulted the fence, carefully clambered down the moss-covered stairs, and examined the slope of the sluice channel.

"It doesn't go anywhere!" she yelled at the top of her lungs, but I kept descending.

I was right: someone could fairly easily exit the castle premises by scampering or sliding down it. Not much more difficult than scaling the low walls around the castle property to the south and east.

"This is not your property," she shrieked, stamping her feet, her crazy-length multicolored pants flapping furiously up and down on her calves. "And it's extremely dangerous." Yet something in her voice told me she was saying it pro forma. From the lips of many a Frenchwoman, this would be the admonition of a *petit chef*, a small-fry administrator or schoolmarm exercising her petty power over her wards. But her manner suggested something else—I wasn't sure what. "And just so you know, that is not where Charles VIII died at such a young age after hitting his head on a low-slung door jam," she lectured me out of the blue like a typical Gallic know-it-all putting me in my place, as though I were an ordinary tourist who had never read anything but a basic guidebook.

"I didn't think so," I told her when I had made my way back up to the esplanade. "Where, by the way, did the inimitable Duke of Lauzun stay during his 'exile' in Amboise?"

The building no longer existed, she told me disparagingly, many of the structures erected on the site having become so dilapidated by the nineteenth century, they were torn down. I was about to inquire which bed the cheeky rascal had hid under while Louis XIV and his mistress took a roll in the hay, but then remembered that that especially piquant episode had occurred at Versailles and was even one of the main reasons why Lauzun had been sent into exile in Amboise!

We eventually arrived at the Logis du Roi (King's Dwelling), which was built by the very first artists and master craftsmen Charles VIII brought back from Italy with him after waging war there. "Why in Italy?" you might ask. For honor's sake, perhaps (the French kings had legal claim, by marriage, to territories in what was not yet a unified country called Italy, but you actually had to conquer them if you wanted them and keep reconquering them if you wanted to hold onto them), and then for the love of art ... and plunder!*

Marie Gaudin seemed to have concluded by this point that I was just some silly tourist who had had the extraordinary luck of knowing somebody who knew the director. I had concluded that she was boring as beans.

Proceeding through the Grande Salle with its incredibly high ceilings, and several elegantly furnished bedrooms, we finally ended up at the stone staircase in which, as she told me all agog, a professor had found his death recently. It was dark, quite narrow, and cordoned off by crimson ropes, like at theaters, a sign indicating that it was not currently open to the public.

162

As might have been expected, the fall had not occurred in the spiral staircase that was almost more square than circular in the Logis du Roi, for the squareness of the outer walls there would have stopped his tumble almost immediately. The more perfectly round staircase in the Louis XII-François I wing—which ran between the Antechamber of the Cordelière,* with its beautifully sculpted fireplace, and the plush Orléans-Penthièvre Study—had undoubtedly guided his plummet ever further downward.

"He obviously failed to grab onto the metal handrail," I commented as we stood in the penumbra, "and the *coup de grâce* was probably delivered by the squared off wall here at the bottom of the spiral."

"I heard he was found all the way at the bottom, against the wall," she said in a toneless voice. "But he might have been battered so badly by banging into one step after another after another after another and repeatedly hitting and crashing his head against the wall," she added, excitedly now, "that he was already dead on arrival. In fact I'm sure of it."

I walked up and down the stairs several times alone. Then I asked the slender girl to try to pass me in the same direction and in the opposite direction, too.

"Who are you?" she now asked.

"I work for an insurance company."

She did what I asked obediently, now that she knew the gruesome death and I were no strangers. I noticed that it was possible to pass, but only with some difficulty, perhaps lending credence to a bump and roll.

"I wouldn't have to do much," she opined eagerly on her second pass, "to have you careening to your death. The slightest contact and you'd be beaten to a pulp, smushed like mashed potatoes."

Was she right? I wondered if any forensic physicist had ever studied whether it would be better to fall down a straight staircase or a circular one—did one have a better chance of being able to stop one's fall on one or the other, and not end up "smushed like mashed potatoes"? And was a tight spiral better or worse than a loose one? Morbid speculations, when you got right down to it, which were interrupted by Marie calling me to join her upstairs.

She was invisible to me as I ascended, and then jumped out at me from behind a turn, making me start as if the hideous specter of the oenologist had suddenly appeared in the shadows. "You see this spot here, Mr. Colombo, it's a blind spot. The staircase continues up beyond

163

where tourists enter it, and someone can easily hide there until his poor unsuspecting victim is already on the stairs and then sneak up behind him like a bloodthirsty vampire," she added. "Like I just did to you."

She appeared straight-laced, but might well, I surmised, be addicted to gory television series like *Game of Thrones* and be into BDSM ... I see that sort of thing every day.

* * *

The state-of-the-art sporting goods store I found in Tours was located in an ancient stone building, and I half expected them to tout "royal hiking boots" and sell *Fleur-de-Lys*-brand sneakers. Banners and monikers recalling France's royal past are so abundant in the area, one might think the king is still meting out justice in one of the nearby palaces!

I browsed the rock climbing and mountaineering aisles, where boots, ropes, and carabiners abounded, all of the latter looking very much alike to me.

"Can I help you?" came an affable voice.

A twentysomething-year-old dressed in a store uniform had materialized between two colossal medieval pillars. He was of medium height, athletic build, and had somewhat long, unkempt, dirty-blond hair that almost smelled of southern Californian surf.

"I'm trying to learn about this little thing I found," I said, taking it out of my pocket and showing it to him. He was about to touch it, so I stopped him, saying, "I'm afraid it has to stay in the plastic bag for the time being."

He scrutinized my face for some moments.

"It may turn out to be material evidence in a case I am investigating," I explained.

"Righteous, *righ-teous!*" he uttered, his surfer locks swishing mischievously. "Looks like pretty typical equipment, though."

"I am wondering whether it is the kind that is used primarily for recreational purposes."

"I don't recognize the brand name, dude," he responded, giving the item greater attention now. "But it has a screwgate and interlock mechanism," he said pointing. That was all Greek to me. He politely took a similar item out of a box on one of the store shelves, and showed me how it worked. Leading me over to a computer on a nearby counter, he added, "Carabiners like this are mostly used for radical sports like hang gliding and paragliding." Placing his fingers on the keyboard, he said, "Can you read the brand name for me?"

"AustriAlpin," I said, and spelled it out.

"Yep. Here it is, man," he commented, pointing to the screen. "It's the Tropos model, designed especially for hang gliding."

I stroked my chin thoughtfully, recalling da Vinci's words, "For once you have tasted flight you will walk the earth with your eyes turned skyward, for there you have been and there you will long to return." I asked the salesman, "Do you yourself hang glide or paraglide?"

He tossed his head to the right, his straggly hair swinging with it. "Not my main gig. I mostly mountain bike and paddle board on the Loire and the Cher," he replied, his eyes opening wide, "but I've done a little here and there."

I drew him toward a window and pointed at a nearby Haussmannian building some six stories tall, with intricate black ironwork balconies against the whitest of sculpted stone, topped by a black slate mansard roof with gables sporting triangular pediments. "Let's say I needed to jump off that building—say, out of that dormer window there—and land safely nearby. What would you recommend I use?"

"You're shitting me!"

"Am not."

"Dude, nothing we sell here!" He brushed his unruly hair back from his forehead, as if it would help him think. "You'd have to go to a totally, totally, totally specialized shop. I'm no expert, but I believe you could use either a mini-hang glider or a mini-paraglider. But, man, you'd want to practice a lot first. Preferably for a few months or years. And hope to hell that the wind would be just right!"

"How bulky are such gliders?"

"Most of them'll fit into a large backpack, like those over there," he said pointing to full-size backpacks for multi-day hiking trips. "But, you know, I've seen some as small as this," he said gesturing with his hands, indicating something about the size of an American football. "The smallest ones could fit into a lady's handbag."

"A lady's handbag?"

"Yeah. *Trans-cend-ent*, huh?"

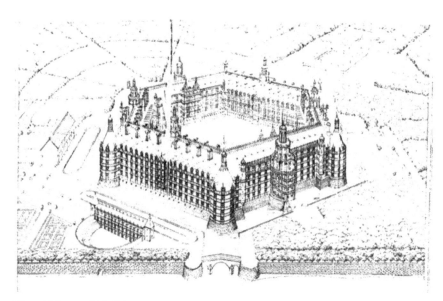

The Abbey of Thélème

CHAPTER ELEVEN

Location unknown

Prohibition is temptation.*

—A certain shrink

"I'm in a huge room, rushing to leave. I can't find my way, and the lights suddenly go out. I finally locate the exit, but someone is there. I turn to see ..." She broke off, hesitating.

"Go on."

"A woman. She's on fire—flames are coming out of her head—and she yells something at me, like 'You stay away!' The next thing I know, I'm falling and can't stop ...

"That's when I woke up, my heart pounding!"

"Hmm ..." I voiced almost inaudibly.

"It seemed like a very long dream, but that's the only part I remember."

Anna appeared barely able to walk without a helping hand today. Yet she remembered the strange man who had placed her datebook and a pen on her bedside table.

"You asked me to write down any dreams I might have, so I wrote about him the minute I awoke."

"Him?"

167

"It wasn't that different from the one I had the night before that too, when I woke up. You made me have this horrible dream again! In my country—"

"Who is the first *him* who comes to mind?" I cut her off, gently patting her forearm.

"What do you mean" Despite her nation's party line regarding dreams, she seemed intrigued.

"You said *him* instead of *dream*—does any *him* pop into your mind?" I reiterated.

She looked away, out the window, deliberately it seemed to me.

"I won't tell anyone."

"He's the worst person I ever met." After a short pause she added, "But he also has a great ... I can't think of the word."

"Probably loves and hates him at the same time," I said to myself. "Now we're getting somewhere." Aloud I asked, "Do you remember his name?"

She shook her head. "He's tall and slim, has dark hair and dark eyes. I think he works with me."

"Enrique?" I ventured.

"Yes, that's right."

"Now, can you think of anyone who might want you to stay away from him?"

"Of course not. No one knows I like him."

"Not even him?"

"I've never let on ..."

I wondered if she truly believed she'd been able to hide her feelings from the man, given Fielding's opinion that "Love may be likened to a disease in this, that when it is denied a vent in one part, it will certainly break out in another."*

"What about the woman on fire?" I asked, trying to elicit further associations to the dream.

"She looked like the devil."

"Are there any devils in your life?"

She contemplated the question for a few moments and then inclined her head. "But I can't remember who."

168

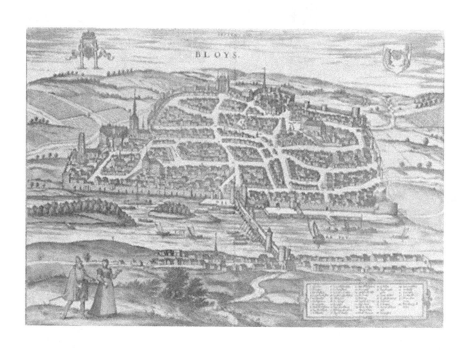

CHAPTER TWELVE

The town of Blois

Warts and all.

—Attributed to Oliver Cromwell

One musician a month is generally enough for me—after all, I've rarely met any with decent manners: most arrive abominably late for dinner dates when they don't forget altogether, and insinuate that it is my fault for having failed to remind them more than twice—but tonight I left one musician only to drive straight to see another, no small fry at that. At the Saturn, I had the front desk buzz Wack's room for me on the off chance he was in.

The jokester/guide/garbage picker/conductor was in, so I proposed we go to a little place I knew just outside of town, *Assa*. Upon arrival, we passed through a forbidding-looking metal door, climbed a dozen steps up to an unexpected raised garden, and entered the dining room overlooking the vast Loire, with its islands, shifting sandbars, and swans gliding here and there. The site is so close to the city and yet so far, offering the kind of peaceful setting only found in this privileged part of France, the banks of its mighty waterways being protected from development for almost their full length. You've probably noticed that

I don't always go easy on the French, which I feel I'm allowed, being one myself, but they do some wonderful things too!

"Bonsoir messieurs," said a youngish, tattooed, and pierced woman in the refined setting of the Michelin-starred restaurant. We were lucky enough to be the only guests in the tasteful dining room with huge windows giving out onto the river. Wack had readily agreed to come with me, although I was not entirely sure why—his evening must have been Françoise-free, and more generally female-free. He nevertheless gave the waitress the thrice over, we ordered our meals—a simple task as we selected the whole shebang, the most extensive tasting menu on offer—and he gestured that he would let me order the wine, not professing to prefer pastis this time. François Cazin's *Le Petit Chambord, Cuvée Renaissance*, a top Cour-Cheverny made from the rare Romorantin grape, was on offer, and I couldn't resist trying it, if only because of the name. It also happened to come from at most ten miles away—talk about local! The fare at *Assa* was French-Japanese fusion, so sake was another possible choice, but I figured we could always order some later. I might need it, I reflected, Wack being no walk in the Azay-le-Rideau park.

"It was pretty brave of you to found your own symphony at such a young age," I opined, after observing that he seemed far more preoccupied with ogling the server wearing overly tight-fitting clothing than with getting to know his distinguished dinner companion.

"It sure beat working under Avid Sapristi!" My eyes widened at this and he went on, "Don't get me wrong—it was a great musical experience, but ... "

"But?" I prompted him.

"But it was scary. I knew if I wanted to survive I had to get out—the guy acted like he owned you."

"Owned *me*?" I queried, knowing full well that was not what he meant, but trying to see if he would own it for himself instead of using the generic "you" form.

He looked a bit confused at first, and then said, "No, owned *me*—like I was his chattel to do with as he pleased."

"And what did it please him to do with you?"

He eyed me narrowly. "Things best left unsaid."

"Few and far between are the things best left unsaid, in my view," I commented once I had tasted the exquisite white wine the waitress had poured, and Wack had stopped watching her as she high-heeled it off.

Had I not been there, I was sure he would have tried to chat her up. Indeed, it struck me that he would have been more eager to converse with any woman at all than he was with me. It wasn't sour grapes on my part—at least I don't think I need to feel loved by all and sundry—just something I sensed about him. Then again, maybe he needed me—or at least someone else—there in order to feel comfortable enough to stare, perchance to flirt … Some feel a need for cover, as it were—or is it strength in numbers?

"Let's just say that Sapristi acts like he can take whatever he wants, and if *he* wants it, *you* must obviously want it too." He whetted his lips with the wine and then downed the entire glass, like a man trying to deep-six his thoughts.

"You didn't?" I inquired, pouring him another.

"Certainly not!" he blurted out. "But when you're young and impressed by someone's stature … I had terrible stage fright at the time—still do … Anyway, when you're just starting out and a big shot like him takes you by surprise, it's hard to know when and how to say no."

I nodded. Wack struck me as uncharacteristically grave tonight. Where was the incorrigible clown I had encountered thus far?

"So much seems to be on the line … "

I waited while he quaffed the second glass, almost without stopping. The man had a thirst for something!

"Your whole future, your whole career in France, Europe, the world," he eventually finished his thought.

"So if you had stayed?"

"It would have been as if I were condoning his unconscionable behavior."

"As if you were turning a blind eye to the fact that Sapristi is just another word for 'rapist'?"

His brow furrowed in perplexity. "Is it?"

"Well, if you wish to be persnickety about it, it's an anagram for 'is rapist.'"

"Avid Is-a-rapist …," he said musingly. "It's built right into his name. Nice."

The amuse-bouche came and the waitress poured us both more wine while Wack goggled at her bare midriff admiringly, it seemed.

"I noticed that Sapristi conducted at Chambord the night before you did," I remarked offhandedly, as I tasted the bite-sized *lamproie à*

173

la chinonaise, river lamprey from the Loire cooked in red Chinon wine, but with an Asian twist: a hint of wasabi and a dash of sansho pepper. It was presented on a two-tiered teak platter and tasted, well, rather indescribable, apart from its soft texture. I employed my chopsticks as I waited for him to respond, wanting to know what words he would choose, and not sure whether to mention that I suspected Sapristi had stormed out just before Wack's performance of Lully, during his flamboyant introduction.

"Yes, we cross paths now and then." He ate the carefully prepared delicacy, nodding his approval as he chewed.

"Is he still angry you left?"

"Oh, I doubt it. He was at first, but since he has an unlimited supply of young, impressionable musicians to grope, I suspect he doesn't even remember anymore."

"People often remember more than you think," I remarked.

"What I'm sure he does remember is that a bassoonist he recruited jumped ship and came to work for me. I bet that still rankles!"

"The one who's gone missing?"

"Exactly. He apparently talked her into coming to France and helped her get all kinds of papers so she could stay. Then, the very minute she received her residence permit a few months ago, she auditioned for an opening *we* had," he added, looking pleased as punch. I guess he had served up his revenge cold, as some say is best, decades after being ambushed by Sapristi. Do people ever forgive and forget?

Our appetizers arrived, being described as raw tuna with hot mustard and truffles. The tiny morsels were propped up on a wooden mask with the unlikeliest of toothpicks.

"She was head and shoulders above the other applicants?" I inquired, eyeing the appetizer suspiciously.

"I wouldn't say that—she was right up there with the best of them, musically," he said expertly, holding up his glass, taking yet another long draft, and giving me a significant look, "but, you know, we don't do blind tastings … A live concert is never just about the music."

"I couldn't agree more," I said, tentatively sampling the fare. "So this missing bassoonist of yours is quite a vision of loveliness?" I poured him another glass of Cour-Cheverny, wondering if he'd soon tire of my fishing or wonder where I was heading with my questions.

"Attractiveness is in the eye of the beholder, of course," he opined, hiccupping, "but I think many appreciate her face and … " He finished

174

his thought with a grandiloquent gesture requiring two hands. I got the distinct impression he was one of her admirers.

"Too many?"

He shot me a quizzical look.

"*Elle est aimable, mais elle se laisse aimer d'un autre*?" I quipped, playing on the line he had cited at his concert from the play *Psyche*, where *aimable*, lovable, also means beautiful (She is lovable/lovely, but she accepts another's love). I avoided suggesting she might be in love with another so as not to twist the knife in the all-too-palpable wound.

"I don't know what she sees in him," he said with a twinge of bitterness in his voice. "Well, I *do*, but she has to know she can have no future with him, he being happily married and all."

I must have looked confused, finding it improbable that Enrique was married and trying to recall if he wore a wedding ring. And how could anyone consider him to be "happily" anything-ed? Then I remembered that Wack had almost fallen over backward at Azay when I'd insinuated that he wanted the concertmaster out of the way so he could have the bassoonist to himself. I knew for a fact that *Civadin* was married.

Wack appeared to have noticed nothing of my confusion, simply draining yet another glass of the white marvel as if he were drinking water, not superb wine to be savored in small sips. I realized that if I were to have anything to drink, I would have to order a second bottle.

"Happily married?" was all I said, it being possible that the bassoonist was involved with some other married man, though why the conductor would think I knew about it was beyond me.

"Let's say that he always seemed to be, up until recently. Orlando and I have worked together for many years and I've never known him to have an affair until this one started a couple of months ago."

So it was Civadin who was involved with Pislova. This suddenly struck me as the only mystery I had solved thus far, and I hadn't even done so myself.

"How does that sit with Madame Civadin?" I eventually asked.

"She doesn't know."

I waited until the waitress, who was eyed anew up and down by he who professed to be in love with another—"What made the man tick?" I wondered—removed the wooden mask, set down our main course of *sandre*, pike perch, caught right in front of the restaurant (it was presented in tiny cubes piled on top of slivers of beets in soy sauce), and disappeared before asking, "So what do you think is going on?"

175

"I wish I knew! I don't have the impression he is that into Anna. My guess is that she pursued him, but it's hard to say. Maybe if I were a mind reader like you … ," he added, looking at me searchingly.

"You think she would have more of a future with you?"

"Well, of course," he nodded emphatically. Then, considering the question more seriously, he gave a laugh, "Not necessarily. I don't exactly have a stellar track record."

"No?"

"Four failed marriages. Well five, if you count the one I had annulled the morning after the wedding—what a fiasco that was!" He took a bite of the incredibly local pike perch and chewed wistfully.

My eyebrows rose.

"Not to mention other dalliances in between that went awry. Do you think I keep picking the wrong women?" the maestro asked with a pity-seeking expression on his face, smiling up at me from his plate like an overgrown baby.

"The wrong women?" Not being of the fairer sex myself, my heart did not go out to him.

"They never turn out to be as savvy and cultured as I think they are at first, never know how to turn a house into a home and take care of their husband." He looked down at his dish. "I'm starting to think I don't even know what love is … I tell myself I'm in love often enough, but maybe it's just that I am captivated by women's beauty."

"A common enough experience," I proffered.

"There's nothing common about it for me—I go completely berserk!"

"And once the captivation wears off?"

"Then, I don't know… It isn't pretty… I get furious at them." He grinned disarmingly.

"Furious? Why?" I asked, as the waitress brought us a second bottle of wine, a biodynamic Cour-Cheverny this time, "Romo" from Domaine des Huards.

He shrugged, still smiling. "If only I knew," he replied, sipping his wine for once instead of chugging it. "It's like they had promised me something and then cheated me out of it."

"Hmm."

"I know it isn't anything they actually do. It's me, it's the way I see them—like they're goddesses at first, when they're just ordinary women—well, not exactly ordinary … "

"And when you discover their humanity?" None of them, I mused silently, could ever take the place of the goddess he probably thought his mother was when he was little and that he'd been on a quest to refind ever since.

"I no longer want anything to do with them." He took a piece of bread out of the basket, and bit into it. "I'm bad, right?" he said after a while. "At first, all I want to do is to win them over—"

"And once you have won them away from someone else, you don't know what to do with them anymore?" I insinuated. He seemed surprised that I had perceived his love of theft, but I went right on, "You're not sure what to do with Françoise already?"

His face turned red, he swallowed another half a glass of white wine, as if he hoped it would hide his Bordeaux-colored cheeks, and stammered, "Françoise? She's a lovely girl."

"Beauty again?"

"Well, life's too short to date dogs!"

"I only hope you don't crush her hopes."

"Her hopes? Ha!" he exclaimed ironically. "They're all about me. I mean," he corrected his Freudian slip, "they're *not* about me. She's just a girl who can't say no—not to men with power, at least."

"Kind of like he himself had been with Sapristi," I found myself thinking, while listening.

"Loves how she feels about herself when she's with big-name conductors and rich patrons of the arts. I've heard about relationships she's been in before with such men, none of which have lasted. Right now, she has some idea of me as big banana—or is it 'top banana'?" he laughed a bit drunkenly at his unintended sexual innuendo—"which is just fine with me." Downing still more Romo (I was sure the heathen hadn't even noticed the change of producer and vintage), he went on more soberly, or at least somberly, "It's not really me she wants. She doesn't love *me*. My mother is probably the only woman who does. Pretty messed up to say that, huh? But no one else loves me for who I am."

He struck me as simultaneously sure and totally unsure of himself. "Who are you?" I asked.

He looked surprised at the question, shoveled another morsel of locally sourced and exotically spiced pike perch into his mouth, and then replied, "I am who I am, warts and all. But she wants me to fit into some idea she has of a perfect man."

177

"When there's no such thing as perfection—no more for men than for women," I opined.

"Exactly," he agreed, clearly relishing the Loire specialty. "They say men don't understand women, but I say women don't understand men."

I had to agree with him there. I sensed that Françoise saw Wack as head honcho when he conducted, but that she'd hate the scared little kid who threatened to come out when awaiting the reviews, the boy who needed his mom's reassurance when the world out there looked cold and dark.

"Maybe women in New York are different," he looked at me hopefully. "Would you introduce me to some?"

I threw my head back and laughed heartily. I wouldn't do that to my worst enemies! Naturally, I didn't tell him that. Instead I ribbed him, "So you've exhausted the supply of available women in Europe?"

He smiled.

"Women are many things, too," I reminded him, "not just incarnations of beauty."

This seemed to perplex him. "Finally!" I thought. People can be so developed in abstruse fields and yet such nincompoops when it comes to real life. "Françoise's a captivating female, a consummate flirt, and a fine flautist—it must be hard for men to resist such a talented mouth," I gave him a knowing look, "—but she's probably also a little girl looking for a daddy to tell her she's his beautiful princess, no matter what she does, and a boss to tell her what to do when she's unsure. Take her little seduction number yesterday at Azay ... "

"Who wants to be with a girl looking for a daddy? or a macho boss?"

"Who wants to be with a boy who thinks his mommy is the only one who really loves him?" I countered. "You want her to love you warts and all, but you draw the line at her warts?"

"I never thought of it that way, I guess ... ," he hiccupped.

"Anyway, it's obvious that Françoise is not the one you want."

"She shouldn't want me, either," he said in a meek voice. "I wouldn't be good to her, I'm sure." He hiccupped again.

"Why is that? You mean you're the problem?" I asked, happy that he seemed to be admitting he played a part in the Kármán vortex street of failed relationships he had left in his wake. "It's not that you keep picking the wrong women?"

Again he looked rather confused. I guess I had jumped the gun, thinking he'd finally changed his tune. "I meant that I'm sure she doesn't have all the requisite qualities and wouldn't be a good fit for me either." He seemed to be trying to sort his thoughts out, looked the incongruously appareled waitress up and down again as she passed by, and attempted to drown his hiccups in sparkling water, his first of the evening.

I had, as you know, heard so many idiocies proclaimed about the importance of *fit* I might have thrown one then and there! As if love were only possible when there was just the right fit between lovers, as if analysis only worked well when there was just the right fit between people—whatever that was! As though the analyst had to have just the right personality to be able to see through the analysand's neurosis, needing to rely on his disposition instead of the old noodle, or as though their problems had to mesh in just the right way for the curative gears to turn to the patient's advantage—how vague could you get? And vague as such notions were in therapy, they were even vaguer when it came to love! Hadn't I heard it said that Zodiac earth signs should marry other earth signs—or was it fire signs? Did that significantly whittle down the list of prospective partners?

"Could any woman possibly have all the requisite qualities? How many are there?" I inquired.

"Dozens." He looked up. "Hundreds."

I eyed him narrowly and he grudgingly cracked a smile.

"Maybe it's not that they fall short of your standards, but it's something about you?"

He scratched his chin doubtfully, as he soaked up the soy sauce around the beet slices with a piece of bread, something you really aren't supposed to do in public—why was I not surprised?

"You keep doing the same thing over and over with all of them."

"You think?" he responded unreflectively. "I think it's that they're not who I think they are."

"Who do you think they are?"

"I don't know … Beautiful, logical, organized, totally independent, sexy beings," he hiccupped yet again, "perfect in every way."

"Why would you keep failing to realize they're not? Doesn't that say something about you—that you're being willfully blind?"

"No, they hide it. They put on a frightfully fine show, too!" He took another serious slug of wine, hiccups be damned. "For a while, at least."

"So when the show is over, you stop being good to them?"

"Definitely."

"What about Anna? Would you stop being good to her, too?"

His face lit up. "Never! I'm sure she's perfect for me. Aren't you? At least, hope springs infernal—I mean eternal," he sputtered.

"Have you ever declared your love to her?" I inquired resignedly.

"She never gives me any cues."

"You have to wait for those?"

"I would never force anyone—"

"Force? Who's talking about force? Declaring your flame might light a fire in her, or throw oil on an already smoldering log."

"Hard to imagine."

"How can you know if you never try?"

"Touché," he conceded. "You're rather clever, aren't you? I could use more people like you in my life, you know, to make me think."

"So you are prepared to try?"

"Maybe, but I can't anyway. She's been missing for four days."

"What if I told you I know where she is?"

The great maestro fell off his chair.

* * *

The towers of a giant fortress appeared all at once on my left and right, so many it was like plane trees lining a narrow country lane. They loomed out of the mist and I could barely make them out as night was falling fast. A huge vehicle came up behind me. I didn't notice it at first because there were no headlights. It suddenly moved to pass me on the left, rammed into my car, and tried to knock me off the road. I was careening toward an enormous tree trunk that was blocking a dirt road leading into the forest—

I awoke sweating and breathing hard.

Sitting up and turning on the light, I looked around me. All was perfectly still. Not a creature was stirring in the house.

I considered the dream's elements and tried to free associate to them: The vehicle was a ... No, it was too dark in the dream to remember precisely—the only two words that came to me were sedan and tank. Sedan, *berline*, in French—Berlin, the Berlin Wall, East-West relations, the cold war, spies ... What about tank? Dank, stank, fish tank, old war movies I'd seen as a child ...

180

No headlights? A man, not a woman? What was that expression: "The lights are on, but nobody's home"? What if the lights aren't on? Playing dead? Truly being dead?

And the lane? Definitely French, far too narrow to be American. Could be almost anywhere in France … I'm not sure why the south came to mind—Provence.

I tried to picture the driver, despite my still somewhat foggy state. Curiously enough, it seems I had glimpsed him in the dream. I let my mind wander. I saw a long beard. Amish? No, not trimmed like that. He had a mustache, too, and the beard was wavy. And long hair, like in the sixties.

Was I dreaming again? No, definitely not. Was it someone from my youth? One of the young men I'd treated back in the day?

I noticed it was getting light out—a new and confusing day was dawning.

CHAPTER THIRTEEN

Fontevrault Abbey

A person doesn't only love himself in others, he also hates himself in others.

—Lichtenberg

The breakfast tables at my B&B were crammed into a small area, and a grand piano taking up half the space was relegated to serving as a dusty shelf for coffee mugs and plants. The hostess showed me the aged sideboard on which industrially produced baguettes (from the local supermarket where the increasingly indolent French now get the lion's share of their daily bread), watery butter, sickly sweet jam, and shriveled-up croissants wrapped in plastic were on offer. And to top off my second nightmare of the day, she cruelly informed me that I had a choice between filtered coffee and Lipton tea. Where were the homemade bread, artisanal butter, and dandelion jam? That is what I had heard they proposed—I guess the place had changed hands in the meantime.

Did I really want to eat a typical French breakfast? If they were going to give you nothing but quick sugars, they should at least be to die for!

I selected the only items I considered not likely to be toxic, a piece of fruit and a slice of nondescript yellow cheese, and chose a table near a window. There was only one other guest breakfasting there at the time, facing the other window, and I broodily tasted the nasty-looking java the ornery proprietor set down in front of me. No amount of milk or sugar was going to change the fact that it was undrinkable, I concluded. I'd have to go into town to find something palatable.

I was wondering how far I would have to drive to find a café with a real espresso maker when a voice exclaimed in American English, "Are you following me?"

"Is *she* following me?" was the thought that immediately occurred to me. "How did you end up here?" was all I asked, as I stood up to greet the voice's owner. It was the formidable coach of U of M's swim team.

"It's only the best bed and breakfast for a hundred miles around."

"I thought so, too, until … ," I said, gesturing to the sideboard.

She shrugged. Americans, I reflected, can never say anything nasty about the food in France. They're cute, but hopelessly out of date. Every-day French fare has been in freefall for decades, so much so that the majority of frogs have almost completely accustomed their taste buds to mass-produced trash. Yet Americans believe that twenty-first-century frogs feast on scrumptious croissants at breakfast, that their bakers continue to knead their own dough, and that classic dishes like *coq au vin* and *crêpes suzettes* are still made in every home.

"Have you been keeping out of trouble, or continuing to swim in insalubrious waters?" I asked.

"What about you?" she riposted.

"Trouble has a way of finding me," I said. "You, too, perhaps. I recommend you watch your back."

I invited her to join me at my table and helped her into a chair.

She smiled. "I've been known to make six-foot-five swimmers break down and cry, so I think can handle myself here. Besides, Lead Investigator Scarface has someone watching me night and day now."

I groaned internally. So I'd ended up in this dump for nothing! "They say to keep your friends close and your enemies closer …" I uttered, as though talking to myself.

"Enemies? He's a bit rough around the edges," she said, making a sweeping hand gesture and spilling the coffee she'd started drinking out of my virtually untouched cup. "Like at the restaurant we went to last night. I had to step in to avoid a scene."

I raised my eyebrows and glanced at the growing coffee stain. I naturally thought her taste in men quite poor, but I could be mistaken. It takes all kinds, after all. "What did you do?" I asked.

"The waiter insisted that my dish wasn't overcooked, and I said I was sorry my French was so awful that I was lost. After all, "blue" means red in French! I apologized and smiled, and everything worked out just fine. The chef himself brought out the replacement dish." Her face evinced self-satisfaction.

"Well done! I mean, nicely done. In France the customer is always wrong."

"And men are so confrontational! It's all about their egos. Happens all the time at swim meets when the opposing teams disagree about a referee call." (She was quite talkative when it came to competition, I thought.) "The male coaches go for the jugular, instead of doing an end run around the problem or looking for a solution that would satisfy both teams."

"Coaching is your true passion?" I asked.

She smiled as she heaped sugar into the remaining coffee in my cup and stirred vigorously. Then she dispassionately added, "I think I can help Scarface get what he wants a lot more adroitly."

I couldn't help but approve her approach, having once said myself that "To run straight at obstacles is to behave just like a bull. The point is to find a different path than the one where the obstacles lie—or, in any case, not to be especially interested in obstacles."* Still, I suspected that what Scarron wanted most was Durtal's job. "That sounds like fun to you?"

"Yes, I enjoy giving a guy what he doesn't have, what he's missing."

"She should be with the prefect," I thought to myself. One would be hard pressed to call that love, I reflected—it gave her a narcissistically gratifying role in which she could feel she was doing something praiseworthy and could maybe even feel superior to her partner—but at least she was giving something (even if it wasn't what she didn't have) …

"And what are *you* missing?" I asked with my signature indiscretion.

"Me?" She reflected, sipping my coffee. "Someone to give something to."

I smiled. Love truly is different things to different people.

"I was married before, you see."

"Oh?"

"To an alpha-male athlete who had it all. I don't think I ever found anything I could offer him."

"No one has it all," I opined.

185

"Maybe not, but I could never figure out what he was missing—unless it was a sense of humor."

The lady of the house came over to us and offered more revolting dirty socks water and industrially processed tea leaves. The swimmer accepted the former, although she suddenly looked confused by the presence of two mugs in front of her. In the end she held up both of them for refilling.

The owner and the solitary breakfaster left and we found ourselves alone in the dining room. Still, the house was centuries old, and doors sometimes existed in unexpected places in such ancient dwellings, so, after observing the Midwesterner for a few moments, I whispered, "Where are you at in your supercomputer negotiations?"

"The guy threatened last night to auction off his wares to the highest bidder if we don't cough up the machine within a week," she said right off the bat.

"If he tries to force your hand by informing the Russians or the Chinese that he has important advances to sell, he'll be placing himself in grave danger: they won't send," I held my tongue for a moment and then completed my sentence, "a nice coach like you to negotiate."

This did not seem to rattle her. Was she made of some kind of Michigan steel?

"He must know they don't pay, they just take," I added.

Calmly glancing out the window, she said, "We'll probably promise right away and then tell him delivery is going to take longer than we thought. He's impatient, but administrative wheels turn slowly."

"Well, I'm sure you will get your innovations in the end, and your team will be even more alpha," I said encouragingly. "By the way, you said you never found anything you could offer your ex-husband, but what did he offer you?"

"Good question, Canal," she replied, a response that is often, in my experience, a prelude to dodging the issue. She lapsed into silence, and receiving the impression something had occurred to her, I tilted my head a bit questioningly. "Security, I guess. It's hard to come by in my world. People betray you, renege on things …"

* * *

Fontevrault is, simply put, the largest abbey in the Western world. Ravaged by the French Revolution, it is now once again the most royal of all royal abbeys. In the greenest of valleys—known for its spring, the Fontaine d'Evrault—no less than five complete *moutiers* (the old French term for monasteries) stood within its walls, each with its own church and cloister, each welcoming a different community—lepers, nurses, daughters of the aristocracy, former prostitutes, and, worst of all, men (there is some debate about the rigid distinction between the third and fourth communities …). Whether or not the domed ceilings of its main church—the size of a cathedral—are original or not, nobody knows. Some say they are almost a thousand years old, others that they are quite recent.

They hold incredible concerts here, and the outbuildings alone can easily house the entire New York Philharmonic! Tonight the Symphonie de Provence was giving their penultimate concert in the vast, unparalleled refectory before heading back to the south of France, and I found the evening's program quite curious and irresistibly intriguing.

The notoriously controversial Robert d'Arbrissel founded the abbey at a time when priests were usually married. But for some mysterious reason, known perhaps only to himself, Robert sought out the company of single women to repeatedly put his chastity to the test, thereby endlessly atoning for his "sins of the flesh." It was not enough for him to flee females and live in the woods like a hermit or in a monastery surrounded only by men. He would sleep naked surrounded by nuns in order to continuously overcome temptation. (Not the sort of trial I would ever impose on myself …)

Despite his wish to lead a solitary contemplative existence, punctuated by torturous nights, he was inundated with followers from all walks of life. They were impressed by his religious fervor, preaching, and opposition to the scandalous, but lucrative, practice of pardons. He eventually accepted to found an abbey which became home to the daughters of kings and was forever run by them.

* * *

Having indulged my wine obsession with private tastings at the nearby Château de Villeneuve and the Domaine Saint-Just, I for once resisted the temptation to buy something in the boutique before visiting a Loire Valley monument. Instead I took a long, lingering walk around Fontevrault Abbey—covering only a small slice of its expansive grounds—hours before the concert was to begin.

I arrived, finally, at the enormous yet ethereal domed church and made my way to the transept. There, in front of me, were the prominently displayed remains and recumbent figures of the abbey's royal patrons: Richard the Lionhearted and his scary family. They exemplify almost every facet of human tragedy. They hated each other, betrayed each other, stole from each other …*

A few British tourists were taking snapshots of Richard—who would have sold London if he'd found a buyer—maybe hoping against hope that, after years of alternating whining and threats, England would finally manage to wangle the august figures from France.

A family of French city slickers approached. "Not bad for a monument out in the boondocks," the husband said.

"And the town! So totally cute," his wife concurred. "*Incroyable!*"

Fleeing such heathens, I hurriedly crossed through the abbey boutique on the way out to the village. Like Odysseus's men trying not to hear the Sirens' song, navigating between the Charybdis of volumes on medieval love potions, witches' brews, herbal remedies, and permaculture on one side and the Scylla of works on Richard the Lionhearted, his mother Eleanor of Aquitaine, different monastic orders, and Romanesque architecture on the other, my eyes nevertheless alighted on a book they were featuring, large stacks of it topped by a copy propped up on a stand. On the cover was da Vinci's famous drawing of a man inscribed in a circle with arms and legs wide apart, showing the proportions of the human body according to Vitruvius. Lifting the handsome publication from the stand, I read the words accompanying the cover image: *A Treatise on the Human Figure* by Leonardo da Vinci.

I flipped through the pages rapidly, noting well-known sketches by da Vinci of human faces—annotated with the proportions of the nose and nostrils, and the distances between the eyes, lips, chin, and ears—and of hands, arms, feet, and legs, their various proportions noted on them. The text accompanying them seemed to spell out da Vinci's mathematization of the human body, head, and face.

I strode over to a saleswoman and queried, "What do you know about this tome?"

Did I sound too eager? She turned away arrogantly and helped a blond Scottish lady select a book on the evil British Plantagenet dynasty, and then a little American boy who wanted to buy purple ink to put in his water pistol.

When his parents yelled and screamed, I spoke more forcefully: "The preface indicated that it was compiled by Francesco Melzi, da Vinci's amanuensis, right?"

"Well … yes. Pipe down, sir!"

I persisted in pestering her. "It was recently unearthed somewhere in Italy" (obviously not in Oxyrhynchus or Heraklion, I thought to myself). "Transcribed and simultaneously published in French and Italian, it just came in a couple of weeks ago. You had never heard of the press, but the book was proposed to you directly by an older man. Isn't that right?" I said all in one breath.

Her lips pinched at a couple of points while I was speaking and her big brown eyes half-closed. "Partially true," the civil servant uttered condescendingly, "except that the preface indicates that the manuscript was part of a huge trove of documents recently discovered in France. It is thought to have once been in François I's library at Fontainebleau." Feeling she had me on the run, she now moved in for the kill, "And it just came in yesterday," she said, obviously expecting me to be impressed that she'd learned so much in twenty-four hours. To drive the final nail in the coffin, she added, "A woman brought it."

"Can you describe her?"

The civil servant sighed. Could the French government ever pay her enough to answer such inane questions, she seemed to wonder. After a pregnant pause, she replied, "She had a thin face, somewhat scraggily gray hair, and was wearing heavy, baggy clothes. Crazy!"

"Crazy?"

"Yeah, it was like a hundred degrees out! Don't you remember?"

"I'd like the publisher's contact information, if you don't mind. And if you receive any more copies in person or hear from that woman again, please let me know right away, Mademoiselle," I said.

She lazily placed my calling card on the counter next to a million souvenirs made in China.

* * *

"Where did you find that bow tie?" a man asked. "Prague? New York? It's divine."

"Do you practice in the bathtub?" asked a younger woman. "Fully dressed? Or …?"

I sidled over to the gaggle of fans, being thirsty as is my wont and they just so happening to be hovering near the outdoor post-concert drinks table. The petulant concertmaster turned toward me—acting like he actually wanted to talk to me—shook my hand, and said, "Mr. Canal, I am quite flattered. At this point I can only believe that you are shadowing us."

I greeted his clique—all Parisians on vacation, I would have wagered—and replied, "Were I in the shadows, you most assuredly would not see me. I believe that the accepted term for someone like myself is *groupie*."

He smiled and took a step away from them, but they all followed.

"Quite an interesting program you prepared for us this evening," I remarked.

"Not I," he protested, "Wack. He was called away suddenly, or more likely *indisposed*."

The young woman smirked and looked at Civadin admiringly.

"Nothing serious, I hope," I said. Wack struck me as a space cadet when it came to love, but as, if anything, overly dedicated when it came to concerts.

"Probably a broken fingernail on his precious pinky," Civadin replied. "Or perhaps he stepped on his lucky baton again."

"You played Lanier, Handel, Scarlatti, and Steffani all in the same concert," I said casually. "Any particular reason?"

A few interested looks were directed at Civadin who regarded me unblinkingly for a moment. "You appear to have figured it out, Mr. Canal."

"Must we assume that it is, not exactly a subliminal message, but a veiled communication of some sort?" I asked.

"You'll have to ask Henri about the connection among the musicians," the concertmaster said, looking supremely uninterested.

"They all had more than one patron," I persevered. "Is Wack working for some foreign power?"

A slight frown attacked his brow as he replied, "He is quite possibly in the employ of the ruler of that region where the waters of the Acheron run deep, as I believe Freud, following Virgil, characterized the nether regions, *n'est-ce pas*?" The concertmaster's Parisian fans were all ears, eating up the abstruse and rarefied allusion. "But you would have to ask *him* about that." Smugly satisfied with having associated Wack with Mephistopheles, he gave a little snicker and the snooty group all laughed just in case something terribly oblique was meant by it.

"I'm not sure anyone would admit to having such connections," I bantered back.

Civadin stroked his chin, still looking pleased as punch.

"But there is a question that I believe I can ask *you*," I went on, despite the crowd, "if it isn't too personal, that is."

He looked at me expectantly—one can, I suppose, be bored even by adoring fans—and I said, "Have you been too busy to shave, or are you now growing a beard?" At Chenonceau, he appeared to have a day or two's stubble, which struck me as a bit odd since he was center stage. Now, a couple of days later, it looked deliberate. "Do you wish to look like a della Robbia?"

The snobby fans gathered around him did their best to hide their puzzlement.

"Your culture does you credit, Mr. Canal," Civadin conceded nobly. "You refer, undoubtedly, to François I's uproarious accident during the Three Kings Day festivities in Romorantin." He turned to his coterie. "François led a mock attack on the home of the 'bean king,' the man who had found the bean in the special Epiphany cake they had shared that day, and was allowed to play king for a day, naming whatever lady he liked as his queen. François could not tolerate this for long and gathered his fearless knights for a pseudo-assault on the man's lodgings. Carried away by the play fighting, one of the defenders threw a smoldering log out the window and accidentally hit François on the head. The doctors had to shave the royal head to allow the wound to heal. So he decided to grow a beard—and his courtiers, not to be outdone, promptly followed suit. The beard figures prominently on Girolamo della Robbia's bust of our beloved Renaissance king—on display at the Met in New York," he concluded magisterially.

"To turn now to your initial question, Mr. Canal, you and I have passed the age of seduction," he went on, with words I found quite unusual for a Frenchman in the prime of life, "and the concern with 'time's winged chariot,' so I, for one, prefer a look that befits my accomplishments." He stroked his whiskers fondly, as if they were a favorite new attribute. I wasn't sure his beard would give him the desired look, given how sparse it was. And the lightness of his hair color did little to help. But I let his silver tongue wag, savoring his recondite references.

"But Maestro, you look ever so young!" said a woman, as if dying to have his baby.

"We are accustomed, in the West," he continued, ignoring the come on, "to associate a full beard with mental stature, whether in philosophy or science. Indeed, our representations of the venerable sages of old are lent an air of seriousness by their abundant pilosity," he proffered pompously.

"Yet the appearance of wisdom hardly need go hand-in-hand with actual learning," I objected.

"'It is as possible for a man to know something without having been at school, as it is to have been at school and to know nothing,'"* he recited from memory.

Yet it was not Fielding's *Tom Jones* that was at the forefront of my mind at that precise moment—it was the frenetic race to acquire ever more diplomas, mere pieces of paper, instead of knowledge.

"I couldn't agree more," he resumed. "Yet such is human nature that the mass takes—or, rather, mistakes—appearance for reality. All the diplomas in the world and patches on the elbows of a corduroy jacket cannot transform an ignoramus into a man of science. Regrettable, perhaps, but—"

Other fans waiting in the wings—all young women this time—began approaching and, before they could interrupt us, I placed my hand on Civadin's forearm and seized the opportunity to say, "I know you told me that I would find nothing about the piece by Mozart you played at Chenonceau, and you were right. But I have also been unable to identify those by Bach and Haydn. Could you enlighten me on that score—or should I say, on those scores?"

"As I told you—"

"Oh there you are, you blue djinn, you!" came a feminine voice from my left, as a soft but determined arm intertwined with mine and tugged on it. "Who let you out of your bottle?" A woman's ribbing is always a joy to me, except when deliberately calculated to obstruct my designs. She added, "And how dare you make serious talk with your bosom buddy here when you could be charming the …" Françoise interrupted her own sentence, perhaps thinking better of the expression she was about to use, "Well, entertaining me!" Glancing at Civadin, she added coyly, "You will excuse him, won't you?"

The concertmaster nodded magnanimously. I never got my answer.

* * *

192

"Men are such selfish, stupid, retarded phonies and frauds!" Françoise declared—gaily on the outside, at least—as she nervously removed her black hairband and shook her head to free her locks. She was wearing yet another designer dress (regimental black again), accessorized with matching gold necklace and earrings that sparkled brightly, and a vivid fuchsia Hermès scarf—*très élégante*.

We were seated at a small table on the awfully quaint *place*—it is anything but square—at the center of the village of Fontevrault directly across from the abbey that is its lord and master. Françoise had taken charge, after she had released the concertmaster from my clutches, and all I was allowed to do was choose where I could enjoy her sweet, loving self afterward. The restaurant I had picked, *Le Comptoir des Vins*, specializes in wine, as the name indicates, and the owners had ditched high-powered jobs in the big city to root out the best organic and biodynamic wines in the country. They knew how to deal with stressed-out professionals and helped me choose one for the flautist. (The nuns who used to live in this unheated abbey apparently loved wine too, for they drank about six liters of it—nine of our contemporary bottles—per day, although the alcohol content wasn't as high as it is now.)

We had alighted upon one of Pabiot's dynamite Pouilly-Fumés— I certainly wasn't going to let a single musician choose anything, especially one who professed not to drink. She claimed to only like red wine and probably knew nothing more than Beaujolais Nouveau. But I was sure she'd enjoy this white anyway on this warm summer night. While waiting for the musicians to pack up their sheet music and instruments and file out of the nine-hundred-year-old abbey, like traveling minstrels of yore, toting their giant theorbos and violas da gamba over the worn cobblestones, I had taken the opportunity to relish the floral nose of the delicate sauvignon blanc and sample it—ambrosia of the gods!

"How such juvenile, dimwitted, sneaky cads ever manage to do anything or organize anything is beyond me," she went on. So that's what she wanted to talk about—men. Who was I to object? After all, she could have picked a far less interesting topic.

It struck me again tonight: whether musicians or not, most people are only too happy to talk about themselves and their own interests, concerns, and perspectives for hours on end. They chat away contentedly as long as you ask them questions, fall silent as soon as you stop, and cannot think of anything to ask you beyond the banal "So, how are you?"—a question rarely followed by additional probing. Which is all fine and good in my line of work—or should I say "lines"?—yet I confess that every now and then it can be a tad exasperating. It wasn't tonight, because my companion was lively and lovely, but I guess it must have gotten to me just a smidgen, otherwise why would I have brought it up only to deny it?

"I keep hoping I'll finally meet one who is a real man, not a mean, immature baby," she suddenly added. She glanced at Pabiot's colorful label and politely opined, "It looks amazing," even though it was conspicuously devoid of images of castles. Then—indifferent to the vintage, the varietal, or even whether it was red, white, or rosé—she directed her gaze to the unusual menu, which she happened to be holding upside down.

The owner—a man who can face down the Coca-Cola addicted crowds, and convince kids and adults alike to try instead a local "cola" made of plants and herbs—came by, looking as trim as ever, and we placed our order. I asked him if he would be so kind as to play a certain song. I suspected he had it in his unequaled collection of French and American jazz vinyls: Annisteen Allen's "I Want a Man." Deep dimples appeared as he grinned and nodded.

"They wear men's clothes, have low voices, and hair on their chins, but ..."

"They all disappoint you sooner or later?"

"It seems to be getting sooner and sooner all the time," she replied, finishing the first glass of the amber ambrosia I had poured for her, without averring tonight that she didn't drink.

"Might we be talking about a certain man with magic hands we both know?" I poured her a fresh glass. "The bloom is already off the rose? The spell he had on you has already worn off?"

"Henri's not the man I thought he was," she said.

"What kind of man did you think he was?" I asked quietly.

"The kind who could leave a prestigious orchestra at the tender age of twenty-five and found his own—no mean feat, especially in France. The kind who can direct thirty unruly musicians with overinflated egos and get them to play beautiful music together. The kind who can organize scores of concerts, hire and fire publicists—you know, a mover and a shaker."

"In short, a man who can do everything and needs no one?"

"Instead, he's pathetically insecure and greedy for reassurance. I don't know how I could've been so in love!"

194

"Perhaps it was not really *him* you were in love with."

Her face evinced surprise, but I wasn't sure whether it was at my uncommonly profound remark or at the giant black slate tile heaped with charcuterie, mostly Loire cheeses (Pouligny-Saint-Pierre, Sainte-Maure-de-Touraine, crottin de Chavignol, Selles-sur-Cher, Valençay, Trèfle), and multicolored vegetables that had just been set down in front of us.

"The greatest deception people suffer is from their opinions," I said, citing da Vinci's claim, "their own preconceptions," I added.

"What in the world does that mean?"

"Perhaps you were in love with a certain idea or ideal of a man, an ideal he did not live up to."

"Precisely. Why can't they be like men are supposed to be?"

I couldn't help smiling and asked provocatively, "You think maybe you fall for the wrong ones?"

"I used to think that, but I'm beginning to think there are no real men out there." Then, glancing at me, she hastily stuttered, "I mean ... Present company excluded, of course."

If you think that disclaimer duped me, you're not really paying attention, now are you? I looked at her dubiously.

Cutting herself a slice of the medieval round raw milk cheese on the slate tile, she said, "I never eat dairy products."

"Just like you don't drink?"

"No, the other woman in me doesn't eat dairy either," she said, cutting herself a second piece.

"Is it a religious thing?" I asked, pretty sure it wasn't. "Or are you vegan?"

"No, it's about cows."

"Cows?"

"I only like the dark-colored ones."

I cocked an eyebrow.

"Milk products make me think of the light-colored ones. They're creepy."

"Everybody's got their thing," I thought to myself. If I had had to guess I would have said she, like so many others repulsed by milk products, probably had qualms about her mother, but there you have it. I suspected it wasn't something I'd gain any clarity about tonight. "So what do you think of the Fourme d'Ambert?"

"Excellent," she nodded. Finally registering the fact that I was looking at her curiously, she added, "It's blue. It doesn't count."

The girl had an explanation for everything! Except maybe for men. I suddenly recalled what I had been about to say before our movable feast arrived. "Perhaps the problem is not with the men you meet but with your idea of them."

"Everyone knows what a real man is," she asserted reflexively, continuing to savor the licit blue cheese, or nondairy dairy.

"And a real woman? What is she?" I asked.

"That's easy: beautiful, kind, willing ..." She smiled broadly.

"Like yourself, then."

She blushed crimson.

"Never needy, whiny, insecure, or scared?"

"I didn't say that," she retorted. "But that's what a man is for—to reassure and protect her."

Interesting ... I was reminded of a line I'd heard back in the seventies about the formidable "modern woman": Claiming as she did to be both free and submissive, capricious and conventional, equal to men and yet in need of their protection, it was less dangerous to confront the thorniest political problems around the globe than her.* I wasn't about to go there. I mean women had the right to be as contradictory as they liked, after all. It didn't make things easy for men, but then who ever said they had to make it easy for them? As long as women understood themselves, why not? But did they?

Then again, why did they have to understand themselves? As if men understood themselves! Women just want whatever they want whenever they want it. Men are usually far more conflicted and can't decide what they want ...

Anyway, are people actually happier if they understand what they want? Maybe in business, because they can then try to go out and get it. But when it comes to love? Don't we all want things we think we don't want and vice versa? And want one thing now and something else later?

As you can see, I was on endlessly slippery ground, so I decided to simply echo back what Françoise had said, "That's what a man is for. Huh? So it's okay for a woman to complain, be unsure of herself, freak out about things, and want to be babied?"

"Yes and no," she replied, gazing inquisitively at the maze of delicacies before us. "We aren't strong and confident all the time."

"So it's because you aren't always strong and confident that you see it as a necessary quality in a man."

Her brow furrowed.

"It's because you despise your own lack of strength and confidence that you consider the lack of strength and confidence in a man to be a fatal flaw."

"What?"

"Flaws, like qualities, are in the eye of the beholder."

"How can you say that? You're mocking everything I just said."

"No, I'm not," I said more gently. "Could it be that the weaknesses you perceive in him bother you so much because you hate them in yourself?"

She made a face like she'd just seen a slug on the delectables we were about to share and quaffed her second glass of wine all in one go.

"Try to think about it," I continued. "Maybe you despise any need in him to be reassured about his musical talent, success, or desirability because you despise your own? If you were confident about all those things, why would it bother you if he wasn't? Wouldn't that just be his problem, not yours?" Was I really, I wondered, the only one who grasped this basic fact? Okay, so they don't teach such obvious truths in college, and it's hardly the stuff of radio talk shows where people get the thumbs up or down based simply on how many listeners agree with you that your boyfriend's a loser.

"Everything we despise in others reflects something we despise in ourselves?"

I raised both eyebrows this time.

"If I am annoyed by an infantile guy's bad taste in socks, it's because it reminds me of my own?" The little skeptic laughed at me, almost choked on a carrot, and ended up hiccupping nonstop like Aristophanes.

This gave me the opportunity to smile at her feeble attempt to dismiss what I was saying, and go on, after refilling both her wine and water glasses, naturally, "If you think a guy's social savvy is his most important quality, it's probably because you feel you lack such savvy. If you felt perfectly at ease in every social setting, why would you care if the guy you are with doesn't?"

She seemed to be internally debating the point, trying not to give too much weight to all this. Ignoring the water, she swallowed half the wine I'd just poured but seemed to capitulate a mite.

"You're going to say, 'Wouldn't that just be his problem, not mine?'"

I nodded, as I signaled to the owner to bring another bottle of the same. "And maybe you secretly admire his fatal flaw of acting like a needy baby because you'd like to act like one yourself but would never allow yourself to."

197

"Every flaw I see in him says as much about me as about him?"

"Maybe more. And when you hate something with a passion, as they say, it usually means you secretly love it too."

* * *

The song I had requested, "I Want a Man," finally came on, and Annisteen Allen's voice wafted out onto the square.

> I want a man who will squeeze me,
> I want a man who will tease me,
> He's got to please me …
> He can hop like a frog,
> Have a nose like a hog,
> He can buzz like a bee,
> Fly like a bird in a tree,
> He can be short and squatty
> Long as he loves nobody but me.

Now *there* was a woman who knew what she wanted and wasn't put off by what most ordinary mortals would consider fatal flaws! François I's nose wasn't exactly like a hog's, but it must have taken some deliberate ignoring on his mistresses' parts. I wasn't sure if Françoise had grasped all of the words—especially that odd rhyme of "squatty" with "nobody"—but she seemed to be listening. Indeed, I had the sense she was reveling in the good old jazz as she held out her glass for me to serve her anew. It isn't done, I know, but she did it anyway. I gave her the last few drops in the bottle.

For once she sipped the exceptionally floral elixir as one ought to. "I would have said it bothers me if a male isn't strong, self-assured, and socially savvy because it means he isn't a real man. An awkward teenager, maybe, but certainly not a man. And what would it say about me if I'm dating a dork?" Her face clouded over and she appeared to be lost in thought.

The new bottle arrived perfectly chilled, and the popping of the cork seemed to shake her out of her daze.

"So that's the question," I remarked, "what would it say about you? You're worried you'll be seen as not so hot if you're with someone who's occasionally insecure?"

"It takes two to make a power cou—" She interrupted herself, "I mean, a popular couple. I can't show up with Forrest Gump in tow!"

"A power couple, you started to say?" I picked up on her censored formulation. "So it's power you're looking for? Not love?"

She looked confused. "That's nonsense! They go hand in glove."

"Do they? Isn't loving someone different from getting off on being with someone powerful?" I'd met many who were fascinated by power in its varied forms—money, prestige, military might, charm—and who ditched friends and family to associate with big kahunas, frantically trying to get close to them, ride their coattails, or at least have some of their aura rub off on them.

"That depends on what you mean by loving someone."

"I mean not just being infatuated, but showing love, engaging in loving acts."

"You're off your chardonnay rocker, jumbling everything together with your tortured logic," she protested. "You can't separate—"

"What an unpleasant surprise."

We both looked up, startled.

"Just my luck—I finally finish packing up all the symphony's equipment, only to find *you* here. I bet the bar's closed too. Well, at least you've been keeping my seat nice and warm for me."

The rudeness of the jackanapes' manners startled me anew. Even compared to the musicians he worked for, who were often impolite, if not downright offensive. I pointed out a free chair at a nearby table and he looked at it as though it were a trap of some kind. I probably hoped he would sit over there and ruin somebody else's evening, and maybe even that the chair would shatter with a terrible crash and Enrique would be swiftly spirited away to sound engineer's hell—I can't recall now if the thought flashed through my mind at the time. (And if you believe that, I'll tell you another.) Misery might love company, but the company didn't have to love misery.

"Still getting wet for this Victorian dinosaur? What the fuck!" he said to Françoise.

"Excuse me, but I'm sitting right here!" I exclaimed, taking him to task for his appalling lack of courtesy, "and my name is Canal, Mister Canal to you." I didn't care if I sounded like Hercule Poirot, relic of a long-lost era.

"Yeah, yeah, Your Royal Snooziness," he feigned a bow as he pulled up a chair and plopped down on it.

"Do you have to be so darn disagreeable all the time?" I asked with forced politeness.

"Do you have to be so goddamned bourgeois?" he barked, refusing to match my urbane tone. "Life sucks and people are assholes." He obviously was not one to jump on the surfboard of life and enjoy riding the waves wherever they might take him. He picked up a piece of ham from the slate in the middle of the table with his fingers and stuffed it in his gaping gullet.

After my tense exchange with Françoise, I didn't have much patience left for Enrique and went straight to the point. "I can understand that you don't like seeing me with Françoise. You obviously have a thing for her, and I can fully understand why. How long are you going to wait before you tell her? You think the universe is going to pick her up and drop her into your lap."

"I, I …," he stuttered.

"Stammering won't get you anywhere. Little boys act mean to girls they like, pulling their hair and lifting their skirts. You think you are demonstrating your affection by acting like you do? Like everything is wrong with the world and everyone in it except you?"

"Oh, I make no exceptions—I'm just as fucking screwed up as the rest. Maybe worse. Definitely worse, in fact."

"So what's your problem—you think Françoise is out of your league?"

He suddenly melted like cheap ice cream left out in the sun. "I'm just a techie with no education, no …" he broke off.

"Really? I thought you needed to have at least a bachelor's to be a sound engineer."

"Well, yeah."

"So you must've gone to college for a few years." He stared at his black shoes. "Or maybe you just told Wack you did."

"College! The lamest shit!"

"Enrique is a fine sound engineer and always does a fabulous job for us," Françoise said, pleading with her eyes for me to stop.

"I'm sure he does. He's just pretending to be someone he's not."

"Well, we're all holograms, robots, really, just following out what we've been programmed to do, for fuck's sake. What about you, Canal? Are—"

"Mr. Canal."

"Sir Canal," he bowed sarcastically. "Aren't you just doing exactly what you were raised to do? Visiting stodgy old castles and going to hear classical music because your parents or friends told you they were marvelous and fascinating? You can't tell me that music gets you hard! It's supposedly so sophisticated, but it's just a bunch of boring, starchy highbrows sitting around congratulating themselves on being better than everyone else." He shot me a black look, yawning conspicuously all the while, without covering his big yap. "What good is it if you can't even tap your foot to it, if it doesn't get your blood boiling and your mojo rising?"

"And what kind of music does that for you?" I asked stiffly.

"Techno, electro, house, trance—those are here to stay," he proclaimed loudly and rammed another piece of prosciutto into his maw.

"I'm sure you don't believe that," I rejoined. "It's the most repetitive music ever made. Except maybe Indian music for meditation or ceremonial purposes. How can you even dance to that stuff?" I didn't care if I sounded like I was a hundred and hopelessly out of touch. The fact is that I like to dance more than most and, when the music is right, I'm usually the last to leave the dance floor.

"It's *made* for dancing!" he cried defiantly.

"A song has to have words and stanzas and choruses," Françoise interjected, "otherwise I can't dance to it either."

"Freaking snobs! I'm not sorry to say it to you," he said looking at me, "but I'll get you to change your mind Françoise, if you let me take you to a club I know."

"He actually asked her out," I marveled to myself. "I guess I managed to push the right button."

"Monsieur Canal," came a strident voice.

The voice came from an automobile that had pulled up right next to us.

I excused myself, laid a few bills on the table, and jumped in the car with Commissioner Le Coq, while the two lovebirds looked on all agog.

CHAPTER FOURTEEN

Saumur Castle

With juice of cursed hebenon in a vial.

—Shakespeare, *Hamlet*

As one woman ripped me from another woman's arms—well, not exactly her arms, her presence at least—I wondered briefly if I had lost control of my life. Did women now call all the shots? Or had they always? Aristophanes (yes, him again) seemed to think they did already eons ago.

"I see you drink rosé with every woman in France," the copper exclaimed, interrupting my musings. "Thank God you mentioned you were going to a concert here this evening. I was sure I would find you out front, having a nip, and you were."

"It was white wine." She appeared to have forgotten that I'd had to content myself with coffee in Langeais while she enjoyed her jovial rosé.

"What do you know about stinkweed?" she asked with no segue.

"Stinkweed? The plant with the pretty white trumpet flowers you find in everyone's backyard?"

"*Datura stramonium*, as it's known in Latin. It's one of what they call the witches' weeds, along with henbane—maybe you've heard that name?"

"Claudius pours it in the King's ear in *Hamlet*." Take it from me—knowledge of literature always comes in handy, sooner or later. "Shakespeare called it 'hebenon.'"

"I knew it!" she exclaimed.

"You knew what? I guess the bard altered the name a bit. It also goes by jimson weed, locoweed, and moonflower."

"Dammit! You should be helping me solve this case instead of drinking and chasing women on every street in France!"

"It also tends to make people crazy, I hear," I added, unperturbed.

"Right again. Teenagers who take stinkweed to get high never take it a second time, the trip is so bad. It's time to focus that brain of yours on serious matters," she snapped.

"And this is leading where?"

"To Saumur."

François I visited Saumur, I reflected in a flash, during his 1518 trek westward through Ussé, Chinon, Montsoreau, Fontevrault, and on to Angers. Did he see the double spiral staircase there—or what we might more legitimately call a staircase within a staircase—the year before breaking ground at Chambord? I was sure he did. Had Leonardo tagged along with his royal patron on this particular trip? He might have. But what did all these stairs have to do with this case? Should I be thinking of "stares" instead? There's no such homonym in French, but still …

Yet François I's visit was almost modern history compared to the site's history. Our old pal Thibault the Trickster fortified an already existing abbey there, which Foulques Nerra proceeded to burn to the ground, I recalled.* A wooden castle soon replaced it, but it too was burnt to a crisp—along with the whole town—by a powerful lord to the south.** I guess fire outperformed firepower at the time. Maybe it still does—think of California's forest fires.

The Angevin counts learned their lesson and built a castle keep out of stone. The stone keep's exact location was finally discovered in 1993. Interesting number, I thought. And where was it? Right in the courtyard of the far more forbidding fortress, erected over six hundred years ago, that still today reaches skyward with its four giant white towers and imposing twenty-six-foot-high ceilings!

"To *L'Orangeraie*, the restaurant at Saumur Castle," I heard the commissioner add after she sped past a huge Dutch motorhome with a funny yellow license plate and a peloton of bicycles hanging off the back.

"Is that where they feed the droogies from *A Clockwork Orange*?"

"It's no laughing matter," she retorted. She seemed to be furious at me, believing I was slacking off. Then again, she might be furious at herself and finding it more satisfying to attribute our lack of progress to me. There might even have been a tinge of self-reproach on my part—for tasting wines and dining out instead of devoting myself to the investigation—that I was attributing to her. You never know for sure. I am, after all, an incorrigible hedonist, in case you hadn't noticed, a firm believer that "all work and no play makes Jacques ..."—well, you know the rest.

She looked at me askance like I was I was a damned nuisance, and as if silently impugning my training and dedication.

I tried to focus. "At Chenonceau, it was *L'Orangerie*, and at Saumur it's *L'Orangeraie* ..."

"One of their diners began looking wildly around the room, as if he were hallucinating. He got physical, too, and eventually passed out—well, not exactly. The medics said he was in a coma by the time they arrived."

"Poison?"

"His symptoms strikingly resemble those caused by stinkweed. The staff did well to stop him from leaving the restaurant. Given how disoriented he was, reeling and staggering about, he might well have fallen from one of the high parapets around the citadel into the moat."

"Maybe that was the plan," I thought to myself.

We were speeding toward Saumur—known as the pearl of the Anjou region—from the north shore of the Loire and could already see the brightly illuminated castle high up on the hill dominating the town. Although a mighty fortress, it somehow managed to appear simultaneously to be a fairy-tale palace, and I thought once again of the famous image of it in the fifteenth-century *Très riches heures du Duc de Berry*, with its forest of sculpted dormer windows, chimneys, and corbeled turrets and bartizans. "The castle of castles," as its PR staff call it now, its hallowed walls are considered so sacred that it took a year and a half for the staff to obtain authorization from the ministry that protects historical monuments to put up a simple "Don't climb on the ramparts" sign.

I wondered what made it different from the other castles. In the gloomy darkness, I realized it certainly didn't fit into alphabetical order. Was there a clue somewhere we were overlooking that had something to do with the castle itself?

Joan of Arc slept there, naturally, after joining forces with Charles VII in Chinon. The palace also hosted such illustrious swashbucklers as Richard the Lionhearted and John Lackland, as well as one of the biggest parties ever held on the planet: the "Nonpareille" thrown by King Saint Louis in 1241 (rivaling Belshazzar's?).

Good King René of Anjou hosted a giant bash of his own there, the "pas de Saumur," in 1446. It wasn't until over five hundred years later that some of the ramparts slid down the hill into the town, but you can be sure they had been weakened by all that jousting and reveling. (Don't worry: unlike Humpty Dumpty, they were able to put them back together again.) Imagine throwing such a great clambake that it goes down in history, receiving its own unique name! My musings were, as you see, going nowhere, unless thinking about what sort of unforgettable, lavish luau I could throw amounted to progress …

We had to approach the castle's steep butte in a roundabout fashion, surrounded as it was by high walls. The restaurant was located in an old stone outbuilding to which a modern glass veranda had been added that gave directly out onto the towering fortress.

The victim—a certain J. Livingston—lived in Washington State, the stiff Angevin commissioner told us. He hadn't reserved a table in advance, and had been willing to accept one inside, ceding the glorious view from the patio to those who had been lucky enough to secure a table there before he arrived around six-thirty in the evening. (That's very early for France, but the restaurant was usually open only during castle visiting hours.) He had joked with the waitress as solitary male diners are wont to do, especially when selecting wine, making her laugh at his poor pronunciation of French names as he tried to say *les Perrières*. But he still had managed to ask the people at a nearby table about the local dessert they had ordered, because it looked very unusual to him, the light and creamy *crémet d'Anjou*. He never got a chance to taste it.

"Maybe he never will," I reflected, for I knew that when the toxicity of the plants is higher than usual or the dose is especially large, stinkweed can lead to death.

After his main course arrived, the maître d' had lost sight of the man— who lived on the other side of the planet in Seattle, and worked for Northrop Grumman—for a few minutes after he dashed into the back, past the polished walnut bar. We asked the commissioner for a copy of the list his team had drawn up of Livingston's fellow patrons that evening and took a gander around the place for ourselves. The dining room was a shambles, with tables overturned and broken glass strewn all about.

Wandering around, I noticed small vases on the tables still standing containing freshly cut flowers, and some of the tables had a second vase on them that was empty. The maître d' explained that a woman would often come in during meals and sell roses to the buoyant crowd. The restaurant would provide vases for the roses, but almost everyone took the flowers home with them. "But it was not Antoinette this evening. It was some other woman."

"Did she come around the same time Livingston went to the men's room?" Le Coq queried, seeming desperate to extract something from the crime scene.

The I-see-a-thousand-tourists-an-hour maître d' merely shrugged his shoulders.

* * *

The crenelated city hall and the stately Counter-Reformation Ardilliers convent we passed at the edge of town could have served as sets for major motion pictures, and Saumur suddenly disappeared in the rear-view mirror as we drove back toward Fontevrault. The Loire was our only companion, the mighty waterway looking like a silver sliver in the darkness. I reflected that I hadn't a clue. Was the river that I so love the thread that connected all these violent incidents?

I felt easier knowing our poisoning victim wasn't dead. Yet Le Coq looked like he had expired right in her arms. I tried to lighten the atmosphere—after all, anxiety doesn't improve one's ability to solve problems, it compromises it. Only psychologists are dumb enough to claim otherwise. (Well, maybe I did once when I solved the so-called three-prisoner problem—long before anyone else, I'm sure—one of those logical conundrums people used to talk about at swank Parisian cocktail parties before the advent of Twitter).

"How are things with your new paramour?" I asked. After their lunch in Chenonceau, arranged by yours truly, the lock and the unfindable key were to dine together tomorrow night.

"I never talk about myself," she declared forlornly.

"You don't?"

"I prefer to talk about others," she explained. "No one listens when you talk about yourself, anyway."

I looked at her. She was not unwise for her age—indeed, she had a point, even if *I* listened. I was, after all, one in a million.

In spite of herself she said, "Started texting me almost every hour from the time we left *L'Auberge*."

I shook my head disapprovingly, a movement she probably couldn't see given the hour. How dark the valley was that night! Saumur Castle's magical lighting was long gone.

"After the first couple of messages, I barely answered anymore, but I got the impression that merely made things worse. Daniel just seemed to get more overwrought."

"Hmm," I grunted. That, at least, was a problem *I'd* never had, I thought, making a mental note to call him later and observing that she'd conveyed something significant about herself while talking about someone else.

CHAPTER FIFTEEN

Montsoreau, Candes, Ussé

Only the paranoid survive.

—Andy Grove

Fontevrault Abbey was still partly illuminated despite the late hour. It offered a sharp contrast to the dark countryside we'd been driving through in somber mood. The village was totally deserted, except for a black cat and a lone woman wearing a long, dark, flowing robe of some kind. She might have passed for the last of the abbesses who ran the place, but was probably a grandmother feeding the feral felines.

We carefully turned into the grand entrance of the recently renovated Logis Bourbon and stopped at the only car left near the high stone walls surrounding the parking lot. There I gave the commissioner the carabiner, still in its plastic bag, for fingerprinting.

"I'm going to ask you another favor," I said, as we stood alone in the peaceful silence of the night. "You live in one of the most beautiful areas in the world, so beautiful that I'll set a novel here if I ever get around to writing one." She gazed at me, her long curly hair shining brightly in the moonlight. "I know you have an embarrassment of riches to choose from," I continued, "but would you meet me in Chinon tomorrow for lunch?"

She refused to drive off until she ensured my car did not explode when I turned the key in the ignition. *Quelle imagination!*

I followed the vehicle of the comely yet *coincée* (reserved, inhibited) copper slowly through the narrow streets of the village, then down the hill to Montsoreau, which was also slumbering under the starry sky. But there we parted ways, she living on the north side of the Loire—perish the thought—and me residing on the south side. Maybe she didn't even truly live in the Valley!

With the river just a few yards to my left, I passed beneath the mighty walls of Montsoreau Castle, whose name everyone in France recognizes, it being forever associated with a man's love for a beautiful married woman, the Lady of Montsoreau, and the vengeance wreaked on him by her heartless husband. Alexandre Dumas apparently took rather a lot of poetic license with the life of the lady, Françoise de Maridor, as writers so often do—it seems she was quite enamored of her husband and bore him numerous children! As Mark Twain famously said, never let the truth get in the way of a good story.

I couldn't understand why the castle itself wasn't better known, when it was the only true Loire castle, its glowing white walls having been formerly lapped directly by the river's waters. Boats could moor at its lowest doors, and the big iron rings they tied up to are still visible. Wine and grain were unloaded directly into its perpetually cool, vaulted, windowless storage cellars, along with highly prized, life-saving salt, essential for animal husbandry and for preserving foods in eras without refrigeration. Contrabanders, trying to escape the unpopular salt tax, ferried the white staple up and down the Loire in specially designed flat-bottomed boats while royal agents tried to sniff them out. Such boats (minus the salt) are the only ones now authorized on a long stretch of the waterway, and they still sail peacefully by the castle, which remains one of the finest examples of largely unadulterated medieval architecture. You really should see it someday—at least the outside, for you'll have quite a surprise when you look inside.

The rising moon shimmered every shade of orange as it admired its own reflection in the river, but hadn't yet begun to eclipse the stars shining brightly over the water. With Montsoreau at my back, I crossed the ancient but invisible Roman boundary between Anjou and Touraine, and entered what I had long considered to be the most picturesque village in the entire Loire Valley: Candes-Saint-Martin. Ascending the narrow street to the main square, I parked briefly—something you can only attempt at night as there's no room for cars—and decided to walk around, admiring the sole truly fortified church in the region, a giant hulking in the darkness of the somnolent scene, protecting the town with its four mighty defensive towers. Villagers and monks alike would climb the narrow spiral staircase to man the collegiate church's machicolated battlements, arrow slits, loopholes, and gun loops when attacked.

I didn't take the time to walk down to the lower village that virtually waded into the swift waters of the Loire and the Vienne rivers, which join forces here, but promised myself I would return soon to stroll through the maze of flowered cobblestone-paved alleyways and gaze at the prospect from the *confluence*, the little beach directly across from the town. The French postal service's engravers came here to preserve in stamps the harmonious way the flock of white stone and black-slate-roofed houses and small castles rise up from the river, hug the massive yet reassuring church on all sides, and climb the hill behind it to its very summit.

Touraine by night—what a delight! I could loudly trumpet it as a new form of tourism, but it's probably better to reserve it for myself and …

Wistfully taking the wheel anew, I tried to concentrate on the investigation, yet my thoughts ineluctably drifted to the beauty and rich symbolism of all that humankind had built here over the centuries. So many incredible sites, all connected historically and architecturally.

"Focus Quesjac," I scolded myself.

"A huge but marvelous failure" someone had once said about our attempt to comprehend prime numbers. Well, my failure was not that huge, for my hypothesis that this case involved them had been refuted only if one assumed the Saumur incident was connected to the others, for it had occurred on July 8th. Yet the crimes, like the primes, seemed to arise at random times and places. Well, the places were actually not as random as all that, monuments open to the public being key. Was it the kings and queens who built these witnesses to the past, the architects who designed them, or the symbolism they embodied that had unleashed someone's ire? I should check if anything had happened at Villesavin or Villeprévost in the last two days, but something had indisputably happened on the seventh at Chenonceau and on the eighth at Saumur. So, unless the incident at Chenonceau was not related to the others, Fibonacci was also out. I had no real lead to go on except—

What the hell? What was happening?

213

The route I was taking was no longer a tiny one between hamlets, but a slightly more trafficked road. The impossibly white headlights—which thankfully most cars in France didn't yet have—of a black BMW were hurting my eyes even just in the rearview mirror. It had been directly behind me a few minutes ago, another car having come between us at the last roundabout.

Streetlights now appeared and the Beamer was no longer in sight. I slowed down as I passed through Ussé with, on my right, the giant fairy-tale castle—visited by François I, with his number one painter, engineer, and architect possibly in tow. Its numerous wings built in different centuries and pepper-pot roofs were not lit up at this late hour, and it looked like a great white whale. Sleeping Beauty Castle, as it is known the world over, was usually hopping, but was fittingly slumbering now. Not a cat stirred as I passed beneath the imposing gardens (designed by Versailles's head landscape architect, Le Nôtre) and on through the town that was dozing peacefully at its feet, awaiting the breathless arrival of Prince Charming on his white stallion.

I had traversed a few more villages, where anyone taking this winding road could have turned off, when xenon headlights abruptly reappeared in my side-view mirror. Was it the same car? At this witching hour, it might be. Up ahead was the Lignières church, famous for the ocher-colored medieval frescoes in its chancel. I wouldn't have time to run in and ring the church bells to raise the alarm, so I decided to take a little detour in order to see if the car with the painfully white beams would follow suit.

It did.

Had someone concluded I was involved in all this? Was some sort of net closing in on me? From being the apparent hunter, it seemed I had become the hunted, like Actæon. From being the predator, I had become the unwitting prey.

I accelerated, and then turned right on a tiny road known primarily to cyclists—the Loire Valley now being a mecca for long- and short-distance bikers. It was the kind of road most American drivers (especially chums from Texas) would scrupulously avoid, feeling it was designed to be a one-way, not a two-way street, and led only to the smallest of hamlets, even if it was a cute one: La-Chapelle-aux-Naux. The lane through it is windy, and almost invisible bumps slow you down—unless, of course, you're not worried about losing your transmission.

The car followed, and I accelerated still more. The road was built on a berm designed to keep the Loire from flooding all of the farmland to the south, which it used to do up until recent times. We soon arrived at the point at which the Cher River, in which the coach from Ann Arbor had taken a little swim, flows into the Loire. The road next parallels the Cher itself toward Villandry, where Hervé Castillo was no doubt dreaming of chess moves or fantasizing about the Riemann zeta function. After a short stretch of terribly bumpy cobblestones, dreaded by cyclists young and old, I pretended to turn right and then very abruptly turned left instead, put the pedal to the metal, and looked out the rearview mirror. The car behind me swerved and went off the road into a ditch.

I dialed 17 (the French equivalent of 911) five minutes later when I arrived at my B&B and told them where they would find the car. I didn't go to take a looksee at the driver myself as I didn't have my gun on me that evening and hoped to see more of the world before I passed over to the other side.

CHAPTER SIXTEEN

The town of Chinon

Sleep is not, death is not;
Who seem to die live.

—Emerson

"There's a call for you, Monsieur Canal—or should I say King François?" A roar of laughter accompanied this new way of addressing me (which I could get used to, by the way), emanating from the husband of the curmudgeonly woman who ran my B&B. He was the antithesis of his life partner—it happens often enough, and maybe has something to do with the maintenance of cosmic balance—and the polar opposite of your typical Parisian hotel owner: a kind, funny *bon vivant*.

"How do you mean?" I asked, putting on my jacket and adjusting my bow tie.

"I'm reading that book you lent me," the one on François I's lady friends. "I didn't realize the king had so many mistresses. And I can't help noticing that, every time there's a call for you, it is from a woman, and she always gives a name like that of one of his mistresses!"

I guess I wasn't the only one who was starting to feel like the clock had been turned back five hundred years, as though I had been transported, by some da-Vinci-inspired time machine, back into the Renaissance world of love, beauty, and daily brushes with death.

"Are you François I's great great great great grandson or his reincarnation?"

"Now don't be jealous," I told him as I made my way to the phone in the lobby (it was actually a glorified mudroom), and he chuckled again. I would be jealous were I in his shoes, though not if I knew the real reasons why these female correspondents were calling. I couldn't attribute their assiduity to my distinguished appearance, perfect manners, or taste in wine, alas! And having had such a close shave last night, I felt a bit more like Henri III or IV—kings assassinated by fanatics—than like François I.

"Inspector Canal," an overwrought voice greeted me. "You asked me to call if I remembered anything." I looked for a door to close in the dark, dank space—perfect for growing mushrooms, not humans—but could find none. I spoke as quietly as I could.

"Indeed, I did." At the time, the pain in the neck at Amboise Castle had seemed to think a few weeks made something ancient history which human memory would never be able to dredge up, and that I was, as usual, a weirdo! But the mind works in mysterious ways and things *can* float back into consciousness, even from decades past. She may have been mocking me inside, but the message I had sent her had nevertheless arrived at its unconscious destination, as it always does.*

"I have to admit, I thought it was incredibly dumb when you recommended that I let my mind drift." (I always have to put up with nonsense like that.) "You told me to give myself a couple of days. It seemed too long ago to me—what, three weeks now?"

"But something did come back?"

"There was someone who struck me around that time," Marie Gaudin replied. "I can't swear it was that exact Wednesday, I'm afraid."

"Go on."

"It was late in the day. I remember that because I was finishing up my last guided tour of the afternoon, shuttling some thirty people out of the Louis XII-François I wing, and you know—a few were eating gelato during the visit, letting it drip everywhere, and one ducked under the rope to touch da Vinci's tomb." The rush of words seemed to hide some kind of embarrassment. "A bunch of them started playing frisbee as we crossed the lawns and one of them tripped pretty badly and took a picture of his foot and sent it to Monaco where he said he knew a specialist at a—"

"Didn't you say François XII?" I chipped in.

"Of course not! There is no François XII."

"Right. Now you were saying you were coming out of the Louis XII-François I wing, and ..."

"So I was shuttling them out into the gardens," she sighed, "and a man was blocking the door, trying to enter just as we were all trying to exit. At first I thought he was from Translovenia—"

"You mean Transylvania?"

"Whatever. Now listen! The tourists I teach are oddballs in every way imaginable, like this Brit who asked if da Vinci's *Mona Lisa* secretly represented the poison-breathing Hydra of Lerné on a goat's body, like it says in *The Da Vinci Code*, and if—"

"Is he the one who struck you?" I asked, cutting short her toxic captivation with vampires and dark creatures whose blood is so venomous you can die just from smelling it.

"Of course not! The one in the doorway. It came back to me yesterday when I was standing in the exact same spot. I can't work here anymore—I'm asking for a transfer," she added breathlessly.

"He threatened you?"

"No, I just can't sleep at night ever since I remembered."

"What?"

"I remembered," she finally uttered. "He had a hump. Like he came from a different time."

Why people are embarrassed to say such things is beyond me, especially a tour guide whose job it is to tell her prisoners about François I's first wife, Claude de France, who had a hump, limp, and strabismus. How could *that* have been the fright of her life, impelling her to ask to be transferred?

"Is that all?" I prompted her, as she seemed to have lapsed into silence in the middle of a thought, which is always a sign of reluctance to say what is on one's mind, maybe even on the tip of one's tongue. "Don't worry if what you want to express strikes you as silly or stupid." After all, we can work wonders with stupidities.*

"I remember thinking he was the most hideous man I had ever seen!"

"Hadn't she seen hundreds of ghastly figures before on TV?" I wondered to myself.

* * *

"Monsieur Canal?" came the same voice as five minutes earlier. "There is another call for you—it's Brigitte Bardot!"

I came around the corner and regarded him with curiosity. It wasn't impossible, as we had mutual acquaintances, but all the same …

The owner handed me the phone and reluctantly exited the mudroom.

It was a man for once.

"Recused himself?" I asked, surprised that the scientist who had been asked to evaluate Bouture's article had just bailed out of the peer review process. "Does that sort of thing often happen so late in the game?" Was the field of oenology, I wondered, so different from others? Or were all the professors so busy advising winemakers—to attach computer chips to bottles of Margaux, for example, in order to guarantee their condition when they sell them in Hong Kong for thirty thousand dollars each—that they had no time left for research?

"Never," Professor Sarment replied, strangely talkative. "People bow out only at the outset, when I first approach them to ask if they'll review a paper. They let me know they are personal friends or foes of the author and can't objectively assess his work."

"The referee's name and number?"

He hemmed and hawed. The French—especially urbanites—don't easily give away personal information. What, did he think I was dangerous or somehow behind this setback for his journal?

"Don't force me to subpoena the information or you'll be spending the day at the county courthouse tomorrow for obstruction of justice," I menaced.

He made it sound like he was searching far and wide for it in his file cabinets, when it was obviously in a computer database. His precious journal was more important to him than people's lives, it seemed.

He finally divulged the reviewer's name at the University of Bordeaux.

"Did this professor Chimmi give any reason for recusing himself?" I asked. I knew that oenologists there thought they were God's gift to the wine world. They sold their services to the highest bidder—often, indeed, to all bidders! Had Chimmi grasped the ramifications of Bouture's groundbreaking research and realized they would displease the very corporations that funded Chimmi's research? That was the way it usually worked in academe, universities having their hands in company pockets and kowtowing to their will.

220

"Pressure regarding the research," the professor said coldly. "He didn't say whether he'd been pressured to praise it or pan it." Sarment sounded distant.

"Pressure? What kind? No more trips to five-star hotels in Argentina and Hong Kong?"

"The man said he was threatened with death by a thousand cuts," Sarment snapped.

"You mean a thousand cuts in funding for gala dinners with celebrities, a thousand less euros for a table at *la Fête de la Fleur*?"*

I heard a click. The professor had hung up on me.

* * *

I quickly placed a call myself before exiting the cubbyhole. It soon went to voicemail. I suspected the prefect was too bent out of shape to answer, news of the events in Saumur having made it into the morning paper I had glanced at in the B&B foyer. Love being my primary preoccupation, I left a brief message.

"Stop texting her!" were my only words to this brain-dead man who had met a willing doe but could end up losing her before dinner.

* * *

"What if the thread that linked all of these incidents was neither prime numbers nor a Fibonacci series but a person? a man? a king?" I wondered, as I took the wheel anew to head for Chinon, happy I'd be driving there in broad daylight. "Could it be François I?" Front and center here was his relationship with Leonardo da Vinci, not with the many women who gravitated around him: mother, sister, wife, and myriad mistresses. In every instance, the *Roi Chevalier* (the Knight King, as he was known, who adored tales of the Knights of the Round Table and fancied himself the head of its French incarnation) had, strangely enough, either built the castle where a crime occurred, frequented it, or confiscated it and then given it away. He had grown up primarily at Amboise Castle and added a wing to it, built Chambord from the ground up, indirectly financed the construction of Chenonceau by his treasurer, Thomas Bohier, lent the Clos Lucé to da Vinci (right after persuading his mother to buy it), and likely brought his entire entourage of ladies, poets, and friends with him to the royal town of Saumur and to Villandry too.

221

I've made a career out of connecting ostensibly unrelated dots, but his possible role here didn't make much sense, even to me! Yet the Symphonie de Provence got me thinking along such lines. The orchestra had not played at absolutely every one of the venues in question, but strange things had undeniably occurred at several of them or a mere twenty minutes away. Their final concert in the area was scheduled for July 10th …

It had all started at Chambord on the staircase François I had sanctioned if not designed himself. Two internationally famous directors had been in the vicinity that evening, Wack having arrived in Blois the day before his concert and Avid Sapristi—Wack's nemesis even after all these years, and a diva to boot, as indicated by his first name read backward—at the castle itself to conduct. Enter one beautiful bassoonist. Was it all about plain old sex?

Wack's life, much to his dismay, revolved around Sapristi's—like the second flight of stairs wrapped around the first at Chambord—in a never-ending spiral. What had happened between him and Sapristi remained unresolved. Was that why Henri was like so many men I hear about these days who wait for the woman to take the first step or try to detect microscopic gestures, cues, or advances they believe she is making? While some men imagine that anything a woman does is intended as a sign to them ("she looked up from her book at the coffee shop and smiled at me—it couldn't have been at the silly dork behind me"; "she scratched her neck to signal a desire to neck with me and me alone"; "I overheard her say the word 'passport,' which meant she was dying for me to invite her on a trip"), others need to be beaten over the head with proof of her interest in order to be jolted out of their paralysis. Was the smooth-talking Wack so afraid of violating someone that he showed nothing? He flirted easily with the most elegant of fans and the trashiest of waitresses—could he, perhaps, show interest only in those in whom he was not truly interested?

It suddenly dawned on me that Sapristi swung the other way. So what could Pislova represent to him? *Flûte!* I must be the one who needs to be beaten over the head with proof as massive as the Empire State Building—the platinum-blond Russian's dream was not about a man!

* * *

Chinon is the real deal. It's where it all started—not the dramas I was investigating, of course, but the conflicts that made England France's hereditary enemy for the better part of a millennium (some might say it's still true today!). The two kingdoms collided in Chinon and two quasi-brothers mercilessly duked it out here. Their story is chock full of deceit and deception.

The British still think they own the place. They come in droves—mostly in the summer, but increasingly all year round—to fill the trunks of their cars with red wine from Chinon, even though the town is forever linked to Joan of Arc, whom they ignominiously burned at the stake.* Nothing can stop them!

The staid virgin warrior came to town, picked the young, disguised, future King Charles VII out of a crowd and changed his life, crowning him in record time and leading the reconquest of his entire kingdom. She is the spiritual queen of Chinon, which she graced with her presence for a whole month of her all-too-brief existence.

The butte in the center of town started out life as a Gallo-Roman stronghold and was fortified by the Counts of Blois, headquartered to the east, before being captured by their sworn enemies, the Counts of Anjou to the west. One of the latter, a true Frenchman, Henry II Plantagenet (Lord of the Saumur region), built most of the dazzlingly white, mile-long fortress we see today before becoming King of England. His whole government was based in Chinon. And his son, Richard the Lionhearted, grew up here and betrayed his father by allying with his cousin, King of France Philippe Auguste. Just another typical family! Richard then allowed himself to be outwitted by Philippe while they were crusading together. Philippe raced back to France and, breaking their "non-aggression pact," besieged and conquered the Lionheart's holdings in the Loire Valley—all's fair in love and war, they say … Chinon was never again to leave the *Domaine Royal*. Which is part of the reason why French kings and their ministers built so many castles in the area.

I parked near the enormous statue of Rabelais, the earthly king of Chinon, that greets every visitor upon arriving in town. A doctor, like me, he penned hilarious tales in order to relieve his patients' suffering. He would, I suspect, have agreed with Raymond Devos' quip "*Le rire est une chose sérieuse avec laquelle il ne faut pas plaisanter*" (Laughter is serious business, and mustn't be joked about, or laughter is no joking matter). Being in Chinon and reading the good doctor's nonsense always makes me feel as jovial as rosé.

* * *

The restaurant I selected, *Un Air d'Antan*, is known for its true old-fashioned French fare. It is located off the beaten track, in a maze of medieval streets overflowing with manor houses adorned with hexagonal spiral staircase towers and pretty round bartizans, and shops festooned with flowers. (The cobblestones will wreak havoc on your high heels, if such is what you tend to wear.) On my way there, I passed an ATM tucked into a fifteenth-century half-timbered house, almost stopped and took a picture of it for my nephew back in the States, and allowed myself to get distracted by menus at several eateries offering the latest in local truffle-laced dishes. I'm sure you're shocked!

A sharp cookie, Le Coq had had no trouble finding the tiny restaurant in the rue Rabelais, and had selected the table in the corner of the courtyard patio with the best view of the door leading back into the restaurant. The owners, Frédérique and Antoine, wouldn't poison us, but, as for the others, you can't be too careful. In the far corner, however, no one could just casually walk by *our* table and surreptitiously sprinkle something on our plates or pour a potion in our beverages. Unless the commissioner assassinated me herself, having had enough of me by now, like so many others ...

Le Coq's hair was straggly (was it even washed?), her bag and shoes didn't match, and she was wearing what looked like a wrinkled pajama top. She seemed rattled, too. I hoped it was by my close encounter last night, which I had mentioned to her on the phone that morning—at least I flattered myself that was the reason she seemed out of sorts.

"You should try the local remedy, gelotherapy," I ribbed her as I greeted her.

"What's that?" she asked curtly.

"Cops," I thought. "What can you do?" Aloud I said, "Chinon is the hometown of the infamous Rabelais."

"I haven't read anything by him since high school," she said with a slight trace of nostalgia in her voice, but still looking sour.

"His stories may be totally crazy, crude, and salacious, but they are side-splittingly funny! And laughter is the best medicine—it's good for the soul." She didn't look amused, so I didn't bother to tell her that the remedy's name came from the Greek *gelos* for laughter (in English it would be funnier to spell it "jellotherapy"). "They sure knew a lot back in Renaissance times."

"You're the one who's going to need to laugh, Inspector," she said. Something was clearly wrong.

"Why is that, Jeanne?" I asked, taking a seat next to hers and calling her by her first name for once.

"There was no vehicle in the ditch when my colleagues arrived on the scene last night."

"No vehicle? How's that possible?"

"I don't know." She glanced briefly at the food menu on the hand-written chalkboard neatly posted near our table, so as not to look at me directly, I thought. I was sure she had already made her choice, and she didn't strike me as the kind of woman who keeps changing her mind about what to get, calling the waiter back two minutes after placing her order to switch it yet again.

"Only a highly skilled driver could have gotten the car out of that mess," I commented, recalling that someone had told me about a local castle owner who had a collection of vintage Ferraris and state-of-the-art four-wheel-drive vehicles for Dakar rallies. Was it Castillo? He didn't seem the type, but the incident had occurred not two miles from Villandry. "The driver must not have been badly injured," I said aloud. "Well, what else have you got?"

"The boys in forensics agreed that the mathematician's crash position at Villandry Castle was a bit unusual, but felt it did not conclusively tell us whether he deliberately jumped, slipped, or was pushed. Oh, and the license plate number you gave me for the car Canaples' contact drove off in—there's no such number," she said peremptorily.

"But I'm sure I wrote it down correctly."

"There's no record of it," she stated icily. "Yet another waste of time."

I guess I hadn't given her much to go on. "What about the coroner's report on Lavillaine?"

"They tell me it hasn't been written up yet—maybe tomorrow. If not, we won't be able to see it 'til Monday." She moved the wine menu over toward me. "Prefect Durtal is going to be furious, for, as fate would have it, our facial recognition software is incompatible with Villandry's obsolete video installation. So we will have to narrow down our list of suspects in the old-fashioned way and then comb through the tape frame by frame."

"I figured as much," I remarked. The lack of good news didn't discourage me from glancing at the varietals and vintages on offer.

She made a reproachful sound to get my attention and I looked up. "There were fingerprints on the carabiner you found, but they don't match those of anyone on file." She extracted the small metal object from her bag and handed it back to me.

"I see we're batting a thousand."

She sighed. "There is one interesting tidbit," she made a face. "The tracking device you found on your car was made by Russian Navigation Technologies and uses the Russian GLONASS global positioning system."

"*Tiens, Tiens*," I muttered. "Interesting …"

"It can, however, be purchased online through dozens of websites."

"Hmm."

The personable owner/waiter came by, nodded indulgently at Le Coq's cursory order and heartily approved mine. I requested two appetizers, gazpacho soup and garden salad, *coq au vin* for my main course, and two desserts, chocolate lava cake and *poires tapées de Rivarennes* (dried pears from the nearby town of Rivarennes that are rehydrated with Loire Valley wine). I simply couldn't decide which appetizer or dessert interested me most. "In honor of Rabelais, a gargantuan feast," I quipped when I noticed her quizzical look. "Anyway, I'm famished! You cut short my dinner last night, I skipped the industrial breakfast on offer this morning, and a restaurant that serves real food is hard to find."

She seemed to stifle some pithily censorious repartee she had no doubt been contemplating, about the number of desserts, perhaps. Women can be so jealous …

"On the instructive side," she remarked, "we have determined that J. Livingston was, indeed, poisoned, and that the type of poison used was a derivative of stinkweed, as the doctors had initially thought."

"What sort of shape is he in? Hallucinating that the hospital food is from the Michelin-starred *Jules Verne* in the Eiffel Tower?"

She shot me a reprimanding look. "He's in stable condition, but still comatose."

Female officers are even more saturnine than male officers, I reflected. "So no help to us yet," I said, trying to sound somber, which is no easy feat in Rabelais's neck of the woods. "Have there been any previous incidents of deliberate stinkweed poisoning?"

"We're looking into it now. It's rarely identified so clearly—luckily the doctor in Saumur happened to have once treated a whole family that ate stinkweed after the father accidentally collected the stuff growing amongst the wild herbs he used to spice up a stew he was making. They thought they saw pink Martians with dreadlocks, blue elephants with multiple trunks wearing tutus, sperm whales dancing the Charleston—pretty wild stuff," she said staidly, failing to relish the story's jellotherapeutic potential. "But that was before they got paranoid and started seeing danger everywhere." She sipped the sparkling water Antoine had poured out for us. "A number of street drugs cause similar symptoms, so it's often hard to know who ingested what."

"Any idea who the one-time flower girl was yet?"

"We should know any minute now," she said smugly.

I sampled Marc Plouzeau's light, lemony, flint-soil-parcel-white Chinon Silice we had ordered, or rather I should say I had ordered, Le Coq having deferred to my knowledge of local producers.

She, too, tasted the delicious chenin blanc—the king of Loire Valley varietals—with pleasure, I thought, but it didn't blunt her ill humor. Still, I never anticipated what was coming.

"I contacted Northrop Grumman when I got home last night and spoke with a very amiable receptionist there," she began.

"One can usually count on Americans to be friendly," I commented placidly. "Was she able to enlighten you as to Livingston's position there?"

"Told me she had never heard of the man," she almost yelled, looking me in the eye. "I felt like a fool!" The floodgates of her fury suddenly opened.

I almost choked on my sparkling frog water. I hadn't asked Le Coq to call the firm, but then again I hadn't volunteered to do so myself. I guess you never know what will prick someone's pride.

"To be thorough, I asked her to check if he had worked for Grumman in the past, even just as a temp or subcontractor."

I wasn't sure to whom she was justifying herself. "So ..."

"They never had any such employee."

My soup and garden salad with Frédérique's secret dressing on it arrived. "Do you want the recipe for this pesto? I'm sure they'd be willing to part with it," I said. Knowing the owners as I did, I was sure they would be kinder than the chefs who accidentally (on purpose) leave out one essential ingredient or step when they tell you a recipe.

"Would you stop talking about food already!"

I assented, reflecting that you never knew in France who was going to be a true gourmet. I know a harpsichordist who astonishes me with his knowledge of champagne and haute cuisine.

"The only clue we have is a slip of paper from Livingston's wallet. He may have come to France for an appointment he was to have with someone in Oiron tomorrow. He'll probably turn out to be a traveling salesman hawking office supplies," she said scornfully.

"Don't be discouraged, my dear. You'll go to the rendezvous in his stead and, if nothing else, you'll see a pretty place, even if it is with me as your only company," I said. "Did you get the list of Livingston's fellow diners last night from the Saumur police force?"

She drew some papers out of her bag and proudly handed them to me. "Here you go," she said. She seemed to like lists, there being something reassuring to her about them.

There were dozens of locals, along with some artists, Parisians, and foreigners.

"What about this one?" I asked, pointing at the name Brinvilliers on the second page.

She looked at her printout. "He's head of security in France for Rosso Inc."

I was sure I'd heard the name in a context from some faraway time.

"Maybe he met with someone about tightening security at Saumur Castle. Vigipirate and all that," she postulated.

"Rosso Inc. is a holding company for the multi-billionaire Jorge Rosso," I remarked. It was strange to hear his name in a quaint setting like *Un Air d'Antan*. He had exploited a sophisticated algorithm to manipulate exchange rates in currency markets, where a series of small movements can lead to a far greater one—one of the fundamental principles of turbulence and chaos theory. The classic example of chaos involves the beating of a butterfly's wings: so-called nonlinearities in the weather can potentially augment those tiny vortices in the air a billionfold and lead to a hurricane somewhere on the other side of the globe! Or, something no one ever seems to mention, prevent one.

I sipped my chenin blanc pensively. "Rosso is the chairman of Sallaud Industries, one of Northrop Grumman's main competitors. Doesn't he also own a bunch of big-name wineries in the Bordeaux region?"

She took out her cell phone and, after several deft movements, exclaimed, "Purchased Chateau Mutton-Rothfeld in 2003, Chateau

Effete in 2008, and the enormous Chateau Evangelus just a few months ago. Quite a haul."

"You won't find those on the menu here," Antoine quipped as he removed our old-fashioned plates. "Too rich for our blood!"

"Those are some of the best-known wineries in Bordeaux," she gasped. "They're not French anymore?"

I couldn't help being irritated. "Don't be naïve, Jeanne. The Chinese and other foreigners have been snapping up famous vineyards in the Bordelais for years. Rosso must be extremely well connected if he managed to acquire those," I mused. "Isn't he is involved in winemaking equipment as well?"

She scanned down the list of his holdings, mumbling names as she went: "Veolia, Schneider, RNT—

"Could that be Russian Navigation Technologies?"

"Could be," she replied, intrigued. "But it could also be Rata Naval Tata's RNT Associates or any number of other firms with the same initials."

"What else have you got?"

"EDF, Frigorifica—"

"Frigorifica, that's it," I interrupted her. "It's a major manufacturer of winemaking equipment, like sorters, presses, and temperature-controlled fermentation vats."

* * *

Her *queue de lotte au beurre blanc*, a beautiful monkfish oozing butter and shallot sauce, and my *coq au vin* arrived. The finely crafted traditional dishes were steaming invitingly before us when Le Coq suddenly twisted to the right, then to the left, then backwards. (I strove to find something to appreciate in the ridiculous modern dance.) "It's the maître d' at *L'Orangeraie* calling." Antoinette had just shown up, she eventually whispered to me. Le Coq scribbled a few notes as she talked.

"A woman she did not know had seen her trudging slowly up the hill to the castle and proposed to sell the roses for her," she said quickly, after hanging up. "The old flower lady trusted in the goodness of human nature, but lo and behold, she never saw the woman, the flowers, or the basket again—she wants her money back!"

We both laughed. At least we had shared one good moment …

"Did she tell you anything else?"

229

"The thief had gray hair and wore bulky clothes," she replied slowly. "Are you sure you went to the right room at that hotel?" she asked pointedly, unconcerned about the non sequitur.

Wow, it seemed that nothing could soften her today. "What do you mean?" I asked, trying to pour two fingers of wine in her glass surreptitiously.

"And stop trying to make me drink," she cried. "The gearheads in the lab had a hell of a time hacking into that laptop you gave me, but they finally managed to do so. Guess what they found?"

I was all ears.

"It isn't her computer."

"What? Why?" I sputtered.

"It is full of aircraft designs and formulas regarding the airflow generated by fighter jet engines. About as far from tuba music as you can get!"

"And yet I found it in the same room with her bassoon and date book," I protested.

"It must've been planted there—people do that in industrial espionage. Or else she was holding it for someone. Losing your grip, I'd say."

"Don't you see," I said, putting my hand forcefully on her forearm, "now we're finally getting somewhere. Tell me about the designs."

She looked at me once again as if I were as dumb as Durtal and the all the other men in her life. Yielding, she responded, "I didn't see them myself. But the boys in the lab said they had the impression the plane designs were based on the kind of mimeticism found in nature. If you see some connection with your blonde, you must really be looking for one."

I didn't know what to tell her, and she wasn't allowing me to ply her with drink (not laced with locoweed) to temper her negativity.

"A penny for your thoughts," she eventually uttered a little more gently. "Unless they are indecent, of course!"

"I'm too old for those, in your book," I quipped, a little depressed. "At Fontevrault last night," I slowly sounded out the syllables of the lovely name, "the Symphonie de Provence played a piece by Nicholas Lanier."

The name obviously didn't register with her.

"Don't worry, he's not very well known, but I'm sure you've heard of Handel." She nodded. "They played something by him too." I sampled the delicate Silice again and went on, "Scarlatti and Steffani were also on the program. They were both immigrants and had similar ins with

230

the rulers in the countries where they took up residence as Lanier and Handel did. They all turned out to be spies! Can you imagine Scarlatti writing six hundred sonatas for the very people he was reporting on?"

She seemed nonplussed.

"Lanier, the British composer, was sent to Italy to buy artwork for King Charles I, but is alleged to have spied along the way. And the Water Music may have been written while Handel was getting the lay of the British political landscape for the eventual Hanoverian successor to Queen Anne."

She remained as closed as a two-hundred-year-old clamshell. Classical music must not have been her bag. "It may sound like ancient history, but musicians are always potentially … shady characters!"

She laughed for the first time that day, then looked at the remains of her modest main course and over at my huge but empty plate. "How do you stay so trim?" she suddenly blurted out. "You eat like a … horse!" (I wondered if "pig" had occurred to her first and she had censored it, which would account for the hesitation.)

"Brainwork burns up a lot of calories," I said sententiously. "Good thing, too, because I love good food."

Her face, comely despite her bad-hair day, took on a furious expression.

"In any case," I said, nibbling on a half-eaten piece of baguette and enjoying it, "being a creative artist has always been a perfect cover, and no art is off-limits. Have you ever heard of Julia Child?" She shook her head. "She was the American celebrity chef who almost single-handedly brought French cuisine to the United States in the nineteen-fifties and sixties. While training at the Cordon Bleu Culinary Institute in Paris, she was simultaneously working for the CIA. It only came out after she died, but she had one of the most successful covers in the history of espionage."

"I always wanted to study at the Cordon Bleu."

"You? Then why didn't you?" I asked, cocking an eyebrow at her.

"My parents. Anyway, I had no idea there was any such spying tradition," she replied regretfully.

"There, there. Don't be sad," I petted her arm sympathetically. "Almost nobody knows about that. But it is a well-established tradition. Architects like da Vinci sketched and studied fortifications, and he himself was suspected of spying by the Florentines for Cesare Borgia. Ever hear of Machiavelli's *The Prince*?"

231

She nodded.

"Borgia, the son of a Pope* and the model for Machiavelli's prince, was just one of the well-known tyrants for whom Leonardo plied his trade. A bit later da Vinci worked for Charles d'Amboise, the French governor of Milan, and thus for France.** Who knows? While Leonardo was drawing pictures and maps of forts in Lombardy for d'Amboise, supposedly in view of restoring and strengthening them, he may have been helping the French prepare to attack those very same forts."

"How so?" she asked.

"Da Vinci showed them all their weak points, which the French could then exploit when the forts fell back into Italian hands, which they almost always did. He may even have been a double agent." The name Vellimachia flitted through my mind. "At one point he seems to have worked *against* the French by informing the Venetians about the state of the French army and their defenses in Lombardy."

"Why him?"

"As an artist, he was able to travel far and wide to see what was being done in other city-states. Even his young protégé Salaì was accused of spying."

A disturbingly modern beep sounded, and Le Coq began anew her contortions in search of reception while I gave the desserts my undivided attention, first the hot then the cold, then back to the hot. Putting her phone down, she looked off into the distance. "Thinking about love?" I wondered. "About men?" Not always the same thing, those two. "About her upcoming date that evening? I wouldn't want to be in her shoes," I reflected.

She tapped away on her screen for a spell, and so I ordered herb tea and coffee for us and chatted briefly with Antoine about his recent hiking trip to the land of druids: Brittany.

The commissioner looked up from her phone and, after Antoine left to attend to other patrons, remarked, "You know, when I was little I was addicted to watching figure skating on TV."

"No, I don't know. How could I?"

She reacted like most people do, by simply ignoring my question. I looked at Jeanne and tried to imagine her on skates in a skimpy, wispy tutu.

"I remember hearing," she went on, "that Olympic athletes, like figure skaters, and top ballet dancers from Russia were suspected of spying. They were able to obtain visas to lots of different countries, and

232

their equipment was always gone over by security personnel with a fine-tooth comb to ensure they didn't have microdots or chips in the blades of their ice skates or the tips of their ballet shoes."

Wondering if I'd examined Pislova's instrument carefully enough, I opined, "A baroque bassoon is a hell of a lot bigger than skates or slippers."

* * *

The majority of men are perceptually challenged when it comes to recognizing and describing faces. Professor Chimmi at the University of Bordeaux gave me a detailed description of the huge hunting knife with which he had been threatened—a flashing blade over a foot long, with a brass and black leather handle—and of the female thug who kept tossing the weapon from one hand to the other expertly as if to show off her deadly dexterity. He spoke intelligently and precisely on the phone with me this afternoon, but the portrait he painted of the knife's wielder was useless.

"Probably some broad Bouture jilted or cheated on, although she was built like a roller derby skater!" he volunteered. "He spends half his time in Russia hawking his trendy organic wares, trades wine for glass bottles when the ruble is tanking, and has a different girlfriend in every Scandinavian port of call. I figure the one who threatened me was looking for payback and decided to hit him where it hurt," he exclaimed with bravado, as if he felt the Don Juan deserved it.

"He's dead, you know," I observed.

"You're joking, aren't you?" He paused and I merely waited. "I saw him just last week at a lecture. A senior chemist from UC Davis came to give a talk in Bordeaux. It was quite interesting, actually—discussed the difference between French and American oak used in aging barrels. Anyway, Bouture came in late and sat down in the back next to some blond bimbo. Showing off, as usual."

"Are you sure it was him?" I asked.

"Of course. I've met the man on umpteen occasions," he sniggered. "I can't believe you thought he was dead."

"Don't you research many of the same questions as Bouture?"

He chortled hollowly. "At this point in my career, I don't have any earth-shattering ideas, unless grape-skin facials at luxury hotels in the area count. I mostly track the health benefits of a couple of glasses of wine per day," he replied. "Listen, I'm teaching a class in five minutes. Call me back when he's really dead." And he rang off.

His description of the knife struck me as overly precise, as if he had deliberately studied one in advance (probably something called a "Mistress Down Under," one of the biggest and with an intriguingly compelling name).

* * *

Putting down the receiver at my B&B, I wondered if anyone ever stayed dead in the Loire Valley. I fished a piece of paper out of my inside jacket pocket and dialed a number. It was not in service. I called the number of the hotel the Anjou police had indicated, but it was that of a butcher shop.

Beginning to see the writing on the wall, I did not give up, as Chimmi might have preferred. Instead I asked the jealous but amicable male host of my lodgings if I could use his computer for a few minutes. The chair was comfy and the connection good, but something leaped into my lap, knocked the keyboard over, and I uttered imprecations that even Renaissance folks would have blushed at. Yet it was just the owner's black cat. Paws covered with mud—it was the countryside, after all—he quickly settled on my lap and I let him stay put while I stared incredulously at the roster of employees at Rosso Inc.'s headquarters in La Defense (Paris's answer to Manhattan's midtown concentration of corporate headquarters, located just outside the city limits). There was no mention whatsoever of a security department, even though they obviously had one, just like every other major corporation in the world. Theirs must have been operated so unconscionably it couldn't even be listed. Brinvilliers didn't exist.

CHAPTER SEVENTEEN

The town of Oiron

Love looks not with the eyes, but with the mind.
—Shakespeare, *A Midsummer's Night Dream*

The scrap of paper found in J. Livingston's wallet indicated a tiny tavern in a village that few people on the planet have ever heard of. Amidst cow pastures and country lanes frequented by more tractors than tourists, the region's inhabitants have stayed put for generations, protected from the outside world by their dense hedgerows. After a long drive through the bush, a slender bell tower emerges in the distance and suddenly one of the biggest Loire Valley castles appears out of nowhere, as if shipwrecked on a desert island.

The inn, *Le Relais du Château*, was located on the only square in the sleepy little town. Anyone lunching on its terrace could see people approaching from all directions. Le Coq reserved a room there the night before with a commanding view of the terrace. At the crack of dawn, evincing even more energy and dedication than usual, she had, as she related it to curious ol' me, slipped out dressed all in black like Grace Kelly (or was it?) to do her spy work.

Well before the appointed hour of noon, I parked in the picturesque tree-shaded parking lot directly in front of the colossal castle's gates, and a funny feeling came over me. "Why?" I wondered. Oiron is a monument like no other, of course, even if it is clearly a Loire Valley one by its style, grandeur, and stone: *tuffeau*. In sheer square footage and mass, the place is bigger than everything else in the entire village put together—indeed, the already substantial castles of Azay-le-Rideau and Amboise could easily fit in its east and west wings respectively, and there would still be room for all of Chenonceau in the main body of the castle to the south (well, okay, I might be exaggerating, but not by much; I recall having once been struck by the fact that Oiron is an anagram of Orion, and even if no mortal could tighten Orion's belt, I felt it a fittingly enormous constellation to associate with the behemoth).

I knocked discreetly on the cat burglar's door. The bugs she had placed at dawn were invisible under the tables—the stage was set—and we began our watch at the window.

A fellow walking with a cane approached the terrace, took a seat, and studied the menu. He had gray hair, dark sunglasses, and wore the kind of blue jumpsuit to which many French farmers and manual laborers are partial. When he addressed the waitress, he spoke hoarsely in the local patois you can hear in isolated parts of the country, and we used their brief conversation to perform a final sound check. "Very exciting," I reflected.

Time passed, but no one stopped. It was almost one and the lone man had finished his lunch and ordered coffee.

"Oh, my baby!" cried a woman. I could clearly make out a sturdy physique and closely cropped red hair.

The old man fidgeted, moved the newspaper he had been reading first one way, then another, but eventually greeted her.

"I told you, no Americans!" she boomed. She seated herself and the chair under her almost collapsed. "What's with your voice today, my love strudel?" she asked, smiling and looking at him longingly.

"I have a sore throat."

"You should let me take care of you, feed you, and bathe you. I'm the only one who's got your back in life." She grinned even more broadly now, revealing horrible black teeth.

The farmer shrugged his shoulders.

"Are you still working for that parasite?" she asked accusingly.

"No, as I've told you repeatedly." The farmer glanced off to his left as a cyclist sped in and out of sight. "He helped me get started when I was a poor ephebe." She rolled her wild eyes. "But a year ago it dawned on me that nobody really cares. You were right, he was exploiting me."

"You wouldn't have needed him if those blood-sucking vampires hadn't destroyed our family castle and killed my father," she retorted. "We didn't need them to liberate us from the Nazis. And to think they never even compensated us, my sweet apple dumpling."

"No one had any money at that time. Everyone knows that."

She looked around the still deserted terrace. "I guess your American is too stupid to even show up," she sniped, obviously savoring her victory. "You are my treasure and I'll never abandon you. And you can never abandon me, you know that!" She rose and her heavyset frame set off in the direction of Oiron Castle. After a few steps she turned and sent him a long, lingering air kiss that displayed her rotting teeth, ending with a sinister smile that gave me the creeps.

If the Americans had shelled their estate, I reflected, they had undoubtedly done so by mistake, believing that the S.S. had occupied it when they were actually at a different estate with a similar name. Lord knew it had happened often enough …

* * *

Le Coq nudged me and pointed out the window. A man dressed all in black was approaching the restaurant terrace baking in the midday sun.

Through a gap between the curtains we watched the man unzip his jacket—making perfectly visible to the newspaper reader a huge revolver that contrasted oddly with the peace of the countryside—and then zip it up again.

"You can't take a crap without us hearing. There isn't a single step you can take," he addressed the farmer, "a call you can place, a bank transfer you can make, or a key you can hit on your computer without us knowing it. Get it?" The square-shouldered man seated himself on the edge of a chair. "You think you're in charge of your life. But we know where you are at every moment, everything you eat, everything you think."

He pointed his index and middle fingers at his eyes and then at the farmer. "We'll be watching. If you so much as dream of exposing you know who, whammo!" Pointing back toward the giant stone palace, he added, "And not just you—your sexy heavyweight champion too. Don't expect the biggest U.S. aerospace firm to spare her."

"Freeze!" the commissioner yelled. She had crept up behind him soundlessly, like a leopard.

* * *

After Le Coq's departure with her prisoner, I sat at a table on the *Relais du Château*'s terrace. I was sipping *un grand crème*, licking my wounds, and trying to get the ol' coconut working properly again.

"How's your ankle?" asked the kindly waitress. On a chain around her neck hung several silver medals of saints, one depicting Saint Martin, the patron saint of innkeepers.

"It still hurts," I replied, rubbing it again.

"Sorry you weren't able to catch that old farmer. Took off like a jackrabbit—pretty amazing—and nobody saw where he went ... We know everyone from around these parts but never saw him before." She smiled at me, curious perhaps what a stranger like me, arrayed in a blazer and bow tie, was doing in this remote place.

I thanked her for her solicitude, and contemplated my coffee as though it were a Greek oracle. Stray thoughts came to mind one after another. Who was J. Livingston? (Was the J. there to evoke Jonathan Livingston Seagull?)

Who was the farmer, and what did Boeing—for it had to be the giant aircraft producer with a huge assembly plant just north of Seattle—have to do with any of this? Boeing was a direct competitor of Northrop Grumman's (which also had offices near Seattle) in the "defense" sector, though it might be better termed the "offense" sector, I reckoned.

I finished my java and ordered a glass of wine. The fruit of the vine stimulates thinking, in me, at least, maybe not in others. Grinning, the waitress poured me a generous glass of Anjou blanc—I noticed the name Passavant on the label—and I sipped the local aromatic chenin meditatively, noting that I was surely *pas si savant*, not as wise or knowledgeable, as I wished.

Pislova's laptop, as I learned from Le Coq's chief engineer that morning, contained no musical scores or pictures of the rakish Henri Wack, but a folder named "J.R." Inside were precise schematics of flying machines—at least they seemed to be planes—but the main focus seemed to be on their "skin." He believed we were dealing with radically new designs for rendering stealth aircraft still more invisible to radar and the human eye. The outer coating was to change color

240

depending on the color of the sky around it, like a chameleon, or to look the same as the jets of the country being attacked. "Pretty damn inventive," I remarked. The engine noise, he informed me, was to resemble the sound of a meteorite hurtling toward Earth—a pretty scary thought, but still more inventive! The very maneuvering of the jets seemed to have been rejiggered to imitate that of a large bird in flight, in accordance with something he called biomimicry. "Hardly your typical approach to invisibility," I commented. It sounded revolutionary to me, and showed a keen interest on the inventor's part in how birds fly and evade predators.

"Every major government and weapons company will be dying to get ahold of the same cutting-edge research" were the guy's last words. Pislova's computer, he warned, contained encrypted email exchanges with addresses domiciled in good ol' Russia. I couldn't get a clear answer as to how many of the designs had been sent to them so far.

Jumping up and running into the restaurant, I asked the startled waitress if I could place a local call. I looked all around to ensure I was alone. Loud cheers came from the television, which was broadcasting a soccer match between the faraway locales of Marseilles and Monaco. When I finally got through, I recognized the voice of the nurse I'd met at the hospital in Blois, and she informed me that the bassoonist had disappeared.

"When?" I asked, dismayed.

"Wednesday morning, sugar," she said cheerily. "There was no trace left of her in the room when I came in at seven a.m. Stunning but stupid," the elderly woman tsk-tsked. "She obviously doesn't give a fig about you, Sir, and you'd be a fool to chase after her."

I thanked her for her concern and rang off. I guess I must have sounded heartbroken to her.

I might be a fool, but Pislova certainly wasn't! Indeed, she might live up to her namesake's reputation of being *la plus savante des belles*, the most learned of beauties. Anne de Pisseleu was known for her knowledge of the arts, sciences, literature, and men—especially how to manipulate them.

Who was, after all, the total idiot who had jogged that vixen's memory, first with her bassoon and then by sending the lustiest musician in town, Wack, to see her at the hospital Tuesday evening after our dinner at *Assa*?

A gaggle of farmhands suddenly materialized near the TV and I returned to my outdoor table. Sipping what was left of my restorative,

I reflected that someone had seemed to be watching my movements with a Russian-made GLONASS tracking device from the beginning. No, I corrected myself, it only started the day I met the latest addition to the Symphonie de Provence at the hospital.

She probably had a handler at the GRU—the successor to Russia's KGB for military espionage the world over—who was keeping a close eye on her. Most agents are assigned one, agencies being unable to trust their spies not to go over to the other side, get "turned," or "go native," especially when their jobs involve sleeping with the enemy. Was her handler now watching me? Or was I being followed by a backup they'd sent, sensing she'd fallen for her "mark" and decided to abort her mission?

The Russians were no slouches, I recalled. They had poisoned double agents in England with nerve gas, disposed of a former agent with radioactive materials put in his tea, and eliminated countless "security risks" and "undesirables." Where others might fail, they pretty much always got their man.

CHAPTER EIGHTEEN

Oiron Castle

Where the master was, the disciple shall come into being.

—Anonymous

The best place to hide out was, I concluded, in the castle itself. The concert I was to attend that evening at Oiron, the Symphonie de Provence's final performance in the Loire Valley, wouldn't be for a couple of hours.

I wasn't truly expecting to find in its boutique a third newly discovered treatise by Leonardo da Vinci (say, the much vaunted one on mechanics based on the Codex Madrid I), and I should perhaps have been looking for one about women and xy-chromosome fools—they might have had one! Instead I merely grilled the cashier who confirmed that it was a slow day even for them. She was alone at the till and I had counted only five cars in the parking lot on my way there.

Venturing out of the small but handsome boutique, I began my tour where others end theirs—in the last part of the castle to be built, "La Tour des Ondes" or Wave Tower, as it is currently known, an amazingly beautiful entrance tower to the west. It used to be the exact same size as the entrance tower to the east, but was expanded for added majesty by the Marquise de Montespan, the Sun King's most famous mistress for many a year. She left his palace in Versailles under suspicion of complicity in the biggest scandal of the 1700s, the "Affaire des Poisons," of which a certain Brinvilliers was the evil linchpin. Which perhaps just goes to show that even murderers can sometimes have taste in art and architecture.

To get to that tower, one proceeds along a gray gravel path made of demolished concrete low-income housing units built in Paris in the 1950s, a fine reuse, if ever there was one, of government-sponsored eyesores. The sound of my solitary steps was quite distinct in the stillness of the esplanade. Crossing the moat, the tower is immediately to the right. Alone, I entered the serene space, which is capacious yet warm. No one was about, so I relaxed and immediately began my usual fun fantasizing: I'd install leather chairs in the first room to the right (a sort of anteroom); a huge desk, comfortable armchair, and fainting couch—or perhaps even a *duchesse brisée*—in the one with the fine windows; and curved book cases all the way around the circular third room, with a ladder on which to stand while selecting among my ever-growing collection of math treatises, philosophical works, and arcane novels from prior centuries. Now that would be some office! I could forget all about my misadventures with coppers, felines, and farmers. Even on a horribly hot day like today, the ground floor of the tower remained marvelously cool and untouched by the world outside.

Still indulging my inner daydreamer, I took the narrow but luminous spiral staircase that is dissimulated in a wall up to the second floor. Its curious feature—a high balcony built into it—affords a view of the creamy white stone entrance hall below. A part of my mind alerted me to the danger I could be in standing at such a balustrade. Yet I didn't want the comforting feeling to dissipate and pushed on, my steps quickening. I entered the enormous round room with a tranquil aura, home of Tom Shannon's "Decentre-Acentre," a gigantic gravity-defying magnetic sculpture. (For the first time ever, I imagined what sort of circular staircase it would fit nicely inside of. Certainly not Chambord's double one.) But nothing in that "Levitation Hall," as it has been dubbed, can compete with the hundred-foot-high exposed timberwork designed only with rulers and compasses—truly mind-blowing. It mesmerized me to the point of forgetting everything else …

I climbed up one more story and found myself still closer to the intricate woodwork. I was right under the roof in a small space that looked like an enchanted attic in children's books. From the oeil-de-boeuf window up there, one has an unobstructed view of the endless country-side. And the fifteen-hundred-year-old fortified Romanesque abbatial church in Saint-Jouin-de-Marnes five miles to the south can be seen as clearly as when the tower, in the garret of which I was standing, was erected, nothing having been built between the two towns in the three intervening centuries. I couldn't help but gaze out at the preserved landscape, all alone in the deserted cozy space. I exited wistfully.

Sweating slightly, I slipped off my blazer while crossing the majestic courtyard to the main part of the beautiful classical castle, the south wing. Once inside, I charily strode through various second-floor rooms, including the King's Bedchamber and a couple of others with odd names, like the Hall of Geometrical Figures and the Hall of Jacqueries—which I hate because of the modern wall-mounted pitchforks and rotating animal skeletons in there, the latter of which I'm always tempted to unplug, and because of its abuse of my name. I was moving faster than usual through the place: being alone was dangerous, I admitted to myself for the first time, almost uttering it aloud.

Where, I wondered, were the people whose cars were parked in the visitors' lot outside? The palace was so enormous, I might never cross paths with them, but then again they could be tarrying in the tiny medieval staircases tucked away in the oldest wings I hadn't yet gotten to—unless they were crouching there in wait … It was just so damn quiet. I suddenly heard a loud noise and spun around—too quickly, for intense pain shot through my body and I cried out.

I wasn't going to be able to hightail it out of there. My ankle was hurting even more now than this afternoon. I'd tripped over an enormous power cable—it had no business being in my way—that was taped to the floor and ripped it loose, making that terrifying noise.

"You idiot!" a voice bellowed. "Look at what you've done!"

It was only fitting that the Hall of Jacqueries had led me to Enrique. He was setting up for the concert that evening which was to be held in the King's Great Hall on the second floor (now bizarrely referred to as the Armory), which may well be the biggest room in any castle ever built. Well, the great hall at Sully Castle in Sully-sur-Loire at the other end of the Loire Valley probably gives it stiff competition, but I personally would not count the latter because they made the room wider than the beams could stand, and eventually had to prop them up with pillars in the middle (requiring them to swallow their pride).

Looking as badass as he could, given his job, Enrique came over to me, shook my hand, and said, "Excuse me, Monsieur Canal, I didn't know it was you."

I couldn't believe my eyes or ears. It was even more shocking than realizing that I'd mistaken a cold-hearted secret agent for a damsel in distress, even if only fleetingly. Was he, too, up to something? Chic Françoise must have agreed to go to some sort of electrocutionary dance club with him, dressed, no doubt, as a duchess in punk's clothing.

I carefully wended my way through the wires, feeling a bit ashamed that I'd allowed myself to be spooked by a young tattooed misanthrope whom I may have misjudged. I slipped surreptitiously into the extraordinary *Cabinet des Muses* (Boudoir of the Muses), which is coyly tucked away in a corner and reminds one, in certain respects, of the phenomenal *Cabinet de Travail* (Study, a.k.a. *Cabinet des Grelots*) at stately Beauregard Castle. I was going to need all nine Greek muses—accompanied by Apollo, Minerva, Mercury, and even the goddess Diana, the huntress—to inspire me to solve this case. Not to mention Zeus—who was guarding over all of them, presiding in his sumptuous Olympus of gilded castings—to protect me from the dangers at every turn.

Alone again in halls worthy of Fontainebleau and Versailles, I let my mind wander off, like my steps. Which is not so bad at Oiron, because its treasures are hidden even on the inside of the castle. None of my friends in America would believe me if I told them that the finest Renaissance Gallery in all of France is found in some godforsaken village in the wilderness of Deux-Sèvres County (or, as I like to call it Deux-Chèvres County, that is Two Goats County, in honor of its acclaimed goat cheeses).

Swiftly crossing the private quarters of the Gouffiers, the castle's main builders, with their striking black, red, and gold wood triangles forming stars overhead, I entered the Gallery, let out a little gasp, and stopped for a minute in awe—every one of the hundreds of paintings in the coffered ceiling had been restored, and the entire Trojan War was splayed on the frescoed walls for me alone …

I had reached the monumental fireplace at the far end of the hall where the war story begins when I detected the presence of another soul. The bespectacled man came over to me. He sported a yellow silk bow tie with blue elephants on it, not so different from my own brightly colored number, under a well-tailored dark blue blazer.

"*Excusez-moi*. This ... this ..." At a loss for words, he gestured the length of the gallery. "Could you possibly enlighten me as to what I am looking at?"

I'm not sure why it seemed to him that I could. Perhaps it was simply because I had been walking so slowly, my hands clasped behind my back.

"I am no tour guide," I replied. ("Nothing scary about him," I thought, but found myself checking the location of the nearest exit all the same.) "But I believe I can say a few words about at least some of the frescoes, if you like." I gestured to the first brightly colored one to the right of the fireplace. "This represents the invincible François I, not depicted for once as a salamander, an amphibian reputed at the time to be born from fire and either to breathe fire like a dragon or put it out with its frosty exhalations" (rather than being known as it is today for autotomy— dropping its tail when attacked to distract predators and for regenerating lost limbs, characteristics I'd made much of at one time).* "The King is portrayed here instead as the winged horse Pegasus symbolizing wisdom and fame, surrounded by the gods of art and war, Apollo and Mars, or possibly Minerva. It's a glorious tribute! François I was, after all, widely viewed as both cultured and intrepid on the battlefield." I stole a glance at the man and he seemed quite engrossed. "This is how Claude Gouffier, the King's 'Grand Ecuyer,' the crown equerry or squire, dedicated the entire gallery to his sovereign." My interlocutor nodded thoughtfully and, as we moved on to the vividly restored fresco to our right, I added, "Gouffier seems to have wanted to constantly remind his visitors of his role as stable master, selecting and training the king's horses, and overseeing the instruction of the nobles of the land in the art of war."

"In this next scene, we see the gods assembled for the wedding of Achilles's parents. Eris, the goddess of Strife, shown here with ugly bat wings, disrupts the festivities by trying to force Jupiter to declare which of the goddesses is the most beautiful." The man smiled. "Jupiter, however, is no fool," I went on, wrapped up in my own story telling, "and orders Mercury to conduct the contestants, Juno, Minerva, and Venus, to Mount Ida where, by Jove, it will fall to the Trojan shepherd Paris to pick the winner." My voice trailed off as I recalled Henri Wack's whistling of an air from *Psyche* at Azay, and reflected how ubiquitous Venus and the problems arising from beauty were in our crazy culture.

249

"Predictably enough, the next scene illustrates the Judgement of Paris—no, not the one in Paris, France in 1976!" The gentleman betrayed no sign that he knew what I was talking about, so I did not prolong this particular tangent. "This Judgement of Paris is far more fateful: Paris designates Venus as the most beautiful of the goddesses, not because she is but because she offers him an irresistible bribe: the love of the most beautiful mortal in the world—Helen, Queen of Sparta."

He yanked at his bow tie as if to free himself of the constrictive garment and groaned. "Irresistible, indeed." I had the sense he knew whereof he moaned, like so many other men who had too oft preferred beauty to bonhomie, but he did not elaborate.

"The foolishness of his act is matched only by the destruction it unleashed. Next," I said, pointing to the brightly colored fresco to our right, with a mountain range as backdrop, "we see the abduction of Helen and are reminded how incredibly potent man's passion for beauty is and the infinite dangers that accompany this fascination, leading him to myriad follies." His demeanor was icy now.

"After that, we have various battles," I continued, guiding the stranger around the gallery, "here the story of Achilles and Patroclus made so much of by Plato in the *Symposium*," we walked on, "then the Trojan Horse and Troy burning." For a few moments, I failed to realize we had come almost full circle, with our backs now to the monumental fireplace. "The last two frescos were repainted almost a century later," I couldn't help adding in concluding our trip back in time. "The first portrays Hercules, and the second Aeneas's perilous journey to the underworld to visit his dead father."

"To visit his father?"

"Yes. We saw Aeneas carrying the elderly Prince Anchises on his back, as they fled Troy in flames, a couple of scenes back," I said, pointing behind us to the intense scene. "The son overcame every obstacle in order to visit him in Hades, as his ancestor had requested."

"Now that's filial piety," he said.

"Virgil describes him as a venerable and great-spirited father. We fathers are probably not all quite as inspiring to our children as he was."

The man abruptly turned away. As he glanced at his watch, I recalled Claude Gouffier's motto, *hic terminus haeret—ici est fixé le terme*—which, just for fun, I had sometimes translated fast and loose in my own mind, not as "the destination is set in stone," "the outcome is fixed," or "the die is cast," as in certain official translations of Virgil's *Aeneid* (where the

250

terminus was Italy, the goal or endpoint of the Trojans' wanderings), but as "the buck stops here." It took on a different connotation in the present context: "your time is up."

He turned back toward me. "I am attending the concert here and it will be beginning shortly," he whispered.

The gallery was suddenly filled with blinding sunlight. "I will be attending as well," I smiled. "I will enjoy listening to Orlando Civadin!"

"I believe it will be Wack."

He seemed to want to leave, and yet I sensed he wanted to add something, something I could not divine.

"The apple doesn't fall far from the tree, I'm afraid," he opined. (I wasn't sure what he meant!) "Civadin, on the contrary, has, I feel, a one-of-a-kind sensibility. You know, he was a child prodigy and won every competition he ever entered."

I began walking with him toward the south wing. Something eluded me in his words—something that should be obvious and yet was indecipherable, much like a *fermesse*.

I confined myself to listening attentively, and he went on, "He's a far better conductor than Wack, but crazy as a loon." He tapped his temple with his fingers. "Thinks he's ..."

I raised my eyebrows, but he didn't finish his thought.

"How do you know so much about him, if you don't mind my asking, Sir?"

"It's a long story ... As long as this gallery," he pointed despondently down the length of the hall. "I'm Anchises."

"Civadin's father?"

"A mere 'sperm donor,' according to his mother. But we poor sidelined souls have to stay involved somehow. We may not openly display our grief like women do, but we suffer terribly when our children are taken from us. 'If you prick us, do we not bleed? And if you wrong us, shall we not revenge?' I eventually found a way."

"Do tell," I prompted, relishing his *Merchant of Venice* citation.

"His mother is positively insane, a real public menace. And she plays the long suffering martyr only too well."

I tried to show no trace of judgment, despite my conviction that it virtually always took two to tango, saying only, "Huh."

He paused for a few moments and then, in a composed voice, volunteered, "When Orlando turned eighteen, I introduced myself to him under the assumed name of Dupont. I granted him carte blanche. I paid for everything. I gave him the world," he cried, looking a bit bonkers himself.

"Quite a sweet offer!" I matched his ardor to keep him talking, one of my old tricks of the trade.

"Yes, he could do whatever he wanted. He had no need to teach, no need to sell his soul to the French Ministry of Culture, no need to become one of those bums they call 'occasional workers' in the entertainment industry. I even saw to the purchase of the Stradivarius he plays from the Shah of Iran," he added scornfully, as if no monarch could possibly be worthy of it. "It's insured for millions."

"What was in it for you?" I couldn't help but ask.

"A chance to see my son blossoming," he replied proudly, "of course."

Did he really expect me to believe that? He hadn't caught my drift in the slightest. I was inclined to roll my eyes, but didn't feel that would encourage him to go on.

His eyes narrowed. "Isn't that enough?"

"You remember our winged horse Pegasus, François I?" I queried. "He gave Leonardo da Vinci free rein because he enjoyed talking with him about everything under the sun and thought him a profound philosopher. Others might wish for more tangible rewards."

There was a pregnant pause.

"I see you haven't understood a word I've said. We'd better be going," he said brusquely, like a man expecting to be instantly obeyed by one and all.

* * *

The concert was something of a blur to me. Lightning—flashing first out one window and then out another, not knowing what to hit in the palace's environs—and crashes of thunder kept interrupting the music. The temperature and horrid humidity had been climbing all day, and the electricity from the earth finally connected with the clouds as the latter released their moisture in torrents. I tried to relax in my chair, nevertheless, feeling lucky, after all that had happened, to be hearing Baroque music performed in a masterpiece of Baroque architecture.

I noted right away the presence of the ever so elegantly attired brunette flautist and the absence of the stunning blond bassoonist, but try as I might to concentrate on the music, I did little more throughout than observe a female gambist I had never seen before. A bright red shawl,

252

revealing half her shoulders, caught my eye. She was playing with gusto and fire, and Wack seemed to pick up the tempo every time he looked at her. It was as if they had decided to outdo the storm raging outside with the intensity of their onstage passion, her body enveloping the instrument in a sensual embrace while giving the conductor a come hither look, driving him completely insane.

I doubted he would be able to turn over a new leaf, do things differently for once, and not delude himself about who this new girl toy was and how perfectly she fit his hundreds of criteria. (A huge crash of thunder exploded directly above us. Had the gods decided to strike Oiron?) Could Wack, I wondered, finally accept and indeed love a woman not just for her qualities, but for what he would think of as her failings too, her flaws, warts, insecurities, self-doubts, and ineptitudes? Maybe he just wasn't *fait pour le mariage*, wasn't marriage material. He obviously had no idea where he was going. Yet the chase was on! One could almost feel his heart pounding harder and harder with desire for this new prey. Did he at least remember her name?

But even Henri's love life, in its quest for as many hinds as Henry the Eighth himself had, could not compete with my urgent need for air, and (instead of illicitly opening a window like Marie Canaples) I ducked out of the hall between a piece I usually enjoy by Vivaldi, the Concerto for Flute, Strings, and Basso Continuo in D major,* and a lovely suite of dances by Carlo Farina.

Just as I reached the top of the straight staircase down, the lights flickered, I was jostled by someone in the darkness, a desperate voice cried "You bastard!" and a lightning flash blinded me momentarily.

* * *

By the time I could see normally again, no longer seeing spots in front of my eyes, all I could make out was a dark figure hurrying away. I tried to follow, but quickly lost it, so deep was the darkness owing to the blackout.

I groped my way down the stairs and found fresh air in the hallway beneath the King's Great Hall. The strains of the symphony were strangely muted down here (they kept on playing, perhaps thanks to those little battery-powered lights on their music stands), and, as I paced back and forth through several movements, I examined my surroundings carefully. Something was afoot, something dark and—

A loud thud reached my ears. It seemed to come from the room nearest the hallway, but I could see nothing in it. I rushed through the two adjoining rooms, tripping over one of the bizarre artworks littering the floor that had no discernible place there—it was some sort of low-lying black rock masquerading as a beanbag couch that was totally invisible in the dim light. I cursed whoever it was that had had the bright idea of putting it there, but still came up empty-handed. It was only when, feeling my way along in the dark, I reached the landing halfway up to the second floor that I realized what had caused the noise. A man lay soundless and motionless on the ground.

The vastness of the castle and the full-throated sounds of the instruments drowned out my cries. Around me all I could see were fantastical winged beasts dangling from wires, mocking me whenever there was a flash of lightning. I checked the man's pulse and breathing and found none. Laying him out flat in order to give him CPR, I felt a warm liquid on his head—it was blood, and there was a lot of it. All over his coat, all over the landing, all over.

* * *

The lights back on, the place seemed under siege with frantic policemen attempting to cordon off the immense palace. I stayed first with the crowd and then with the officers. We had to try to move quickly, even though the assassin—I was sure *this* was no accident—might well have left the premises immediately after doing the deed.

An incensed Henri Wack reluctantly but methodically indicated which musicians had been excused during Farina's suite of dances, and all but five of the thirty-some musicians were allowed to leave. Among the five remaining were Françoise Foix and all of the violinists, including his archenemy.

Luckily for us, there had been no intermission, so most of the two hundred people in the audience had never left the room. They had been asked to remain seated when the sirens began blaring, becoming hostages of the hulking castle far from everyone and everything.

Some in the crowd glared at me furiously, others cringed in fear, prisoners of their seats. I looked each and every one of them over as carefully as I could—checking hair color, makeup, glasses, clothing, everything—before dismissing them, half-expecting every time to spot an exotic blonde or a more elusive character. I began at the front of the King's Great Hall and, after scrutinizing each face and ensuring that several people sitting nearby would vouch that this person had not left the room during the concert, released them one by one into the Hall of Jacqueries.

Instead of a blonde, I spotted a baggily dressed woman with a thin face and tousled gray hair, and then a familiar face, in unfamiliarly refined attire, sitting in the back row. The swimmer's nicely tailored dress, revealing her long muscular back, probably came from a swank shop in the center of Tours.

Corralling two hundred people out of the giant palace and leading them off the property so that no one could surreptitiously join the cortege was no mean feat. The local dicks took exactly twenty at a time, two officers escorting each group.

Le Coq and Durtal finally arrived, looking like they'd come straight from the Oscars!

"You will have to search over fifty rooms," I told them. "It's possible people bought tickets but did not attend the concert. The place is full of hidden staircases and *entresols*" (floors between floors), "not to mention offices and other spaces closed to the public." They were in for a long systematic top-to-bottom search of the castle after their hopefully romantic dinner out. The place seemed more gigantic than ever.

As the bells of the nearby church rang out eleven-thirty, only a handful of people remained. But just then, Durtal's team returned to the King's Great Hall with a woman in black they had found in the tiny maid's quarters, now known as the "Taboo Mystery Bedchamber," at the top of a windy wooden staircase not far from the fatal straight staircase. Simultaneously, the Deux-Sévrien polizei—having noticed a discrepancy between the number of cars remaining in the castle parking lot and the number of suspects, and redoubling their efforts combing through the castle grounds, despite the darkness and continued rain—escorted in a limping, mud-splattered woman with long gray hair. She had no ticket for the performance on her, just a general entry ticket to visit the castle.

"What is that *bitch* doing here?" the woman thundered, looking daggers at the woman from the Taboo Mystery Bedchamber.

Civadin jumped off the stage and ran to the hobbling woman's side. "What are *you* doing here?" he admonished. "And what have you done to yourself?"

255

"I was taking a walk in the park by the cedars and someone shoved me," she bellowed. "I hurt my ankle and couldn't get up. It was her!" she pointed. "That usurper, that Cremaniac has always hated me!"

"You threw that slut at him to break us up!" the other woman growled back.

The fireplug lunged at the woman in black, but Durtal grabbed the illicit visitor and escorted her furious frame out the door still yelling.

CHAPTER NINETEEN

The King's Bedchamber at Oiron Castle

Nothing can be loved or hated unless it is first known.

—Leonardo da Vinci

"*E troppo!*"* the woman wrested from the Taboo Mystery Bedchamber wailed, tears streaming down her cheeks. She removed the round, oversized black spectacles she was wearing, pushed back the black silk scarf covering her ginger hair, and eagerly accepted the handkerchief I handed her.

"Why are you hiding your face?" I asked, my voice echoing off the high ceilings, as Durtal, Le Coq, and I hurriedly placed chairs in a small makeshift circle in the King's Bedchamber. The girl had hidden her finest features.

"What are you doing here, Madame?" I asked, more quietly this time. "You remember me from Chenonceau, don't you? You called me Mr. Cannelloni in your lovely language." Realizing I knew her, the gendarmes merely looked on.

She slumped forward, depressed. "First it was that horrid bassoonist. Now another whore, lined up by his mommy!" she sobbed.

"That woman who called you a 'bitch' is your mother-in-law?"

"She's always hated me!" she now screeched. That was exactly what Civadin's mother had said about Cremona (although the in-law had included a neologistic hapax, Cremaniac, in her formulation). "Figures that if she sends a hussy his way, he'll leave me and be all hers again."

"Had history repeated itself?" I wondered. Had Civadin's mother acted just like François I's mother who threw a captivating Jezebel into her son's arms to get rid of a mistress she felt had too much power over him? Well, it wouldn't have been to get her son to give up a *mistress* in Civadin's case.

"Mother-in-laws!" I ejaculated.

*"Mi rompe les scatole!"**

"You dropped this at Chambord, by the way," I added offhandedly, handing her a small object as if she had just let it slip to the floor. Durtal looked blankly at the nondescript piece of metal but let me go on.

"Oh *grazie*," she said, turning it over in her hands, adorned only with a simple wedding band.

"So it *is* yours!" I cried, smiling to myself. Pislova's dream had conjured up the truth.

*"Ma che cos'è?"*** she asked defiantly. "I've never even been to Chamborrrdo. I don't go to my husband's concerts."

"So how come you were at Chenonceau? No one could have missed you in your oh-so-discreet gown ... and jewelry!"

"That was an exception," she explained. "He said I could come that time, for once. And excuse me for dressing up! *Le francese non le fanno mai pui!"****

"You don't always dress to kill. You're also an athlete. And you aren't always the dutiful wife who never interferes in her husband's affairs, now are you?"

"Scusi?" she replied unflappably, taking a diminutive compact from her handbag, checking her mascara, and wiping away some smears with my handkerchief.

Without giving the two cops a chance to intervene, I asked, "Madame, do you know Charles Bouture?"

The Italian shook her head.

"J. Livingston?"

Same motion.

"Marie Canaples?"

"*Non li conosco.*"*

"What about Sidney Lavillaine?"

"*Si.* He's the ridiculous-looking boy on TV. He would do better to buy his clothes from Armani for juniors!"

"Dupont?" Durtal queried. For the mystery man on the landing was the one I'd spoken with in the Renaissance Gallery, as I'd told the prefect, and that was the only name we knew for him. Cash and a password-protected smartphone were all we found in his pockets.

"*Che stronzo!*"** she exclaimed.

"Really? Isn't your entire designer wardrobe paid for by Dupont?" I inquired.

"I warned Orlando again and again not to work for him, but would he listen to a woman?" was her response. "Much less a real one?" she added, running her hands up and down the sides of her curvaceous body. "Not a chance!" she continued. "We owe that *cazzo* nothing!"***

"What were you doing here tonight, hiding in the maid's quarters?" I asked anew.

"I came to hear the concert, *caro mio*, but I didn't want Orlando to know. I told you—he doesn't want me to come! And I've never seen this palazzo before. *Bellissimo!* Such culture—look at this," she pointed a delicate hand at the extremely ornate white and gold ceiling. "It's Primaticcio."

"You couldn't possibly have heard the concert from that far-off room," Durtal asserted, looking spellbound, and not endeavoring to hide it, by the Italian who had switched in a flash from desperate housewife to sexy seductress. I had the sense she would be cleared and on a plane back to Milan's haute couture runways in a second if it was up to him.

"You couldn't have heard the music from that room, so don't toy with us," I reiterated in response to her silence.

"*Si! Non!*" After a few moments, she added, "Is it a crime to try to hold onto your husband?"

"So *that's* why you took matters into your own hands," I concluded. "You calculated the height of the roof at Chambord, the direction you'd need to head—due north—pushed Anna Pislova down the stairs, and then flew with your mini-paraglider off the parapet."

Cremona, I reflected admiringly, had been far more successful in flight than da Vinci had been the day he flew the cumbersome glider he had designed, based on his study of birds' wings, and came crashing to earth in Italy. I don't know why, but it suddenly occurred to me why the name Cremona sounded familiar to me: it was rumored that da Vinci had had an affair with a courtesan by that name when he was in Rome. This Cremona was playing a different role—doing her best to ensure that her adored husband had no courtesans by his side!

"Nobody takes my man away from me!" the Italian exclaimed, clicking her compact shut.

* * *

A pale drenched figure resembling a specter appeared in one door of the King's Bedchamber as Cremona was escorted out the other to the nearby Cabinet des Muses.

The Italian fashionista was, I sensed, like Lear claimed he was, "more sinned against than sinning." She never laid a hand on Pislova, she insisted, just frightened her ...

"How's Marie Canaples holding up?" the shade asked.

"What are you doing here?" Durtal queried.

"I'm her ride home."

"I thought you were helping the Deux-Sévrien police," I remarked.

"I am. The local officers are overwhelmed. Some even got lost in the castle earlier," Scarron snickered lamely.

"I hear you left in the middle of the concert. Walked out on your date?" I quipped. "Couldn't face the music?"

Unsure what I was referring to, it took him a while to answer. "I ducked out during the harvest season, I mean the summer. Oh, you know, the third Zodiac sign of that seasons symphony. Had to go to the john."

"The people near you said it was during the second piece," I averred (and not bothering to remind him it was one of Vivaldi's flute concerti, not the Four Seasons, we'd heard tonight). Canaples, who had been sitting next to him, was the one who had blabbed.

"I never know if it is just a movement or the whole piece that has ended. Who can tell the difference? Right guys?" He pulled up a chair, seated himself, and his legs, I noted, were motionless again tonight.

I decided to change tack and go way out on a limb, but I hoped, like Polonius, to "take this carp of truth" with my "bait of falsehood." It was a strategy that had served me well in the past—propose unlikely hypotheses that could nevertheless ferret out the truth. I had assembled quite a bag of tricks over the years that were useful in winkling things out of people, *not all* of which involved alcohol.

"Did you treat Madame le Sous-Préfet to lunch at L'Orangerie to suck up to her behind your boss' back? You certainly weren't there on Monday for *dinner* with your *father*."

"That's preposterous," he squawked. (I was impressed he knew the word.)

"Answer the question!" Durtal commanded, his eyes wide in astonishment.

"I can't stand that woman!" he went on. "It was just some broad."

"Then what the hell were you doing in Chenonceau that evening?" the prefect boomed, pounding his fist on a nearby table.

"I have a connection there ..."

* * *

Scarron's insinuation at Chambord that the girl on the stairs was undoubtedly "high as a kite" or "tripping on" some substance, and at Chenonceau that Canaples had taken something that made her think she could fly, now made sense: he had been attributing his own hidden proclivities to them.

Maybe plowing the fields, planting, and harvesting helped people manage their nervous energy in pre-pharmaceutical times, I reflected. Or maybe they simply weren't as "amped-up," as one of my former couchlings (as I liked to refer to them affectionately) used to put it— or "jacked-up," an expression I abhor for obvious reasons—as they are today, psychiatrists taxing them with lack of "affect regulation," which sounds pretty sinister to me whether you have it or not. Maybe people used to have their regulating mechanisms on the inside, in the form of something they had assimilated—a law requiring some sort of sacrifice—and didn't need to artificially control their feelings by turning to something outside themselves, whether drugs, bondage games, or what have you. Then again, alcohol has been around for quite some time ...

* * *

"Is the 'broad' you had lunch with your connection?" yours truly inquired.

"Her? No, she's just some bimbo," Scarron now laughed. (Was he high even as we spoke?)

"What is that supposed to mean?" asked the galled prefect with a hole in his soul.

"It's nothing. Just casual, polyamorous."

"Poly-what?" Durtal queried testily. Le Coq looked away, embarrassedly, it seemed, to be witnessing this scene.

"You know, it's an open relationship—we can see other people. I said it was my father because I didn't want the American to know about her." The scoundrel almost blushed.

Having heard more than enough about such short-lived, atom-bomb-like relationships (and reflecting silently that if an abrasive bloke like Scarron could have multiple girlfriends, Durtal should have no trouble being the next Sean Connery), I opined, "Drugs and women can be pretty expensive."

"*Life's* expensive," Scarron retorted. "*Family's* expensive," he added, taking a quick look at the gilded ceilings above us and suddenly waxing loquacious. "We lost everything years ago." He seemed transported back in time. "The whole reason I went into law enforcement was to try to stop traders from manipulating markets."

"Why did you want to reform the world of finance?"

He gave me a disgusted but possibly candid look for once.

"My father got wiped out by unscrupulous currency traders and didn't survive the blow. I wanted to clean things up, but the AMF wouldn't hire me.* They claimed I was too emotional about money. Traders destroy young kids and families everywhere, not just tycoons in London and New York."

"What exactly did you want to fix? High finance or your family?" I asked archly.

"Messing with markets hurts real people. It can bankrupt plenty of honest folk … My life is still a shambles."

As he rose to his feet and headed for the exit, he bumped into a castle staffer carrying a tray of mugs and hot coffee that Zeus had conjured up from the belly of the beast. Not one to apologize, Scarron turned toward the prefect and unleashed, "Your precious Inspector Canal left the concert even before I did—why don't you ask *him* what he's doing here? He knows everything and everyone, he's everywhere, and he's always there before the rest of us."

"Bang!" went the massive door as he slammed it on the way out.

* * *

Durtal's phone buzzed and he left the room for a few minutes. Upon his return, he closed the towering wooden door and lowered himself onto one of the incongruously modern chairs across from mine set up in the extravagant decor. "You were trying to find out all about me too, weren't you? Why were you drawing me out about my ex-wife? You even got me to tell you my favorite joke at the Relais de Chambord. Why? To learn how to manipulate me? The barmaid there was hanging on to our every word. Did you pay her to spy on me?" he thundered in the mostly empty gilded room, his voice bouncing off a hundred gold and blue mythological figures and exotic animals on the ceiling. "It seems like you've been galivanting around since the beginning of the investigation and yet you know everything before we do." Glaring at me, he added, "Did you let the guy die tonight? Maybe you already know who killed him!"

What could I say? "I didn't. I even tried to perform CPR on Dupont to revive him." I presumed the prefect would never have heard of people who attack someone and then try to undo what they have just done, feeling guilty for it immediately after having satisfied their aggressive wishes, their affectionate feelings for the victim returning to the fore. We humans are bizarre creatures, after all! Unfortunately, no one had witnessed my attempt to bring him back to life—all they saw was blood on my hands.

"Stranger things have happened …," he asserted. "And now it turns out that you know Lavillaine very well."

My jaw dropped.

"The two of you wrote an article together and are both members of a private, hush-hush math club in Manhattan."

"Actually," Le Coq interjected quietly, "Castillo told us Inspector Canal works on topology."

"Yes, topology," the prefect repeated emphatically. "In fact, you mentioned topological space the very first time we met at Chambord. Yet you pretended you didn't recognize Lavillaine and that you had never even heard of him before the incident at Villandry."

Canaples was suddenly pushed into the room by the Deux-Sévrien guards. She was loudly threatening to contact the U.S. Embassy in Paris, the Attorney General of Michigan, and even the Commander-in-Chief himself at the White House.

* * *

"You just can't stop ruining my trip here, can you?" she said, looking the grand prefect straight in the eye.

"Still in France, Miss Canaples?" Durtal inquired, annoyed.

"Not this again!" She shot the prefect a venomous look and then a quizzical look at me. "I want to go home! I'm just a tourist now." She took her phone out of her purse, said "Excuse me" matter-of-factly, and shot a few pictures of the overhead paintings of Mars, Minerva, Icarus, and the Three Fates surrounded by huge, intricate, gilded plaster frames. "These are unbelievable! Who built this place? The Marquise of Poisons I read about in my guidebook?"

Much like Canaples' ex-husband, Durtal obviously didn't appreciate her verve and sense of humor. (So what if her information was not strictly accurate?) He opened the door and ordered her to wait outside a few more minutes. She glared at him, looking like she'd love to poison him.

* * *

"Are you going to continue to maintain you'd never seen the famous mathematician before that night at Villandry?" Durtal shouted at me.

"Canal told us," Le Coq said, "he'd been in Champagne before coming to the Loire Valley, and even told me how many cases he'd shipped back to New York! But he was actually in Bordeaux and attended a lecture Lavillaine gave there. I have it from a reliable source—the same source who saw the fist fight between Couard and Bouture with his own eyes."

"Lavillaine and I may have both published articles in the same journal once," I responded evenly and deliberately. "But that's all."

"That's all?" Le Coq echoed.

"Your source is not as unimpeachable as you think."

"It is reliable," Durtal averred angrily. "I can call him in a second and he'll repeat the exact same thing, word for word."

"What does that have to do with reliability?" I spoke more forcefully. (I could have highlighted the *lie* in reliability which most people overlook, but reckoned it wasn't the time or place.) "People jump to conclusions every day. They pretty much always believe whatever it's most convenient to believe," I stated slowly, while looking at them intently. How could I convince them? They were probably hearing this simple verity for the first time. "Does your source even know what I look like?"

"More of your bullshit rhetoric!" Durtal growled. "You use perverse methods to get into people's heads."

"Everyone, absolutely everyone, makes serious mistakes—"

"There you go again with your twisted twaddle!" the prefect interrupted.

"Everyone makes mistakes," I persevered, "when they believe whatever is easiest to believe." I knew this unfortunately wasn't my best line of defense, since no one ever wants to assume responsibility for making mistakes. I took out my wallet. "Would you like to see the receipts for my champagne purchases and my hotel near Epernay?"

Finding no takers (and figuring Le Coq was thinking "Enough with the champagne already!"), I changed tack: "Don't write me off just yet. In any case, I'm not going anywhere, so you can always book me later." I adjusted my bow tie. "Let me help interrogate the others." They goggled at me and seemed to be at a loss for words. "I believe I have a knack for asking the right questions, helpful questions."

"Do you now?" Durtal inquired mockingly.

A rather long silence ensued. Once you're accused of a crime, it's almost impossible to *prove* your innocence unless you can prove that someone else did it. I had my work cut out for me.

"Almost nobody really listens anymore," I finally proffered. "But I listen intently to everything people say, and everything they seem about to say but don't, then get them to spill."

* * *

"What are you doing here, Miss Canaples," Durtal inquired without much enthusiasm, "so far from your Olympic swimming pools and fantastic racers?"

"Inspector Canal recommended that I visit the castle and attend the concert tonight," the woman uttered as lightning lit up the immense wheat fields beyond the moat and the room flashed white. "I'm just touring around." A loud crash followed.

"What do you know about topology?" he asked.

She looked slightly surprised. "I don't study deformable spaces," she replied.

267

"And yet you know the technical term," Le Coq remarked. "Rather extraordinary for a swim coach!"

"I know nothing about topology. I came to France to buy something, that's all. I'm surrounded by professors and hear about plenty of fields."

"But I can't understand why you're still here. There's got to be more to the story," the prefect asserted.

"There isn't! The swim team is my life and I'll do anything to help them."

"Anything?" I echoed.

"I have to protect my girls. I don't understand why *you* can't understand! The teenagers and twenty-year-olds I train are not well. They are unable to work out on certain days because they're too weak or ill," she said heatedly.

"What does that have to do with anything?" Le Coq objected.

"Monsanto, Dow, Corteva, DuPont, and Syngenta are killing them with junk they put in their bodies every day. Even though I carefully recruit for our team, almost every swimmer turns out to have bizarre hormonal or thyroid problems. None of the swimmers had any such problems two generations ago. I have to keep mine alive and whip them into shape, but they're being poisoned!"

Le Coq glanced at her coffee cup and the energy bar next to it.

"We *aren't* here to talk about the health of girls in Michigan!" she said sharply.

"I'm just trying to help my athletes get a new competitive edge. That's my job."

"Perhaps there is something personal in all this, too?" I queried. Her tone had, after all, been surprisingly vehement. "A dearth of medals?"

"I set a world record for backstroke in my sophomore year at UC Berkeley, I'll have you know," she rejoined. "I would have had plenty— my coach expected me to be the next Janet Evans!"

"I remember her," Le Coq said. "And she looked healthy enough to me."

Canaples fiddled with her purse and said, "Well that was thirty years ago."

"You had no career as a swimmer," the commissioner went on aggressively, after glancing at the screen of the laptop open before her. "How could you possibly coach a top team?"

"A wealthy alumnus reneged on his promised donation to the Berkeley team and my scholarship got cancelled. I had to work full-time to stay in school, which meant I couldn't swim anymore," Canaples replied bitterly. "I read in the papers that the shares of corporations he invested in had plummeted because of some environmental misconduct in Europe. Anyway, he dumped us, saying that the team wasn't 'diverse' enough," she continued. "But the athletic director at U of M believed in me and gave me a chance."

"Life has a way of putting things right," I commented.

"How do you explain your total lack of jet lag?" Le Coq renewed her attack.

"Easy. My swim team competes in every U.S. time zone from Maine to Alaska to Honolulu. I'm so used to traveling, I can sleep any time, any place."

"Where did you go during the second piece?" the commissioner persisted.

"To the ladies room. I hope that is allowed in this country."

"Which staircase did you take?"

"The one over this way," she replied, pointing toward the door at the back of the room we were in that led out to the straight flights.

"Did you encounter anyone?"

"I wish I had—the place is so gigantic I almost got lost!"

* * *

They had gazed into a heart of luminous stone.

The three "second" violinists, tired and spooked, all told the same story: they had hung out together near the regal semicircular staircase on the opposite side of the King's Great Hall, contemplated its hollow central core, and seen the concertmaster, with a worried look on his face, go down those steps and return shortly before the sirens began to howl. We released them from the sequestered stone giant in the remote countryside, sending them back to Seuilly Abbey, their new and much closer home away from home since leaving the Saturn in Blois.

* * *

"Are you a competitive swimmer?" asked Le Coq.

"No, I can't swim," said the thin-faced, gray-haired woman, whose name was Ren Claude and who lived in Chinon and worked at the municipal pool there.

269

"Are you aware we just interviewed a world record setter?"

"What do I care?" she replied belligerently, her little silver pin sparkling as she shook her head. "I just work the cash register."

"Why did you come to the concert tonight?" Durtal inquired firmly. "Isn't it rather far from where you live?"

"I like classical music but I can't stand being in crowded spaces. The concert hall here is spacious. I go to Easter mass at Fontevrault because it's in a large church."

"Do you know *L'Orangeraie*?" I asked. "It isn't far from Fontevrault."

"I can't afford restaurants."

At least she knew it was a restaurant, I thought. "How do you feel about flowers?" She rolled her eyes. "What about Leonardo da Vinci?" I heard the commissioner snort.

Ren Claude eyed me cautiously. "Something big must have happened here tonight," she commented.

"What did you imagine?" I asked, Curious George that I am.

"Poetic justice!"

"Poetic justice?" I echoed, after recognizing the pin she was wearing.

"I mean, this place just screams out for it. Haven't you noticed the giant scales of justice hanging above us everywhere, warning us? The Greek goddess Themis brutally punishes mortals when they trespass the moral law." She sounded worked up and ready to fight.

"Where did you go during the second piece tonight?" I inquired.

"Which one was that?"

"Farina's suite of dances."

"Oh, that one—I didn't go anywhere then. I left for the ladies' when I thought the piece by Vivaldi was over. I can never figure out how many movements there are in each concerto, and thought it was finished."

"Yet you said you like classical music."

"Doesn't mean I know everything. I heard the whole Farina—all three movements." She looked off toward the exit, and I took the opportunity to hold up four fingers for Durtal and Le Coq to see, there being in fact four movements in that particular suite, even if the fourth had been interrupted tonight.

"A rich man died here tonight," I remarked.

"Some capitalist finally got his just desserts? What, whacked by one of the branches of the Lebanon cedars out front, falling in the storm? No, it must've happened when the lights flickered and then went out altogether!"

"You're the one who killed him?" Le Coq asked excitedly.

"Honey," she replied, looking the commissioner straight in the eye. "Ask yourself one thing before you book me: who are your real friends? Who in the Loire Valley has your back when you go to sleep at night?"

"You?"

"Certainly not Wall Street tycoons, the engineers running the nuclear reactors in Avoine and Saint-Laurent that leak radioactive tritium into the river every month, or the businesses that dump all kinds of other toxic stuff into your drinking water and get away with it. They'd just as soon turn you into a corpse!"

"You seem to think you are under suspicion," I commented, "but we just want your account of tonight's events."

"Was the CEO of EDF* hit by lightning?" she went on, giving her imagination free rein. "Or did some fat cat investor in Pfizer take a tumble down the stairs? I'd love to give 'em a push!"

"Let her go," I said, having heard enough.

Durtal, who couldn't have cared less about her grand ideals, was about to concur when Le Coq suddenly cried, "What? Just when we finally have something ... someone ... a lead?"

I signaled to Durtal and he agreed to dismiss her.

"Don't try to dupe us again!" Le Coq hurled at me after the door closed behind Ren Claude. "What could you possibly know about that woman?"

"She's part of an ecoterrorist group that snuck into the nuclear power plant near Chinon." Glancing at Durtal, I added, "I did some research after our little chat over breakfast at the Relais de Chambord. She was probably the one who squirted pink ink on the engineers in the main control room to demonstrate how easy it is for anyone to waltz right in and take over. She's killed rich guys like Dupont alright ... in her dreams."

* * *

"I hate the music, so I get the fuck out of Dodge whenever I can," a damp-looking Enrique replied when I asked him why the audio technician would leave during the concert, the Symphonie de Provence's first performance ever at Oiron. "Went to the crapper for ten minutes. It's just a job."

He was met with surprised looks.

271

"I'm not the only one who hates it. Françoise Foix"—here he looked specifically at me, savoring the moment—"only admits she prefers jazz when there are no bigwigs or snobs around. You saw it yourself at that bourgeois wine bar you took her to!"

"I'm surprised you don't prefer salsa, reggae, or merengue to EDM," I remarked.

"Are you all crazy about Edith Piaf?" he asked, his eyes sweeping the three of us. We shook our heads in unison.

"Still, ten minutes is a pretty long break," I commented, "Mightn't you have to make some adjustments during the adagio?"

"Well, I did have a smoke as well."

We waited silently.

"Okay, I had a few hits of weed," Enrique added matter-of-factly. "I wouldn't need it if they were playing Goa or punk."

"Where did you smoke?" asked the prefect.

"Out back. It's wicked dark near the moat," he explained, grinning. "I wasn't the only one either. I left right around the same time as a guy seated in the last row."

"Did you see anyone when you came back?"

"No one."

"How long have you been with the Symphonie de Provence?" I asked.

"Long enough to know better."

"How would you characterize your relations with the concertmaster?"

"They bite."

"Bite?" Durtal reiterated.

"Yes, they bite," he said, rolling his eyes.

"Why? Is Civadin a beast after concerts? A party animal? A womanizer? A secret bourgeois trafficker in period piccolos for the rich maestro, Wack?" I proposed.

He didn't even crack a smile, looking at me strangely instead. "Not exactly the happy-go-lucky type." I couldn't believe he said it without batting an eye. "He's a stickler who never had to give a single violin lesson his whole life, doesn't lift a finger to help me, and claims he is 'elevating the masses.' The conductor's more fun, if snobs like that can be fun," he added as an aside.

"You really expect us to believe you have to work for a living?" asked Le Coq.

"I do."

"When your uncle owns Embraer?"

"What?!"

"Have you ever heard of Northrop Grumman?" Jeanne went on.

Enrique fell silent for once, then seemed to yield. "Yes, it's a major competitor of Embraer's."

"What do you know about DuPont?"

"One of the biggest chemical producers in the galaxy."

"You know Sallaud Industries?"

"Builds cutting-edge stealth fighter jets with depleted uranium in them."

"What's the deal with you and your uncle?"

"He tried to groom me to take over the business by bribing me—first with ice cream, and later with money and even Ferraris," he replied calmly. "But I chose to make my own life and follow my own rules. I couldn't give a rat's ass about being rich! If I have to put up with know-it-alls who are stuck in the past playing 'positive organs,' well that's just the way it goes."

"Isn't it true that your father is also one of the wealthiest men in Brazil, Mr. Castro? Or should I say, Marquis de Castro?" Looking up from her screen, the commissioner paused for effect.

The man who spit on castles and everyone who liked classical music was of noble birth? "How delightfully twisted," I reflected silently.

A burp was Enrique's only reply.

* * *

Our next interrogatee tugged on her well-tailored little black dress as she crossed her legs. A black pump with a big preppy-looking bow on it jiggled in the air, while she twirled her strand of lustrous triple-A pearls with a finger. She was so expensively dressed that I found myself wondering how a self-declared fancy-pants hater like Enrique could truly fancy Françoise. Love is so peculiar! Then again, the boy obviously protested too much—unconsciously loved what he so plangently professed to hate. Don't we all? Maybe the lowly techie was even secretly paying for all her Fifth Avenue outfits from a trust fund.

"Where did you go during the second piece?" Durtal began.

"Downstairs," she replied placidly.

"Be more precise."

"If you must know, I went to the chapel," she said haughtily.

"To the chapel?"

"Yes, to pray," she asserted.

"For something in particular?"

"That's between God and me."

I have been blessed with a rather geographical memory and can walk through many a castle in my mind, recalling which room lies where and how the various wings are laid out with respect to the compass rose. "All you can do is glance in the chapel from the outside. Where did you really go, Françoise?"

She said nothing.

"A secret tryst?" She looked down.

"Obviously not with Henri Wack. I guess he is no longer your cup of tea. And I had hoped I might be next," I feigned dismay. "I guess I did not make the grade." The chapel is close to the giant semicircular staircase the violinists said the concertmaster had descended. All I'd have to do is wangle a confession from him and she'd be off the hook. A good thing, too, because I preferred to think of her as a charmingly nutty boy-hating "manizer" than as a …

She smiled wanly. "A girl's taste in tea can always change," she replied, fiddling with her pearls again. The baubles seemed to mean something. Were they the family jewels? A gift from a prince? Their quality was uncannily high and their sheen unique.

"Especially if she's used to drinking hers from a samovar," I added. "Your grandfather, who was in the French resistance, went over to Russia's side after World War II, right? And he served as a spy throughout the Cold War. Some even say he was a double agent. How long have you actually been with the symphony?"

"Three months. Before that I was—"

"In the GRU? You worked for FATRAS, Ms. Foix," the commissioner interjected as she scrolled through a few screens on her flickering laptop, "a major arms manufacturer."

"I worked for FATRAS, briefly, yes."

"In fact, you were the personal secretary of the head of a large department there. Weren't you spying on them for Russia?"

Françoise seethed.

Le Coq looked her right in the eye. "You only took this low-paying job with the symphony to assist and even protect Pislova."

"Pislova? What? No! *J'avais du piston* at FATRAS, a family connection who helped me get the job."

With her style and looks, she needed a lot of money—indeed, her wardrobe was far too expensive to be afforded on her pittance as a flautist—but I doubted she needed any *piston*!

The commissioner looked at the laptop again and remarked, "Your department at FATRAS was invisibility to radar, a highly classified area." The commissioner looked at the screen again. "It says here that you 'accessed files for which you had no authorization.'"

"I hope God can vouch for you," I said in a serious tone of voice.

* * *

"As a matter of fact, I do know Charles Bouture," the concertmaster replied, while showing some surprise at my question. "A fine scientist and not a bad winemaker."

"He's dead." Okay, I knew he might not be, but I could always clear that up later.

His face appeared to fall. "Was he here tonight? Is that why we are all being detained?"

"He was about to publish his latest research. Any idea who might want to stop him?" I inquired, noticing that he sat on the metal folding chair with his back straight-as-an-arrow.

"What did it show?" the musician asked.

"It showed … something unexpected," I replied.

"Did it, now?" Civadin seemed cool, calm, and collected at present.

"You aren't always Orlando Civadin, are you?" I said, changing tack slightly. I scrutinized his face and went on, "People don't always see the real you, do they?"

I hoped he would respond before Durtal and Le Coq grilled me, as it would have been too time-consuming to explain my conclusions relying on hair-length, intensity of facial expression, and musculature stemming from my idiosyncratic reverie-based working methods.

"At Amboise Castle, for example," I added, peering intently at the silent virtuoso.

"I haven't seen it since I took Cremona to attend *la commedia dell'arte* there during our honeymoon many years ago," he answered, speaking softly. "But I did make an appearance in one of my vilest disguises at

L'Auberge du Bon Laboureur in Chenonceau a couple of days ago," he added, smiling as if remembering a real coup. His handsome face and long locks seemed to belong to an alternate reality.

"Not exactly Brad Pitt," sniggered Durtal, looking shocked even though he must have run into bizarre people from all walks of life before.

"I generally prefer to remain anonymous," the man replied. "I have too much going on, too many activities ..."

I raised my eyebrows.

"It helps," he said cryptically. "Most people steer clear of ugliness. I find it compelling." Le Coq looked up at him. "And no one's jealous of a poor hideous soul, with a hump to boot, who's trying to change the world. In any case, ugly faces are very useful, Monsieur le Préfet," he added, clearly captivated by them. "A guy I used to work for had a chauffeur. I often saw him get out of the car to open and close the door for his boss. He was probably the most unsightly man I had ever seen. Don't get me wrong—I'm not like Leonardo da Vinci who thought ugliness on the outside necessarily went hand in hand with moral depravity on the inside. But I chose to imitate that specific look because I thought it was the one most diametrically opposed to my own." This from a man who professed to have passed the age of seduction. People truly are nothing but a bundle of living, breathing contradictions well into adulthood, even former child prodigies—assuming, that is, he was telling us the truth.

"So how are you trying to change the world?" inquired Le Coq.

"At times, by developing algorithms." (I couldn't help but imagine Al Gore rhythmically dancing the Macarena when he said the word, but tried to focus.)

"So 'at times' you're not just a musician, but a mathematician too?" the prefect asked.

"Affirmative."

"Any specific field?" I inquired.

"Turbulence at present."

"Turbulence," I reiterated, "which is, some say, the most important unsolved problem in physics—"

"You said you want to change the world," Durtal interrupted me. "Using your expertise? I want straight answers, not digressions."

"Yes. The new-model jets being sold today are largely untested. The Federal Aviation Administration and the European Aviation Safety Administration let commercial airline pilots test the aircraft for their

276

manufacturers, hoping against hope that any remaining problems won't be catastrophic and can be corrected through retrofits after delivery. I am utilizing this planetary experiment."

There was a chill in the room.

What was he talking about? I was aware that unproven prototypes were rushed out the door by executives falling over themselves to please shareholders. They put tremendous pressure on their engineers to make good on billions in R&D investments. It's one of the financial realities of the business.

Many other companies did much the same, as I well knew, releasing new largely untested medications, the Food and Drug Administration tacitly allowing pharmaceutical firms to use the general public as guinea pigs in their longitudinal "studies" (and even assuming legal liability when there were class-action suits against their most dangerous vaccines). Cashing in on gargantuan investments in R&D in the business world is an imperative like "publish or perish" in academia.

"Utilizing this experiment? What? How? While wearing a disguise?" Le Coq queried, seeming at a loss to decide what question to ask.

"I doubt my algorithms for modeling turbulence are much more sophisticated than the ones jet manufacturers already have at their disposal," the sometime hunchback remarked. "But they have allowed me, I believe, to uncover something. I know what they know. Yet none of the documents necessary to prove it can be obtained without subpoenas or hacking into their mainframes—not an easy task for the police, or even for me!" he added, not so modestly. "Only WikiLeaks might be able to pull it off."

"Are we talking about the same algorithms that you were hoping to sell at noon today?" I asked.

"Only a few of them."

"Only a few of them, but Northrop Grumman is a major-league player."

"Wait, how do you know about that?"

"Just tell us what you discovered," I insisted firmly. "Or are you simply aiming for Wiki whistleblower fame?"

"No! I take the world's biggest airliner builders to task in an article that will be coming out shortly."

Uproars did, I knew, regularly occur when risks that were known to certain high-ups at aircraft companies weren't addressed. The malfunctioning of rudders, bespoke software, and space-age batteries eventually led planes to fall out of the sky. Was that what Civadin was talking about?

"What the hell did you discover already?" the prefect snapped.

* * *

A woman from the Deux-Sévrien police force poked her head in the door and gestured toward us with an index finger. Durtal, Le Coq, and I gathered around her in the hallway.

She whispered, "A stretch limousine pulled up in front of the castle entrance a few minutes ago. The driver from Poitiers came to pick up a client who was supposed to call him hours ago to bring him back to his hotel, a certain J. Rosso—a dark-haired man in a blue jacket, yellow bow tie, and glasses." The name echoed sinisterly in the cavernous corridor.

"Your Monsieur Dupont is Jorge Rosso?" cried Lecoq, suddenly dumbfounded.

"It looks that way," I nodded.

* * *

We found Civadin in an exceedingly odd position upon our return—stretched out between two incongruous metal folding chairs in the middle of the room, his head and shoulders on one, his feet on the other, his torso and hips straight as an arrow between them, like James Coburn in *Our Man Flint*. He rose and scratched his head for a moment.

"Who was this man?" I silently wondered, inviting him to take a seat.

"What exactly happened here tonight?" the concertmaster asked. "Was Charles Bouture killed?"

"He was, but not tonight. He was on the verge of publishing some groundbreaking research," I said. "I thought you might know who'd want to suppress his work."

"Well, what did this 'groundbreaking research' of his show?" There was a touch of irony in his voice.

"How to vastly simplify vinification techniques so that expensive temperature-controlled vats won't be necessary in winemaking," I replied.

"Well, then, *cui bono*? If we follow the money, it was probably those who stand to lose the most: a firm called Frigorifica. And from what I hear, the people there are not above employing force."

278

"Do you know J. Rosso?" Le Coq asked the concertmaster impulsively.

"Which one?" was his answer.

"You know more than one J. Rosso?" Durtal dared inquire.

"Yes, I know two."

Durtal looked thoroughly exasperated. The limousine driver's docket simply read J. Rosso, and we all at once realized it could have been the infamous magnate, but it might, instead, have been Jean Rosso, Jacques Rosso, or even Jean-Jacques Rosso!

This piece of news sounded bad to me. I wondered if the world was sturdy enough to withstand two Rossos …

Le Coq stifled an exclamation.

Civadin breathed in sharply, "Is this some kind of a joke?"

He was met only with incredulous looks.

"Are you saying you know the *infamous* Jorge Rosso, R.O.S.S.O.?" the commissioner asked.

"I do."

* * *

I had to duck out of the King's Bedchamber in search of fresh air and to marshall my thoughts. The rain had mostly stopped and, removing my jacket and bow tie—and even my metal-framed glasses, which wouldn't stay put on my nose—I paced up and down the Horse Arcade that formed one side of the castle courtyard. The perfectly vaulted ceilings and the images of the king's finest steeds on its walls were almost invisible at this witching hour.

Everything I'd read and heard about Jorge Rosso came flooding back to mind. He was no ordinary billionaire trying to bring clean drinking water to the entire planet. He publicly proclaimed that his goal was to promote world peace. But the man shook up currency markets deliberately for his own benefit, bankrupting people far and wide, some of whom had maybe even been at tonight's concert.

Peace, equality, tolerance, love, and understanding among different peoples—Rosso publicly epitomized all of those owing to his mountains of self-aggrandizing propaganda. But with his massive wealth and stranglehold tactics, he forced massive numbers of people to leave their homelands and emigrate—to Europe, above all, where they overwhelmed the ability of nations to integrate and assimilate them—which, not surprisingly, led to the opposite of love and tolerance. And the total blenderizing of radically different peoples' customs and traditions, which he aided and abetted, led to one global consumer culture—to which the companies he owned or controlled conveniently catered. Quite a racket!

Heading up FATRAS for years, he was currently the controlling shareholder of Sallaud Industries which was working on the next generation of stealth bombers, hoping to leapfrog the current state-of-the-art aircraft produced by Northrop Grumman. Like scientists and politicians whom I considered to be insane for asserting that if everyone had the atom bomb, no one would use it, Rosso claimed that if everyone had his fighter jets, no one would use them and peace would reign forever after.

The only obstacle to achieving that would be government policies restricting sales to certain willing buyers considered to be enemies of the state … He obviously didn't give a damn about the poor countries that couldn't afford his billion-dollar wares—his goal was simply to sell as many bombers as possible to the rich.

Everyone knows that the temptation to use arms, once a country has them, is almost irresistible. Manufacturers even encourage such use as it is the only way to test their weapons in the field and demonstrate their superiority to other companies' offerings. That made Rosso's platform a perfect example of Orwellian doublespeak.

Belying his public celebration of diversity, his actions tended to reduce all difference to the same, the many to the One—as if in some perverted form of Neoplatonism. Save the world by destroying it, foster diversity by making everyone identical, preserve cultural difference through total uniformization of tastes and goods—more doublespeak.

Some might say that, being French, I was especially allergic to everything uniform—in other words, insipid—and his brand of homogenization (Americanization) went hand in hand with the decline of France and the ascendancy of English over French. But so what?

Had Rosso Machiavellianly acquired prestigious billion-dollar "first growth" vineyards in Bordeaux over the past thirty years to combat insipidity? Hardly. Probably just wanted to be a major player in super-expensive wines. But Bouture's research would level the playing field for small-scale and third-world winemakers, and the ensuing flooding of the market with good quality wines would seriously diminish the value of Rosso's acreage. Not to mention the sales of Frigorifica's fermentation vats. When the almighty dollar was at stake, you could be sure that all of Rosso's supposedly moral and social principles would go out the window!

I suddenly stopped pacing. "Why did a famous mathematician disappear at Villandry," I wondered, "only to reappear in Shanghai?" Was it because of his work on turbulence? The Chinese would, of course, want it, but so would Rosso.

And what was I thinking? Sallaud industries was not restricted like Grumman was by U.S. policies dictating who you could sell to. Rosso could sell his weapons to whomsoever he liked, just like he could sell standardized junk to the entire planet through his empire of multinationals.

Yet the mogul was, I had read, a major investor in Airbus, not Boeing. Maybe he'd told his gun-toting goon to allude to Boeing to hide his identity. Civadin's paper was, after all, going to tar both companies with the same brush. Had he sent another of his thugs, a female this time, to poison Livingston?

I knew of no vested interest in sports on Rosso's part, although he probably owned shares in a number of sporting goods makers. Had Canaples jumped out the window to divert attention from something else she was up to? Was anyone truly honest? She might very well have had a second mission in coming to France: to stop Livingston from getting information on turbulence and invisibility that her university's physics department wanted. All's fair in love, academe, and the Olympics?

* * *

"Was one of the two Rossos still hiding in some nook or cranny in the castle?" I wondered as I returned to the interrogation room, filled with a sense of foreboding.

"So you said you know two Rossos," I addressed Civadin open-endedly.

"I have that dubious honor."

My eyebrows shot up. "Huh."

"Javier Rosso showed up at a concert I gave some years ago and we struck up a friendship. He is a true gentleman, very warm and caring," he averred as he rose charily from his chair and began gesturing broadly as he paced the floor before us. "Indeed, an avuncular sort of guy. Honest, upright, an overall good egg." Civadin's vocabulary truly harkened back to another time, befitting the setting, I reflected, and he appeared to enjoy having an audience. "Gives anything shady a wide

281

berth. He is well respected in his field, even though he shuns the lime-light. He figured out not long ago that he had a twin when he began to read about Jorge in the newspapers. Didn't like what he read either.

"The two brothers are—if you will allow me a possibly inapposite metaphor that just occurred to me—like those two staircases at Chambord Castle that wrap around each other as they ascend and descend, but never meet." He stroked his nascent beard. It was as if da Vinci himself had just spoken. How uncanny!

"So don't believe the lies told in those stupid studies," he turned toward me, as if seeking a likeminded soul, "claiming that identical twins are astoundingly alike, even when raised separately."*

"Yes," I concurred, "they almost never bother to discuss the ones who aren't. Psychologists are fixated on sameness."

Civadin stopped pacing for a moment and then added, "I apologize, for, just as I suspected, my simile wasn't terribly apt. The flights of stairs at Chambord are identical, whereas Jorge and Javier could hardly be more antipodal, except in their style of dress." Looking up, he remarked, "In any case, the very imperfection of the analogies and metaphors we construct is stimulating, forcing us, as it does, to rethink things."

I guess he always spoke like that. I, for one, appreciated his refined phraseology, and at least he didn't buy the explanations I had some-times heard proposed for the double spiral at Chambord—good and evil eternally wrapped around each other, the ascent to heaven inextricably tied to the descent into hell, and all that bunkum.

I poured myself another cup of coffee, a habit I'd undoubtedly acquired in America, land of the bottomless cup. "You seem to love one and hate the other," I remarked, chagrined that I hadn't thought to check if the man on the landing was accoutered *exactly* like the one I'd spoken with in the Renaissance Gallery, never for a moment having suspected he might have a doppelgänger.

"Javier became a sort of father to me—the father I never had. Jorge never tried to understand me," the concertmaster added ruefully, "so I decided to break off my financial dealings with him last year and to devote myself to my art and science."

"Yet," I remarked, "diamond bracelets and designer dresses don't exactly grow on trees."

"The money was nice for a while, but it's no substitute for a heart." He suddenly dropped dejectedly onto his chair.

Civadin had perhaps wanted to invent for himself a good father—following Nietzsche's dictum—since he hadn't had one, but the fiction couldn't hold. And it was plain he didn't endorse Kierkegaard's notion that hard work allows one to give birth to one's own father, allowing one to dispense with a real one, or get over never having had one. Orlando still wanted a paternal figure in his life and the avuncular Javier was better than nothing.

The climax of the toccata having passed, he continued, "I didn't break off my dealings with my father out of solidarity with my mother against the 'monster,' as she called him, but for my own piece of mind."

Having denied something none of us had suggested, I had to wonder if he hadn't refused the allowance Jorge had been supplying precisely out of solidarity with his mother.

"What do tonight's events have to do with the Rossos?" the concertmaster inquired.

"First tell us what your algorithms revealed," demanded Durtal.

Civadin rose to his feet and stretched his arms upwards into a gravity-defying pose. "The real reasons for the crashes of dozens of airliners. My analysis of those crashes will soon be coming out in *The Journal of Aviation Technology and Engineering*. The whole world will know once it does. Assuming I make it out of here tonight," he added.

"Why wouldn't you?" I inquired, reflecting that turbulence seemed to await us at every turn in this investigation, whether in the water, atmosphere, or relationships. "Just tell us where you went during the concert tonight and you'll be a free man."

"During the concert? I went to the chapel," he smiled.

* * *

"I didn't break off my dealings with my father out of solidarity with my mother"—Civadin's unprovoked denial still rang in my ears. Did he realize how many people sabotage or cut off their relations with one parent out of solidarity with the other? And how sad he looked when he said it?

The Queen Mother load would, I suspected, need to be handled with great care, and I gestured to Durtal and Le Coq to sit near the mammoth mullion windows so they wouldn't be in her direct line of sight. Yours truly began from what must have struck them as another "twisted" angle. The time had come to be surpassingly careful.

"How is your ankle feeling, Madame Breizh?" I asked, as if reading her name off the clipboard Le Coq had just passed me.

"A bit better, thank you. Your associate here," she indicated the commissioner, "gave me a nice little pink pill."

"I'm glad to hear it," I said, smiling kindly. "Unlike the others, I work for the Loire Valley Tourist Office, and we would be delighted to know your opinion on a few matters. How do you like our unique castles in the area? Do they live up to your expectations? And which period do you like the most?"

Although surprised at my questions, she replied eagerly, "My favorite is a very unusual one. It can only be seen in engravings today. Maybe the Cardinal of Richelieu was too avant-garde, but you don't expect the likes of a Parisian palace! He must have been a marvelous man," she exclaimed. "And I'd recommend you not tell anyone about the castle in Champigny-sur-Veude, because, you know, the Japanese might try to steal every last piece of it again."

I feigned note-taking and then looked up at her expectantly.

"Villandry is another of my favorites. I love to visit the gardens there."

"Oh, so you've been to the Loire before?"

"Countless times," she said. "Especially to see the Clos Lucé, my absolute favorite."

"You don't say! Are you an artist, by any chance?"

"Me? No, I have no artistic talent whatsoever."

"You must know Amboise Castle as well, then."

"No, I don't."

"What do you think of the gardens at Chenonceau?"

"The Medici Garden is quite nice. The much larger one built by Diane de Poitiers has always bored me. If it weren't bordered by the Cher River, I'd think they should just plow it under and turn it into a poppy field."

"The Cher does add a lot," I opined. I appreciated the larger garden more than she did, if nothing else because I have a soft spot for the gardeners there who employ only natural pest-control techniques, like hedgehogs to eat slugs and ladybugs to eat aphids.

"And the river is not nearly as deep as people think," she remarked. "If you dive in from almost anywhere, chances are you'll hit your head on the rocks on the bottom. I was there just last week and the water was lower than I ever saw it before."

284

"I was there recently myself, but I can't remember if it was before or after that big rain we had here."

"I was there Saturday, the day *after* the rain, but nothing ran off into the river."

"What do you think of the new gold *fleur-de-lys* on the tower at Saumur Castle?"

"I've only seen pictures of it. I can't believe they managed to put it up there! I bet Americans paid for all the gold leaf."

"What do you like best at Villandry?" I moved on to the next site on my imaginary checklist of the Valley of the Kings turned Vale of Blood.

"Oh, that's easy. The view of the whole valley and the lit up court-yards and moats from the north terrace during the *Mille Feux* festival. It's so pretty."

"It's a bit dangerous, though, don't you think?"

"Yes, the slightest misstep and one could take a fatal fall. And after all, *personne n'est à l'abri d'un accident*" (anyone can have an accident). She grinned a broad, cruel smile that exposed ugly black teeth.

"Oh, I think it would take a bit more than a misstep—a little push, I'd warrant."

"Well, only a very small push," she remarked, shifting her arms and shoulders and shaking her head, which released a lock of red hair from beneath a very damp gray wig.

"Why him?" I asked pointblank, before anyone else could get a word in.

"The plagiarist?" she replied matter-of-factly. "He gave a talk in Lyon and he stole Orlando's ideas! He deserved to die." She uttered these words with no trace of uncertainty.

"You didn't think your son could handle the situation himself?"

"My son can be a total idiot at times! He couldn't save himself if his life depended on it." The redundancy of her statement didn't seem to trouble her in the least. "By the time he was done trying to imagine how someone else could have come up with the same amazing formulas, the conniving Lavillaine would have already taken credit for everything. The snake had hacked into Orlando's computer. My son is the greatest genius in history and it's crucial that such brilliant work not end up in the hands of traitors."

"Who are the traitors?" I queried.

"The Americans, of course. They ruin everything."

"They do?"

"Obviously. The Russians would have liberated us in 1945 if the Americans hadn't butted in, turned our homes and cities into rubble, and made us into their clones."

The Marshall Plan and all that, of course …

"I found Orlando a good Russian buyer. High up in research and development in the United Aircraft Corporation," she recited proudly. "I even found him a bigwig," she beamed, "from the Russian Olympic team for his work on swimming who was willing to give him that crazy thing he needs."

"What thing?" I asked.

"A really fast calculator."

"Did he tell you what he wanted it for? Inventing new strokes?"

"No, silly. For his music. He analyzes the style of his favorite composers and creates new compositions in their style. Says he needs more computing power to improve the compositions."

That explained the mystery of the bizarre pieces the symphony had performed at Chenonceau. What was his angle? "Have there been any other occasions on which you had to help him out?" I asked.

"Countless occasions," she bragged. "Interlopers would usually back off right away, but some people are deaf. Anyway, there was always one buyer we disagreed about, and I had never able to get to him before—" she broke off.

A shiver went through my body, and I put my jacket back on, draped my yellow bow tie around my collar, and removed my glasses from my shirt pocket and put them on my nose, as though they, too, might warm me up.

Mrs. Breizh looked as though she were seeing a revenant.

That's when it dawned on me. "There but for the grace of God go I," I said to myself.

The woman whom most people would have thought perfectly normal, albeit a bit excitable when it came to her son, had mistaken me for Rosso and, if not for the lightning bolt that illuminated my face in that dark hallway, would have killed me in cold blood.

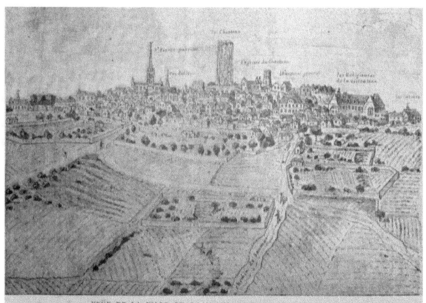

VEÜE DE LA VILLE ET CHASTEAU DE LOUDUN EN POICTOU

CHAPTER TWENTY

Return to Abbey Road

The idea that something or someone is irreplaceable frequently leads to an endless series, because every surrogate falls short.*

—Freud

My pumpkin-colored carriage, with a hundred and eighty-four horses chomping at the bit, awaited, so I offered to drive the motley crew of musicians back to their lodgings at nine-hundred-year-old Seuilly Abbey (which doesn't look a day over five hundred).

"What in the name of Handel's last sock just happened to my concert?" Wack asked obstreperously as we left the parking lot. The castle was still ablaze with emergency lighting, police cars were strewn all around the front gates, and we had to circumvent a fire truck blocking the road (the French always call the fire department whenever there is an emergency of any kind). But only one thing had occurred in the enigmatic palace tonight: the maestro's brilliant performance had been interrupted.

"Someone just jostled Jorge Rosso," I replied jokily (and presuming that Mrs. Breizh had not mistakenly conked his twin brother, about whose existence she may have known nothing).

"What?" cried the conductor. "Rosso attended my concert and no one introduced me to him? Why, he could sponsor a whole season of my symphony with a flick of the pen! Do you have any idea how many ducats I would need to put on *Psyche* the way it should really be performed?"

"Well, I'm afraid he won't be able to serve anyone as a generous benefactor now, if he ever did. He didn't survive the crash."

Wack looked crestfallen. "You don't know what you're missing—you only saw the bargain-basement version. Tell them, Orlando. We need wonderful people to donate mountains of moola to give the world what *Psyche* deserves!"

I turned slightly toward the concertmaster. "Would you prefer I not say anything?"

"Go on … ," he replied with a lump in his throat.

"Rosso would have done far better to underwrite your lavish production of *Psyche*, my dear conductor, but was instead the invisible force behind many evil projects, which sent far more than one innocent girl to hell with no hope of return."

"Hello? He claims to be for peace on earth and good will toward men," Enrique quipped.

"And for fairness and equality," Françoise sniggered. "Everyone knows that!"

"Yes, a man of myriad contradictions," I remarked, "like so many." Even in this very car, I reflected silently. "Working for 'peace and love,' this angel of death wanted Orlando's research on turbulence—do you mind if I call you by your first name?"

His blond locks stirred a little as he shook his head lugubriously.

"—in order to be able to kill even more people with ever more undetectable stealth fighter jets. Orlando is a true Renaissance Man, both musician and mathematician. You all remember Anna Pislova, don't you? A foreign power sent her to obtain his research for free, which she did."

"I thought she was hot!" Enrique volunteered.

"Pig!" cried Françoise. Turning to me, she asked, "Is that why you came to the Loire, to stop Pislova?"

"I was asked to help the police because of certain unusual goings-on. Almost immediately after I arrived, someone pushed a French mathematician by the name of Lavillaine off a ledge at Villandry Castle." Assuming Mrs. Breizh got the right man, I reflected silently. "And an American swim coach out a window at Chenonceau Castle two days later."

The audio technician whistled. "Scary bitch!"

"Wow, the bleached blonde killed Lavillaine?" Françoise exclaimed, overjoyed.

"No, the scary bitch wasn't her. Pislova was not one of those ordinary-seeming people we occasionally encounter who turns out to be a complete psycho."

Françoise pouted, disappointed.

"You mean it was Rosso?" Françoise inquired.

"No, it wasn't him either."

"Then who killed Lavillaine?" asked Enrique. "He was a funny dude, with those creepy crawlers on his jacket. Why would anyone want to kill *him*?"

"He was killed because of algorithms pertaining to the turbulence generated by jet engines," I answered.

"Mucho dinero at stake," ironized Enrique.

"What about the swim coach?" asked the flutist. "Is she the American you questioned? I heard in the King's Great Hall that she was from Mississippi and designed alligator-skin underwear."

"This story is getting screwier and screwier," the audio technician opined.

"She was shoved in the Cher, *ma chère*, because of fluid mechanics. A mother's 'love' did it all. A mother was convinced her only son's research on turbulence was being plagiarized by a famous mathematician, she wanted to deprive a U.S. team of his research on swimming because she hates Americans, and tonight she found a way to keep Rosso from ever exploiting her pride and joy again."

"Quite the wacko!" Enrique remarked heedlessly as Civadin bowed his head.

"What about my beautiful Anna?" Wack abruptly asked, oblivious to his second-in-command's distress.

"I swear you have a one-track mind, Henri," cried Françoise. "How can you be so dense?"

"She was Slavic and sexy," the conductor opined. "Don't you think I should hire that blond Bulgarian violinist who auditioned last week?"

I'd encountered egocentric people in my time, but not many as self-absorbed as Wack. No wonder he felt so alone! He kept hoping each new female to appear on his radar would make up for what he felt he had lost, his mother as goddess no doubt, instead of grappling with her irreplaceability. I guess he would never realize that trying to get back

291

what you think you've lost leads you to lose everything—even what you still have.

"Or should I hire the Finnish girl instead?"

His question having been ignored by one and all, the maestro turned toward Civadin and exclaimed, "Why couldn't you just follow your dream of becoming a soloist instead of mucking around in far-flung fields?"

"That's *your* dream, *your* fantasy, not mine," Orlando said sharply. Wack seemed to be on the receiving end of Civadin's hitherto suppressed fury at his mother (and at himself to boot), but appeared oblivious to that fact.

"What? Nobody goes to the Tchaikovsky Competition if they don't want to pursue a career as a solo violinist," the conductor said in a high-pitched voice.

"Well I did. I wanted to see what all the hype was about. I barely even practiced, unlike what you'd have done if you signed up for a competition," Orlando replied heatedly.

"Yeah, right," Wack retorted. "You probably played eight hours a day in a freezing cold room to simulate the balmy conditions in Moscow in June."

"Practice doesn't always make perfect," I interjected calmly.

"It can make you note perfect, but totally lacking in magic," Françoise chipped in. "You can work a piece until it is technically flawless, and there it lies, inert, uninspired, and uninspiring," she added, sighing softly.

"Better to miss a few notes than give a lifeless performance and kill your audience with boredom," Wack concurred pettily.

"Don't talk about killing or anything lifeless, okay!" As she shrieked, Françoise's pearls jiggled hysterically. "Not tonight!"

"Sometimes you perform better when you don't feel you have much at stake," I opined. "There is such a thing as trying too hard."

"Like I said," Wack went on, "it has to be fun, otherwise it's dead, lifeless, and a killjoy."

I wondered if Françoise was going to strangle him with her triple-A strand.

Turning to Henri, Orlando said, "You were the one who always wanted to be a soloist. What stopped you from pursuing a career as one? You can't possibly have fantasized about directing a band of divas and hotheads!"

"Why would I have taken up the recorder if I wanted a career as a soloist?" Henri bellowed. "People call my instrument a joke! How many guest recorder players can you name?"

I turned onto the main road north toward the Loire now, while listening intently to two of the world's top musicians bickering like an old married couple in a movie.

"Christopher Ball, Jan Van Hoecke—" Orlando almost yelled.

"Alison Melville," interrupted Françoise.

"Anna Fusek," chimed in Enrique. "I'd like to see her play punk naked!" It seemed the hydra-tattooed kid from the fabulously rich family knew more about classical music than he let on.

"So what really stopped you?" Orlando blared from the back seat.

Henri mumbled.

"Sapristi had his symphony, so you were damn well going to have yours?" I ventured.

Fiddling with the buttons on the passenger door and finally opening the window a crack, Wack ejaculated, "What is this nonsense about Anna Pislova? Are you trying to tell me that she wasn't interested in me at all?"

I glanced at Enrique in the rearview mirror and said, "Sorry maestro, but she was only interested in Orlando's innovations and Goa-lovers."

"Say what?" cried Mr. Ray of Sunshine. "Despite all the big shots in the orchestra, she liked me? Just my luck to find out only now. I must have the worst Karma in the galaxy," he carped, and this time I had the sense he really meant it, not like before when his griping sounded rehearsed and perfunctory.

"I hope they nab her at the border and get back that amazing music stand I gave her," the conductor said with great generosity.

"French borders are like Swiss cheese, you ninny," Françoise remarked, "full of holes."

"She is undoubtedly long gone. You've lost your chance to wring her neck," I added.

* * *

We were fast approaching the ill-famed town of Loudun, which was easy to spot from afar. The town, known for its nuns "possessed by the devil" and its inhabitants' use of poison to settle internecine disputes, is located atop a hill in the middle of a vast fertile plain. Its castle keep soaring above the wicked burg was still illuminated and my gang of four would fit right in.

We entered the medieval town center and, after questioning the few nocturnal strollers out well after midnight, I steered the car into a labyrinth of windy little one-way streets in search of the one place open at that hour: *Le Morning Lounge*. We finally spotted its dim lights and, after letting my passengers out, I maneuvered into a tiny parking space on a narrow cobblestone street.

Gathering around an oval wood table, Enrique seated himself squarely between myself and Françoise and we took the risk of ordering our respective Loudunian brews. I noticed Orlando, who probably needed a good stiff drink, wince when he tasted his. The knucklehead had ordered a tipple known in France as an *Americano*, thinking perhaps that it would be as sweet as the deal he had cut with A²'s swim team, but which turned out to be awfully bitter—the irony of the thing wasn't lost on me. Lo and behold, he went on drinking anyway!

"Why don't you let me order for you?" I had ordered cognac, although the brand on offer was no great shakes. It didn't much matter tonight, in my view: it was the minimum forty percent alcohol content we needed!

"I pride myself on finishing whatever I start," he replied. He sipped his bitter pool water yet again and screwed up his eyes, his nose wrinkling.

"Whether bad drinks or other things," I quipped, wondering if he would drain the cup of bitterness right to the dregs.

Civadin took a serious swig of the cognac the waiter placed before him and his face relaxed. "You mean the books? First-rate sleuthing," he remarked, holding up his glass to me, and I sensed his iciness begin to thaw.

"Elementary, my dear Watson." We clinked glasses.

"Did you know, Françoise," I asked, "that Da Vinci's *Treatise on Sculpture* and his *Treatise on the Human Figure* were just published? Turning toward Orlando, I asked, "What inspired you to complete them anonymously and invent a bogus publishing house in an abandoned warehouse district near Taviano in Puglia?"

The general mood finally began to lighten—in no little measure, perhaps, owing to the second round of drinks I had ordered—and the concertmaster's anger seemed to dissipate. "When you study some-one's work as much as I have studied da Vinci's, you begin to have the impression that you can fill in the blanks he left in his writings. You begin to imagine that you know what he himself would have said if only he'd taken the time to do so."

"And yet," I rejoined with delight at this change in topic, "as you just said, it is something you imagine, something you project onto his work, something you—"

He interrupted me, "Something *I* would say but which, while the master might recognize it as in continuity with his own train of thought and style, he would never have said himself. You are right. Had Leonardo wanted to write something in keeping with his own already established ideas, it would have been child's play for him to do so, sup-plying a sort of *tessera*. Instead, he was obviously seeking something radically different, something discontinuous," he said enigmatically.

"Fascinating," Françoise commented, looking at the concertmaster admiringly.

The lone waiter came over with more refills and I asked him to leave the bottle with us. For better or for worse, their brand of rotgut was beginning to taste alright.

"Indeed," I remarked, impressed with the concertmaster's grasp of the mindset of someone whose name was almost a perfect anagram of his own, "da Vinci was always trying to break new ground. Recall his warn-ing, 'Poor is the disciple who does not surpass his master.'"

Enrique whistled, but Wack frowned at this, perhaps thinking about his relationship with a certain conductor.

"He even strove to out-da-Vinci da Vinci," I went on and heard the waiter laugh behind me, even though we were the last remaining cus-tomers now and were preventing him from turning in. He'd probably had his fill of talk of Leonardo this summer. "What was predictable was never good enough for him. Some suffer from a tyrannical push to be normal or ordinary. He suffered from a relentless ambition to be extraordinary—as great as the immortal Archimedes."

"Men. Never happy," Françoise exclaimed derisively, glancing at me fleetingly.

Wack, staring at his glass, spoke up, "If Rosso had made a donation to the symphony, I wouldn't have to work so hard." He appeared to be fed up with being eclipsed by some Renaissance doodler.

"Anything the Florentine set in stone, or on paper or canvas," I continued, "had to be astonishing, breaking with what others before him had done. A bit like Mozart. No computer, no matter how many calculations it can perform per second, can ever produce a composition that truly sounds like Wolfgang. A computer can never inject soul into a piece, or delight us with the element of surprise." I eyed Orlando narrowly and he nodded. "You yourself might be able to do so, but no machine ever could, even if you fooled a lot of people."

"You mean that new piece we had to learn was not actually a long-lost concerto by Mozart?" Françoise cried.

"No, nor was the piece by Haydn or the one by Bach," I replied. "Orlando was testing us to see if we would detect the ruse," I added.

"Oh!" sneered Françoise. "No wonder ..."

"How dare you use *my* symphony like that!" Wack glared at him.

"I dared, yet no one on stage noticed, and only one spectator," the concertmaster informed us, "which was instructive. It makes you wonder if people are really listening," he mused aloud. "But who cares? It was fun for me."

Wack, looking positively furious, cried, "You're insane and demented! A real menace!" He hiccupped loudly.

I alone seemed to appreciate this unexpectedly ludic facet of Orlando's character.

"Leonardo hoped to figure out how to square the circle," the concertmaster went on anyway, seemingly encouraged by my tolerance of his utter and total lack of orthodoxy. "I hope to accomplish things that may be less impossible. Like mathematicians the world over, I long to prove Riemann's hypothesis or the Hodge conjecture, or both— why not! *Je veux toujours être sûr de développer ma démesure*" (I want to ensure that I always give free rein to my over-the-top-ness, my lack of moderation).

"Well at least you're not excessively modest!" Françoise quipped. "What will be next? A flakey pie crust that is foolproof?"

"I'm working on it," he replied without missing a beat.

"It's important to follow your most outrageous bents," I remarked. *Ce garçon gagne à être connu* (the better I know this guy, the more I like him), I thought to myself.

"I may be hubristic, but I'm not like Leonardo," Civadin chortled, sounding rather deep in his cups now. "Da Vinci had a serious problem—"

"Like you don't?" Wack roared after taking another slug of the forty percent liquor.

Orlando, who did the same, was clearly having fun and became insistent, "Forget about that stupid concert and let me finish. Da Vinci's problem, as I see it, hic, at least one of his problems, is that he wished to supersede all his predecessors even before knowing their work inside out."

"Everyone knows that," Wack proffered superciliously. I was sure he didn't.

"Still, don't you see that to think outside the box, you have to first discern what's in it? You must grasp the rules before breaking them and, like the great Newton himself, master the work of the giants on whose shoulders you stand if you truly intend to add to it, much less go beyond it." He hiccupped again and poured himself another glass of firewater, appearing to be really enjoying himself now, even if this late-night conversation was going to give rise to three more years of fighting with Wack onstage. "But Leonardo suffered from 'the anxiety of influence,' as Bloom called it, the fear of being influenced by others. And he suffered from it well before the critic—who was himself a product of what Auden called 'the age of anxiety'—claimed it began in his bleak vision of the *raison d'être* of all artistic creativity."

No one said a word. Only Civadin could include the poet W. H. Auden and Harold Bloom in a discussion of da Vinci while inebriated, I reflected, genuinely impressed. Orlando was no run-of-the-mill quant.

"You should listen to Terrorvision's album *How to Make Friends and Influence People*," Enrique eventually blurted out. He pulled out his smart phone, brought something up on the screen, and commenced swaying back and forth on his chair.

"Tons of young poets refuse to read others' work," the concertmaster went on addressing me, "for fear they'll unwittingly model their own on it or borrow from it."

"Fuck such snobs!" Enrique erupted. His broken-record-style contributions were getting old fast, yet I had a newfound fondness for him after hearing that he'd said no to pecuniary temptations few resist.

"As if originality were the only thing in the whole world that counted," I responded to Orlando. "Instead of beauty or profundity." I had never thought much of Steve Jobs' grammatically egregious advertising slogan, "Think different." And it could hardly be considered beautiful, even if it was performative.

Enrique smiled at Françoise, but the belle simply shrugged her shoulders.

"Leonardo was only human," the violinist sighed, "and the sole avenue he found for clearing a mental space for himself was, at times, to blind himself to his predecessors' work, wishing to be beholden to no one—to sire himself, as it were, to be a truly self-begotten man."

Another angel passed.

"So, in the end, are you praising him or criticizing him?" Françoise finally inquired. She sounded quite lost in the polymath's unusual discourse.

After removing his spectacles and wiping them with a napkin, the concertmaster continued, "You decide. Da Vinci did not, however, suffer from the opposite problem, even though many erroneously say he did. He wasn't afraid of what so many fear today: he wasn't worried about people stealing *his* ideas."

"Didn't he write backwards to stop people from reading his notes?" the flutist asked, staring at the menu as if imagining how impossible it would be to decipher if it were written right to left.

"That's what I always heard," interjected Henri, looking totally discombobulated.

Françoise's eyes returned to Civadin's face, as if to find the answer there. We were all rapt, he seeming so knowledgeable about the enigmatic genius.

"No, he wrote backwards spontaneously, like many other lefties, right from the tenderest of ages—just like me," he added. "In Leonardo's case it had nothing to do with paranoia about people plagiarizing him, *ma chère Françoise*. Those who claim that it did blithely impose contemporary notions of intellectual property on Renaissance practices, another example of projection. It was a different time—all that counted was beauty," he looked intently at the flutist, "and nobody gave a farthing whence your inspiration flowed. That's why we love the Loire Valley—the only rule here was to delight the eye, and everyone borrowed from everyone else," he enthused.

All eyes turned to Françoise. Her beauty and classic style were a fitting homage to the ladies that many a masterpiece in the area had been built to delight and impress.

"Artworks often were not even signed back then," I remarked. "The artists who painted your lovely portrait would remain anonymous, and myriad hands in a specific workshop or studio would contribute to it.

Yet today everyone wants something signed by Rembrandt or Michelangelo—as if it were the signature that was worth all those millions, not the painting itself."

"Typical bourgeois bullshit," Enrique opined, looking up from his phone. "At Christie's, my uncle bought a world-famous signature on one of the ugliest paintings I've ever seen."

I gazed up at the *Morning Lounge*'s beams. Maybe this house, like so many in Loudun, had been built during the Renaissance or even before, and had treasures hidden in its entrails. Like—why not?—Leonardo's first sketch of the Mona Lisa!

"Those who claim Leonardo was worried about being copied," I commented, "are probably apprehensive about their own originality, anxious they themselves are plagiarizing others."

I didn't bring up the old story of the nutty patient an analyst once had who was convinced he was always plagiarizing others (naturally, his favorite dish was "fresh brains"). The patient could not, I reflected silently, have had such a symptom five centuries earlier. And those who claim that Leonardo's boy toy, Salaì, deliberately duped people into thinking he was selling them genuine da Vincis when he had painted them himself might also be projecting—artists made copies of each other's paintings all the time! Wasn't it T. S. Eliot who said that the mature poet steals—steals what is best in his predecessors' work and makes it his own?

"Is nothing we hear about da Vinci true?" Françoise asked wide-eyed.

"Very little, I'm afraid," Civadin replied.

"I need to read some of the books on Leonardo you've studied," she remarked.

"Reader beware—if we were to list the number of wacky things that have been said about the artist, we would be here all night," I opined. "It's one of my *bêtes noires*. Infuriates me."

"Oh, tell me about your *bête noire*," Françoise entreated, "and then I might forgive you."

I searched my memory banks for a particularly absurd example. "Merejkovski's wild speculations about da Vinci set the stage for Freud's," I began. "I suspect that Sigmund's obsession with Leonardo's childhood dream about a kite—a bird called *nibbio* in Italian—was related to his own interest in his nephew's disappearing game with a 'bobbin.' *Nibbio* is a near anagram of the word for bobbin in Italian, *bobino*, and Freud, who prided himself on his knowledge of Italian,

299

bizarrely thought *nibbio* meant 'vulture.' God only knows where he got that from!"

My table companions looked at me uncomprehendingly, and I have to admit that it was all a bit obscure. I do have a tendency to go on at times …

"To Leonardo," I raised my glass, "and to his dreams!"

We all clinked glasses.

"Still, Françoise," I continued, "I don't see how you can, in good conscience, base an in-depth analysis of someone's personality on the only dream we know he ever had, especially someone who lived hundreds of years before us and never wrote an autobiography."

"I thought a person's dreams revealed a great deal," the flutist objected.

"They do, when we can get the dreamer to associate to them, to tell us what each element in the dream brings to mind. When we can't, and try to interpret them anyway, we merely give free rein to our own imaginations." Freud, I felt, had done just that far too often.

"You sure talk a lot about projection!" said Françoise.

"Many are fascinated by Leonardo the man, but all we really have to go by is his work."

"Work?" Wack protested, coming out of one of his trances. "Stop talking about work," he said sullenly, his virtuoso fingers cutting through the air. "I'm going to chuck it all and you'll be out of a job. I'm fed up with this goddamned symphony business!"

"Isn't art about the divine, not the individual?" Françoise asked, ignoring the threat.

Orlando wasn't deterred by his employer either. "All we have to go by is da Vinci's work," he repeated the unpopular truth I'd stated. "I myself have always been far more interested in his opus than in his life." His face suddenly turned grave and he looked at us one by one. "Yet his work strikes me as *nombriliste*, as smacking of 'navel-gazing'— an endless pursuit for himself alone."

Françoise gasped and Wack snorted. Was Orlando, people around the table seemed to be wondering, going to dare to condemn the man idolized by the entire planet?

"Don't say that at Amboise, the Clos Lucé, or the Louvre!" Françoise warned, shooting him a suggestive look.

"But if you never share your discoveries with others, what good are they?" he went on. "Why study architecture, lay out principles of mechanics, and learn about the functioning of the human body? People marvel at the fact that da Vinci came up with ideas for flying machines and submarines centuries before they were ever built, but his speculations about them were known to virtually no one. How can one say he influenced people in multiple fields when almost no one ever saw his sketches? It makes you wonder why he was studying things so sedulously and what he intended to do with his finds, if anything."

"I've never heard anyone say that before," Françoise said. "Are you ... " She turned to me. "Is he right?" I nodded.

"In the eighteenth century, Françoise, there was a brilliant mathematician by the name of Euler," Civadin continued. "Like Leonardo, he was highly prolific—perhaps not surprisingly, he, too, had a king who gave him carte blanche, Frederick the Great."

"Prussia was not terribly artistic," the French flutist quipped scornfully.

"Perhaps not, but Euler's field was math," I remarked. "In any case, his king didn't stay on board long."

"Such cozy arrangements rarely last forever—da Vinci's only lasted three years, and my own ... well." The others' brows creased in confusion, but the concertmaster just went on, "Euler's complete works total scores of large volumes, many of which have yet to be fully explored."

"Like da Vinci's," said Françoise.

"Indeed." Orlando cradled the cognac glass in his hand, as if to warm its contents. "Some say Euler was the most prolific mathematician of all times. His notebooks contain all kinds of mathematical ideas, from simple games like magic squares, and ways to make maps, place sails on ships, and simplify mathematical notation, to speculations about the most complex problems in virtually every area of mathematics known at the time. But at least Euler, like Fermat, shared his results with people—"

"Except that Fermat," I chipped in, "claimed his book margins weren't big enough for him to indicate how he arrived at his results, which certainly sounds like a crock of five-alarm chili."

I heard everyone laugh for the first time all evening. "But at least both shared their conclusions, *mon cher*," Orlando retorted. "Euler was obviously working things out in his notebooks, and maybe just didn't have time to spread the wealth, so to speak, despite the many assistants who helped him publish his work."

Françoise, looking up from her cocktail, shifted languidly in her chair. The math talk seemed to fascinate her—or was it the mastermind who intrigued her? Her silk scarf slipped conspicuously from her shoulders to the floor.

The bar was quite dark now, and the waiter still seemed to be eavesdropping on our discussion of human foibles.

"The tragic result in Leonardo's case was that the wealth simply went to waste," Civadin added, sipping his cognac. "Some of it literally rotted."

Françoise and Enrique looked ready to object to something so unthinkable, while Wack gave signs of having drifted off to sleep.

"Much of the paper is virtually illegible today," the violinist—unruffled and looking heavenward—continued, "and certain researchers say a great deal more of it was simply lost. In the end, no one was able to benefit from most of what Leonardo worked so hard at."

"When I was at Chambord, I heard he left behind tens of thousands of sketches and scribbles, enough to keep specialists busy deciphering them for five hundred years already," Françoise remarked to Orlando.

"Nothing more than an historical record of the time," he observed disdainfully.

"You won't make many friends criticizing the genius of geniuses like that," Françoise said. "Certainly not in Paris or New York, or to magnates who own da Vincis."

"But one does have to wonder what the point of all that dogged activity was," I remarked. Out of the corner of my eye, I saw the waiter smirk, evincing Schadenfreude at the unfortunate fate of Leonardo's notebooks.

"Still, he has, *ma chère*, handily bested the three hundred years James Joyce said it would take critics to unpack *Finnegans Wake*," Orlando opined, lifting his glass and looking directly at Françoise.

"Fin again's what?" growled Enrique. He stood up and said he was going outside for a smoke. "Françoise, come with me. I need to bum a cigarette off you." Turning to the rest of us, he added, "You're such narcissists, with your highfalutin references. You should stop talking and see who can drink who under the table!"

"To narcissism," I said, raising my glass to Orlando, as the audio technician and the flutist exited *Le Morning Lounge* and as Wack's eyelids shut quite decisively.

I was sure it would be a waste of time to tell the audio technician that virtually everyone on the planet is narcissistic—it's a vital component of our nature as human beings. "Narcissism" has become an almost meaningless term in our times. It is little more than a psychobabblesque put-down used, these days, to insult anyone you don't like, having largely replaced "selfishness." So Enrique wasn't being terribly original. And he was as narcissistic as any of us—his narcissism just manifested itself differently. I confess that I preferred others' manifestations of theirs to his!

He would probably tax Leonardo with "mental masturbation," for I suspected that Leonardo got a kind of private buzz out of comprehending natural phenomena and inventing hitherto unknown gadgets. But is indulging in solitary satisfaction so bad? Maybe, if the lion's share of his kick derived from thinking himself superior to others. But even then, is it a crime? Or just a bit petty? Do all our satisfactions have to be shared?

Orlando's cell phone rang, so I pushed my chair back a bit to give him space and gazed out the window at the narrow lane. The smokers were the only souls afoot and might have been mistaken for a pair of thieves, all dressed in black as they were. Then again, maybe they *were* both crooks of one kind or another ...

The concertmaster interrupted my musings, and relief was evident in his voice. "Javier is alive and well."

"I'll drink to that," I said, clinking my glass with his, as Wack began snoring, even as he mumbled about ducats, blondes, and wringing necks.

Civadin smiled and drank deeply, glad, too, perhaps, that the conductor was finally down for the count. I unabashedly poured him another round, tipping the last drops of the bottle into his glass.

"You know, finishing things may not be all it's cracked up to be," I opined, only slightly out of left field. "It might even be overrated at times." I sipped my cognac and looked at him intently to see how he would react to such an unpopular idea. "Not everything had to serve a purpose, after all, did it?" I mused silently. Aloud, I said, "I hope you at least kept some pictures of your version of *The Adoration of the Magi* for your scrapbook. It was quite impressive."

"You thought so?" He examined my face closely.

"Uncannily Leonardesque."

"Rest assured," he said, "I have all the pictures I could possibly want, plus the ones you received from Claudine Thoury."

"The ones *I* received?" I snorted.

"Everything is so damn digitized these days. Nothing stays personal anymore—not even my ever-so-carefully-encrypted data."

"How dare you invade my privacy!" I cried, feigning indignation. "Drink up," I added after a pause. "You're scaring me." Civadin complied and downed his glass in one fell swoop.

"Shall we?" I began rising to my feet.

Orlando followed me and we waited for the barman to ring us up in front of a classic poster of Catherine Deneuve.

The concertmaster studied the image for some time and then volunteered, "Henri was right for once: Anna Pislova *was* stunningly beautiful. I didn't know why she threw herself at me like that, but stupidly assumed she had something of a father complex and just went with it." He chuckled and hiccupped. "'Drunkards tell all, and sometimes more,' as Fraunce put it so long ago."

"More?" I uttered, gazing at the lovely blond actress and relishing anew the "geek's" vast knowledge of literature.

"You see, feminine beauty is not irresistible to me," he averred. "It's all fine and good, but it is not what captivates and inspires me. I think Anna found me quite bizarre. She obviously wasn't in love, even if she did know how to keep me interested. This all probably sounds rather outlandish."

"Hardly, my good man," I replied genially. "It's an age-old story." Like Anne de Pisseleu, I reflected, the bassoonist knew how to intrigue a man to get what she wanted from him, which was something quite other than love.

"My special connection is with Cremona," he asserted. "She recognizes things in me that I don't even notice in myself. And I believe I do the same for her, or at least I flatter myself in thinking I know the little tics and fears in that insanely wonderful creature better than she does herself, that I know when she's really engrossed in something and when she is light years away in her head, and when she is relating to me as a man and when for her we are primarily friends … " He had a dreamy look in his eyes as he gazed out the window.

Another voice sounded, "Few know as much about their partners." The waiter had suddenly materialized near the two of us late-night chatterboxes. "'Great love springs from great knowledge of the beloved object, and if you know it but little you will be able to love it but little or not at all.' That will be a hundred and fifty euros."

I guess Loudun harbors more than just hidden treasure in the basements of its ancient abodes, but closet poets, too. I'd heard that line by da Vinci before. As we left the bar, I remembered what old man Freud had considered that a mound of malarkey, love being for him either romantic infatuation fueled by our sublimated sex drive or animal-like attachment to someone who takes care of us like our parents once did. To his mind, love had nothing whatsoever to do with knowledge of our beloved. Maybe the Italian master had experienced something the Austrian physician had never been so fortunate as to have encountered. Perhaps Civadin too ...

"I've messed it all up," he added, looking down at his feet.

The course of true love never did run smooth, I reflected. "She is obviously willing to fight to keep you," I opined aloud. "She believes your mother threw the bassoonist in your path to try to break the two of you up."

"It might be an illusion worth maintaining," he pondered aloud.

"Hmm ... "

His eyebrows shot up at my grunt.

"Would such perfidy be compatible with your special connection?" I queried.

CHAPTER TWENTY-ONE

Seuilly Abbey

Ce que le vin nous cause de folie
Commence & finit en un jour;
Mais quand un Cœur est enivré d'amour,
Souvent c'est pour toute la vie.
(The madness wine brings begins and ends in a day,
but when our hearts are drunk with love it is often forever.)
—Lully, *Psyché*

Coach Canaples had already been up for hours, probably run a half-marathon in alligator-skin underwear, finished her breakfast, and was about to go pack when, considerably worse for late-night wear, I slunk down to the dining room of my B&B. I was lucky she was still dawdling there over her coffee, for I had vastly overslept the clearly defined breakfast hours.

Funny that an aged computer could make somebody so happy! She was not part of an exclusive club or think tank in Boston or New York, like Castillo might be. And yet an ordinary human being like her, out of love for her swimmers, had managed to secure an incredibly rare lightning-fast calculator to swap with Civadin. The U of M's Department of Particle Physics had just recently acquired a new one, was willing to dispense with the dinosaur and might even—if his work turned out to be half as innovative as it seemed—see to it that the sometime hunchback was offered a professorship in the Midwest, far from the clement climate of Provence. Maybe the edge Canaples was about to procure for her protégés would go some little way to making up for the medals she felt she herself had been robbed of.

"But could she be happy with a lying drug addict?" I wondered when she informed me she wouldn't be heading back to Ann Arbor alone. She'd made it clear she'd had plenty of experience cracking tough nuts on the swim team. And what was it she'd said the other day? She enjoyed giving a guy what he didn't have, what he was missing? If that was love, she'd have her hands full with Scarron! Would her ministrations staunch his polyamorous quest? And would she be able to rest easy in the harness?

"Do men work as hard, put as much on the line as women?" I asked myself. "Take Cremona!"

* * *

Left to my own devices after Marie's departure, I imbibed the only coffee available—it was still atrocious, but I hoped it would have a salutary effect on my splitting headache—and sat watching the river run out the window.

A professorship in physics—how hilarious! That, I was sure, wouldn't suit Civadin's restless and wide-ranging spirit in the least. He dug, planted, and reaped in far too many fields to settle anywhere in the modern-day academy, perhaps the least broadminded institution of all time, I reflected sadly. Indeed, he fit more than anyone I'd ever met before the perennial fantasy of a "universal genius," someone who can supposedly do anything and everything (I know a few women who wish their husbands could be like that!). People liked to think of da Vinci as one, and Lord knows not many others have been considered to be such—maybe Aristotle?

The black cat of the house had been moseying nearby and now jumped into my lap. I stroked the kitty's fluffy fur and returned to my reflections, fueled by last night's encounter with such a rare individual.

What is a genius? Someone who makes serious new contributions, someone extraordinarily curious, or someone who just looks more closely at things than others? Aristotle's powers of observation were not terribly keen apropos the natural world—plants and animal behavior, for example—but he had made an impact in quite a few areas: politics, ethics, metaphysics, poetics, logic, rhetoric, and the list goes on.

Einstein was a genius when it came to math and physics—or so it was generally agreed—Bach when it came to music, and Jim Carrey and Louis de Funès when it came to physical comedy (some agreed, anyway), but they were hardly considered Renaissance men.

Why, I wondered as I gazed at the black and white cows wading into the water on the opposite bank, did people have such a fantasy in the first place? Was it owing to that ugly word "specialization"? Or rather "overspecialization." At resplendent Notre-Dame de Cunault further downstream along the Loire, I once heard the former teacher of a now-accomplished musician point out—to the audience's apparent amazement—that his protégé was not only a world-class trumpetist, but also a topnotch French horn player, and that he could play piano and violin quite well and even sing rather competently.

Yet, for centuries educated women were expected to draw, play the piano, sing, dance, and discuss literature and history, in addition to doing just about everything in *Beeton's Book of Household Management*! And even today, men from all walks of life like to be able to impress women at a party by sitting down at the piano and belting out a few recognizable tunes. But fewer and fewer people are even the slightest bit polyvalent in our times. "Why is that?" I asked the kitty.

Today most musicians will assure you that the level of expertise demanded of them is so high that no one can play more than one instrument. And the repertoire—Baroque, classical, romantic, avant-garde, modern, postmodern, post-postmodern, metamodern—is supposedly too vast for any one person to master. Almost none of them learn to compose or even to improvise tolerably well. Can all of that be chalked up to overspecialization, or could it simply be that, compared to earlier eras, the majority of performers today are … lazy? Well, at least I know a *few* who aren't.

Spilling java on my tie—luckily it was the one Jeanne had justly criticized as not suiting me in the least (so why was I wearing it again, you might ask? was I still mulling over what went wrong with the woman who gave it to me?)—I thought that, as strange a bird as I was, I still usually dressed alright (even if a photo of me in somewhat extravagant garb once appeared in the papers in New York). Certainly not as quirkily as Lavillaine! His attire was hardly that of your average mathematician, if there was such a thing. But then he was anything but average.

Analysis, harmonic analysis, algebra, geometry, non-Euclidean geometry, algebraic geometry, ultrametric geometry, probability, statistics, partial differential equations, topology, logic, set theory, and mathematical physics—Lavillaine had been adept at establishing links among these variegated branches. Was this rare creature alive or gone forever? I still didn't know. Such breadth was far more common centuries ago, perhaps at least in part because most mathematicians used, like Einstein, to believe in pre-existing harmonies in the universe and thus sought such harmonies in different branches and even different sciences.

Physics, chemistry, biology, linguistics, anthropology, psychoanalysis—indeed, any field that had been around for more than 100 years—suffered from the same problem of ever growing scope. In the seventeenth century, Ben Jonson argued that every art requires considerable time and effort. But our post-Enlightenment-era friends and family tout "genius," some mysterious, presumably innate gift few of us have. Why? Is it because art is hard work? (Of course, you're not allowed to say that today.)

So-called genius leapfrogs a dilemma that is heart-wrenching to some, but exhilarating to others: It takes so long to master even just one small branch of a science that no one can easily embrace the whole tree, much less several. Yet certain people love knowing there will always be something new for them to discover. Einstein and maybe Stephen Hawkins are among the few recognized as having been able to see the forest for the trees (or, to change metaphors, as having had a bird's eye view of their fields), but I doubt they would have claimed to be equally conversant with anatomy, art, music, history, literature, linguistics, and philosophy …

What, in the end, do we hope for from a Renaissance man, from a universal genius? Do we consider such a person to be godlike, able to embrace all areas of human endeavor and thus able to see the bigger picture, to fathom the universe and our place in it, unlike the rest of us mere mortals? Maybe we want to believe such people exist so that they will explain the cosmos to us, and enlighten us as to the meaning of life, our reason for being on this earth. Da Vinci never did, to the best of my knowledge …

* * *

Françoise and I were to rendezvous that afternoon in the tiny village of Seuilly. There I would see the bundle of contradictions, but who was as delicious to look at as a glass of rosé after a divine concert at the stunning Grand'Cour manor house nearby. I couldn't help but think of Rabelais's Picrocholine Wars, which began when the bakers from Lerné, a neighboring village, refused to sell their *fouaces*—a thick sort of pocket bread still made today into which you can slip local goat cheese, rillettes, or foie gras—to a couple of Seuilly's shepherds.

As I drove, I spotted signs for the towns, villages, and hamlets around Chinon whose names are found in libraries the world over, having sent their native sons to fight in the fouace wars—Seuilly and Lerné, of course, where the mother of all *casus belli* arose, La Roche Clermault, where one of the main battles was fought, Le Vau Breton, Les Roches-Saint-Paul, and Huismes—along with the names of countless fairy-tale castles like Coulaine and Le Coudray-Montpensier. Even in my modern car, I expected a giant and his army to spring into action at any moment, or a horse befitting such a goliath to wash my vehicle off the road and into a nearby river with its formidable urinary flow.

François I's sister loved Rabelais's Lewis Carroll-like nonsense. The princess read it by the Gothic windows in her study in the almost square Lacataye stronghold in Mont-de-Marsan south of Bordeaux, even as she penned her own famous tales of love and seduction. But his gelotherapeutic books—with their wise and unwise reflections on marriage and sex, compendia of colorful colloquialisms from every dialect spoken within a thousand miles, and drunken dithyrambic delirium—were banned one after the other by the Church.

Gently spurring on my steed, I thanked the princess for having accomplished what few other women have managed: to convince a man to do something! She talked her brother François into supporting the humanist movement by allowing Rabelais's work to be published despite the ban, and may even have helped get the jellotherapist named to the royal court in 1543. Rabelais, for his part, likely based his description of Gargantua's education on that of the Knight King himself!

As a baby, Rabelais's infamous Gargantua required the milk of a hundred cows to quench his redoubtable thirst (his first words had, after all, been *à boire!*—"bring me something to drink!"). Yet the giant allowed himself to get ensnared, like François I with his archrival Charles V of Spain, in an interminable conflict between two miniscule villages that were as alike as two peas in a pod and whose histories intertwined like the twin flights of stairs at Chambord Castle.

Was the eternal human predicament embodied in that double spiral? Two strands circling around each other, like the snakes around the caduceus, the staff carried by Hermes (that fleet of foot messenger of the gods, guide for the dead, and protector of a motley assortment of merchants, shepherds, gamblers, liars, and thieves). They were bound to give rise to every form of dualistic, black-and-white thinking: good and evil, madness and sanity, man and woman, love and hatred, heaven and hell … And writers had not spared us any of them over the centuries, projecting onto the beautiful architectural achievement whatever recondite Manichean or divine nonsense they had floating about in their heads.

Does the sleepy village of Seuilly embody good and the still sleepier village of Lerné evil? What about the double helix-ly identical Rosso brothers, Javier and Jorge? Were they personifications of good and bad? Polar opposites they appeared to be, but was anyone all good, apart perhaps from a few saintly figures like Gandhi and Mother Teresa? And, when asked, most such figures denied being all good—and shouldn't *they* know? Was anyone all evil? After all I had heard about Jorge, he seemed to verge on evil incarnate, but isn't there an admixture of good and bad in just about everyone?

Civadin's parents had been circling around each other for decades in a sort of double death spiral, never meeting but their lives enmeshed nevertheless—was one completely sane and the other mad, one all love and the other all hatred, one all sweetness and light and the other pure evil? That hardly seemed likely to me. A smothering form of love and blatant insanity seemed characteristic of his mother, whereas so-called rational self-interest and myriad inconsistent ideals seemed to go hand in hand with some warped form of paternal affection on his father's part … Which was good, which bad? Did they form a circle? An ouroboros? Or rather a Möbius strip?

Swans, like the ones I'd seen at Chenonceau, might be able to do it, but could human beings like Durtal and Le Coq, to pick another couple, circle and dance around each other harmoniously like the two flights of stairs at Chambord—which, although configured alike, are decorated differently—and inspire and feed off each other like the several artists in Verrocchio's workshop did? (Who knows—maybe watching swan pairs wrap their necks around each other gave someone the idea for that staircase! And perhaps it *was* da Vinci who had the idea, given the tiny drawing I discovered in a yellowing castle brochure stuck behind a shelf at my B&B, showing either a double spiral staircase or a double Archimedean screw for pumping water ...)* Was the prefect doomed to repeatedly tread on the commissioner's toes instead of twirling her languorously? He wasn't looking for a tango partner, but rather for someone to *boucher les trous chez lui*, someone to fulfill him, seal all his holes, staunch the emptiness in his life. Durtal wasn't looking to samba with someone, to foxtrot, mambo, bump, twist, grind, or what have you. He preferred a frontal assault and was seeking saturation—someone to plug into his pre-existing life, which was lacking in so many ways, and make it all better. He struck me as a sort of Bermuda Triangle for the unwary ...

How can a woman respond? Jeanne might like the brawny, not overly brainy type, but what about the strong on the outside, desperate on the inside type? Could she engage him in a dance and avoid being pulled into the turbulent vortex of the bottomless sinkhole in his soul? While not as strong as "the navel of the sea," the so-called *Horrenda Caribdis* of literary fame—the Mokstraumen maelstrom off the coast of Norway described by Jules Verne and Edgar Allan Poe—it might still suck her in and leave her (no Olympian, she) swimming for dear life.

Yes, I admit, I'm not optimistic. I wouldn't reckon their probability of working things out—especially if I constructed a Markov chain including all the other pairs I'd encountered in the course of this investigation—at higher than, say, five, eight, or thirteen percent, depending on how much Fibonacci wine I'd been drinking! (You probably think there is no such vino, but there is.) But then again, their specific chances didn't depend on the success or failure of the couples that had come together and splintered apart before them.

Maybe Hervé Castillo, the enigmatic owner of Villandry, would cross paths with Le Coq again. They shared a great many interests—maybe those could serve them as a central core, like the one to which the separate flights of the da Vinci staircase are attached? But, as Shakespeare pointed out, "reason and love keep little company together now-a-days." Had they ever? Would they ever?

If the majestic ceilings at Chambord had been twice as high as they already were (which would make them disproportionately tall), the builders could have included three or four intertwining flights of stairs and all of this silly dualistic, Manichaean speculation would have been avoided. Hadn't a famous Frenchman once said that it took three to love, not two? (Far simpler than Freud's notion that it took six: two partners and all four of their parents!) The twin Rossos had unwittingly been circling around each other, but a third party had been there all along: the child to whom they were, not coupled, but *troisés* ("thirded").*

Two staircases, like those at Chambord, are enough for partners to ogle each other through the regularly spaced slits in the core without ever meeting. That can spark their desire and keep them interested—but is that *l'âmour*?** Is that a relationship? Is that even a dance? Tango requires a third and perhaps even a fourth—the dancers must gaze at someone other than their partner to keep things interesting! At Chambord there is always a *mur*, a wall, between them, giving rise to *l'amur*, as I sometimes spelled it.*** Can't we hope for something more? But what?

Isn't love a dance, a dance in which the partners are sometimes in synch, sometimes not, sometimes stepping on each other's toes, sometimes swirling uncontrollably, sometimes tripping over their own feet and falling flat on their faces? A dance in which one or both rug-cutters may at times be preoccupied with their own performance, the admiration of others, or what other terpsichoreans are doing—so preoccupied as to miss more than just a beat, allowing their partner to spin like a whirling dervish right off the dance floor, careening into wallflowers or even into the punch bowl? A dance of changing rhythms, respirations, speeds, moods, intensities, proximities? A dance in which sometimes neither one knows the time-honored steps, and can do no better than wing it? A dance in which the partners may not have the same vision, tells, culture, or stamina, and in which the canonical has to give way to improvisation?

The Ancient Greeks believed that when you fall in love, it is a message from the gods, a confirmation that Cupid himself has intervened in your life. Is Hermes, Cupid's sometime messenger, whose staff is topped with two intertwined serpents, trying to tell us something through Chambord's double helix? Known to the Romans as Mercury, this god can be as volatile as the weather itself in the Loire Valley. Still, he is associated with balanced exchange and reciprocity—as when he received his snake-infested caduceus from his half-brother Apollo in exchange for music, music in the form of a tortoiseshell lyre—not to mention writing and eloquence …

His mighty staff is reputed to awaken the sleeping and even the dead, and it certainly seems to have brought the dead back to life in this case! Is it, as some claim, a symbol of two adders basely copulating? Or is it, as others believe, two vipers entwined in mortal combat which, being separated by Hermes's wand, become a sign of peace? War and peace, love as a struggle to the death—such ancient symbols certainly have a way of accumulating contradictory meanings.

Does Chambord's double spiral mean everything and nothing? A glorious emptiness? What if it had been built with "chirality," as topologists called it, one flight being right-handed, the other left-handed, one descending as in the Middle Ages, the other as in the Renaissance? The staircases would not have fit together—just as a glove made for your left hand does not fit your right hand—or intertwined. (Just try to design a stairwell—known in French as *une cage d'escalier*—in which to encase them!) Their symbolism might then have been more complex: Man and woman do not go together like jam and bread or horse and carriage, good and evil are not cut from one cloth, heaven and hell are not of the same order.

The investigation sparked by the "stare-cases" had been confusing. I hadn't known if we were dealing with a concatenation of unrelated events or if there was a highly sophisticated logic that escaped me. It turned out that the incidents had revolved around one center. Orlando—having *les défauts de ses qualités*, flaws intrinsic to his qualities, being apt to get so engrossed in his work that he didn't notice what was brewing—was unaware of his own centrality. Like Nero fiddling while Rome burns? No, more like a cook so intent upon putting the finishing touches on a magnificent dish that he doesn't notice that the building that houses his kitchen has caught fire!

The man was perhaps blithely or indeed *willfully* unaware of the passions he and his work had unleashed (why on earth had he been studying invisibility in the first place, with its inevitable military applications?), unaware of the crimes that had been committed not always in his best interest, but rather for the benefit of those planets that gravitated around him, their sun.

His mother and his father, his mother and his wife (funny coincidence how they, who hated each other so viscerally, both ambushed their prey at the head of staircases—like mother, like daughter-in-law?), his wife and his mistress had all been warring over Civadin for months, if not decades—four not-always-heavenly bodies revolving around a supernova, an exploding star reaching its maximum luminosity …

I had suspected the concertmaster of being involved somehow, but had failed to grasp the gravitational pull of the elliptically interacting elements in his solar system. Yet, had I more quickly seen clearly—or rather, to jettison the silly vision metaphor, calculated better—Jorge Rosso, the likely key to so many unanswered questions, might still be alive.

Was it his hideous chauffeur who killed the professor of oenology (assuming it was Bouture who died that day at Amboise)? Or was it Herbert Couard or another disgruntled kingpin "winemaker"? My next stop would have to be—no, not Savennières as planned to meet up with my friend, the pope of biodynamic viticulture, but—Bordeaux. And a preliminary trip to the coroner's office was imperative.

It was not unthinkable that the thug in black had been instructed by the evil twin to mention "the biggest U.S. aerospace firm" to deviously provide Airbus' investor with plausible deniability. After all, I had thought it. Was he the one who had tried to drive me off the road, or at least follow me back to my lodgings?

The investigation felt to me like a never-ending double spiral, impossible to conclude …

The road I was traveling, having gotten narrower and narrower, calmly wound its way among the fields, passing exquisite castles and manor houses.

Would I have to resign myself to never knowing whether Leonardo designed the staircase himself, or had a hand in its design? Maybe, but so what? Did it really matter who had created a thing of such beauty? That's a question worth raising in my travelogue to the artists of our times. Perhaps the idea had emerged from a brainstorming session between the king, his chief architect, and Domenico da Cortona, or from someone else history has not recorded, like the many unknown painters who dreamt and toiled in Titian's and Raphael's workshops. What shocked me most was that no one had ever built another like it. Is true art inimitable?

And why, we might wonder, didn't people focus instead on the castle's far more intricate schema, that of spirals within spirals? Was that the secret key to Chambord? The palace was designed to make a complete revolution, after all, and circular flights wound their way up and down each of the round corner towers that rotated ninety degrees with respect to the one next to it. Twists within twists, like multi-vortex tornados—small twisters revolving around an empty center. How typical that we never notice what is right under our noses … Without a bird's eye view of a fancy-dress ball, all we see are couples spinning around each other, missing their circular movement around the dance hall—or converted roller rink, if they're doing the Texas two-step!

Yours truly was convinced that the quarter turns of the corner towers had been dictated by a simple wish: to offer private entrances to each of the apartments in those towers. Hallways were, after all, an Italian invention. Prior to the sixteenth century, a scantily clad girl in France had to walk through numerous people's rooms to get to her lover's, not a great plan for a hostelry, and certainly not for a royal residence! And no one—well, except for the most prurient or voyeuristic—would have wanted to have to pass at Chambord through someone else's larger rectangular apartment to get to his own circular one. A door had thus been planned at the end of each of the four galleries (or arms) that formed the giant Greek cross, opening out to the right onto a passageway—partly covered, partly exposed to rain, snow, and biting winds—that led to the nearest tower, forming a sort of proto-hallway, or hallway *avant la lettre*. This was the most elegant architectural solution (was it François I himself who alighted upon it or who at least demanded of his fellow architects a floor plan that respected his privacy?) and it allowed all of the towers to be handsomely identical with respect to the larger structure. Well, it would have, if they hadn't decided to tack on a wing to the east before raising the northeast tower! (I guess the king was seeking still greater privacy, wanting a whole wing for his sovereign self.)*

I might be right, but then truth is not always provable, as Gödel demonstrated. Maybe all the speculation about the architects' obsession with rotational motion, twisting and spiraling, had arisen much later, reflecting onlookers' own internal turmoil, flightiness, and inability to sit still, like turbulent children. Instead of a model of peaceful harmony, they preferred to view Chambord as spinning out of control like their own adult lives did at times, ready to fly off the handle, or rise to new heights!

* * *

I may occasionally be overindulgent with the fairer sex—I do have my faults—but I am not the sort to take a woman's fury lying down.

317

Françoise and I were sitting in the garden at old Seuilly Abbey. "I thought we were friends," she cried.

I glanced over at Coudray-Montpensier Castle. Like everyone else who sees its imposing towers, I dream of one day living there. A two-second TV shot of the place as bikers from the Tour de France sped by some years back kindled a million fantasies! Right nearby us were a few stray grapevines planted to remind everyone of Brother John's heroic protection of Grandgousier's vineyard there in *Gargantua*.

"You know that was a totally trumped-up charge at FATRAS, and it was ages ago," she went on as if Le Coq's insinuation last night still hurt. "My boss was three times my age, but wouldn't take no for an answer. I finally slapped him in the face good and hard one day—*that's* what got me fired!"

I put a friendly hand on her arm. "I apologize for accusing you of being another Anna Chapman or Maria Butina—of being involved in sexpionage." She reddened and opened her versatile mouth as if to speak, but I went on. "Yet," I said rather formally, and I admit I felt a bit silly adding this, "when a suffering soul seeks solace, an analyst's love for the unconscious must take precedence over his love for the patient. So, too, in police investigations, the inspector's love of truth must take precedence over his love for the suspect."

"But what the hell *is* truth?" she exclaimed, twisting her lustrous strand of pearls.

"A thorny topic," I concurred. "But I think you'll agree that you either cudgeled Jorge Rosso on the head or you didn't and someone else did."

"I might have done it if I had known he was there—after all, he let that perverted boss of mine fabricate charges against me. Who knows, maybe I even did it without realizing it, in some sort of fugue state," she added daringly.

"All of which goes to show you had a motive, a perfectly conscious one. But the fact remains that someone else did it while you were having your little tryst with …"

Rage suddenly flared anew in her eyes.

"You don't expect me to believe you are really and truly interested in Orlando, do you?"

"And why wouldn't I be?"

She sounded desperate, which made me feel pity for her, and I'm not prone to that feeling—I'm even quite suspicious of it, given how much condescension it tends to bring with it.

"Because you're not really interested in anyone, are you?" During my lovely drive from the B&B to the abbey, I had wondered if even the President of the United States, a fabulously rich prince, or James Bond would be potent enough to hold her attention enduringly. What, after all, would happen if he failed to get reelected, lost his shirt, or broke his trigger finger? Would she drop him like a smelly old sock, so fast, indeed, that he wouldn't know what hit him?

"As if you were any better! Always ready to *tirer votre épingle du jeu*, take your ball and go home, stay above the fray, uninvolved, invulnerable. What kind of life is that?"

"Good question," I replied unperturbedly. That was her point of view, even if she knew not whereof she spoke. "Anyway, you're an incorrigible flirt."

"You're another."

"Touché."

"*Je pensais que vous m'aimiez ... ,*" she paused, trying to read my face, "*bien.*"

"I do," I replied vaguely, rather than confirming that I loved her, as the part of her statement before the pause suggested, or merely liked her, as the addition of *bien* to *aimer* suggested. It's one of those odd French locutions that forever trips up foreigners.

"Maybe I'm interested in *you*," she said slowly. "You're obviously the man in charge." At this, she leaned in and pressed her lips to mine. I didn't push her away, but when she had finished, I told her I had to go.

"To go?" she pouted.

"I have a date."

"A date? Impossible!" she exclaimed.

Like Françoise, you perhaps think I always remain on the sidelines, safe from emotional entanglements. And like Durtal, you perhaps wondered earlier on what I had been up to prior to the concert at Oiron—shouldn't I have been investigating something?

Well I was, but ...

On Wednesday, I met with the lovely, witty director of the Clos Lucé—ostensibly to go through the castle with a fine-tooth comb in search of a remote-controlled painting device or robot that might still be hidden there, but more importantly because I liked her and wanted to get to know her better. I had noticed the conspicuous bareness of Claudine Thoury's left-hand ring finger—hardly proof of no prior engagement, but promising—and we had lunched by the old bread oven in the diminutive dining room at the *Pâtisserie Bigot* in Amboise, Renaissance music playing in the background. She was, as I half expected and wholly hoped, funnier and zanier than when at the office, and those are qualities I greatly appreciate. Many view me as quite an eccentric fellow, and it might surprise you that I can be overly serious—at least in my own eyes. So it is nice to be around people who counterbalance that and know how to bring out my inner nut!

Thursday night I took her to *Le Bout du Monde* (Land's End) in Berthenay—nothing fancy, but real food, cooked on location, presented beautifully, and a top-notch cellar stocked by two wine addicts I know. It is located, moreover, just a few feet from Ol' Man River—the Loire that just keeps rolling along from the *Massif Central* to the Atlantic, where it shares its royal waters with the benighted world.

Our dinner conversation there had been just as lively as our lunch, but more intimate, and tonight I was taking her to the right bank of the Loire, to a little place I knew in Langeais—after a short canoe trip on the majestic river itself.

Would I fall into one of the many traps love lays, one of the old snares that had waylaid my previous *amours*? Would I trip into one of the muddy puddles in which Foix, Civadin, Wack, Castro, and *tutti quanti* had already soiled their feet in recent weeks? What could possibly stop Thoury and I from stumbling into some major silliness of our own, our boat getting caught in one of the many dangerous eddies in the river of life? And if—or, rather, when—we did, would we be able to hold fast to the rudder and navigate it?

What sort of dance could Claudine and I hope for? One like the swans at Chenonceau? No, we aren't made for that sort of symbiosis and harmony—we are speaking beings, after all, and words make us lie even as we strive to tell the truth and tell the truth even when we intend to lie. I am doomed to misunderstand what she tells me, however slightly, and she me. I will never grasp exactly what she wants, nor she what I want, for both of us know ourselves imperfectly and ask for things we don't really desire or that can't possibly satisfy us. But maybe, just maybe, we will be able to work around that, live with that …

So now you know. It isn't the whole truth—no one speaks the whole truth, no matter how hard he tries—but it's a pretty good start, in my humble opinion.

It's time for me to get going! *Allez en selle!* (Saddle up!)

320

ENDNOTES

Page 1.   From Jacques Lacan, Seminar XVI: *From One Other to the other* (Cambridge: Polity, forthcoming).

Page 2.   Some say there are "only" four hundred and twenty-six rooms at Chambord.

Page 7.   Each of the three syllables of *tri-ni-tas* (Trinity) were written in a different circle, and *unitas* was inscribed in the center where all three rings overlapped.

Page 7.   Spintronics is a technology that exploits electron spin and charge.

Page 13.   For Canal's dealings with Olivetti, Ponlevek, and other of New York's finest, see *The Adventures of Inspector Canal, Death by Analysis, The Purloined Love,* and *Odor di Murderer/Scent of a Killer* (London: Karnac, 2010, 2013, 2014).

Page 17.   The upstart built the initial Manoir du Cloux (later expanded into the Clos Lucé) in 1471.

Page 22.   "Twenty times on the loom" is a line from Nicolas Boileau's *L'Art poétique*: "*Vingt fois sur le métier remettez votre ouvrage.*"

Page 23.   It took a hundred and thirty-two years for the first fragmentary edition of a *Treatise on Painting* to fall from the presses.

Page 31.   "It is a crime for a lovable girl not to love": "*Lors qu'on est aimable/ C'est un crime de n'aimer pas*" (*Psyche*, Act II, Scene 5). Consider, too:

"Chacun est obligé d'aimer/A son tour/Et plus on a dequoy charmer/Plus on doit à l'Amour" (Act II, Scene 6): "Everyone is obliged to love in turn, and the more charming one is, the more one owes to Love."

Page 36. The castle mound at Villandry was called *Gemmes*.

Page 41. Many thanks to Henri Carvallo for allowing me to use the drawing of Villandry Castle and its inspiring gardens on page 38 and for sharing the castle's secrets with me. At least some of them...

Page 45. The Romans called Tours "Cæsarodunum" and it isn't that hard to guess why.

Page 46. It appears quite likely that Covid-19 is one of their Franken-progeny that got away from them.

Page 49. Probably untranslatable, but the following might give some idea of the meaning: "A woman is not something you can just become overnight," or "One doesn't become a woman by accident."

Page 52. The prescient French researcher was Michel Ranjard (†1983).

Page 53. Neither the arcades nor the corner towers were, in the end, included in the Medici Palace, and corner towers already had a long history in military architecture: consider Le Val en Corrèze, for example; even Chenonceau has corner turrets, albeit skinny cantilevered ones. The later sixteenth-century Château de Mon-bazillac has a similar layout to that of Chambord, minus the central plan and the double-spiral staircase.

Page 53. Du Cerceau's renowned tome on architecture is *Les plus excellents bastiments de France*.

Page 54. Da Vinci died in May 1519, the first stone was laid at Chambord in September 1519, and the decision was obviously made *after* the foundations including the latrines were laid out, as they confirm the original rotating design.

Page 57. Many thanks to Joel Osteen for this joke.

Page 62. February 21, 1518.

Page 65. On Nicholas of Cusa, see *The Portable Medieval Reader* (New York: Viking, 1949, p. 668).

Page 76. The cousin to whom Langeais was given was François of Orleans, the son of Joan of Arc's companion in arms, John of Orleans.

Page 80. From the back label of a rosé made by Frédéric Brochet of the Domaine Ampelidae.

Page 81. Many thanks to Isabelle Saporta's *VinoBusiness* (Paris: Albin Michel, 2014); in English, see *VinoBusiness: The Cloudy World of French Wine* (New York: Grove, 2016).

Page 102. Some say there are two hundred and eighty-two chimneys at Chambord.

Page 103. The *fermesse isolé* was also part of a code that Cardinal Mazarin (who served as French prime minister while the Sun King was too young to govern) and the Sun King's mother (Anne of Austria, regent after her husband Louis XIII died) used when they wrote to each other.

Page 116. The Elysian Fields (*Champs Élysées*) were where the luckiest of the Ancient Greeks went when they died, having been rendered immortal by the gods.

Page 119. On a score that made its way from a Cistercian monastery in Krzeszów, Poland, during World War II, see "The Case of the Lost Object" in *The Adventures of Inspector Canal*.

Page 135. Cf. Jacques Lacan, Seminar III, *The Psychoses*, p. 163: "Misunderstanding is the very basis of interhuman discourse (*le fondement même du discours interhumain est le malentendu*)."

Page 140. Mary of York was the little sister of Henry the Eighth of England, the man of many wives.

Page 140. See Christiane Gil's entertaining book, *Les Femmes de François Ier* (Paris: Pygmalion, 2005), a few passages from which I have paraphrased here.

Page 143. One can't square the circle with just a compass and a ruler because *pi* is not an algebraic irrational, but rather a transcendental number.

Page 153. A citation from Don Zagier.

Page 154. See Jacques Lacan, Seminar XVIII, *D'un discours qui ne serait pas du semblant*, p. 105: "*Quelque chose auquel on ne comprend rien, c'est tout l'espoir, c'est le signe qu'on en est affecté. Heureusement qu'on a rien compris, parce qu'on ne peut jamais comprendre que ce qu'on a déjà dans la tête.*"

Page 157. Richelieu found the occupants of Amboise Castle too powerful for his taste, as he did at so many other castles, leaving a trail of butchered masterpieces in his wake.

Page 157. Fouquet built Vaux-le-Vicomte, with its thousands of acres of French gardens and its mile-long canals designed by Le Nôtre (France's most famous landscape architect).

Page 162. Architecture buffs might be interested to know that the Logis' construction can be followed step by step thanks to one of the ancestors of a friend of mine, the canon Quirit de Coulaine, who saved a register documenting the materials and artisans involved at each stage (my friend's grandmother was kind enough to gift it to the castle). The Logis forms the north wing of the castle da Vinci himself frequented.

Page 163.   The rope girdle or belt that Franciscan monks wore around their waists was called a *cordelière*, and it is represented on the monumental mantelpiece in that antechamber.

Page 167.   Jacques Lacan, Seminar X, *L'angoisse*, p. 67.

Page 168.   Henry Fielding's opinion can be found in *Tom Jones*, Book V, Chapter 2.

Page 185.   On obstacles, see Jacques Lacan, Seminar XVI: "To run straight at the obstacles placed before you is to behave just like a bull. The point is to find a different path than the one where the obstacles lie—or, in any case, not to be especially interested in obstacles."

Page 188.   Richard the Lionhearted's scary family included, for example, Isabelle d'Angoulême, John Lackland's wife.

Page 192.   Fielding's quip is from *Tom Jones*, Book VII, Chapter XII.

Page 196.   On the formidable "modern woman," see the film *Les femmes* with Brigitte Bardot.

Page 204.   Foulques Nerra burned the abbey to the ground in 1026.

Page 204.   The powerful lord to the south was Guy of Poitiers, and he burned the town to a crisp in 1058.

Page 218.   Unless one is a Derridean.

Page 219.   See Lacan, Seminar XX, *Encore*, p. 22.

Page 221.   *La Fête de la Fleur* is the biggest annual bash held in the Bordeaux region, bringing together the shakers and movers of the wine business.

Page 223.   Not absolutely every historian believes Joan of Arc was burned at the stake.

Page 232.   Borgia was the son of Pope Alexander VI.

Page 232.   Charles d'Amboise's sovereign was Louis XII of France.

Page 249.   François I's pseudo-Latin motto was *nutrisco et extinguo* (or *extingo*, as seen at Azay-le-Rideau Castle): nourish and extinguish, meaning, perhaps, I nourish the good and extinguish the bad (in myself and/or others) or I feed off fire and extinguish it.

Page 253.   RV 427.

Page 259.   *E troppo*: It's too much.

Page 260.   *Mi rompe les scatole*: She busts my chops (or: She's a pain in the ass).

Page 260.   *Ma che cos'è*: What the heck is it?

Page 260.   *Le francese non le fanno mai pui*: French women never do it anymore.

Page 261.   *Non li conosco*: I don't know them.

Page 261.   *Che stronzo*: What a shithead.

Page 261.   *Cazzo*: prick or asshole.

Page 264.   AMF: *Autorité des marchés financiers*, the French equivalent of the SEC in the U.S.

Page 271.   EDF (*Électricité de France*) is the major French nuclear power company.

Page 282.   As R. C. Lewontin reminds us in his *Biology as Ideology* (New York: HarperCollins, 1991), Sir Cyril Burt's well-known study of identical twins was a total fabrication, the data having been thoroughly falsified. It constituted one of the biggest scandals in the history of psychology (surely not the last).

Page 289.   The passage by Freud is from "A Special Type of Choice of Object Made by Men" (1910).

Page 313.   The drawing appears to be part of the collection held at the Bibliothèque de l'Institut de France.

Page 314.   Lacan, Seminar XXI, *Les non-dupes errent* (class given on March 19, 1974).

Page 314.   Lacan, Seminar XX, p. 78.

Page 314.   Lacan, Seminar XX, p. 4.

Page 317.   And perhaps it finally dawned on François I that he had failed to include a chapel in his blueprints and that a wing to the west modeled on the new one to the east would maintain the symmetry of the north façade and save him from having to get all muddy when walking over to the village church that was all of three hundred yards away!

See the floorplan of Chambord on page 82.

CPSIA information can be obtained
at www.ICGtesting.com
Printed in the USA
JSHW030028270922
31047JS00003B/3